MIXED BLESSINGS

MIXED BLESSINGS

A NOVEL

PETER SOMERVILLE-LARGE

SOMERVILLE PRESS

Somerville Press Ltd,
Dromore, Bantry,
Co. Cork, Ireland

First published in 2012 by Somerville Press Ltd

Designed by Jane Stark
seamistgraphics@gmail.com
Typeset in Adobe Garamond Pro

ISBN: 978 0 9562231 8 0

Printed and bound in Spain
by GraphyCems, Villa Tuerta, Navarra

To Juliet

PROLOGUE

Paul's father didn't have to go off to fight. He could stay at home in a country spineless enough not to take on Hitler. But most of his friends, people in the Kildare Street Club, and people like Jack Bailey and Freddy Barnsworth whom he went shooting with, had gone over to England to join the forces. It was high time he went as well.

This would be an encore for him. He had been in the army before, only resigning his commission when Grandad died and he had to come back and run the place. He might get some proper fighting this time; he had missed the Great War by a couple of years.

Mummy would stay at home, keeping the house going and seeing to the estate.

The evening before his father left Paul was summoned to the study. On the wall along the corridor, beyond the engravings of *Scotland for Ever* and *The Return from Inkerman*, were regimental photographs, lines of officers and the colonel in the centre. Daddy stood at the back, young, but recognisable.

'Come in and close the door.'

Paul looked around at the roll top desk, the rent table, bookshelves, full of titles like *With Road and Gun in Baluchistan*. He could hear the clock on the chimney piece ticking away. Usually the study was out of bounds. The last time he was in here he was given a lecture on not getting up at the right time, and generally hanging around the house instead of revising his school work.

Wooster was farting and the smell of the smoke from Daddy's pipe and the Labrador's farts combined to make the atmosphere poisonous. Daddy was poking the fire which was made up of logs from fallen trees and turf from the estate's own bog high up on the mountains. The men collected it during the summer, grumbling because, they said, they were afraid of the Great Boo.

Paul was ordered to look through the basket and pick out a log.

'Far too big – don't you know anything about lighting fires?'

Daddy pushed Paul to one side and found something smaller which he laid tenderly on the smoking mess in the fireplace.

'I want to talk to you. If this war continues I may be away for some years.'

'Yes, Daddy.'

'No one knows how long it will be before we have trumped Hitler.'

'No, Daddy.'

'If I'm sent overseas there won't be any question of leave.'

'No, Daddy.'

'You'll be alone with your mother during school holidays.'

'Yes, Daddy.'

'Take care of her, old boy.'

'I will.'

'You'll do exactly what she says?'

'I will.'

'Promise?'

They were silent for a moment.

'You'll go to mass regularly when you are on holiday.' It meant going with the maids. 'I've written to Mr Good and you'll continue the same way.'

'Yes, Daddy.'

'I don't like it. One of these days you will be old enough to make up your own mind.'

The arrangement, which had been going on for years, was supposed to be civilised. One Sunday Paul was supposed to attend a Protestant church, the next he should go to mass. And when he was old enough he would decide whether to be Catholic or Protestant.

Daddy hesitated. 'Now everything will have to wait until I get back.'

'Yes.'

'Unless you've made your mind up?'

'I don't know.'

Daddy sighed. 'You'll talk about it to Father Hogan, won't you?'

'Yes, Daddy.'

'Another thing . . . I want you to think very carefully about what I am going to say.'

His moustache twitched as he struggled with his words. They were both embarrassed as he lectured . . . masturbation . . . girls . . . temptations . . . He spoke for some time. It was stuff Paul knew about from school.

'. . . And look after your mother.'

He walked over to the desk where he opened up one of the innumerable little drawers.

'This should come in useful.'

In his hairy hand with the signet ring on the little finger was a ten pound note. Golly! Paul had never had a fraction of so much money in his life.

'Thanks!' None of his friends had ever been given that much. Was it pocket money? Was it a sort of payment for looking after Mummy? Was it for the whole war?

Later he hid the note in the tin box which contained his best stamps.

That night for the first time he wondered what life would be like without his father. He worried in case Daddy might be wounded or even killed. He thought a bit about Mummy. She would have to do more with her life than messing with horses and dogs, gardening, and embroidering tapestries for chairs.

He also inspected his willy with a torch.

Daddy would take the train up to Dublin, have a meal at Jammet's and then go out to Dun Laoghaire to catch the mailboat. In London he would order a uniform fitting for his figure which was a bit round in front. His old uniform had become far too small; the trousers rose above his socks.

He would be off with his old regiment to fight the Hun. Run Adolf, run Adolf, run, run run.

It would be good for Paul and Mummy to have the house to themselves. That thought was secret.

Next morning the rain continued with fits of gusty wind rattling the window and a greyness over the park trees outside. Mummy ordered Agnes to light a fire in the dining room.

They ate the breakfast fry which came up in the lift from the kitchen in the basement. They were silent, all three of them, munching eggs and bacon.

After breakfast Daddy went down to the basement to say goodbye to Cook and the maids. He was going, really going.

Paul waited while Dempsey went upstairs with Mummy to fetch the leather suitcases. The inner hall contained Daddy's fishing gear, and Paul's own rod. The river ran through the estate and the two of them would stand on the bank watching for the rise. When Daddy cast, nearly every time the fly would settle on the ring made by the fish. Paul had learned a bit from him and had landed three trout altogether. The last one, caught this summer, he managed to get to the bank in a landing net by himself. Well done, old boy.

Daddy had promised that Paul could go with him to Lough Mask when the mayfly were up, or down to the Blackwater after salmon. But any fishing expedition would have to wait ages until Hitler was licked. Perhaps he would fish by himself? His eyes filled with tears which he wiped away furiously. Not that Mummy and Daddy would notice.

Dempsey piled the suitcases in the boot, and now they were sitting in the Rover watching the windscreen wipers working sluggishly. Daddy was driving, of course; Mummy would drive back. Next week she would take Paul to the station for school and that would be the last journey the car would do. Dempsey and one of the farm hands would put the car up on blocks for the duration. No more petrol. Mummy would use her bicycle or take out the governess cart.

They drove down the avenue. The car was misting up inside. From where Paul sat in the back, Wooster curled up beside him, he couldn't hear what they were saying because of the noise of the engine. His father was doing most of the talking – from time to time his head would turn to the left and he could see his lips moving. It did not look like any sort of loving talk about how much he would miss her or how much he loved her. It looked like instructions. Do this and that . . . Don't let something or other happen . . . see to it . . . Paul leaned forward and listened. Something about ploughing. You will see Paul goes to mass. And he heard distinctly – 'Think seriously about getting a tutor in the holidays. We don't want another report like the last one.'

He could examine the backs of their heads. Mummy's hair was gathered in a snood. For the first time he realised his father was going bald and there was a small round sunburned patch right in the centre of his hair which was mostly grey. The patch shone back at him and he wondered if Daddy would be quite bald when he returned.

Perhaps he wouldn't come back at all. Paul leaned against the sleeping dog and imagined Redmond coming up from the village on his bicycle carrying a telegram. Would Mummy cry? Of course she would. Would he cry? Probably.

Then he would really have to take care of her.

He wondered what he could buy with the ten pounds.

The rain had stopped by the time they came to the station which stood just outside the town. Duggan the porter put his father's two bags on a trolley and preceded them to the ticket office.

'One single first class to Dublin.'

'Right you are, Major,' said Furney the station master.

A couple of old women in black shawls carrying baskets waited on the platform, the only other passengers.

The train was running late. 'Typical,' his father said.

They sat in the waiting room with its brown photographs of Irish beauty spots. After a bit Daddy said: 'Paul, why don't you get yourself a bar of chocolate?' He handed over some coins.

More money. Much more than he needed for chocolate.

Out on the platform the two old women sat chatting to a couple of farmers who had joined them. Their peaked caps were pulled down over their eyes, and they were smoking. Paul smelt whiffs of tobacco and manure.

The machines, painted dark green, were in a line. One held chocolate bars, another was filled with coloured sweets and a third printed your name on a metal tag. He put in a penny and pulled out chocolate filled with peppermint cream. In the distance a whistle sounded.

'She's coming,' called out one of the farmers and the station master and porter appeared.

Just then he thought of printing out his father's name. He put in sixpence and began stamping out the letters.

Major G.L.Blake-Willoughby. It was slow work much slower than he thought it would be.

W . . . I . . . L . . . L . . . Horrible double-barrelled name.

'Paul!'

The train had arrived steaming as if it had a bad cold. Doors creaked open and one or two people stepped down. Puffs of blackened steam went up overhead.

'Paul!'

'You'd better make it quick, Major,' said Furney.

'. . . B . . . Y.'

When he had pulled out the tag and turned round Duggan was being given a tip.

'What the hell have you been doing?'

'It's your name, Daddy.'

'Thanks, old boy.' His voice was different. He pocketed the piece of metal before pecking Paul on both cheeks the way Frenchmen are supposed to do. He hugged Mummy.

Paul didn't know if he had spelt everything right.

Goodbye, goodbye they all said and then his father climbed in and slammed the door. He let down the window by the leather strap that held it and then leaned out so that he could wave to Mummy and Paul as long as the train was in sight.

CHAPTER ONE

After three years absence Daddy had dwindled to a photograph of a cross-armed figure in uniform and a series of sharp letters on blue airmail forms marked *Opened by Censor*.

'My dear Paul, I hope you have enjoyed your holidays. Your mother has sent on your report. I needn't stress how disappointed I am in your general progress. You seem to have made very little effort at your work. "*Could try harder*" and "*Shows little interest in this subject*" are just not good enough, particularly since you will be taking School Certificate next year. I am seriously thinking of sending you to one of the schools Father Hogan recommends if your studies do not show a general improvement.

'Of course he is more concerned with your spiritual progress. He has always regarded the fact that I let you attend a Protestant school in deference to your mother's wishes as simple defiance of the will of the church. Perhaps if I had taken his advice and sent you to Holy Name your educational results would have been more satisfactory. It is a pity that the war put an end to the Stonyhurst plan. Remember that although standards at St George's may not be quite up to those of an English school, there is no excuse for laziness. Boys only a few years older than yourself are taking up responsible positions in the war effort.

'To pass to more cheerful subjects. I am well, quite recovered from my bout of dysentery. I am hoping that my next spell of leave coincides with the cold weather so that I can get away for a trip to Cairo. The regiment . . .' The censor's blue pencil erased some lines '. . . and next time you write try and put more news about yourself in your letter. With fondest regards, Daddy.'

Paul often received letters like this. He wondered how many of his friends at school got similar rebukes from far off places. Their fathers had also gone off to fight like Crusaders and had been away for a long time.

Once again he buried the thought of how simple things would be if Daddy were to die gallantly in battle, perhaps get an MC or even a VC, a posthumous one, or just simply get shot.

His mother was in the kitchen feeding the dogs which surrounded her, salivating and shivering with hunger. They were smooth and fluffy, pug-nosed and long muzzled, or old with white faces and a squirming gaiety which endured in old age, old old puppies.

Two wild-haired maids, hovered in the background, Bernadette cutting crosses in Brussels sprouts, Agnes washing tea cups in cold water. Cook carried the preserving pan out of the lower oven of the Aga where the sheep's head had been simmering overnight. The skull had been malleted by the butcher and it sagged as his mother lifted it out. Head meat peeled off the cheekbones in gelatine strips floating away from smashed bones; the dripping gravy was strained through a sieve to catch fragments and dripped onto stale bread. Blue-black eyes gazed up reproachful, indestructible after twelve hours cooking.

'Did you get a letter from Daddy?' Paul asked.

'I haven't looked at it yet.'

He wondered how much she read of her own fortnightly air letters whose photographed handwriting was so small.

'He's awfully cross about my report.'

'Oh. Is he?' She hadn't read that properly either, or she would never have sent it on to him. 'You'll have to try harder. We don't want to give him an excuse to take you away from St George's.'

'Father Hogan's been writing to him.'

'Later,' she said warningly. Cook and the maids were too curious. They prayed for him, Paul knew.

Cats, piled against the Aga like sprats, moved suddenly to the smell of herring. Mummy put aside the roe for Miss Mew, her favourite Persian. Cats aged better than the dogs. They usually remained agile until they were perhaps sixteen or seventeen, and then suddenly in a month they would shrivel up, their fur staring, their joints stiff. Until then they seemed everlasting, unless they were killed off by accident. Cars weren't a threat these days, but traps and poison might get them. Or . . . the kitten, which liked to retire to the cool oven of the Aga for warmth, when the door was open was shut in, poor braised pussy.

'We'd better pack after I've finished. Go and get your trunk and take it upstairs.'

He left the kitchen and moved past the dark onion-smelling basement rooms. One was filled with trays of newly gathered apples, another with mounds of potatoes. A third housed the boiler, too expensive to use; the radiators upstairs were cold, clogged with dust like half-filleted fish bones.

Past the dairy, always freezing. After milking, a couple of zinc buckets were dumped there for the house; the rest of the milk went to people on the estate. Past the terrible rooms where Cook and the maids slept; past their lavatory, locked, unused, choked. 'Put an eel down it, ma'am,' Dempsey had suggested, but eels were in short supply. The maids had used jerry pots for years.

In the last room was his brass bound trunk and tuck box which had been thrown there at the beginning of the holidays. Mice had trotted over the bottom of the tuck box looking for crumbs and he turned it upside down, shaking out black droppings. This afternoon it would be filled with cake, which would last a few days and the sweets and chocolate he had scrounged. Pots of blackberry jam were better than nothing and Mummy had managed to obtain some oranges from the cargo of fruit which had recently come into the Dublin docks.

It was always lovely being with Mummy, but the summer had gone slowly. Fishing and bicycling down the avenue to the village and back had taken up time; so had helping with the harvest, and mooching around with Joe Roche from the gate lodge. Often Joe and Paul accompanied Tim Daly when Tim went after rabbits which were a good source of income since he sent them off to Wales. The Welsh were mad for them, the poor crathers, with their rationing and there not being a morsel of meat to eat across the water. With his two skinny ferrets Tim earned plenty catching Welsh chickens.

'Did ye know, Paul, a lady rabbit can have fifty babies a year?'

Too many ended up in the kitchen and Cook served them up at least once a week.

Every day his mother asked him to exercise Pavlova, the devilish ex-polo pony who disliked her outings as much as he did. But he liked to please Mummy, and braced himself each morning carrying saddle and bridle, approaching field or stable or wherever Pav might be, ready to fight him every time. He didn't have to exercise Parade; Mummy wouldn't trust him with her hunter, but took him out herself early every morning while Paul lounged in bed.

When it rained he stayed indoors reading old volumes of *Punch* or *The Illustrated London News*, or trying to teach the parrot to swear, or playing billiards against himself, always nervous of damaging the green baize. He had made no effort to do his holiday tasks and probably there would be hell to pay.

He dragged his trunk upstairs through the sumptuous squalor of the big rooms whitened under the fine dust of dog's hair. Past the drawing room, where the parrot sulked in its cage. The drawing room was known as Siberia.

'Half the drawing rooms in Ireland are called Siberia,' Mummy had said when she came here as a bride.

'This one is the biggest and coldest,' Daddy had told her.

'It might well be.'

'Wait until you see the ballroom.' If you were playing tennis outside and it began to rain you could move into the ballroom and continue. Circles covered the tables where vases had rested for years; a chair sagged, its warp trailing on the floor. Lyre backs, scallop shells, devil's masks, serpentine legs, ball and claw feet, Nelson trimmings of wooden ropes were scratched and peppered with holes. Paul sometimes wondered if Mummy loved animals so much that she refused to have wood worm treated.

The chandelier in the hall was so thick in dust it did not glitter at all. The skull and horns of the Irish elk were just as dusty. The mirror, topped by a golden eagle and edged with golden laurel, was chipped and mercury wrinkled up behind the convex glass. When you looked at your reflection it was distorted so that you resembled a horse. Antelope horns loomed among dark portraits, and swords were bunched like bursting suns. There was a parcel covered with stamps on the hall table that had never been opened.

The staircase ascended like a soufflé before it divided in two; he lugged the trunk up one stair at a time, round and up the right-hand fork.

His mother helped him pack.

'I suppose Father Hogan's been complaining again about the arrangement being unfair. He should mind his own business.'

'He thinks it's more than unfair. It's against the rules of the church. He thinks I'm going to Hell because Daddy wants to avoid a squabble and you consider Holy Name socially inferior.'

'I consider nothing of the sort. It's just that I don't want to see you in the hands of the clerics the way your father is.'

She folded a shirt into which she had sewn a name tape with neat black stitches. 'They're quite different in England. Attitudes are much more liberal and civilised. Look at the fuss they make over here. Always some row – and Father Hogan still fuming about Confirmation even after he was allowed to let you take First Communion.'

'I wouldn't have minded Stonyhurst.'

'Well you couldn't go. Blame it on the war and U-boats.' She added, 'And your father. He insists you should stay in Ireland.'

'People went to school in England during the last war, didn't they?'

'Yes, they did. None of this stay at home nonsense.'

'They could get torpedoed.'

'You've got to take some risks in war time. Over here we have no idea what things are like.'

'A mailboat sank in the last war, didn't it?'

'I suppose it did.'

'Hundreds of people were drowned. Dempsey knew someone on it. This man, his friend, got on the boat at eight o'clock in the morning and was back in bed by ten o'clock after he had a ducking outside Dun Laoghaire harbour.'

'Kingstown. I dare say. You shouldn't spend so much time talking to Dempsey, he's got work to do.' She bundled grey clothes into the trunk which was stamped with his father's initials. 'Father Hogan will be ringing up St George's all term badgering Mr Good.'

'It's supposed to be half and half and the Protestant half is doing better.'

'You've been to mass plenty of times these holidays.'

'Twice.'

'Oh. How would Father Hogan get to know about that?'

'I suppose from Father McCabe.'

'Nosy bloody lot. '

'He only takes an interest because he thinks I'm going to be damned.'

'Nonsense, it's just because he can't bear to lose a high-class soul. He's always specialised in elegant conversions, people like Lady Ballyragget and Mrs Cooper. A fisher of people's souls, and you're a little sprat. I wish all the fishing didn't make him keep writing to your father and worrying him. If we're not careful you'll end up at Holy Name.'

'I wonder what that would be like?'

'Quite awful. Terrible accents. Boys get TB. Daddy went there for a term before they had the sense to send him to England. You don't want to have to find out.'

Wearing her black and white uniform, Agnes presented the chicken which had come up from the basement in the lift before she retired to the corner to watch them eat. In the old days a footman would have done that.

Agnes had been with the family for many years. She was the reason the house had not been burnt during the Troubles. The men who came up in the dark with the petrol had all been local. None of them wanted to be first to cross the threshold.

'Ah, leave it be.' Matt Brady who was among them fancied Agnes. Paul could never understand why.

'Fuck them anyway' someone said, but the house was saved.

'A pity,' Mummy said from time to time. 'Grandfather might have got compensation and built something more manageable.'

Matt went off to America and Agnes heard nothing more from him. So she stayed on. Perhaps unrequited love made her grim.

Mummy carved. 'Here you are, darling, *le nez du pape*.' Roast chicken was his treat before going back to school and so were raspberries and meringues for pudding.

Plates were put on the floor for the dogs who worked efficiently at the remains. The dishes, deceptively clean, descended in the lift to the kitchen where some were washed, others not.

He woke with the rooks. Mummy was going to bring him to Dublin in the governess cart. She hadn't been to Dublin for ages.

Trunk and tuck box were loaded by Regan while Mummy issued directions in her high voice. She looked vestal today, her skirts hidden under her tweed coat, her pretty face wrapped in her Hermes scarf. The dogs thumped their tails sadly, the maids waved goodbye and the men touched their caps as she flicked Jessie into action and the governess cart moved off.

'I wish Regan wouldn't call me Master,' Paul grumbled. It was not only Regan; everyone called him that.

'When people like Regan are dead, there will be no one left to speak respectfully. One will be lucky enough to get sir or madam.'

At the end of the avenue Paul got out and opened the gate. When his father had been home Mrs Roche would come out of the lodge and open up, and then stand respectfully with her head bowed. Even at midnight.

They trotted through the gateposts which were topped with lions. Outside, the governess cart made its way through the village, past the two churches, past Toss Doyle's, then beyond by the raw gap where the crossroads dancing platform had been dug up. Not a car in sight; it could have been a hundred years ago.

Between cajoling Jessie, his mother chatted away. There was the religious thing. Her own family were stalwart Church of Ireland.

'You can't imagine the trouble we had when Daddy and I got married. My father kept saying I hate to see an old family going this way. He thought I was letting down the side. Marrying a Catholic.'

'Why did you go on with it if it was so difficult?'

She released the drag of the cart as they moved downhill. 'I loved Daddy, you see, and he loved me. That was what no one seemed to understand.'

It was beyond Paul as well. 'You could have saved yourself a lot of trouble.'

'I might have avoided that ghastly wedding. Ten minutes in a side chapel. My mother with tears running down her face. My father looking as if he was watching an execution. The other lot didn't like it either. No letter from the Pope saying how pleased he was.'

She was still prattling as Jessie trotted along the empty road towards the Dublin suburbs. He had heard much of it before.

'Grandpa met Granny when he was recovering from enteric after Ladysmith.' She sighed. 'How many men *hors de combat* have been nabbed by nurses?' She was inclined to repeat herself. He knew she didn't like nurses along with a whole lot of other people – anyone from Scotland, anyone who fed crumbs to birds, or put the names of their houses on their gates, or ate sandwiches, or went after honours like the OBE, or, even worse, accepted honorary degrees, people who said someone had passed away rather than died, people who kept poodles, people who grew floribunda roses or preferred geraniums to pelargoniums, de Valera, Lord Mountbatten, the Queen of England. Nurses in particular. Granny in particular.

'Grandpa used to say, "Some are born in the church, some are received into the church, others have it thrust upon them." It wasn't really a joke. He knew he was weak, you see, and when Granny insisted, he agreed to become a Catholic. So Daddy, as their son, was also bound to be a Catholic. And then Aunt Delia going the whole hog by becoming a nun. And Uncle Eddie refusing to go into a Protestant church, even for a funeral. I was quite tempted not to attend his. You're lucky. You don't have to be a Catholic.'

'I'm almost one.'

'I hope not. I hope you'll make the right decision in due course. I got more and more bad tempered after you came along. There was always something to annoy, things like your first nanny baptising you with tap water just after you were born. She was sacked of course.'

'But I did get baptised afterwards.'

'Yes. Too bad.'

He was told once again about the ceremony which was attended by nuns and priests. 'Uncle Eddie driving a selection of clerics up to the church with a smug look on his face as if he was chauffeuring cherubim and seraphim. They gathered round the font in their black and white like a chessboard. There was Aunt Delia – Mother Trinitas or whatever, in her wimple held together with little hat pins. No hair underneath, of course, shaved off.'

'Were none of your relations there at all?'

'They were still keeping away.'

Same old story.

'And after that your other nanny carrying you off to mass when she was given half the chance.'

Many people adored their nannies, but Paul had been an exception. Perhaps if she hadn't beaten him so often with her hairbrush. It was one thing to be beaten by Daddy. Why had he never told on her? The only thing good to be said about that first awful business of going to prep school was that Nanny had to leave.

'The arguments when I went back on what I had signed were terrible.'

'You were breaking a promise.'

'That was why there were so many rows, what Daddy likes to call differences of opinion. Sometimes I think Daddy went away at a very good moment.'

'You mean the war was a lucky thing?'

They reached the outskirts of Dublin. Plumes of lavender-blue smoke arose from chimneys and a soft turf smell dominated the city. No coal – only the great avenue of turf in Phoenix Park, piled twenty feet high kept away the autumn cold. The governess cart passed the German Embassy in Northumberland Road dangling its red and black swastika flag, and drove to Merrion Square, finishing at Goffs, the livery people whose business had experienced an unexpected revival.

'Thirty miles,' Mummy said, patting Jessie who would be comfortably stabled. 'Good girl. Get a good rest. Remember it's thirty miles back.'

After settling into the Shelbourne, they went to a film. Mummy grumbled at the queue.

'You can always go to the flicks at home.' She was right; there was a cinema in Mountsilver village. But it wasn't the same thing. This was the Royal where you got some real life thrown in, an organ that rose out of the floor and songs to sing, as you followed the bouncing ball on the screen. And after that a *Road to . . .* film. Films were often jerky because of the frequent cuts by the censor, not a military censor, merely a love censor. But this evening he didn't seem to have cut out anything said by Bing Crosby or Bob Hope or

Dorothy Lamour and Paul and Mummy laughed and laughed.

Next morning they walked down Grafton Street to Switzers for shirts and socks. The salesman put the money into a cup which he wound onto a wire; a handle sent it flying up towards the little signal box where a girl crouched, shooting change downwards to all parts of the shop.

They went on to fetch Paul's new herringbone suit in the shop that announced *Tailors and Military Outfitters* on a worn brass plate. A chart of old British uniforms hung behind the long counter with its inlaid brass rule, huge scissors and books of tweed samples, now unobtainable.

The suit went with his grey viyella shirt and St George's striped tie. Sleeves and cuffs were reinforced with leather. 'You've grown, Mr Blake-Willoughby,' grumbled Mr Brennan as he always did. 'Still, not a bad fit. That's a nice piece of stuff. Won't be any more for the duration.' He had some hoarded, tailoring having become a miserable business. When Paul was younger he had tried to persuade him to postpone going into longs which needed more material.

No money paid out here, it went on the bill.

Time for the taxi. 'Goodbye darling, I'm sure everything will go well. Won't be long until Christmas.'

She went on her way. She would stock up on cigarettes from Fox's, not, alas, the Balkan Sobranies she had smoked before the war. But Fox's usually had something for her. The less cigarettes she got hold of, the more embroidery she would do. A sojourn in the shop in Dawson Street that sold embroidery wool. She would buy two pounds of Hafner's sausages and look at the hats in Brown Thomas.

The wretched manager at the Provincial Bank of Ireland could wait. Instead she would attend a meeting of the Protestant Magdalen society. There were far less Protestant unmarried mothers than Catholics, so the committee could afford to be fussy and the Magdalen Home only took in first falls. The debate would continue on whether the girls should wear the uniforms that dated back to the eighteenth century.

Afterwards she would have another night at the Shelbourne before driving Jessie home the following day. By then Paul would have been back in St George's for many hours.

CHAPTER TWO

Holding his ear trumpet, Mr Good stood welcoming parents and newcomers. His qualifications as Headmaster were a first in Classics and forty years experience of governing a million Indians. Perhaps that was why he talked to people as if they were half-witted children, semi-deaf like himself. His slow speech with long pauses between words was natural to him, carrying an innuendo of some deep hidden meaning in everything he said. Parents did not like being addressed in this way; they dumped their children and departed.

The taxi carrying Paul and his belongings wound through flower beds planted with cabbages which the boys would soon be eating. He counted the sheep grazing in the field beyond – fourteen, which should be all right if one was slaughtered each week. The taxi driver swore as he made his way along the drive. Last term, boys who had not been selected for the cricket team had been put to work covering the potholes with concrete. The planks that held the concrete in place had not been removed and the concrete swelled over them so cars rattled uneasily over the uneven surface.

Many boys – not always new boys – who had screwed up courage for this awful moment, burst into tears, crushed by the sight of the sinister building with crenellations and flaking walls. Mr Good stroked his beard, greeted parents and directed boys inside to where matron, her uniform clean and starched this first day of term, took charge of tuck boxes. Others were temporarily diverted from their misery by watching arrivals. Some cars had swept up the drive with gas bags tied to their roofs, bulbous envelopes swaying in the wind. The Mercer brothers were brought to school in a coal burning car with two smoking cylinders in the back. After it stopped their father had to pull out a sack from the boot and recharge the engine with coke. Two juniors came in a pony and trap but this was a social error, and they would be teased. Sidecars, traps, broughams, landaus and brakes pulled out of sheds for the duration of the Emergency were to be avoided on the first day of term.

The hour before the evening meal was one of leisure. Some boys retired to the bogs to smoke or weep. Others slumped around empty classrooms reading *Hotspur*, while a few like Jackson and O'Hara were renewing old friendships, walking across the quadrangle hand in hand. Paul wandered around to the yard where people had collected to watch the execution of new boys. Like many other similar institutions St George's prided itself on preserving ancient rituals. Although Mr Good disapproved of ceremonies which were a touch barbaric, he allowed them to continue so long as no one was hurt. Such traditions had their advantages, and this particular toughening up of the individual boy was part of the ethos of any good public school.

Sheridan, the head prefect, and Vaughan, a red-haired freckled senior, supervised the operation, directing each victim to lie prone on the ground and stick his head through a hole in the yard wall. A sliding door would descend on his neck as he tried to free himself in a frenzy of wriggling.

'He's blubbing.'

'I think that one's had enough.'

'You're a spoilsport, Hamilton. You say that every time.'

'Why not give Hamilton a beheading? We could lift the door a little higher.'

Hamilton evaded the wild lunge towards him and disappeared.

'We'll get at him later. Back to business.' Sheridan consulted a list of names. 'Thorne, Burgess, Blennerhasset, Jeffers . . . where's Jeffers?'

'Here.' A tall figure, wearing a blue blazer stood apart, smoking a cigarette.

'But I thought . . . we thought . . . you were a new master.' Most terms there were new masters who watched executions, enjoying the hardening off process.

'Jeffers . . . you aren't related to Bully Jeffers?' Bully Jeffers was the Good's son-in-law, husband of their daughter, Joan.

'I'm his brother.'

'You're a bit old, aren't you to be a new boy?'

'Eighteen in the summer.'

That was older than anyone else present. He looked strong enough to thrash anyone in the school.

'I'm waiting, see, for call-up.' The deep broken voice had a Cockney intonation. 'I'm going into the RAF as soon as I can. Finished school back in London. Hanging around. Jim thought it might be a good idea if I was evacuated.'

'Jim?'

'My brother.'

Gosh! Bully sank in their estimation. Jim! He had married Mr Good's daughter, after which the Goods brought him over to Ireland and St George's. Bully had not turned out too badly, elevated to games master, teaching maths and science and caning his way to a terrifying superiority.

'He thought I might learn something sitting and listening in the senior classes. I told him balls, but it's his big idea, see?'

Sheridan said, 'I suppose there's no need in your case to undergo the usual initiation.' He almost forgot the second half of the ceremony – that was to throw new boys into a bathtub filled with rancid green water.

'No . . . please . . .' The pleading of each child sounded like a squeak. But one quick swing sent each one plunging through the slime. As he came up to take a breath full of decay, he was ducked a second time. Through his gasps voices could reach him.

'All right, that'll do. Pull the little brute out.'

'Send him upstairs quickly. Remember Parkes?' Parkes had developed pleurisy.

A few people objected to these rites. Matron disliked drying and pressing half a dozen new tweed suits at the beginning of each term. Some of the masters did not approve. Fingers Erskine sometimes thrashed seniors whom he found bullying. He was kind to most juniors – too kind.

Paul stood outside the washroom with Beamish inspecting hands, his first duty as assistant prefect.

'Back,' he said to a junior. 'Nails.' People could be caned for persistently dirty hands. There was some embarrassment dealing with friends, whose mitts were passed over quickly with a furtive nod.

'Back,' he said to another junior called Cunningham. Nanny had gone on to Cunningham after she had left Paul carrying a wonderful reference from Mummy. One day he must ask Cunningham how often he got beaten with a hairbrush.

Beamish talked across the assembly line. 'Congrats on becoming a prefect!'

Paul blushed, his ears going red. For many boys 'assistant prefect' was a demeaning title, but it was still absurd the pleasure that authority gave. Handing out tuck on Sundays was an extra privilege and with everything in short supply, a few extra bars of chocolate or a packet of biscuits snipped from matron's supply could make the difference between famine and plenty.

'Mass Sunday week?' he asked. He had a long standing friendship with Beamish, largely because of their similar situations. Like him, Beamish was the product of a mixed marriage; like him, for many years his parents had defied *ne temere*, and pussyfooted about giving their son a choice. Both sets of parents described themselves as enlightened. 'The boy must make up his own mind' Beamish's had said, and so had Paul's; as a result Beamish and Paul clung together, going to mass and Matins every other Sunday, having little talks with Mr Rowse, the school clergyman. This relationship produced a sort of friendship.

Beamish looked down at several pairs of hands, concentrating on evenly spaced gestures of palm up, back, up. After a minute he lifted his head and shouted: 'No. Never again.'

'What do you mean?'

'I've made a decision. At last. Mum and Daddy said I could if I wanted it that way.' His sing song Cork accent was pronounced. He gave a little bow. 'You are speaking to a genuine Protestant.'

'You're not!'

'Mum's mad at me. My godfather is leaving me money if I don't turn, actually.' He pronounced actually in four precise syllables the Cork way.

'Lucky bugger!' Paul was surprised at his surge of envy. Money. Such simple pressure for Beamish to make up his mind.

'Daddy said he was tired of civilised behaviour. Giving the boy every chance, you know the line. High time his mind was made up.'

Inspection was over and Paul and Beamish were walking towards the dining room. Paul felt buffeted.

'They had a final flare up about the innocent child. Mum in tears, my father saying he was fighting about me.'

'What do you feel like now?'

Beamish took off his glasses and wiped them on his shirt. 'To be honest, BW, I don't give a damn one way or the other. But it's a relief.'

Food for thought.

'Mum made my father write to her P.P. You should have seen the letter they got back. He fairly let rip. Hell, stuff about her sacred pledge. And now she can't go to chapel.'

'That seems hard.'

'He'll come round, they'll all come round. There's still my sisters.'

The dining room was dark with pitch pine panelling and stained glass crests belonging to the pretentious landowner who had built St George's as his seigneurial residence. An incomplete set of Malton prints of Dublin, spotted with damp from steaming meals, did not hide the squalor. The skivs jostled round the tables clattering knives and forks.

A new master, wearing a pair of baggy corduroys and a jacket with holes at the elbows, was guarding the door against the crush.

'We want tea! We want tea!'

'Easy . . . it's not six yet . . .'

'Back!' the foremost yelled and the wave receded slightly. But it was the momentum of a battering ram.

'We want tea!'

'Please! Half a minute more!'

'THAT'S ENOUGH OF THAT!' The dense pressure eased and the boys were suddenly spaced out as if they were on a tightened string of elastic.

'BARBARIANS!' Bully Jeffers was beating his way through.

'You OK?' he asked the new master.

'Er . . . yes . . .'

'No experience of teaching?'

'Oh no . . . afraid not. I'm working for my finals . . .'

'When are your exams?'

'June.'

'Quite a while until June.' Bully grinned wolfishly.

Mr Good regularly employed undergraduates, not only because they came cheap, but because any sort of staff was hard to come by, since so many people were off to the war. He had appointed two undergraduate students this term who had failed examinations at Trinity.

From the bell tower six o'clock struck with bogus solemnity. 'Let 'em go!' Bully raised his voice and boys pressed forward through the doors. His baton rippled against their passing bodies.

Boys looked for their place names, which had been worked out by Mrs Good who had distributed trouble makers, keeping them far apart and seating them next to the meek and servile. Another five minutes passed before the Goods' stately entry. Time to eye the new boys at the junior table presided over by matron, bewildered and crimsoned first by torture, now by soft glances and passed notes. Jeffers Minor sat among them, conspicuous in the flaxen-haired group because of his height. But he was ignored by those who only had eyes for the darlings, the bijoux.

Whispers could be heard, I think he's sweet.

Seated at the high table, Paul had his back to most of the school. He braced himself to face the Goods, particularly Mrs Good, who for four years had kept a close eye on him and on Beamish, in their particular dilemma of choice. Now Beamish had deserted and Paul was left alone to face Mr Good's favouritism and Mrs Good's fierce smile and false sympathy.

As Headmaster chucked his knife on his plate for silence and grace she gazed around checking numbers, the rations laid out beside each boy, napkins, table linen, and the stain and shine of the skivs' uniforms. Next came the weary responsible glance and the smile for Paul, even as another prefect pushed her chair into place.

There was a reek of onions – or was it body odour? – as Josie, the oldest skiv, dumped a cracked tureen before Mrs Good. A shallow dip to cover the willow pattern was enough for most boys, although favourites like Paul, received a full ladle. They were ready for potatoes which the boys were taught to crumble into the soup. This was all very well at the high table under the Goods' eye, but there were difficulties elsewhere. When wooden bowls were placed at the heads of tables, the strongest seized them and emptied them, leaving scarred remains for the others. Howls of protest resulted when Moore, the captain of the boxing team, took two thirds of his table's portion, leering over the slimy mound at the new master's feeble attempts to ensure fair distribution.

Soup was followed by sausages; for years boys had used their imagination as to their contents. There were more potatoes. Beside Paul, Vaughan mashed them down and made a volcano into which he dabbed half his week's butter ration which melted into a thick yellow pool. This term, Paul resolved, as he did at the beginning of every term, he would space his own rations better. They were placed before each boy on a small uniform metal tray – butter, sugar, rose hip and apple jam. Many boys like Vaughan, devoured the butter and jam at one sitting and had to spread their bread with a sprinkling of sugar for the next six days. A few ate their rations sparingly and evenly; in later life they would hold down steady jobs and rear happy families.

Next week Matron would take the Juniors on a country walk to scour the hedges for the current crop of hips. It would be a change from pulling up ragweed. Vaughan once observed that Hips and Haws would be a good name for a theatrical revue.

Formal conversation was difficult at the high table, partly because of the shouts below, partly because of Mr Good's ear trumpet. After the soup he had to put down his knife and fork and pick it up every time he addressed a boy. He could always hear Mrs Good's whispers; the way he nodded to her murmurs was as mystifying as a dog responding to a silent whistle.

'Henderson, hold up your hands!' he shouted suddenly into the well beneath, after she had noticed boys at the table along the west wall pushing potato skins down behind the radiators. Henderson's hands were crammed and filthy with dust. 'You will come to my study immediately after the meal.' The school roared; he would be beaten before *The Nine O'clock News*.

Mr Good calmed down and blandly continued his questioning of young loyalists for news of relatives. It was a way of acquiring a little background knowledge of the war, rather better than reading the censored press.

'Your brother . . . in the Fleet Air Arm, Vaughan? Metcalf? Your father promoted . . . brigadier? Excellent, boy, excellent!'

'Blake-Willoughby?' The trumpet wavered towards Paul. 'Your father in the Middle East? Whereabouts?'

'Uh . . . Cairo . . .'

'Fitzgibbon?'

'Uh . . . India, Sir . . . Ootacamund, Sir.'

'Where?'

'OOTACAMUND.'

'Ah, fancy, Ooty. Fitzgibbon's father is in Ooty, dear.'

'Such a lovely spot – so like England it made us homesick.' Mrs Good came from Surrey.

'When I was a young man', Mr Good said, 'I used to hunt the jackal in Ooty.' As he exchanged the trumpet for a forkful of egg Mrs Good counted the boys who rolled their eyes in mock amazement.

Plates were changed for shape.

'From what I hear I cannot help feeling that conditions in India are changing for the worse all the time.'

'Do you mean because of the war, Sir?' asked Hamilton.

'What? No, gentlemen, nothing to do with the war. It is the discontent that has come with a new generation of malcontents. Gandhi has done considerable harm. One could draw comparisons with this country. What disasters Ireland has faced since she was left in the hands of half-educated mischief makers!'

'What disasters?' asked Hamilton.

Mr Good frowned as the trumpet moved. 'The economic crises of the last decade. The sad experience of farmers struggling to make a living – the result of deliberate isolation. Which continues so unfortunately to this day when Ireland persists in her dangerous policy of neutrality.'

'But Sir,' Hamilton persisted, 'Why can't we go on staying out of the war?'

'Because in the crusade against evil no one country can afford such a luxury.'

'Switzerland does.'

'Switzerland has no more moral justification than Ireland does.'

'I don't see why, Sir. We don't want to fight. Why should we have to give our harbours to English ships? Why can't we just go on like we are?'

If Hamilton's father hadn't been a brewer in Guinness, Mr Good might have come down hard on the wretched boy.

'Because, Hamilton, the leaders of this country ignore moral standards.'

The shape appeared, pink. It could come in one of three colours, chocolate, pink and white, Murphy before the bath, Murphy in the bath and Murphy after the bath. All colours tasted the same.

'There must always be standards, not only on a national scale, but on a more personal level. Among ourselves in our school. What does a country need to maintain its standards, Blake-Willoughby?'

Paul dithered.

'I'm surprised at you, Blake-Willoughby, you should know the answer.' He gave his favourite the usual understanding smile which Paul had to suffer regularly. 'Any other boy?'

'Laws, Sir?'

Curtin's father owned a hardware store, but Mr Good gave him his due. 'Well done, boy. And, gentlemen, what do we have in St George's which are our own laws?' He pushed Curtin the trumpet.

'Rules, Sir?'

'Quite right. When rules are broken there is a lowering of our standards. That is why when Henderson behaves like a savage he must be punished.'

Mr Good folded his napkin and the rest of the table and then the school did likewise. Before the thunder of chairs being scraped back boys concentrated like laundresses on napkin folding, thrusting each threadbare piece of linen into individual rings of silver brought from home or of coloured celluloid, or of wood carved during many painful hours in woodwork classes. Several of the wooden circles featured regimental crests. For two weeks, before an exchange for something clean, each ring identified a napkin with its particular pattern of egg or beetroot stains, grease rings and snot marks.

Mr Good beckoned Henderson.

CHAPTER THREE

In Green Dorm boys followed Jeffers Minor as he unpacked oval tortoiseshell hair brushes, and a round tin of cigarettes decorated with a sailor's head. They admired other signs of his maturity, the blue pyjamas so different from their striped cotton, his signet ring, the luxuriance around his parts, the ashtray stolen from the Gresham Hotel.

'You won't be allowed to use that.' Sheridan was alarmed at the challenge to his position of senior prefect.

'Whose to stop me?' Jeffers lit a Players immediately.

'Mr Good for one.'

'Fuck him.' The fore and middle fingers of his right hand were chestnut brown. 'As if I'd take any notice. He told Jim that me staying here was an opportunity to turn me into a gentleman.'

Jim! Old Bully!

'I won't be in this place long, so I'm not worrying about rules.'

'Oo! Wow!'

'Jim was the one who fixed it for me to come to Airr-ah. He said Mum, I can get Alan a cushy berth while he's waiting for call-up, see.'

'Cushy!'

'The least I bloody well expected was to have a room to myself.'

'Too bad,' Sheridan sneered.

'I'll be out of here as quickly as poss . . . into the RAF.'

'You'll really be off to fight the Jerries . . .'

'I'm going into bombing. Flatten what's left of Germany.' He stubbed out the cigarette on his personal ashtray and terminated the audience.

'Good night, chaps.' The giant shape turned over in bed.

A lot of boys lay thinking about food. Tomorrow would not be so bad since Matron would have gone through tuck boxes looked for items that would spoil like pressed tongue, ham and sausages, supplied by careless parents. The boxes belonging to new boys would go far to make up tomorrow's evening meal. On Sunday the school would have joints boiled on Saturday and heated up. This was because of the gas shortage – there was never enough gas to do proper Sunday roasts. The mutton might look grey, but it tasted OK. If it was there.

Boys remembered the time, to be precise, two days after the 24th May 1941.

On the flagstaff outside the school entrance a Union Jack, limp in the rain, had hung at half mast; Mr Good had run it up himself that morning.

'England must have surrendered!'

The school had to be careful about its flag because people everywhere got upset over the Union Jack. Youths roamed streets gouging Union Jacks out of the bonnet of Morris cars while householders phoned the gardaí when they noticed the proud flag over St George's. After the sinking of the Bismarck two guards bicycled up the drive and the offending article was removed from the masthead, wrapped in a brown paper parcel and taken away. However, there were spares.

The 24th of May 1941 was the first time the Union Jack had flown at half mast.

'Hitler's won!'

'The king's died!'

Mr Good looked pale. 'Gentlemen –yesterday *HMS Hood* was sunk by the Japanese.' After the hushed pause he continued: 'This is a black day for the Allied cause. I think you will agree it is fitting for us to make a small personal sacrifice in order to remember the greater and more worthy one made by our sailors. It has been decided that the school will abstain from meat for four weeks.'

At least these days the Allies seemed to be winning the war.

Green Dorm knew about Mrs Good's economies. Leftover fish was sent up by the fishmongers on Friday evening. The school had its fast day on Saturday when herring was served, even after O'Malley had choked on bones and nearly died. Occasionally horse meat was on the menu. Bread made with potato flour were a staple, while Mrs Good believed in the widespread use of potatoes for nourishing growing boys. Potatoes had kept the peasantry healthy apart from one regrettable lapse.

Paul was not thinking about food. He was contemplating Beamish's desertion, trying not to regard it as treachery. Now he would have to listen to Mr Rowse by himself and he would have to go to mass every other Sunday on his own.

Or he could do the same thing as Beamish had done, make the surrender, make up his mind one way or the other. He could tell everyone he had decided to become a Protestant. He wouldn't much care what sort of a row Father Hogan might kick up. Mummy would like it. That would be a good enough reason, in spite of having to put up with the smug satisfaction of Mr and Mrs Good.

But if he chose to join Beamish and become a Protestant he would have to read all the furious things his father would write on crackling airmail paper. And some time, since the Allies were crossing France and the Japs couldn't be feeling all that comfortable, Daddy would be coming home.

Suppose he chose to be a Catholic? Daddy would be pleased enough and so would Aunt Delia and Father Hogan. When Daddy had insisted on First Communion all the rows with Mummy had begun.

He could hear his mother's voice.

'Don't let them get you, Paul. When you're older you'll understand how tiresome they are . . . how wrong Daddy is . . .'

The best thing was to leave any decision for the time being.

The Goods must be pleased. They would probably be talking about Beamish right this minute. Paul could see them settled in the study, which was familiar to him after numerous nagging interviews and beatings. In spite of being a favourite of Mr Good, once he was beaten with a Don Bradman cricket bat. The room was clerical in atmosphere, partly because of the Gothic wainscotting, partly because past headmasters had been clergymen and had left traces of their calling behind, hymn books with petunia-coloured edges which were mixed up with Lord Robert's *Forty Years in India* and Mr Good's Latin authors. He had brought back trophies from India, an ivory paper knife along which elephants marched, brass bells with claw sides and a brass figure which he never noticed was obscene.

Paul imagined what they might be saying. '. . . Excellent . . . good sense has prevailed . . . pity it isn't Blake-Willoughby . . . Beamish . . . such a different background . . . the chandler's shop in Cork . . .'

'. . . Beamish . . . the name . . . worse than the tribe of Smiths . . . If you go to Cork and stop a respectable man you don't know and say to him "What dreadful weather, Mr Beamish" chances are you would be right.'

Both Paul and Beamish had heard Mr Good say that on several occasions – it was his idea of a joke.

'. . . Better than nothing . . . Beamish safely gathered in . . .' They'd be arranging a hasty sort of Confirmation for him – hurried cramming of catechism, late laying of hands on his greasy head.

'And now we'll have to make a really big effort with Blake-Willoughby . . .'

And Mrs. Good would be saying something like '. . . Rowse is ineffectual . . . we must get him to take more interest in the boy's spiritual welfare. . .'

And Mr Good answering 'Rowse is no match for Father Hogan.'

And Mrs Good saying, 'Those nuns make far too much fuss. I wish they wouldn't give him all those sweets.'

And Mr Good saying, 'We can hardly forbid him going to that convent considering his aunt is the mother superior.'

And Mrs Good saying, 'They're out to get him.'

And Mr Good saying, 'All we can do is to give him a little encouragement this end . . .'

It occurred to him why he had become a prefect.

He struggled to change the direction of his thoughts by thinking of home. Home had its drawbacks – brown garlands of damp stains . . . cold . . . draughts ambushing . . . cobwebs blowing leisurely . . . mice moving like comets . . . dogs' mess camouflaged by pattern in carpet . . . He longed for all of it. He longed to be moving through those huge rooms which was taking a walk.

And there would be the old pleasures when this lousy term was over – rabbiting with Tim . . . taking pot shots at pheasants . . . getting up late, really late . . . roast beef, rare the way he and Mummy liked it . . . horseradish – lashings of horseradish dug up from the walled garden and whipped with cream from one of the cows . . . sitting in the study close to the fire behind the pierced grate . . . Christmas . . .

He slept.

The first of ninety eight days of the autumn term rolled out, beginning with porridge like mud and tea which contained a dab of gravy browning to give it more colour.

This year school work would be harder because sixth form was studying for School Certificate – English School Certificate of course, not the inferior Irish version. There was rugby practice in rain and the following day a cross-country run in harder rain.

No letter from Mummy, she never wrote. But Daddy's usual arrived.

'Dear Paul, I am sorry I have not heard from you for some time. I trust you are not too busy to send me a note affirming you are attending mass as agreed and visiting Father Hogan regularly. I have written to Mr Good. I have also written to your mother.

'It seems the time is coming when the Axis faces defeat. After that my duties as a soldier will come to an end and I look forward to returning to Ireland when we will discuss not only the supremely important matter of your faith, but your future. I hope that your school work shows an improvement this term. It is a relatively short time until you take exams that will define the path you will take in life. Please answer this letter promptly. With fond regards, Daddy.'

Sunday brought a change of rhythm to school routine. It was a day for clean shirts and the weekly underwear. After breakfast boys wrote letters. Mrs Good supervised, helping with spelling and subject matter and doing the initial censoring. But the most miserable junior hid his sorrows and filled up his page of lined paper with lies and requests for food.

At a quarter past ten Mr Jeffers inspected the shine on every pair of oxblood shoes and checked that caps were exactly squared off on every head. Boys in threes – twos were forbidden – marched off down the drive and across the tramlines weaving through the crowd which was going the other way to mass.

The church was big and the school added nicely to the two or three old people gathered there in Jesus' name. Above them walls were covered with memorials which varied between marble testaments of virtue to briefer more recent tablets of misted brass recalling dead soldiers. *Dulce et decorum est pro patria mori.* Patria wasn't Ireland.

Once again Paul thanked God he had declined to join the choir in spite of Mrs Good's attempts at persuasion. It doesn't matter if you are tone deaf, Blake-Willoughby. It's the spirit that counts. There they were, the fools, the sissies, having come down early from school dressed in their purple cassocks and tight ruffed collars. Mr Rowse – whose Christian name was Gideon – herded them from behind to O Worship the King.

Mr Rowse read and prayed and gave his sermon. He came from Belfast and during the summer marched with his lodge, wearing an orange bib over his dog collar.

'Recently I was visiting the counties along our northern border,' he said in his harsh northern accent. 'I made a simple comparison. The fields of our northern neighbours were filled with the bustle and joys of harvesting; they were neat and well cared for. Now this was not true of those farms that I observed which were owned or tended by Roman Catholics down in Airr-ah. Here was neglect. The land was undrained and covered with reeds and noxious weeds. I observed ragweed everywhere. What is the reason? Are these fields any the less fertile?' And so on.

The boys paid little attention, since they had heard him before. They fidgeted in their pews, fighting silently with their neighbours, masturbating, biting their nails, examining the contents of their pockets, string, pencil sharpeners, marbles, snotty handkerchiefs. At times like this Paul thought joining Daddy's lot might not be a bad thing.

CHAPTER FOUR

He made the first visit of the term to his Aunt Delia, or Mother Trinitas. At her convent Father Hogan would be waiting to administer instruction. This had been going on all his school life.

'Lucky bastard,' said boys condemned to another cross-country run.

'Take care, boy.' Mr Good stood on the front steps and watched him out of sight like a Roman citizen seeing Regulus off to the Carthaginians. He didn't give Paul his fare. The other side could do that.

At the terminus the driver was pulling the rod round to face the other way while the conductor flipped the seats back. The tram was two-headed like a pushmi-pullyu with identical bow fronts and stairs which spiralled round the simple zigzag stop and go apparatus. When it finished its journey the driver picked up his newspaper and walked down to the other end and passengers began using the reverse stairs.

Paul climbed to the top amid a rain of sparks from the overhead wire which had just met the rod. He settled down in the front seat where he could see the tracks disappearing before him. The tram filled up and the sulphurous smell of wet dirty clothes pervaded top and bottom. It clanged and rattled fiercely through streets full of sombre public houses, little newsagents that kept late hours and sold most things, and cold crowded betting shops. Battered houses had bulging walls and needed repointing; some would fall down sooner or later. Behind their grey net curtains families rationed their fuel. Hairy-hoofed drovers' horses clip-clopped through the afternoon.

At Nelson's Pillar old women rocked prams filled with flowers and children shook collecting boxes. Worried housewives, their pregnancies emphasised by coats of puce and bright green, turned down Henry Street towards Moore Street. Paul took another tram. He knew he had reached the convent without even gazing out of the window, for down the rows of seats there was a movement like wind over corn of people crossing themselves.

Like St George's, the convent had been built as a gentleman's residence before the little red houses caught up with it and surrounded it. Then the gentleman fled, leaving his house to nuns. They doubled its size, turning it from a single Georgian block to an L shape then to a T and finally an H. They ran a nursing home for the elderly and trained novices to go overseas to Africa. They distributed food to underfed school children and bewildered old people.

They looked after a chapel of Perpetual Adoration in which the faithful could participate in the devotion of the Blessed Sacrament. ('It's *not* perpetual,' Mummy said, 'it keeps shop hours'.)

The nun who opened the door smiled and made him feel important as she led him down long corridors whose linoleum smelt pleasantly of Mansion House. He liked the pale opulence of the litmus-coloured walls against which clung shells filled with holy water. At every corner there was a cheerful statue of a saint or some member of the Holy Family. Best of all he liked the comfort of the huge drawing room in which the fire was a foot deep in glowing coals which sent heat to distant corners where old folk were talking to relatives. He was placed on a deep-sprung sofa before all the coals of Castlecomber. It was a pity Father Hogan had to come along and ruin things.

His aunt, Mother Superior and ruler of all she surveyed, swept in for a few moments regal chatter. Nodding to right and left, smiling and coiffed, she resembled the duchess in *Alice in Wonderland.*

'How is your dear Father?'

'He's OK. He had dysentery but he's better.'

'I know that you always remember him in your prayers.'

'Oh yes.'

'And your dear mother?' Mummy and Aunt Delia hadn't been on speaking terms since the business about First Communion.

'She's OK.'

'I have a little present I'd like to give you.' Not another rosary, Paul hoped. 'It's from Sister Mary of Peace – she's the dear little person who makes the nice cakes for your tea.' ('They always talk about themselves in diminutives as if they were a race of pygmies,' Mummy said.) 'She wondered if you'd like this rosary to help you with your prayers.'

'Thanks. Decent of her.'

Aunt Delia departed graciously as tea was brought in on a trolley by the same Sister Mary of Peace, all gentle smiles.

'Thanks. And thanks for the rosary. It's great.' The tea looked good as usual.

Still smiling, Sister Mary retreated. Behind her Father Hogan arrived, small and bespectacled, a slight frown above his brown eyes contrasting with his amiable manner.

'Ah, Paul, how are you, my boy?' He would find the next half hour as tedious as Paul would.

Father Hogan had a reputation for conducting pleasant conversions, oiling and easing open the gates of Paradise, smoothing away doubts about Virgin Birth and Papal infallibility. His converts were likely to be female admirers of Monsignor Knox. But he was a relative of Paul's family, and it was inevitable that he should be called in to look after the boy's spiritual welfare.

From the start he had been handicapped by his cousin's 'civilised' approach to Paul's education.

'Give the boy a choice, eh?' the Major had said, or rather, shouted. 'Of course Paul should be brought up in the church. I agree. It's only Diana being tricky.' He had guffawed. He might be Catholic, cradle Catholic, but he remained akin to the Ascendancy.

Father Hogan could not think of the Anglo-Irish without a shiver of dislike. It was not only the patronage that was so unpleasant nor the snobbery. Paul's mother came from the sort of background where people went around saying how kind their ancestors had been to their starving tenants. Showering them with food throughout the famine. According to them there was no such thing as a wicked landlord. Most of them were mean – they made people in Aberdeen seem like spendthrifts. And despising everyone. Calling the most respectable sorts of people natives or peasants. And they insisted their servants always loved them. Loyal. That was a word that should be confined to those people in the north of Ireland.

As he poured himself a cup of tea and looked across at Paul stuffing himself he remembered the boy's father saying before he left: 'Do your best, old chap. I leave it in your hands. Don't mind telling you that Diana has the other side lined up.' The Major talked as if by clinging to Rome himself he gave a special lustre to the Catholic church. But he was a Protestant at heart.

It was typical of the liberal conscience to believe you could choose your religion as if you were deciding between a bull's eye and a marshmallow.

In spite of that woman, there had been the triumph of Paul's First Communion. But before the good work could be completed the boy's father had gone off to war leaving his son's education in the hands of his wife. There was the continued problem of Confirmation – that important event in the boy's religious life had thus far been ignored. He should have been confirmed years ago. It did the Major little good that far away in tropical climes his conscience started to tick like the works of a rusty clock and he worried abut Paul's soul. Father Hogan received as many letters from him as Paul did.

Of course the heavy guns could be brought in – interference from the hierarchy would soon put an end to Protestant pretensions. The Archbishop could be informed. So far, the Archbishop – who terrified Father Hogan – hadn't heard about Paul's dilemma.

There should be no more of the old foolishness whereby educated families divided up their children by sex, boys becoming Protestant, girls Catholic. Why condemn small boys to Hell? Why should this lad be an exception to *ne temere* which had every force?

Father Hogan's dilemma had increased since he had heard about Beamish's choice. But heavy-handed publicity, possibly degenerating into abuse in the correspondence of newspapers, particularly *The Irish Times*, would be undesirable.

There should be easier ways of cutting the calf out of the herd. If the boy was kept interested, the return of his father from abroad should solve every problem. May that day be soon!

Meanwhile conversation, let alone conversion was difficult.

'What a beautiful rosary,' he ventured.

'Sister Mary of Peace gave it to me.'

'It's an old one – coral. Many old rosaries were made of coral – or amber or hollow silver beads.'

'Mm . . .' Paul was eating a scone.

'You're fortunate in possessing something so beautiful to pray with. At the time this was made a rosary was a precious possession. I forget, do you take sugar?'

'Yes, please.' At St George's Paul abstained from the exhausting scrum for the sugar bowl. Today he took three lumps.

'Poor families often had to recite the rosary with the aid of notched sticks or perhaps with beads made of rowan berries. They might even use knotted twine or a handful of stones dropped one by one into heaps of ten.'

Paul took another scone.

'The custom of using the rosary as a guide to our prayers was introduced into Ireland by Dominicans who brought it from Spain. It was in that country that there arose the beautiful idea of dedicating this form of prayer as a symbolic garland of roses to the Queen of Heaven.'

'Mmmh . . .'

Father Hogan poured himself tea. 'Your father worries a lot about you, Paul. Is it true you are still taking scripture classes at St George's?'

'Oh yes. Exodus this term. Poor old Pharaoh.'

'You shouldn't be taking scripture at all. Your father told Mr Good explicitly. The Old Testament gives you quite the wrong slant on Christian doctrine. You're whole education has been a monstrous breach of faith. Your father, God forgive him . . .' his voice lowered to a mutter.

He usually lost his temper talking to Paul, who said hastily, 'Father, I wonder if you would explain a bit more about the Pope?' The best way of passing these sessions was to pin old Hogan down to instruction. He had learned how to fill these afternoons with questions about Our Lady, the calendar of the saints and suchlike.

'What about the Holy Father?'

'Boys at school say it's not right to worship him.'

'No one worships him, Paul.'

'He's never wrong, is he?'

'That's not correct at all. Lads like your school chums have inherited these foolish ideas about the Holy Father because their parents and ancestors have made him a symbol of all they see wrong in the Church.'

Paul took a piece of cake.

'Perhaps you have boys from Ulster at your school?'

'One or two.'

'You must ignore any signs of bigotry that you hear. Up there the opposition to the authority of the Holy Father arouses primitive instincts of hate. Their shouts of No Popery and To Hell with the Pope have an affinity with the emotions Hitler is able to conjure up from the masses who listen to him. And there are those crude songs . . .'

'Like *We'll Kick the Pope Right over Dolly's Brae*?' Paul asked carelessly.

'Where did you learn that?'

'. . . There's a boy called Dixon . . .'

'You must avoid chums who impart sniggering insults of holy matters. I suppose it was this Dixon who told you that we worship the Pope?'

'Um . . .'

'We do not, Paul. What you must remember is that the Holy Father is an ordinary man like you and me. But his position is special, not just because his rule is supreme over millions of Catholics throughout the world, but because his sacred trust has been handed down from St Peter . . .'

Food and fire made Paul sleepy. He missed bits of what he was being told, but knew he had heard it before.

'. . . Another thing.' Father Hogan was looking at him through his glasses. 'If you join the Catholic church you'll feel more Irish.'

This was a new one which made him sit up. 'I *am* Irish.'

For generations his family had lived in the same house and farmed the same land, and if his grandfather had changed his religion and become an RC, surely this didn't mean that the people before him were any the less Irish? The fat red tomes of *Burke's Landed Gentry*, which his father used to call the Good Books, declared him and his family Irish, also giving him the comfortable sense that he had inherited a superior lineage to anyone else. But was he Irish or Irish enough?

Father Hogan knew he had scored a point, and knew there was more to it than the fact that Paul's parents relied on *Burke's* to give a good account of themselves.

'It's not who you know, but who you are.'

'Daddy's Irish, isn't he? He's Catholic.'

'Yes, Paul.'

'But he's gone off to fight for England.'

Father Hogan sighed, as he sighed often talking to Paul, going over the same puerile arguments. He thought wistfully of the submissive ladies to whom he had recently been giving instruction.

There was the other reoccurring worry. 'Father, are all Protestants damned?' This was something they had tackled a number of times, and as usual Father Hogan preferred to put the idea on hold.

'I wouldn't say that,' he smiled, but there was no denying the threat. The question of salvation had to be brought up very gently. He made the little speech he gave to most of his converts. 'There's a lot of ignorance talked about Protestants and in my opinion most of it is nonsense. Many live better lives than Catholics and I have known a number of them whom our Church would regard as role models.'

'My mother is Church of Ireland.'

'Indeed she is, and a very decent person of whom I have the highest respect,' Father Hogan lied.

The trolley was almost empty of food; it was time to go. The question of Confirmation had not risen this time, but it would be brought up later in the term, that was for sure. Nag, nag. And no mention of Beamish. Was it possible he hadn't heard? Never. Was the subject a touchy one?

As usual both of them felt a deep sense of relief as they got up. Paul thought he would give up all the cake in the world not to have to take part in these afternoon talks. Father Hogan thought something similar.

They went to pray in the chapel, a shining pink and blue haven, except for the story laid out by the Stations which was sad and disturbing. Time to go to Aunt Delia's study to say goodbye and receive more presents – a book entitled *Helpful Thoughts at Prayer*, a box of chocolates, *Chatterbox* and a silver pencil.

'God bless you!'

'They couldn't object to those, now, could they?' Father Hogan said as he walked with Paul to the tram stop. He guessed some of Paul's difficulties. 'But don't be ashamed of your rosary.'

'No, Father.'

'Did you enjoy Bob Hope and Bing Crosby, by the way?'

'Yes. How did you know . . . ?

'A little bird told me.'

'Thanks Father for everything. It was a super tea.'

'That was your aunt's doing. Remember to write her a letter to say thank you. You have no idea how much such small efforts at politeness are appreciated.'

'Yes, Father.' He must have written dozens of times to his aunt. They were easier letters than those to Daddy.

Father Hogan read his mind. 'Remember me to your father when you write. God bless.' Watching the lanky schoolboy figure board the tram it occurred to him that Paul had grown far too old for *Chatterbox*.

Wagtails were collecting in the trees at the Parnell Square end of O'Connell Street. Cinemas were lit up, queues were forming and street lamps glowed against the lemon sunset; while the rest of Europe was in darkness Dublin sparkled with light.

Paul trudged up the drive of St George's. He went straight to his locker where he put *Helpful Thoughts at Prayer* and the rosary beside the lists of his school marks. In the holidays – only eleven weeks to go – he would take the rosary home and give it to Agnes. Or had he given her one before? There was always Cook and Bernadette. He tried to remember.

After a little hesitation he took *Chatterbox*, chocolates and pencil to the common room. He offered the chocolates around and gave *Chatterbox* to Lestrange to pass on to Blennerhasset, the bijou he was courting. He took out the pencil.

'They are really out to get you,' Dixon said. 'Look at the hallmark. It's real silver all right.'

'More like tin!'

'Nonsense it's silver – the Druids are prepared to invest in BW.'

'Beamish is missing out.' But Beamish never had an aunt who was a mother superior. He looked sulky; the friendship between him and Paul was strained to breaking.

Dixon asked, 'Did your man talk about the Pope?'

'A bit.'

Others joined in. 'Did they bless you?'

'Spray you with holy water?'

'Oh shut up!' He had to go through this every time.

'You're selling your soul, BW, for chocolate cake.'

CHAPTER FIVE

Mr Good was well aware of the presence in his school of what he called calf love. 'I needn't tell you, gentlemen, that here in St George's we pride ourselves on our reputation for clean living and moral honesty. Any boys found to be indulging in practices of an objectionable nature will be expelled.' But he had let Fingers Erskine, who had managed to make himself indispensable, stay on year after year.

For a number of terms Paul had been a regular visitor to Fingers' tea parties when favourites would knock on his door, well aware of their impending degradation. A sign announced N.B. Erskine, MA. The MA was the easy one from Trinity which could be bought for ten pounds by anyone who had previously acquired any sort of BA. Mr Good had one. The N.B. stood for Neil Brabazon; those whom Mr Erskine particularly loved could call him Neil.

Small, beaky faced, his nose like a parrot's beak, Fingers wore check trousers, a yellow waistcoat and a ragged tweed jacket edged with leather under his dishevelled gown. There would be four or five boys there already, some sitting on the big sofa covered with faded printed linen, some lounging by the fire, and some blushing unfortunate in Fingers' lap.

'Tea first . . . so terrible the shortage . . . If ever it's available again during my lifetime I shall bathe in Lapsang Souchong . . . Draw the curtains, Blake-Willoughby . . . it's so much more interesting listening to music in the dark, don't you think . . . we won't go classical yet . . . let's just have a few mood setters . . . Noel Coward and Paul Robeson . . . move over and let me sit between you . . . turn off Robeson now, that beautiful rich voice precludes any sort of conversation . . .'

'Please sir . . .'

'Oh sorry . . .' He would discuss art in his low melodious voice. 'Henry Moore . . . marvellous pictures he does of people sheltering from bombs in the Underground . . . All those powerful stylised forms! . . . Sorry . . . come here, Metcalf . . . Van Gogh . . . marvellous . . . the agony of madness . . . now let's listen to some beautiful music . . . we'll go classical just for a little bit, and I know even the most insensitive ear won't find it tedious . . . sorry . . . move over, Hamilton . . .'

You could not escape Finger's restless hands when you were young, not even in the Scouts, which were a summer version of his winter tea parties. The St George's troop were disciples of Lord Baden-Powell, unlike the Catholic scouts who explored different parts of the Dublin mountains and wore uniforms adorned with small crosses. Paul quite liked the Baden-Powell image, the crisp khaki shirt with shoulder tags, the protruding green ribbon of his sock suspenders, the thick leather belt, the scarf, the squeezed lemon hat.

Pity about Fingers who also wore a crisp uniform and carried a silver whistle. The camp fire was lit beside the playing fields and hunter's stew was made with a special allowance of meat from Mrs Good. Smells of gravy and smoke drifted through the trees, firelight flickered on youthful faces. The troop held hands and sang the school song.

'Oh boys, give me that verse again!'

Why did no one squeal?

When Paul prayed to his Janus-faced God, he gave thanks that he had grown too old for Fingers' attentions.

Religion never went away. He endured the alternative dreary Sunday attendance, the fortnightly walk to the Catholic church beyond the tram stop, where, since he was usually late, and the church was filled to overflowing he stood outside with other latecomers and let the Latin words drift out of the Gothic doors.

Religion even came into games.

Paul played rugby well enough to find himself awarded colours. He would be playing against the school's chief rivals. Holy Name had good games masters, priests who tucked their skirts between their legs and coached ferociously well. St George's had been beaten every year since 1938.

Hope sprang eternal and today the team displayed their annual enthusiasm. Once again they would face Holy Name. Once again a bus would be miraculously provided. Bully would accompany them; so would Mr Rowse, who always went on school games trips. His prayers, if he said them, never did the team any good.

There was school spirit discernible among those who were not actually playing.

'Good luck, St George's.'

'Crucify them!'

The team smiled and waved as the bus rolled away. Their boots were smeared with Dubbin and on the pockets of their blazers the school crest glittered in a sunburst. Along with Lestrange and Featherstonehaugh who had also got their colours, Paul wore a black velvet cap threaded with silver tassels.

Jeffers Minor, disdained to wear his. New blood, he was the great hope for a victory.

From the back of the bus Drip Lee led off with the Eddystone Light. Between songs Jeffers Minor, cigarette in hand, told dirty stories which were greeted with roars of laughter. Occasionally Bully looked round from his seat beside Mr Rowse and screamed at his brother:

'Shut your bloody mouth!'

The bus passed horses and donkeys and carts returning home from creameries. Women in gumboots carried tin buckets towards green lion-headed pumps that spat water for their household needs. They drove through a pub-filled town, desolate after a fair, full of wet dung and straw and frightened calves huddled in the rain. A mile on, the bus turned into a drive stretching between imposing iron gates.

Noise ceased abruptly. Every year boys were awed by the replica of St George's they had come so far to visit. Paul observed the same crenellated front, the towers, the spiked railings.

On the steps were grouped half a dozen boys and some figures in skirts carrying umbrellas.

'Now, boys, this is a match we're going to win.' Bully had left his homily late and had to talk quickly. 'School expects it. I want to see clean play above all. Any fouls, any misbehaviour and the whole team will be punished.'

One year he hadn't waited until they got back to St George's but beat them all on the bus.

The door beside the driver slid open and a purple face peered in over a black buttoned habit.

'Hello, Father Doran.'

'Welcome, St George's, welcome! What a day!'

'Out you lot,' bellowed Bully. They seized their bags, brushed past the priest and the boy who held the umbrella over him and ran to the shelter of the porch. Senior Holy Name boys in pale blue blazers awaited them.

'I'm Captain. McCaffrey.'

'Sheridan. Captain.'

The teams gazed at each other suspiciously.

'Ground's a bit soft.'

'We're used to that.'

Cooking smells, dominated by cabbage, similar to those of St George's greeted them as they stepped inside. They were led down corridors lined with pictures of past headmasters like the assembly hall at St George's. But Holy Name's headmasters were clerical men of strong and holy nature, some of whom seem to have attained a very high reputation. Their portraits in the Italianate style were touched with the same mystical light as the peevish representation of Jesus showing His heart. Through a classroom where His mother's statue was preserved in a glass case like a stuffed bird, they came to cavernous changing rooms.

'See you out on the pitch.'

'All right, we know the way.'

The door closed and a tremor of relief passed among the St George's team.

Dixon took down the crucifix that hung on the wall and passed it round. It was given to Paul for comment but he refused to be drawn.

Neither did Beamish have anything to say and Sheridan replaced it.

'Hurry up.' He swaggered round the lockers in his striped red and white singlet and newly ironed white pants, so soon to be tattered and torn. The others were slow, reluctant to face the rain. Lestrange delayed putting on his socks while he ecstatically scratched his athlete's foot. Jackson sat on a bench letting minutes drift by, juggling his false tooth round his mouth. Drip Lee and O'Leary continued their foolish game of pretending they were blind. It was more difficult in strange surroundings, and they kept crashing into Beamish who was groping for a safe place to put his spectacles while the game was in progress.

Paul adjusted his elastic garters so that they held his stockings in place and fumbled with the long white laces that zigzagged up his boots.

There was a rush at the last minute when a blue-clad figure opened the door and enquired sweetly, 'Not ready yet?'

The rain had lessened to a spray blown in horizontal gusts across the pitch. Along the towlines Holy Name boys shivered in their belted mackintoshes, stamping their feet, waving their arms to keep warm, already giving the odd shout of encouragement as their team in Marian blue stripes pranced about punching the ball. St George's only supporters, Mr Jeffers and Mr Rowse were silent, enveloped in clerics and umbrellas.

The referee, who wore a skirt (unfair! muttered the St George's team) tossed a coin and Sheridan called wrongly. Holy Name decided to take the kick. The whistle blew and their forwards thundered down the field, hefty boys with bulging shoulders, properly equipped with ear pads to protect them in the scrimmage. During the first short vicious encounter Beamish, who had fallen on the ball, received a punch in the groin. First blood.

Paul's instant thought was 'That'll teach him to become a Protestant!'

While the two interlocked packs heaved together, Paul tried to put in the ball.

'Push you bastards!'

'Shove, St George's, shove!'

'Push, you fockers!'

There was a mingled odour of mud, sweat and brilliantine which St George's considered a Catholic smell. In the centre chains with holy medals dangled. Paul rattled around legs looking for an opening. From the heads jammed inextricably together came more shouts.

'Jesus Christ, will ye get off my leg!'

'Shove yerself – I'm nowhere near yer focking leg . . .'

'Ball, ye little bugger . . .'

'Jesus, will yez look how long it fucking takes him . . .'

St George's had always admired Holy Name's fluency of language. These days Jeffers Minor swore, of course, but otherwise there was no tradition at St George's for such torrents of words.

'Oh, fuck off!' Sheridan caught the trick quickly enough, as, leaning on the supporting shoulders of his two front-line forwards, he managed to hook the ball into the back. Seeing it emerge from the scrum, Paul managed to pass it to Lestrange, the inside right, who made a quick leap forward, only to be brutally tackled. There was another scrum. Now Holy Name hooked and their scrum half took the ball, passing it to the fly half, who gave it a quick boot to touch. Before it was over it was picked up by the wing and before anyone could stop him he was over the line. The cheering that greeted the try increased to a frenzy when the ball went soaring over the goal posts.

'Jesus Christ, they're keen,' grumbled O'Leary as they walked down the field listening to the noise.

Black clad figures detached themselves from the group around Mr Jeffers and Mr Rowse and ran up and down waving their arms.

'You'd think they didn't beat us every time.'

Sheridan assumed his captain's part with commendable enthusiasm.

'Let's have more hard work. Less playing around. Less mucking about.' He pointed a finger at Paul. 'For God's sake mark the out half!' That was the pimpled hearty who several times already had buried his knee in St George's testicles. 'And you, Jeffers,' he shouted, 'What did you play back in London? Hopscotch? Don't just stand there gazing up at the sky.'

When the whistle blew for half time Holy Name was leading by ten points. Bully came scowling onto the pitch, furious at St George's as usual being beaten to the jolly patter of priests.

'A hell of a lot of good you are!' he shouted at his brother who refused to be downhearted. To the rest, punching one gloved hand against the other leather palm, he screamed: 'You want to try new tactics. Give it to them. Slash them. Break them. Who's to notice the odd foul?' Certainly not the referee. Apart from groin injuries, Lestrange had been bitten on the ear, Jackson's nose was bleeding, and Drip Lee had a black eye.

On the other side of the halfway line they could see Father Doran addressing the Holy Name team. He would be saying they're even worse than last year, but that's no excuse to ease up. Tackle hard run straight . . . show them whose really top.

The referee picked up courage to leave the shelter of umbrellas. The whistle blew for the second half and the game resumed with casual ferocity. Holy Name was strengthened by the screaming enthusiasm of its supporters.

Lestrange took the kick, a long low arc which failed to reach touch, and the ball was passed to the Holy Name three quarters. They moved up the field with graceful easy motions passing and finishing the movement with a sharp kick for touch.

During the line out that followed Jeffers Minor stretched up and for once was able to seize the ball. The enemy pack leaped on him.

'Get the bastard!'

He let go, the fool, and the ball was lost in a tussle of bodies to emerge suddenly at Paul's feet. He ran for touch with nothing seemingly to stop him, aware of the siren wave of shouting from the sidelines. Ahead of him a line of pollarded trees with cauliflower heads behind the goal posts were coming nearer. A few more yards and suddenly the wind was knocked out of him.

He was on the ground surrounded by forwards of both sides.

'Easy, easy!'

'Get off the ball, ye focker!'

There were kicks and trampling legs and he was beneath them, a piece of carrion fought over by dogs. He was knocked out.

He awoke on the grass behind the touchline. Soft rain cooled his face and behind it he could see patches of cerulean blue, uniforms of the gloating crowd. Bully and Father Doran were bending over him.

'Held onto the ball too long.'

'Are ye all right? Will ye go back onto the field?' Father Doran asked persuasively. 'That's the fellow. Give him a cheer, boys, for a good sport!'

Paul ran ten yards and fell down again.

'Will ye get him out of there, or we'll be here all evening!'

He was quite ill, too ill to enjoy the showers after the game. For years St George's wondered sulkily if they had been built with the aid of Vatican funds. Few schools could afford the luxury of allowing boys to run off the mud of the rugby field in steaming water, and a visit to the shower room was almost compensation for any afternoon's defeat.

While the Holy Name team, modestly attired in bathing suits, waited their turn impatiently, St George's boys frisked and frolicked naked. They were joined by Mr Rowse, who arrived to commiserate in his loud Northern accent – he found Holy Name's annual trouncing of St George's particularly painful. As usual, he undressed and joined them in the showers. In the splashing, all together now, ho ho, gasp, in spite of his headache, Paul observed once again how very hairy were Mr Rowse's chest and arms.

Later there was a substantial tea served in the assembly hall, presided over by another portrait of Jesus pointing to His heart. Visiting teams usually ate well; even at St George's they were served with chocolate biscuits instead of the usual potato bread and margarine and runny rhubarb jam. Paul could touch nothing. Afterwards he sat in the front of the bus trying not to be sick, listening to Mr Rowse and Bully grumbling at the driver. The team sat behind subdued by defeat, future punishment and incipient colds.

Paul had a blissful week in San. 'You can spend one more night,' Matron said. She had caught him malingering. Nearly every boy who came to San tried something with toothpaste or the thermometer held against the hot bottle.

'I said a prayer for you when I heard you were ill,' Father Hogan told him the following Wednesday.

'How did you hear?'

'Father Doran sent me a note.' The network continued to watch him. 'By the way, how do you like Holy Name?'

'They've got lovely showers.'

'They're getting money for a swimming pool. Father Doran's a grand fellow, isn't he? Great spirit his boys have. He's a rare good sport. How much did they beat you by?'

'Twenty-seven to nine.'

'Oh, a grand win. Another scalp under his belt. He'll be pleased, He's a great wag. Do you know what he calls that match with St George's? The Battle for the Counter Reformation.'

CHAPTER SIX

Mummy came to the station in the governess cart. She waited, whip in hand, while he scrambled in beside her. She pecked his cold cheek. In the cold he caught a waft of scent. She was in her tweed coat, her silk Hermes headscarf around her head.

With no car, life was as it used to be fifty years ago, a succession of slow horse-drawn journeys. This was a cold one, and he had no gloves. He sat shivering next to Bubbles who was also shivering. There was so much to say, and yet, when it came down to it, so little. Nothing he could really tell her. Keep one's mouth shut and endure. And Mummy was finding it cold to talk in the chill air, so that she concentrated on getting a bit of speed out of Jessie.

They drove in silence through a forestry plantation. Occasionally he could see the ruins of farmhouses and the edges of what had once been fields. They passed a ruined Protestant church, a square tower beside a shoe box open to the sky. They drove between fields where rushes grew; when the rushes were cut they came back again like a man who neglected shaving.

The road stretched ahead and Jessie's little hoofs clopped along and the wheels clattered. If you were in a car all this would take five minutes. He hunched his shoulders, thinking about cars, Daddy's Rover up on blocks, Dr Waters' Ford, only to be asked for in dire emergencies, even the bus that had taken the team to Holy Name.

In the distance he could make out the winter trees of Mountsilver which stood out above barren fields. They reached the town smelling of burning turf and passed the Catholic church with its silver railings where he should attend mass far more often than he did. He opened his coat, took off the school tie and pushed it into his overcoat pocket. Nearly there.

'I hope you'll keep yourself amused,' Mummy said as usual. It was twilight when they turned through the gate pillars. Before they reached the house Bubbles leaped down and ran ahead, swerving at the fork in the avenue – to the right was the yards and outbuildings, to the left the house, big and grey. She joined the swarm of barking dogs which rushed to meet them. Paul recognised Borzoi, Wooster, his father's Labrador, (Daddy's other Labrador, Jeeves, had perished from a kick delivered by Pav), Bug the pug, and Rascal, the mongrel who killed hens. There were other dogs, a brindle greyhound and two nondescript puppies.

'Aren't they sweet?'

The tally had crept up steadily since his father's departure.

'Welcome back, Master Paul.' Grim as usual, Agnes waited behind the front door.

The hall gave out its musty smell and the portraits looked as if they were sniffing in disgust.

Mummy never had fires lit until late in autumn, sharing Lady Gregory's bad habit of not having indoor fires until the dahlias had been cut down by frost. Even in midwinter windows were kept wide open since it had always been Mummy's opinion that there was no better antidote for sickness than plenty of fresh air. This evening, fortunately the cold was too extreme even for her, the windows were closed and the fire in the breakfast room blazed satisfactorily.

The armchairs on which they sat were protected by a Spanish leather screen which was once in the dining room where gentlemen used to retire behind it to fill chamber pots. Last winter Mummy had moved it into the study reluctantly, because she thought it vulgar to change furniture around.

A selection of dogs had made its way inside and was curled up before the fender. Bowls of forced hyacinths were in bloom. The chandelier gave out subdued light; bulbs were missing. In the magazine rack were the *Radio Times* and copies of *Country Life* illustrated with scenes of the English countryside and portraits of long-haired girls in uniform engaged to be married. Christmas cards, mostly fairly plain except for small designs figuring regimental crests, were stretched between the carriage clock and behind cracked china figures and an armless shepherdess standing on the chimney piece above the marble frieze featuring sphinxes and lyres.

Panting, Agnes carried in the Sheffield tray.

'Is there anything else, Ma'am?'

'No, that will be all.'

She shuffled off in her wrinkled stockings and creaking black shoes out and down the steep flight of stone steps to the kitchen, the way to perdition.

Paul watched his mother pour from the dented silver teapot tea that was nearly as weak as what he had to drink at St George's, but that was no one's fault. Everyone in Ireland had to drink tea the colour of weak pee even if it was served in Rockingham cups. He ate scones with melted butter and a choice of raspberry jam or honey from Timmons' beehives and Country Shop cake to mark his arrival home.

He gave Mummy a censored account of his activities over the term, concentrating on being made a prefect, and getting onto the first team. Neither mentioned Daddy at all. Nor did they talk about religion – with Christmas coming you could hardly escape it, but both he and Mummy would do their best to let it take a back seat. No need to bring up Father Hogan. No need to mention Beamish's decision, not yet.

'My concussion's better.'

'Concussion?'

'Didn't they tell you?'

'Mrs Good did ring and mention you had been kept in the San for a couple of days.'

'A week.'

'As long as that?'

'I was quite ill. I was knocked out. I was dizzy for ages.'

'But you're all right now?'

'Not too bad. My head aches a bit sometimes.'

'You'll be all right for the hunt on Stephen's Day?'

Nothing was perfect. But hunting was not for ten days at least. And now – he basked in the glow of the fire.

Soon they had to leave it, when he accompanied Mummy down to the kitchen to say hello to Bernadette and Cook and watch while Mummy did the dogs' dinner.

In the dining room he sat on her latest tapestry seat, the umpteenth dining room chair – the whole house would be plastered with her embroidery if she lived long enough. Standing in her corner Agnes watched them in the dim light as they ate rare roast beef, Yorkshire pudding and horseradish, just what Paul had imagined night after night in Green dorm during thirteen weeks of term. Queen of puddings followed.

And then back to the breakfast room where the fire had to be built up again. There was a mark on one of the armchairs on which, long ago, Bubbles had given birth to puppies. The tall stained-oak Gothic wireless had a grill which shimmered like a coat of mail. For a time last year it had been out of action, since mice had built a nest among the valves getting warmer and cosier as the news rumbled on. Now all was well.

They used to listen to Lord Haw Haw, something Daddy would never have allowed. But Lord Haw Haw seemed to have given up lately, and now it was time for the news. Some people, like the Beamish's, whom Paul had once stayed with, stood up when God Save the King was played. Mummy sewed away while Paul switched on and Big Ben heralded a break through the isolation of the Emergency. Valves squeaked and the noble voice Paul had not heard since the summer said 'This is the BBC Home Service.'

The news wasn't very good. The air war might be OK, lots of cities being bombed, but ground combat wasn't going well. Germans were counter attacking in some sort of mountain campaign in France.

'Oh dear,' Mummy said, putting away her tapestry and lighting a cigarette.

The war might last longer and it would take longer for Daddy to come home.

He went to bed really late. His bedroom was called Minden. Lying under many layers of blankets, a hot water bottle at his feet, wearing a pullover over his pyjamas, he felt content.

Mummy came in to say good night. 'Anything you need, darling?'

He had thrown off his clothes in a heap and he had not unpacked neatly. Shoes, socks, dirty shirts and pyjamas – the school did no washing during the last week of term – were thrown out of his trunk in every direction.

'I'll get Agnes to tidy up a bit in the morning.'

The click of the light, the click of the door. He could switch on and read all he wanted if he liked. He lay under his blankets and thought of school. When would it ever end?

He could see Mr Rowse muscling his way through the rugby team into the showers, soaping the hairy bits under his arms until the water went cold.

'Gentlemen,' Mr Good was saying, waving his ear trumpet, 'Because of the tragic German advance in the Ardennes instigated by Hitler I have decided to cut down your meat ration.'

'I have a letter from your father which will bring you no joy,' Father Hogan intoned.

He woke to find his mother by his bed with a cup of cooling tea.

'You must have been tired so I let you sleep on.'

'Thanks.'

He put on his polo neck jumper and felt for the first time that life at St George's was finally set aside with the foul school clothes which Bernadette would have to wash. In the chilled bathroom he scrubbed his teeth; perhaps he would have a bath this evening, something that took much of the day to arrange by the time the brass cylinder heated and the tap coughed out its dribble of boiling water. He peered in the blurred mirror. Pity about his spots and the bits of hair beginning to grow on his face didn't look very nice.

In the passage a paraffin heater gave out its smell and very little heat. On the floor above he could hear Bernadette and Agnes singing as they went about their work polishing and cleaning. In the breakfast room the hot plate was waiting for him, and the table set – patterned plates, a glass bowl filled with Christmas roses. More wonderful food – kippers and bread and honey.

He took out any dogs that had not accompanied Mummy to wherever she was and walked over the estate, meeting people, seeing if anything had changed. Nothing much. There were the vestiges of the schemes his father had tried out to make the place pay better – the big plot of sandy earth that recalled the years of asparagus, the fields marking the years of the suckler calves, the empty greenhouses. Only Mummy's conservatory was used now, where she took care of the heliotrope and plumbago and datura, and when the grapes were ripe cut them with her silver scissors.

Mick and John Doyle the ploughman were busy making briquettes from coal dust in preparation for lighting up the central heating boiler on Christmas Day. Paul greeted them and Fitzpatrick the steward, who wore his shiny blue suit with the watch chain looping around his waistcoat and the same – could it be the same? – striped shirt fastened with a stud at the collar. He was a slow moving slow thinking man with a chiselled face gazing out on the world with the look of crafty suspicion that belonged to a stone statue.

'Good to see you back, Master Paul,' he lied.

The walled garden was tidied up, its gravel paths made decent – that was also part of the festive celebrations. Mummy had done most of the work. She was there now, watched by favourite dogs, gardening as usual, you'd think uselessly, since there wasn't a flower that Paul could see. But she would coax the usual stuff to bloom in time, iris stylosa, Christmas roses galore, winter jasmine, all for the delight of the ghastly people who would be turning up for Christmas dinner.

He went to the stables where the horses looked out, Parade, Jessie, the plough horses and Pav. Daddy had sold his hunter before he went off to war. Too expensive to keep an idle animal. Tomorrow Paul would have to exercise Pav, taking over from Mummy. But Mummy would continue to take care of Parade. It was amazing how she found time between gardening and telling people what to do.

The cricket field had gone back to being ploughed and sown with the wretched wheat demanded by the government. Kavanagh had been the star of the team Daddy kept going for years. Kavanagh had also enjoyed Gaelic games, playing hurley at the same time he played cricket, something the GAA forbade. Cricket was foreign, garrison, English, the slow game of the oppressor, but it struggled on in the villages and towns round about, and Kavanagh loved it. For a time he continued on Daddy's team, disguising himself with a wig and a false moustache, until his opponents spotted him by his bowling action and shopped him to the GAA people. No more cricket, no more hurling for Kavanagh after that.

Like cricket, tennis had died with the war. Paul could remember summer tennis parties and his father's efforts to turn him into a player. Mummy had converted the court into a hen run where hens ran around with crazily feathered bantams. It seemed a matter of time before foxes or Rascal figured out the surrounding wire mesh and initiated a slaughter. Meanwhile the poultry had weathered two years scratching up the lawn where once the neat white lines of the court had been laid out. In return the hens laid eggs all spring, that would be pickled in brine or whatever; by this time of year all those preserved eggs tasted a bit off, especially when boiled and once you took the top off there was a faint sulphurous whiff.

Every now and then Mick would go in with his axe and kill a bird which wasn't doing its duty. He'd be after the turkey soon. Dragging its feathers like umbrella ribs, its red face and wattles looking proudly out of it bronze ruff like some sort of old Queen Elizabeth, that turkey didn't know what was coming to him. Paul would probably attend the execution.

He felt a twinge of boredom – something that came to him every holidays these days.

The lie-ins in the morning were marvellous. Daddy would never have allowed any sort of lie-in – he would be hammering at the door before eight o'clock. There would have been the orders over the day. You are not trying hard enough. Skulking meant idleness and so did hanging around. No reading – indoors with a book on a fine day like this? No lying in the hay, Paul, you have to give a help haymaking. No wasting time in idleness talking to Mick. Holiday homework? At least two hours every day, and Daddy testing him, and correcting mistakes. Sessions with Father Hogan, who would be invited down to stay so that Paul could learn the odd prayer.

And problems started when he brought a friend home. Nearly always something went wrong – they were caught having a cigarette, or something broke, or his friend behaved with a caddish indifference to standard good manners, or his family wasn't up to scratch.

'I don't want you to invite that boy again.'

Mummy could be just as difficult. He'd been through several friends before deciding it was not worthwhile inviting anyone to stay. Lestrange earned her disapproval when he woke up and shrieked. 'No one takes any notice of the ghosts.' Paul wasn't to blame or for the fact that Jackson's father was in the Signals or for Beamish's family shop in Cork.

'He belongs to the sort of family who put a white horse over their front door to show they are Protestant.'

'We've got a picture of King William on a horse.'

'That's different. It's a brown horse.'

'Daddy's Catholic.'

'The family started off Protestant. It's a good picture. Think of King William as a big house pin-up.'

'I'd rather have Rita Hayward.'

The only boy his parents had approved of had been Lenyx. Had it helped that Mummy had known Lenyx's mother way back when they were girls? Probably. Lenyx had been a good friend until last year when he went off to Rugby. A number of parents preferred to send their boys to public school in England, risking sacrifice, submarines and drowning three times a year rather than have them continue in Mr Good's establishment.

Pavlova. He never got used to the ordeal of getting the saddle on her back and stuffing the bit in her mouth before taking her out on a hack that she always made dangerous. She was as nasty as ever, fighting him on the bit, giving a carefree buck every now and again and when the time came to return from hacking, galloping as fast as she could towards home, resisting his attempts to stop him, determined to kill him by bashing his skull against the stable door. That really would be concussion. Once again he had to jump to save his head before she made it. Although it was satisfactory to say to Mummy, Oh yes, I took Pav for a hack this morning, his dread for the Stephen's Day meet became worse, in danger of spoiling Christmas pleasure.

It was almost a relief when rain kept him indoors. Bernadette went round the house putting buckets under the drips.

'Every big house has a leaking roof,' Mummy said to Daddy when she first came here.

'This big house has more drips than others.' Daddy had told her.

Paul sat in Daddy's study reading *Punch* and *The Illustrated London News* in bound volumes. 'The Queen's visit to Sheffield.' 'Our correspondent in Canada.' 'Mourning garments.' He tried to teach the parrot to swear. He read P.G.Wodehouse and Agatha Christie.

He played the gramophone in the breakfast room. When its doors were open music poured out of a wooden grill. Triangular Bakelite dishes embedded in plum-coloured felt contained old needles to scratch away at records. Needles were hard to get in wartime. He would up the handle that protruded from the rosewood cabinet like a deformed arm and watched the sharp rotations of the half moon bearing the white dog's profile. He listened to noisy songs by the Andrews Sisters, Lesley Hutchinson crooning *When They Begin the Beguine*, Rudy Vallée, Mummy's favourites. He never touched Daddy's stuff, Beethoven and Gilbert and Sullivan.

His report came. 'We don't want to spoil Christmas.' The loathsome details of failure didn't bother Mummy – they were for Daddy to rage about. She had plenty of letters from him. 'See the rath field is ploughed again for winter wheat.' 'You'll have to find more ways of cutting down on current expenses.' 'Father Hogan informs me . . .' The letters joined the report in the confusion of her desk drawer along with bills and an unopened envelope with Father Hogan's handwriting.

The best times were the evenings before and after dinner, sitting before the fire, reading *Country Life*, listening to the wireless, or playing cribbage. Every evening Mummy dabbed wool through her canvas until nine o'clock when the wireless was switched on and she lit a cigarette. Was it possible all that D-Day effort and pushing across France might be scuppered by a new German advance and things would go on and on? What about Daddy?

Three days before Christmas Paul and Mummy were standing around the ladder in the hall seeing it being moved from place to place while the men brought in holly and ivy. They climbed up and wound trails of ivy around the paintings and prints and stuffed heads, antlers of deer and sheep shot by people in the family who had been out in India and the vast antlers of the Irish elk. It wasn't an easy job, in fact quite dangerous. Daddy used to supervise fussily.

There had been a bad moment before Christmas 1938, when Duggan fell off the step ladder in the big drawing room and brought down a painting of the Grand Canal in Venice which Mummy and Daddy always hoped was by Canaletto. Duggan broke his arm. Clumsy oaf. Daddy didn't have him back after he recovered.

'Can I help? Can I go up the ladder?'

'No,' Mummy said, which was ridiculous considering he was nearly sixteen. 'Daddy would never allow it.' She said that last year and the year before.

The house took on the look of a forest, winding lianas capable of holding monkeys hanging down everywhere, and dull prints of splay-legged horses performing at steeplechases brightened up by the scarlet of holly berries. Swirls of ivy topped the glass cases of stuffed birds, one of which was extinct. Each miniature got a holly leaf and the parrot's cage was crowned with a knot of ivy leaves. Even the ball room, which was never used, had its ration of greenery. Mummy found the Father Christmas outfit to wrap around the suit of armour in the outer hall, the red cap and false beard being an old joke for as long as Paul could remember.

And then in the afternoon as the gloom of the winter evening was setting in, there was the glory and drama of the Christmas tree, the great heaving as Mick, Johnny Murphy, Dempsey, Dan Roche, Paul and even Fitzpatrick, who let down his dignity for this moment, assembled and made the effort of getting the giant sitka from the grove above the river through the outer hall into the inner hall where it was propped up in the corner. Agnes, Bernadette and Cook came up and joined in the excitement as if a liner were being launched. The dogs barked. All the cardboard boxes came down from the attic and the tinsel and glass balls got their annual outing. Mummy let Paul use the step ladder to decorate the tree. She sat on her shooting stick and told him where to put things. Here – to the left – up there – Paul was better at it than the men, and she forgot the dangers of ladder climbing.

Gold and silver tinsel raining down, hiding green needles, and scores of decorations that had accumulated over forty years found their place. Enough things covered the tree so that it shone like an altar piece. There were no vulgar fairy lights. The silver balls had to be tied on fairly high since Rascal had a habit of seizing any he could reach and crunching them into silver pieces. It was lucky that Daddy had no opportunity of knowing Rascal or he would go the same way as the turkey which had died that morning.

CHAPTER SEVEN

'Do we have to go?'

'You say that every year.'

"I can't see why I have to join in the lady bountiful business.'

'It's only the Roches.'

He should be grateful he had been spared visits to other estate cottages, to Mrs Doyle with the rheumy eyes, or Mrs Dunphy who lived more or less in solitude after Dunphy was sent to Newcastle Hospital with TB, or O'Shea who would give up drink for the day when he heard Mummy was coming.

They did not have to go beyond the demesne since the Roches lived in the gate lodge, a building with latticed windows and high sloping roof which was very small to accommodate five children, and their parents. Chickens and geese were foraging in the front and behind a wire fence greyhounds were whining.

Paul and his mother got out and Joe prepared to put away the pony and trap.

'How are ye?' Joe smiled, his false teeth gleaming. He and Philly, his elder brother, now working in England, had their teeth ripped out before they were fifteen.

'Hello.' Paul and Joe were the same age, and they had been companions during the past two summers – swimming at the brown pool, climbing trees, exercising Joe's father's greyhounds, helping with the ferrets, smoking Woodbines.

'When are you off?' Mummy asked.

'In the New Year, Ma'am'.

'Where are you going?' Paul asked. No one had told him.

'England.' More room in the lodge for the rest of the Roches. Damn. Paul would miss him. He should have come up here sooner to see him, instead of now, on Christmas Eve, lugging the bloody hamper.

The little room was bright and swept and newly polished. There was a smell of freshly baked pot oven bread mixed with smouldering turf.

'Good of you to come, Ma'am.'

'Nonsense Bridget. We enjoy seeing you. Don't we, Paul?'

Although Mrs Roche wasn't much more than forty she looked older, like a small frightened ageing bird; the black shawl she wore didn't help. Bringing up all those children with very little money could hardly be easy, even if Roche's job on the estate was secure.

Jesus pointing to His heart looked down as Paul and his mother sat at the long wooden table, covered in their honour with a freshly laundered table cloth. No one else sat; Mrs Roche and the children stood and watched them eat. The Willow Pattern china plates and delicate tea cups and linen napkins were for them alone. So was the tea; Mrs Roche must have used half the household ration.

'You must be starving, Master Paul.' How he hated Master. Joe was the only person on the estate who didn't call him that. It could be worse – she might address him as Your Honour. Everything was home-made from the country butter – could he detect a hair in it? – to the scones, cake and rhubarb jam. Any hesitation and Mrs Roche was all over him.

'Sure you're not eating a solitary thing, Master Paul.' She darted forward and another scone was thrust at him. The children continued to watch.

'Terrible that rain.'

'It's brightened up now.'

'Will it be fine for Christmas?'

'It will, I'm sure. '

'More tea, Master Paul?'

'Whereabouts in England is Philly, Joe?'

'South Shields, Ma'am.'

'He must be pleased you're joining him.'

'Yes, Ma'am.'

'What will you be doing, Joe?'

'I'll be in the factory alongside Phil, Ma'am. Munitions.'

'Ah. Helping to end the war.'

'Yes, Ma'am.'

'They pay well,' Mrs Roche said.

Another long silence. Another cup of tea for both of them.

Mummy said, 'Grasshopper has settled in well.'

'Is that a fact?' For the first time the children looked interested.

'He's a good dog.'

'He is that.'

Only when they were satiated were they allowed to go home. In the cold, clouds coming out of their mouths as they spoke, they exchanged thanks and happy Christmases and wished Joe well for his journey to England. Mummy gave him five pounds.

Over for another year. Perhaps next year Paul would put his foot down. After Christmas he would look up Joe before he went off.

'What a wonderful tea. I love Bridget's scones.'

He had to climb down to pee. So did Mummy; he didn't look. When they were on the move again he asked, 'Where is South Shields?'

'I haven't the faintest idea.'

'Who is Grasshopper?' But he guessed it was the new greyhound. A slow greyhound.

'I was just in time to stop that bloody Roche from getting rid of him.' In the bottom of the river were a number of Dan Roche's unsuccessful dogs with stones round their necks.

He lay under the blankets and heavy quilt, biting the sheet, watching the light outside the window slowly soften the darkness. There was the rustle of a mouse in the corner. It was many years since Mummy left a stocking at the end of his bed so that Father Christmas would fill it up. He used to wonder if the old fellow was connected to the ho ho bird that topped the big mirror in the drawing room. He must have wasted time on his global flight signalling out Minden from Plassey and Malplaquet and other glorious days for the British army after which the bedrooms were named.

He remembered the gifts, the annuals, penknives, games, whistles, wind-up toys. It was nice believing in him.

You had to believe in God as well.

He got up at last, went to the window and drew the curtains. The cold was bearable this morning, because Dempsey had lit the central heating boiler and the fat radiators were warm. In the fields outside an animal coughed. Cook and the maids were taking out their bicycles to go to mass. It was three years since he last went to Christmas mass with Daddy. He felt guilty as he shouted, wishing them Happy Christmas and they waved and called back, Happy Christmas, Master Paul. They would return smartly after mass to cook the dinner for nine people before they got to eat a bit of turkey themselves.

He shaved, the razor dodging the obstacles of his spots. He put on his tweed suit and the only tie he possessed which was not a school tie.

Mummy wore her dark green skirt and jacket with Daddy's regimental brooch picked out in diamonds on the collar – churchgoing clothes. They ate breakfast hastily since everything about Christmas was a rush. They took another trip in the trap down to the gate and beyond to where the dour little church waited for them. Why do Protestant bells have a different sound from Catholic bells? Catholic bells are sharp and tinny, urgently reminding the faithful of their duty, while Protestant ones are deep and soporific. Or perhaps that was because old Mr Hudson was pulling wearily on the rope.

Paul recognised some members of Protestant farming families and a few whom Mummy called kindred spirits, which was shorthand for people of our class. Delighted at the annual increase in his congregation, the Canon preached for nearly half an hour. Paul wished he was attending mass down the road which Father McCabe would be conducting briskly. It would be over by now and the maids would be back in the kitchen. Beside him Mummy sat and worried about Christmas lunch, even though she did not have to cook it. She should punish the Canon by putting sixpence in the collection basket instead of the seasonal five pounds. Paul closed his eyes and thought hard about punishing the Canon by becoming a Catholic.

Heads were drooping, the women were looking at their watches, their children were kicking each other in their pews. At last, finally, unbelievably, thanking God, hoping the Canon would choke on his turkey, they rose to their feet for Hark the Herald.

Cook was in tears. 'Rascal's after getting to the ham.'

It looked a mess, but had been rescued before the very worst had happened.

'Put it under the tap, give it a scrub, and carve it straight away. This side isn't so bad. And shut up all dogs.'

The usual old friends and relations were coming to lunch. They were as much a seasonal fixture as the tree and the decorations.

'Oh Diana, meat!' Mary Rooke, who was very poor, would cry when Mummy invited her over. Being Lady Mary Rooke made no difference to her poverty. She lived in a caravan on the outskirts of Dublin and made a desperate living as a gardener. There was very little money in the sort of gardening she did for people living in Foxrock, although Mummy said her flowers and planting were as good, if not better than her own.

Another hunger marcher was the Countess who was rich but mean, living widowed in her castle. The Count, who had only had a Papal title had died long ago. Once, so it was said, the Countess had been a chorus girl. She could not have Christmas alone, even with her lover, and she had been coming here for as long as Paul could remember. Mummy kept up with her for all sorts of reasons.

She was the first to arrive, driving up in her big American Chevrolet bringing Sam Seymour, her lover for the time being, who looked too old to get his leg over. She lived miles away; where in heaven's name did she manage to get the petrol? Probably Sam arranged it. Probably that was why she permitted him to stay with her. As usual she had brought her Pekinese. Rouge, jewellery, knockout scent and the snapping dog clutched to her bosom approached Paul and he braced himself for the kiss.

'Happy Epiphany!' She always said that instead of Happy Christmas. And as usual, 'How big you've grown!'

Other guests came together in Trigger Dobbs's Ford V8 which had been converted to run on charcoal. Five people were crammed in, Mary

Rooke, Donald and Valerie who was Daddy's second cousin whom Mummy and Daddy loathed, and, of course Trigger and his wife Helen whose hair looked as if it had been done with an egg beater. Trigger had one eye which was the reason why he was not off fighting. Once he had been in a pub and taking out the false one, tapped it on the bar counter to get attention. The girl who had been doing the serving fainted.

Not only the missing eye, but the charcoal made his Ford V8 go erratically. Smoke came out of the back and a hiss of steam.

'Don't worry girls!' Trigger's voice could be heard, 'It's only cooling down! Stay where you are!'

There was a bang.

'Are you all right?'

From the back of the car came faint voices.

'Open the door!'

Fumes had half asphyxiated them and they had to be revived with drink.

'Last Wednesday Trigger set fire to a sheep on the Curragh,' Helen said.

'Nosy bastard,' Trigger added. 'Came up when I was riddling. Went off in flames bleating.'

How well the old place looked with light streaming through newly cleaned windows! Dempsey waited in the dining room, dressed in a black jacket to act butler, a role for which Mummy gave him two quid and a couple of packets of Sweet Afton. She had not persuaded him to wear a footman's uniform or to wash his hands. Agnes helped him without getting any bonus, although she had already received her Christmas present, an extra week's wages. But Dempsey had got that as well.

Ancestors looked down, a military gentleman in a red coat, a bishop and a lady in a silk gown who had a moustache. The best of the Snaffles were here, *The Finest View in Europe* and *The Worst View in Europe, the dhrink died out of me on the wrong side of Becher's*. The room was cold as ever in spite of the fire and the central heating and the Countess had done well not taking off the fox fur round her neck, the fox's head snapping at its tail. Everyone else shivered.

The cutlery shone, the forks tasting of Silvo. Mummy had placed flowers all over the place, too many for Trigger's taste; the place looked like a bloody funeral parlour.

'Oh Diana, turkey!' exclaimed Mary Rooke, shouting across the Christmas roses. So it was, and just as well, since the slices of ham were only passable. Paul was stuck between the Countess and Mary Rooke on the side of the table away from the fire. The Pekinese, huddled against the fender, was the only being in the room who was warm.

Trigger ceased fumbling with his flies and carved. Things were getting cold by the time Dempsey and Agnes handed round the potatoes, celery and the pretty Brussels sprouts dyed Kelly green after cook had thrown handfuls of bread soda into the saucepan.

The Countess chattered as she munched. 'Cooking Christmas dinner isn't hard. Nothing like a soufflé.'

Paul would pass that remark on to Mummy.

'I didn't see you at mass.'

'I went with Mummy this time. '

'Have you taken your Confirmation yet?'

Nosy old bitch. She meant Catholic Confirmation, and since she was another of Daddy's spies, and a friend of Father Hogan, knew perfectly well he hadn't.

'Not yet.'

'High time you did, young man. How old are you?'

'Fourteen,' he lied, adding, 'We're waiting for Daddy to come home.'

He watched her putting a piece of ham in her mouth. 'I had a sweet letter from your father. He worries a lot about you.'

'He'll be here next Christmas . . .'

'Please God!'

He turned and talked to Mary Rooke, who was also eating the ham. 'Ham, I haven't had ham for months. More turkey! Pass the Cumberland sauce.' She cleaned out the sauceboat.

The plum pudding appeared. It was Paul's duty to light it with brandy in a darkened spoon. They were all watching him.

'Hold it steady!'

The match spluttered and went out. He tried again.

'Don't they teach you anything at school?'

Trigger took the spoon and placed it over a candle until the blue flame appeared to cheers.

Mary Rooke got the silver wishbone and Paul wondered what she wished for. Crackers were pulled. Grey hair and bald heads were topped with paper hats. Jokes were read out. *Why was the Egyptian boy worried? Because his daddy was a mummy. Where do you find giant snails? On the ends of giant's fingers.* There was port and Benedictine together with weak coffee – how did Mummy manage to find such things, but she always did?

Trigger led the toast to absent friends, Daddy in particular. Here's to 1945 being the last year of the war.

After dinner they moved to the drawing room which was almost as cold as the dining room where Paul distributed and received presents. He gave Mummy a bottle of Je Reviens, for which he had saved over the year from his pocket money. On his last visit to his aunt at the convent he had got off the bus and rushed into Clearys.

He didn't expect much from anyone especially at this time and dutifully gave thanks for home-made fudge from Valerie, a set of Halma from Trigger and Helen and from the Countess an atlas which had come straight off her bookshelf. Nothing from Mary Rooke, of course, who gave Mummy a handful of cuttings of unusual flowers. But Mummy came up trumps – in addition to the usual five pounds and the jumper knitted by Mrs Dempsey, she gave him a new bicycle, hidden behind the heavy curtains.

Pity he had to receive it so publicly. Thanks Mummy, and he blew her a kiss. This was very good – the old bike was rusty and so small he had been riding it with the greatest difficulty. And nice to have a smashing Raleigh.

Diana, you must find ways of cutting down on expenses.

'Oh what a lucky boy!'

It was time for them to leave, t.g.

'See you at mass,' said the Countess. He would ride down on his new bike. There was a delay when the Pekinese went missing.

'Oh Diana, what a wonderful day,' shouted Mary Rooke. Mummy had given her some turkey slices and Christmas pudding to take with her. Donald and Valerie got some as well.

They stood in the darkness waving away the Countess and Sam. Sam had drunk more whiskeys than were good for him. So had Trigger who found his torch and from the boot of the Ford took out a bag of charcoal which needed time to light. As he revved up the engine the poisonous smell reached the porch.

'Tally Ho! Everyone on board!'

Helen, Mary Rooke, Donald and Valerie made their way over the gravel and crept inside, winding down windows as the Ford spluttered and went off into the night. Mary Rooke's voice could be heard faintly. '. . . wonderful day!'

'I don't envy them,' Paul and his mother said simultaneously.

'Hurray, hurray they've gone!'

After the dogs were released and fed they sat in the sitting room and had a plate of spiced beef beside the fire. The maids and cook had done the washing up and bicycled off in the darkness to their relations and there was no one in the house except themselves. They listened to the King's speech – his stammer was pretty bad.

Mummy had a fit of conscience and rummaged in her desk for Daddy's latest letters. They were much more informative than usual, and lists of things to do around the estate were kept to the minimum. Daddy must have felt the Christmas spirit. He was in Egypt, writing from the Gezira Club 'where the clean limbed sons of England loll about in uniform, take their drinks and talk to the girls.'

'Sounds like he's having fun.'

'He's going to miss the war when he comes home.'

Paul went to the blasted Stephen's Day hunt, although all he wanted to do was to go about on the new bike. Instead, since Mummy expected it, there was getting up in darkness, Pav to saddle and bridle, and the challenge of not getting unseated. She calmed down when she was trotting beside Parade, whom Mummy rode side-saddle.

Rain began falling as they set off, and it took them an hour's hack through mud and overhanging branches of trees before they joined the meet. Numbers were small, a few more than a dozen out, three of them small children, since no one had motor transport.

Mr Lawless, the Master and Paddy Ahern, the whip, had already arrived with the van pulled by two horses which contained the hounds. After the hounds were let out, the horses were unhitched and saddled and bridled.

Pav began her usual display of another bad habit, back kicking at any horse that came close.

'Steady on . . .'

'Get back.'

'Whoa . . .'

'Look after your horse, young man – rein him in' – a crabby faced woman with a veiled bowler hat was shouting through the rain as Pav lashed out once more. Mummy had disappeared. Luckily the horn sounded and the thick wedge of riders followed the Master, up a lane and into an open field. Mr Lawless was a superbly good rider, but there were those who thought he ought to be away fighting the Hun rather than staying at home gallivanting on horseback.

At the gate a wild looking farmer in a ragged overcoat held together with string thumped every passing horse, intoning, 'Get on out of that!' and, 'There she goes!'

They pushed through and galloped after the hounds in the direction of Piggot's Hill. Pav decided to behave herself and Paul jumped two easy fences, following Mummy who bounded elegantly ahead. Then he was facing a large bank. He pressed in his knees, leaned forward and urged Pav to do her best. Perhaps a more confident rider could have persuaded her, but Pav's good moods never lasted, and she swerved, tossing him into a pool of water.

Humiliation came with the arrival of Dr Waters with his usual smile of sympathy. The good doctor made it his duty to ride at the back of the field retrieving people or ministering to them. The smile was the one he directed at crying children.

'Nothing broken, I hope?'

Paul got to his feet before the doctor could dismount. 'I'm fine, thanks.'

For a moment Dr Waters watched him limp. 'Sure?' He gave another smile, directed his horse at the bank and was away.

Pav had disappeared.

Covered in water and mud, Paul limped back to where the meet had begun and waited. Dusk was beginning to fall by the time the hunt returned flushed with success. A small girl had been blooded and Dr Waters was leading Pav. Mr Lawless and Paddy Ahern rounded up the hounds and shooed them into the van before mounting again and making for Nolan's pub for hot whiskeys.

'Pity you missed the kill,' Mummy said.

As they passed Nolan's they noticed the horses belonging to the Master and whip lying on their sides in exhaustion.

'Just as well they are both on a long rein.'

Next day Paul's head ached – concussion again? – and he felt stiff as a board. But he took his new bike and rode it down to the village to mass. There was no sign of the Countess.

CHAPTER EIGHT

In Green Dorm there was stupendous news.

Fingers Erskine was gone. Gone for ever. Left St George's. How? What happened?

'Leech squealed.'

'Leech had nightmares over Christmas.'

'Tears.'

'Hysterics.'

'His father complained.'

'Fingers went too far.'

'Dismissed.'

'Sacked.'

Leech Blood-Watson was in second year. Brave little chap. Paul knew all about what must have happened to him. It had happened regularly to plenty of people but this was the first time anyone had made a fuss. Paul remembered every detail of his own experience four years ago. Hartigan's birthday treat. Mr Fallon's cottage.

They had set out in the little van Fingers had borrowed. From where they sat they could see the buttocks of the gas bag overlapping the roof and pressing down on the windows. If it burst, Fingers told them with a guffaw, they would be instantly wrapped in flame.

Paul remembered every stage of the journey, driving past the encampment full of shivering tinkers whose frost-stiffened rags draped the hedges, turning by the quarries filled with burnt flowers of buddleia, and up towards the mountains. It was bleak country of vermin – magpies swooped and foxes hunted through the gorse. Once Fingers stopped to watch a man exercising his greyhounds, setting them after the hare he took out of a sack.

They drove up into the mountains. There was a chink of bottles in the back.

'What are those, Sir?'

'Oh, cider, since this is a celebration.' Fingers believed in the Scout's motto Be Prepared, since each bottle was laced with Jameson.

Mr Fallon, a friend of Fingers, was an artist who earned a charwoman's wages at the College of Art teaching Dublin housewives to draw from the antique. Consequently his cabin was neglected and brown water ran from the thatch down the lime-washed walls.

'In England thatched roofs are respectable,' Fingers said, climbing out of the car with the cider. 'Among the affluent they show discernment and taste of a limited nature. In Ireland they are a signal of poverty.'

The padlock on the door was rusted and had to be broken with a stone. Inside the long room with its dresser and inglenook sweated with damp which had climbed up the walls staining some watercolours of Connemara.

'To work. We'll do our good deed.' They had swept up some of the plaster that sprinkled the floor and threw away the mess in the zinc bucket that had rotted to compost. They had disposed of the fur inside long-unwashed teacups and the rat that had died in the milk saucepan. Then they found a supply of wood and turf – 'John won't mind' – and made a huge blaze.

'No need to light the lamp. Firelight is so lovely.' Two rugs were brought out of the van and spread on the floor. 'Smoke anyone? It is rather a special occasion. Now to hand round the booze.'

The next couple of hours had been energetic. Then Fingers went to the door of the cabin to look down on the city and the rim of lights to Howth circling the blackness of Dublin Bay.

'Oh dear, it's nearly six o'clock. We must hurry boys, or we'll be late for prayers.'

The next day Hartigan, who had a bad hangover, had threatened to blow the gaff.

'You can't possibly,' he was told. 'There'd be the hell's own row. Anyway it would be beastly of you considering it was your birthday treat.'

Now, years later, at last, Leech had told all.

They were silent for a minute remembering the boy scouts, the winter tea parties.

'Poor old Fingers. Wonder what he'll do.'

'He's off to England to a public school. Goody gave him a great reference. No hard feelings.'

'Public?'

'Eton, Harrow, maybe Charterhouse. It's now or never for him. No competition. They're mad for teachers because of the war.'

Paul had ridden forty odd miles to school on his new bicycle while his trunk was sent on by train. He used the new freedom the bicycle gave him to bicycle to mass. In February he raced across town to Aunt Delia and Father Hogan.

Father Hogan was morose, immersed in the depression of Lent. People only wore their ashen faces for a day, but the marks on their foreheads were tokens of sorrow for the whole winter.

Once again the season seem to emphasise Ireland's isolation. At the war's end young men were still fleeing desolate neutrality to cross the water to work or fight. Those who stayed at home felt they were living in the eye of the storm, trapped in its stifling calm, the great winds around them. At a time when Timoshenko was driving Germans over the snow, Lenten pastorals attacked the problem of the pagan influences in dance halls.

A little feverish from influenza, Father Hogan gave Paul some Lenten literature and dismissed him, not before trying a little gentle persuasion. '. . . Wouldn't it be a nice surprise for your father when he comes back to find you have made the correct decision?'

'. . . I know he is deeply hurt to learn that you are still outside the faith.'

Deeply hurt meant bloody angry.

How good it was, Paul felt, to climb on his bike and whizz back across Dublin.

Mrs Good paused in her task of cutting off the unused parts of letters whose paper could be adapted for the sending of brief notes.

Mr Good read a newly delivered letter. 'I thought it a good idea for the Bishop to have a word with Blake-Willoughby. Here's what he says: "...I remember that particular family tragedy well; people were horrified when the boy's grandfather chose to be persuaded by his wife to leave the Church of Ireland. I had no idea of the present conflict. How sad that Mrs Blake-Willoughby was weak enough to allow the boy to take First Communion. I wonder what hold this has given the other side? Of course I will use my influence in every way. I would be pleased to see the boy at any time for tea. I would suggest a weekday afternoon."'

'Excellent,' said Mrs Good. 'With any luck we'll have him back with Beamish.'

On his next half holiday Paul was packed off to the Bishop's residence, a lavishly maintained Georgian mansion a short distance from St George's. The bishop was filthy rich, having married an American heiress. Paul knew him well by sight, having seen him every other Sunday in church receiving Holy Communion, first in line. Outside, with the rest of the school, he had regularly peered into his Daimler, past the inscrutable chauffeur.

He cycled through the gates of the bishop's residence and up the half mile of avenue, past the Italian garden, past the rose garden, past the sunken garden where two follies and copies of Roman statues were dimly visible in the frost and imported shrubs were covered with straw and sacking. The stucco front of the house stretched impressively on either side of the portico, concealing stately living rooms and twenty empty bedrooms.

He leaned the bicycle against a column and the double doors were opened by a footman who led him into a marble hall. It was warm! Really warm so that he took off his coat without hesitation. He hadn't felt this warm for weeks – not even Aunt Delia's convent bothered to heat halls and staircases. The American heiress.

He followed the footman past a couple of marble statues through a series of silent rooms. Occasionally a clock ticked or tinkled as they walked by buhl cabinets and gilded portraits to the study where a tiny bow-legged figure, stood in front of a fire.

The bishop was old and trembling and his cracked voice shook as he greeted Paul. He wore a frock coat and his gaiters were anchored with buckle shoes; the purple of his vest was dimly reflected in the amethysts of his pectoral cross, which were like water to which a drop of beetroot juice had been added.

No sign of the heiress. Was she dead? In America? Divorced? Did bishops get divorced? Perhaps she had just taken the Daimler into Dublin. Paul remembered that she never came to church with the Bishop.

'. . . I knew your grandfather nearly forty years ago. We used to meet at the Club.'

'Uh . . .'

'Forty years must seem a very long time to you, Philip. Around the turn of the century.'

'Sir . . .'

'In those days boys like yourself, Philip, dressed formally at school. Black jackets and striped trousers and top hats on Sundays.'

'Really, Sir?'

'You should address me as My Lord.'

The Bishop caught Paul's eye gazing at the photographs and signed portraits on a table with curvy legs. A queen throttled in jewellery looked out of a Fabergé frame. Two smiling girls in sailor hats cuddled small dogs; 'à cher Freddy' they had written 'Olga et Helena.'

He pointed out a moustached military figure, 'You know who that is, Philip?'

'No, My Lord.' Should he correct him and admit he was Paul?

'That's the Kaiser. You can see his withered arm.' The Kaiser had signed his name with a flourish with his other arm.

'Gosh.'

'A civilised man compared to Hitler. Some people feel it might have been better for the world if Germany had won the Great War. The country would have been the spared years of misery which led directly to the present awful conflict.

'. . . Possibly an unpatriotic conclusion, Philip. but remember from this corner of the world we can view Europe and our great sister island with a detachment that is not possible elsewhere.'

The old boy settled in a wing chair. Perched on damask the other side of the fire, Paul blinked and listened.

'. . . Of course my ministry became complicated when I met and married my dear wife and undertook the management of her property. Not easy – a case of the eye of the needle . . .'

'. . . Since my wife departed this life' – so she was dead – 'I have found managing the estate leaves less time for clerical duties. They are confined to charitable committees and, of course, attending the synod.'

Suddenly the Bishop turned to the business of Paul becoming a Protestant. 'It is time you made up your mind, my boy and came into the fold. No more of this nonsense of going to mass every so often.'

'. . . No, my Lord.'

'We must always be on our toes . . . .' He tapped the arm of his chair with a bleached white knuckle. '. . . they have their tricks, Philip. I remember once in my parish there was a small farmer, a Protestant who had married an RC. Now when this old fellow was on his final sickbed I used to visit him frequently.'

He got up and held onto the edge of the Bossi chimney piece.

'To my astonishment one day I received a letter from the local RC priest to say that as he had the happiness of receiving Mr Camier into the Catholic church he trusted that I would discontinue my visits. My poor old friend had been baptised and anointed when unconscious!'

'Oh!'

'However, Philip, he recovered! And how angry he was at being forcibly perverted as he described it.'

Paul laughed dutifully.

The Bishop walked over to Olga and Helena for a moment and then tottered back, all the time talking.

'I used to converse frequently with our postman, a dear fellow, and RC of course. Do you know what he said to me once? He said that the Catholic religion was mighty comforting but mighty expensive. "Mr Foley," I said to him, "has it ever occurred to you to consider how much more prosperous, abiding and successful in war and commerce Protestant nations are than RC ones?" "Yes sir", said he, "You have your portion in this life!"'

Laugh. Laugh again.

'I thought he had me for a moment. But then I remembered that fine verse from Timothy where St Paul says "Godliness hath the promise of this life that now is and of that which is to come."'

The footman came in and whispered in his ear.

'Tea.'

The old boy stood for a few moments gathering strength before leading the way into the conservatory which was filled with tropical plants. The tea table, covered with a damask cloth stood among ferns and orchids, and behind it a maid in white uniform waited to pour out from the silver tea pot.

'Now Philip, I hope I needn't tell you to begin.'

There were cakes, meringues bulging with cream, a crenellated scarlet jelly, eclairs and cherry cake. There was ice-cream and fresh pineapple chunks, while crumpets and toast were kept hot in silver warmers. The butler spooned out jelly tinged with rum. The tea had an aromatic flavour and came from China. But when?

And what about Lent?

Paul had eaten a lot in the cause of religion, but nothing approaching this feast. The memory of Aunt Delia's teas faded instantly; the convent's menu could not compete with the bishop's. Where had his wealth procured such rarely seen delicacies?

'Bananas!'

The Bishop sat down in a wicker armchair to watch him dabbing cream over his face like soapsuds, eating greedily, indiscriminately. He mopped sweat off his forehead. The hot pipes in the conservatory combined with the water from the lily pond which gardeners sprayed around the greenery every day contributed to the stuffy jungle atmosphere.

'Certainly in the old days in places where Protestants were numerous and confident, mixed marriages seemed to be working in our favour. I mean places like Greystones or Avoca where the parish consists largely of descendants of Cornish miners. They came over to work the copper and silver. Did you know, Philip, that the communion vessels there are fashioned from silver mined in the area?'

Paul shook his head, his mouth full.

'. . . I say again, Philip be on your guard. You are too young to realise the implications of their worship of the mass. I do not think the wording of the thirty-nine articles is too strong when they talk of blasphemous fables and dangerous deceits.'

Paul scarcely listened. Greed overcame caution.

'. . . I am sorry they persuaded you into taking First Communion. It is a step which our own church very sensibly postpones until Confirmation when a boy can understand the seriousness of what he is undertaking. There are other grave differences which I won't go into. Consider, Philip, the worship commonly paid to the BVM in the RC church contrasted with our own reverent gratitude to the Mother of our Lord.'

Now Paul's stomach was straining against his trouser buttons. The hot wafts of damp air, the freesias, the Lapsang Souchong and the clotted cream were too rich a combination.

'Try some of that preserve. From our own strawberries. We provide what we can. I have given up the Italian garden since the emergency began. We grow vegetables there instead. And the front lawn has been put to the plough. Winter wheat . . .'

'Please Sir, my Lord, may I be excused?'

The Bishop did not realise anything was wrong, but the butler and maid watched Paul rush over to the pool. As he leaned over the space between the discs of water lily leaves a gold fish gazed up at him, but in a moment was obscured by the yellow wave of the feast he had eaten.

'Paul never brings anything back,' Beamish complained. Up until last term he, too, had been fêted and fed, but now as a result of his own decision he was half starved like everyone else.

'He does sometimes,' amended Dixon. 'The occasional RC sweetie.'

'It's not easy. If I ask Mother Trinitas if I could take away something she will say she prefers to give cakes and stuff to some hungry little boys she knows if I don't want them.'

'You don't ask, BW, you steal.'

'There aren't any cakes at my aunt's place. Lent.'

'But the bishop's different? Yesterday you could have put things down your shirt or something.'

'I didn't feel like it.' Sweating and groaning in the Bishop's Daimler, his bicycle strapped to the boot, he had not been thinking of his friends. 'Perhaps I will next time I go.'

'Next time?'

'He wants to see me again.'

'He wants you safe inside before he dies,' Beamish said. 'Like the old fella in the bible. Lord now lettest thy servant depart in peace.'

'I suppose that makes BW Jesus,' sneered Dixon.

'Beamish committed himself too soon,' Sheridan commented. 'My God, BW, you're on the pig's back. You can go on playing them all off until you're grown up, you lucky sod. '

'I hear you disgraced yourself when you visited the Bishop,' Father Hogan said.

You'd think one of the perks of that rich old man would be to have Protestant servants.

Mr Good announced in assembly the news that our distinguished neighbour so much loved by all of us had passed away.

'Who?'

'Bishop . . . Daimler,' someone murmured. Poor old fellow – had to die some time.

'You killed him,' Beamish hissed at Paul, who wondered a bit. So much talk from so old a little man might have exhausted him. And he was really old – ninety? Ninety-five?

CHAPTER NINE

Paul's birthday took place just after half-term, and his mother sent him ten pounds. He never bothered to tell her that gifts of money were against school rules.

His father's regular letter arrived.

'HQ Ghazni. Dear Paul, I know you are reflecting that upon reaching your sixteenth year you are on the verge of manhood . . . .Father Hogan continues to be troubled by your inability to take your religion seriously. When I return, which, please God, will be in the near future, I trust you will have made up your mind, and will go along the proper path. Meanwhile put every effort into your exams since a reasonable success is immensely important when you are facing up to the future. With love from Daddy.'

He might have sent a fiver.

Paul thought that he didn't have a hope of passing more than one or two exams, and nor did anyone else for that matter. There were those who had sung for joy when Fingers departed, and to the majority of boys Leech Blood-Watson was a hero. However, sixth form cursed the little brat, since they knew very well that Fingers was the only master with the energy and knowledge to push them towards any degree of success when it came to exams.

Mr ffrench, the wretched master who had taken over from Fingers was useless. He was not even a Trinity undergraduate. He was ignorant. Totally. The boys were aware that the series of books he kept open on his desk enabled him to keep just ahead of them in knowledge. The Latin crib. The maths problems with the answers given at the end pages. They sniggered at the two little f's in his surname and called him Fireball. ffireball.

People had seen Paul open the envelope with his mother's present. 'Ten quid . . . lucky bugger . . .' He hid the note in a gym shoe in the back of his locker.

That evening Jeffers Minor approached him. Jeffers was still at St George's, some delay about his call up. Bully Jeffers ignored him and had not even noticed his brother had grown a moustache like Hitler's.

'You've a bike?' Jeffers asked.

'Bike? Yes . . .'

'How about a trip into town tomorrow?'

'Town?'

'Dublin.'

The height of adventure. Of risk.

'After lights?'

'Natch.'

'We'd go to a pub?'

'That's the idea.'

Paul took a deep breath. 'OK then.'

'Grease your bike well and examine the tyres carefully. The last thing you want is a puncture.'

'What about Red Eye?' The night watchman.

'He's OK. Every now and then I throw him a packet of fags. Keeps him happy.'

Most of Green Dorm was aware that Jeffers Minor went into Dublin regularly. At least twice a week he would get out of his iron bed in the darkness and disappear into the chill of winter. And then at two or three or even four in the morning there would be footsteps and panting and creaking as he got back in his bed. Some heard him, some didn't. Sometimes he would ask someone to go along with him, usually Erskine or Cusack who got decent amounts of pocket money.

Sheridan was a conscientious head prefect, who would never have condoned such goings-on, but he slept as soon as his head touched his pillow, and when he was awake failed to notice that before lights out Jeffers and whoever was going with him climbed into bed under their sheets and blankets fully clothed.

No one told.

This evening Paul also went to bed in his clothes. Lying awake, watching the slow movement of the luminous hands of his watch, he felt qualms because he, too, was a prefect. But he was flattered. And there was the excitement.

As soon as they heard Sheridan's snores the three of them moved. Erskine had given up on the expeditions – Funk! – so it was Jeffers, Paul, and Cusack, who groped their way down the long flight of stone steps and into the basement where Jeffers lit a match and found the key to the back door hanging on a hook on the dresser. Then outside, and a sprint across to the bicycle shed. Unlocking his chain in the dark, Paul thought that another reason besides the fact he had money that Jeffers may have chosen him was height. He hadn't just picked him out because he liked company. And the same was true of Erskine and Cusack who were also tall in addition to being well heeled. Jeffers must feel that they were more likely to pass for adults in his pub.

'Dirty your face,' he whispered to Paul, striking more matches for light. 'It'll make you look older.' Mud. He produced two fedoras and a couple of mackintoshes he had pinched earlier in the day from the masters' cloakroom. These thefts had become routine. 'Pull the hats down over your face as much as you can. They'll have to be returned. Got your money? Ready? If you get a puncture you'll have to be left behind.'

There was a moon and a cold fresh wind that blew away sleep. They freewheeled down the avenue past the turreted lodge where Red Eye lurked, Jeffers leading them in swift single file. It took about twenty minutes to cycle past the comfortable bow-fronted suburbs, to the city and the pub Jeffers frequented. It was situated in a side street near the cinemas, singled out by the name of the publican in gilded wooden letters.

Jeffers hustled them inside past the long bar spaced with snuffling silent drinkers and pushed them into the snug with its high wooden walls. Built to conceal women, it was cupboard sized with a long narrow bench running down one side. Opposite was a shelf narrower still, so that glasses and bottles balanced along it were in constant danger of being brushed off onto the floor, which was stained and speckled with the flattened remains of cigarettes.

An old man who wore a winged collar and was wrapped in an apron that covered him from bosom to ankles opened the top half of the creaking stable door that divided the snug from the bar.

'Publican's father,' Jeffers muttered. 'Put your heads down. Don't open your mouths.' Loudly he said 'What'll you have? Two glasses and a pint of stout, please, Mr Brennan. Give us your money,' he hissed and Paul handed over his tenner.

The snug was at right angles to the back of the bar where they could see young Mr Brennan side stepping up and down, taking orders, while his father poured out their drinks scooping at each glass with a wooden spoon to rid it of froth. Then the old boy's shaking hand delivered the glasses one at a time over the door. Another delay and finally came the change – Jeffers reached for it, but Paul got there first and pocketed the note and half crowns.

If he had the choice he would not have picked stout. He'd tried a gaseous black bottle with Joe Roche and had hated it. This was his introduction to draught, a taste of burnt paper sieved through the sudsy head.

They sat in a row listening to the sounds from over the partition, grumbles mostly, mingled with the loud narrative of an airman home on leave. Sometimes people opened the door and peered in; a woman with black diamonds on her sleeve who was very drunk sat with them for a few minutes before getting up and wandering away outside again.

'Another round, Mr Brennan,' Jeffers called out.

'I'll have cider,' Paul said. Cusack paid. Paul studied the paint on the yellowed woodwork and the faded cigarette advertisement out of date since prices had gone up.

'Do you come to this place every time?' he asked.

Jeffers wiped the froth off his mouth. 'I stay here a couple of rounds. Then if I don't have a bunch of kids on my tail, I go off to the Four Provinces.'

The snug door opened again and two more people came in, young men, one dark, the other with red hair which grew in little curls, pubic fashion, close to his head. At the sight of the newcomers Jeffers' face lit up, then withered in embarrassment.

'I thought you weren't coming this week.'

'Ginger got off. Whose deese?'

'That's Blake-Willoughby.'

'Christ . . . he a lord or something?'

'The one in the corner is Cusack.'

'Kids!'

Jeffers introduced the newcomers : 'Rapey Ginger and Bart' and added quickly, 'What'll you have?'

Bart smiled. 'A drop of the hard.'

'Your round, Paul,' and Paul watched his half crowns turn into whiskey, at the same time finding another glass of cider placed in the shelf before him. Now there was plenty of chat in the snug, the newcomers ribbing Jeffers. They lighted up cigarettes – Paul and Cusack did as well – and talked about drink at length. Ginger claimed he could tell Guinness from the southern stouts, Murphy or Beamish although he did not offer to prove it, accepting another short instead. They discussed girls, pretty ones, shy ones, English ones, willing ones, all conquests. Ginger boasted how he had been up in the juvenile courts for carnal knowledge.

Paul rose to his feet.

'I've got to go to the bogs.'

'For God's sake don't let anyone see you.'

He put on the fedora and belted the mackintosh. 'Keep your head down.' He crept out of the snug into the crowd. There was no indication where he should go, but an atmosphere emanated from a wrought iron spiral staircase that twisted down by a corner of the bar. He descended and found that he was right.

He peed between two swaying old men. The walls were covered with graffiti. 'John Charles for Pope' someone had written in tribute to the Archbishop. He found 'Hitler is Dev's cousin, I think' and 'The future of Ireland is in your hands' which he thought very funny. He would write it up in the St George's bogs.

He circled his way upstairs. There was a stir in the air as young Mr Brennan blinked the lights and began his wailing evening dismissal. 'Now gents, please . . .' Paul bent his head and pushed his way through drinkers concentrating on their last glass. Suddenly a shout stopped him. 'You!' He looked up and there was young Mr Brennan's angry face framed against a background of brown fitted drawers, brass taps and stout barrels.

It was a matter of his licence.

'There's more in the snug,' an informer observed.

After they had been thrown out Jeffers turned on Paul.

'I don't see that it matters. It was time anyway.'

'I won't be able to go back because of you, you little bastard. Neither will Ginger or Bart.'

'His dad didn't mind serving us.'

'That's because he's half blind.'

'Will we fill in the little focker?' Ginger asked, but Jeffers, who was basically a kind person, dissuaded them and they drifted off.

'They're going dancing,' Jeffers said crossly.

'You go if you like,' Cusack offered.

'I'd better see you fools home.' But he hesitated. 'How much have you got left?'

Paul still had a five pound note in his pocket, while Cusack could muster three quid. Jeffers stood silent, under the light of a street lamp. He lit another cigarette and smoked half of it before appearing to make up his mind.

'We can but try. In for a penny, in for a pound. Follow me. Bring your bikes.'

They pedalled along for about five minutes past some very dilapidated houses to the destination chosen by Jeffers.

'Don't open your mouths.' He banged on a shabby Georgian door which creaked open as a fat bald man peered out.

'It's me, Mr O'Toole, with a few friends.'

They were hustled inside towards a dark passage with slippery steps leading downstairs.

'Mind your heads.'

There was a party going on below. A woman screamed amid raucous laughter.

'It's Dolly Fossett's,' Jeffers said.

Everyone had heard of Dolly Fossett's, even the most junior boys at St George's.

'Is Mr O'Toole his real name?'

'Nah . . . Course not . . . Shut up. And let me do the talking.'

When Jeffers knocked at the basement door a fat woman wearing a low cut dress with puffed sleeves answered.

'Ten bob each.'

'Any chance of a reduction?'

'Are you joking?'

Jeffers paid up with Paul's fiver – no change – and they followed her, filing into a very crowded room, where they found a small table – the last one available.

'Keep on your coats and hats,' Jeffers said, offering them cigarettes. It was very hot; loud music from a gramophone and a lot of women were giggling and screeching. One of them came up to where they had settled down. Her dress was low cut like that of the lady at the door and she was perspiring in the heat.

'What are you having, dears?'

'The usual,' Jeffers said.

She was frowning. 'Are you a bit young?'

'No,' Jeffers said firmly, putting his hand up to his moustache.

'If you say so. What's your name, Babyface?' It was Paul she was looking at and he blushed. 'I'm not going to eat you.' She was leaning over the table and he could look straight into her breasts.

'Kids.' But she didn't seem to mind. She went off and the boys sat silent, smoking away, watching the people around them, listening to jokes and laughter and music, gauging the summer dresses, smelling Coty scent. This was the life. Tarts! Prostitutes!

If someone came along now this minute and told them to leave, they still would have had a good time, a unique time.

The woman returned with a tray full of tea cups decorated with a rose pattern and put them down in front of them.

'Thirty bob.' Cusack paid. It seemed a lot to pay for tea, especially tea without milk. Paul picked up his cup, took a draught and choked. It wasn't tea, it was whiskey.

They were so hot they defied Jeffers and took off their mackintoshes and hats before continuing to sit smoking and watching as men got up and danced, shuffling around with different women. The thumping music was deafening and clouds of tobacco smoke made it difficult to see. But it was marvellous, terrific, although Paul wished one of those women would ask him to dance – a dance here would justify to some extent all those lessons he had endured from Miss Watson all those years. He could do slow, quick quick slow with the best of them – so could Cusack, for that matter. But no one came near them.

Having finished what was in his teacup, Jeffers was getting restless. Perhaps he too would like a dance? He fished into his trouser pocket, pulled out the change he had in it and examined it for a minute or two.

'You still in funds?' Paul shook his head. 'How about you, Cusack – I'll pay you back.' Cusack reluctantly produced the two pounds he had left, and whined, 'I don't want any more whiskey.' Jeffers took no notice, but beckoned the lady who had brought them the tea cups and whispered in her ear. She nodded.

'You sit here, I won't be long.' And off he went somewhere.

Time passed and Paul and Cusack were not bored, although Cusack moaned about having no more money. Paul didn't mind, he thought his money well spent, every penny. A brothel . . . a whore house . . . a house of ill fame . . . Dolly Fossett's! What a tale to tell Green Dorm.

Except he was beginning to get worried about time – it was nearly two o'clock by his watch. Would they ever get back? Hurry up, Jeffers, what the hell could he be doing. But Paul knew quite well what he was doing.

They heard shouting in the far corner, loud shouting, louder than the noise of music and the noisy women. And a loud sound of crying.

'PLEASE . . . PLEASE!'

No one took any notice. There were only a couple of dancers on the floor at this stage, and through the smoke they could make out the back of a stout man on his knees in front of a lady who appeared to be quite elderly, in spite of her long blond hair.

'FORGIVE ME!' The man was shouting. 'FORGIVE ME!' You could

see the dark streaks at the lady's parting where the hair had grown out. The hair ended in yellow curls. She had wrinkles and mascara round her eyes made her look like a panda. Through bright red lips she was shouting – 'NOT AT ALL! NEVER. NOT A BASTARD LIKE YOU.'

The sobs grew louder. 'PLEASE, PLEASE . . .'

'SHUT YER GOB YE OULD FOOL!'

'I'M SORRY . . . I'M SORRY.'

'I'LL TEACH YOU! COME WITH ME AND I'LL GIVE YOU WHAT YOU DESERVE.'

'OH NO . . . NO . . . NO . . . FORGIVE ME . . .' Sob.

'I HAVE THE WHIP HANDY!'

Jeffers Minor reappeared looking pleased with himself.

Then the stout man on his knees turned round.

'Oh my God!'

Jeffers turned white as he recognised his brother.

'Jim!'

Paul and Cusack recognised him as well. The bulgy eyes. Bully Jeffers the disciplinarian being disciplined.

'OH MY GOD!'

'Let's get the hell out of here!'

Grabbing coats – they left the hats behind – the boys got to their feet and two of the teacups fell to the floor and smashed. They ran through the cigarette smoke, past the dancers, through the door, up the stairs past Mr O'Toole and out. They ran for their bicycles, and Jeffers and Cusack feverishly unlocked theirs. But Paul's wasn't there. His brand new bike . . . the chain sawed through . . . stolen.

'You'll have to walk or take a taxi or something,' Jeffers Minor called out as he and Cusack whizzed away.

CHAPTER TEN

'I always thought St George's was a wretched place . . . I never cared for Mr Good. I never trust men who wear beards . . . What were you doing? . . . If it hadn't been for the war you would have gone to England.'

Later came her refrain: 'We won't tell Daddy.'

Fat chance Daddy wouldn't find out Paul had been expelled. Father Hogan's spies were everywhere, even in an unsavoury brothel. But more likely Mr Good would have spread the word and Father Hogan would have received a letter dictated by Mrs Good. 'I wash my hands of the boy.' The Catholics are welcome to him.

Mummy showed him Mr Good's letter which was what you might expect: '. . . sullied his role as prefect . . . very much regret . . . old family shamed . . .' Paul made out the faded typescript with difficulty since the Goods kept typewriter ribbons until they fell to pieces.

No mention of D.F.'s and Mummy hadn't heard of the place.

He knew he must have really exasperated the Goods, considering his term's fees were always paid by banker's order and Mummy's father had been a lord. He supposed he was lucky not to be stripped of his prefect's honours in public like Dreyfus.

The unfairness of it! He recalled coming back from the city to St George's in a taxi in the darkness, Bully at his side, neither of them saying a word. Bully was breathing heavily, those pop eyes closed, tears on his red cheeks. Paul was in the depths of misery, not because of being found in D.F.'s, but because of the loss of his bike.

'Say a word and expect the worst,' Bully mouthed when the taxi reached the front porch of St George's and Mrs Good appeared in her dressing gown and grey hair in pigtails.

Paul made the mistake of trusting Bully to smooth things over.

Cusack was safe in bed after furiously pedalling back to school and getting there in time, while back in Dublin some gurrier had nicked Paul's own lovely bike. Jeffers Minor was OK as well, getting the hell out of St George's the very next day, out of reach of his brother and back to England before Paul had packed his bags.

Bully, who must have the world's record for sobering up quickly, told his story of finding the lad trespassing in the slums of Dublin outside a whore house instead of being asleep in the dormitory where he was prefect . . .

Of course Paul should have squealed. He should have said a word, shouted many words, FORGIVE ME . . . FORGIVE ME . . . PLEASE . . . PLEASE . . . Like a fool he had kept his mouth shut until it was too late to spill the beans.

Mummy was really peeved about the loss of the bicycle.

'From now on you'll have to do a lot of walking.'

At the end of the letter Mr Good recommended Mr Julian ffrench as a tutor to Paul if Mrs Blake-Willoughby wished for Paul to continue his studies for School Certificate. Mr ffrench would be prepared to undertake temporary tutorial duties for lodgings and a modest fee.

Mr Good must be desperate and Fireball must be proving more useless than ever at teaching sixth form. Mr Julian ffrench was a no-good second-rate useless sad sack who knew nothing, zero, naught, nil.

Bully must have taken over entirely, increasing his work-load in fear and trembling of discovery.

Again Paul remembered him kneeling and howling before the old whore.

'ffrench – he must be related to Jack and Laura,' Mummy trilled. Once your name was known you blew your cover.

Fireball turned up next week; his arrival meant another trip to the station in the governess cart. Before they were back at the house Mummy and he were on first name terms. Diana. Julian.

'He's a gent,' Mummy said after Julian had retired to Plassey which Agnes had swept and polished, providing clean towels and sheets. Two hot water bottles (stone) were put in his bed. After dinner when they all retired to the study for the news, Paul watched to see if Fireball made any sort of attempt to stand up for God Save the King. Not at all, he sat firmly in the wing chair. They listened to the news which was exciting these days.

'Frankfurt and Kustrien? The Russians will get to Berlin first.'

Mummy challenged Fireball to cribbage while Paul sulkily read the latest *Country Life* which assured him that better days were coming when Rose's Lime Juice and Black Magic chocolates would be readily obtainable. Mummy shuffled the cards with slick efficiency. When petrol was available it would be back to bridge fours.

From day one Julian got on with Mummy like a house on fire. Kindred spirits. Like-minded people. He had an engaging manner, at least she thought so. He was dark with dark brown eyes and girlish lashes and she thought him handsome. She laughed at his stupid jokes. He liked her taste in music, and they listened to her favourite songs on the gramophone. *Hunting tigers out in India . . . It's no good stroking them and saying puss puss . . .*

Cook liked the way he praised her cooking, while he made the maids giggle.

He helped Mummy with the dogs' dinners. He was bloody rude when he first saw Cook and Bernadette chopping up cabbage and peeling potatoes, green leaves and squirming peel falling to the floor. At least they were not wearing gumboots as they did when the basement threatened to flood. A cat dozed between them on the deal table while behind, on the window sill, little heaps of used tea were drying out. Fly papers hanging like lianas had room for more victims making m's and w's under the kippered ceiling. Agnes' little wireless, out of which John McCormack was bellowing a song, shone with grease. Mr Lamb, the pet lamb tottered about. Agnes was pushing fatty pieces of meat through a rusty mincer.

Fireball sniffed the pot which Cook heaved out of the Aga.

'Etna or Vesuvius might as soon be found in England as such a kitchen.'

'Really, Julian . . . *pas devant* . . .'

'Arthur Young said it, not me.'

'Who?'

The greyhounds, the puppies, now grown into mongrels, Rascal, Wooster Bug, Borzoi and Bubbles waited panting. Behind them stalked the cats, the second shift. Before peeling off head meat and throwing it on the bread in the basin Mummy was mixing, Fireball made a joke about Arab feasts and sheep's eyes which neither Paul nor the maids – and probably not Mummy – understood.

Paul was invited to call him by his first name.

For four hours in the morning and two in the late afternoon he was coached by Julian.

Oceanum interea surgens Aurora reliquit. At what time of day is the scene set?

The long bow brought victory at Crécy and Agincourt. Discuss.

'Why isn't he away fighting?'

Paul had joined his mother in her bedroom, which seemed to be the one place Fireball didn't penetrate. As yet.

She sat at her dressing table looking into her triple mirror, curling the ends of her hair, dousing herself in Je Reviens, his Je Reviens, damn it.

'Julian volunteered first thing in 1940. Then this awful weak heart . . .'

No proper fighting. No war wound.

'Daddy fought in Italy, didn't he?'

'It doesn't seem to have shortened the war.'

'At least he fought.' He glowered at her triple image.

'Julian worked in the civil service in Cambridge. Poor pet, his health wasn't up to it.'

'He seems fine now.'

'He's better.'

'How did he end up . . . teaching at St George's?' If you could call it teaching. He almost said being a rotten teacher.

'Just a stop gap.'

'What are you paying him?'

'None of your business.' She painted lipstick on the corner of her mouth with her little finger. 'Julian's a lot cheaper than paying fees to St George's.' She talked through lips curled round her teeth. 'It's up to you to work hard and pass your exams and please Daddy.'

Four hours in the morning, two in the afternoon.

Brutus is an honourable man. Discuss the irony in Mark Anthony's speech.

Qu'est-ce qui arrive après la guerre? Écrivez en cinq cents paroles un essai sur le sujet de la Paix.

I'll sing to him, each spring to him . . .

Fireball could ride well, proof he was one of us. Much good it had done him at St George's. He talked about hunts with the Scarteens or Duhallows and Mummy lapped it up. They hunted the St Patrick's Day hunt, the last of the season, she on Parade, he spreading his fat bottom across a subdued Pav whom he steered with no nonsense. Pav's back would give out. There was no mount for Paul.

He didn't mind, not really. He had a cold and rain was falling. He took the opportunity to sneak into Plassey, lifting his feet carefully over Borzoi who had developed the habit of sleeping across doorways. If you stepped on him he would shriek before taking a bite out of your leg. Sheila had left and gone to an aircraft factory in England because of Borzoi. Doing his bit, Fireball said when he heard.

Fireball's shaving things were laid out on a chest of drawers, the badger brush and razor blades that had to be sharpened in a glass dish. Paul picked one up – blunt. No wonder the bastard's cheeks grew dark around six o'clock, together with the evening. Cologne. Mouthwash to combat bad breath. Three pairs of highly polished shoes stretched by trees. He noted the piles of books relating to School Certificate which Fireball had consulted while he was at St George's and now used to be ahead of his solitary pupil. The old school tie – Oundle? Haileybury? – the bottle of Jameson half empty.

Paul picked up a packet of Craven A and considered stealing a cigarette. Five left – better not take a risk, they were probably counted. Here was an English identity card – Fireball was eight years younger than Mummy.

He listened to the rain and found he was missing St Patrick's Day at St George's. Everyone wore shamrock, even Mrs Good. The school went out and searched for it in the fields beyond the rugby pitch and the senior prefect gave Mr Good a great bunch which he wore while he gave his annual assurance that St Patrick was an English gentleman.

'Wonderful day out,' Mummy said after they returned and were drinking sherry before the sitting-room fire. Paul was allowed a glass. Fireball described every hill and valley through which the fox had fled.

Mummy and Daddy had met on the hunting field.

'We killed at Five Mile Cross,' Mummy said.

'Didn't you get wet?'

'Part of the fun.'

Her love of animals was selective. There was no place in her heart for foxes or rabbits or the chickens which Mick chased with his axe or the buckets of kittens he drowned, or the pig Mr O'Shea came up from the butchers to kill, watched by grinning women and children from the estate. Last year Paul had been Mummy's helper, handling shivering dogs and flea-bitten cats. The routine was the same, a telephone call from some stranger. 'Ma'am, I have a bitch on heat. She'll have to be put down . . . a mongrel, Ma'am.' And never any home to go to. And Mummy a soft touch.

Paul had fed the monkey which the Countess sent over in a laundry basket. It tore down curtains, peed worse than the dogs and tried to kill the parrot which bit off half its ear. Easier to kill a cat. Agnes found the mass of white fur and blood in the far corner of the drawing room.

'It put the heart across me, Madam.'

'Thank-you, Agnes.'

The monkey went back to the Countess. 'Horrid woman!'

Mummy had never known the fate of the white peacock which began to shriek at dawn. Bad luck was attributed to the beautiful bird – the hay harvest ruined, Fahy's accident, the bomb that fell on Dublin, Mrs O'Callaghan dying – first her swollen legs, then her chest. Joe told Paul his family ate it – tough as leather.

It was Paul who had to stand as aid and witness to the donkey's execution, since Mummy had been too upset. There was nothing to be done for the poor creature, rescued too late from tinkers. The hobble and boat-shaped hoofs were horrible. Mr O'Brien turned up rubbing his dirty hands, his eyes gleaming over their bags, his grin revealing missing teeth.

Paul was called upon to help, taking the limping animal by the halter, pulling it towards the van. As a vet Mr O'Brien was allocated plenty of petrol.

'Hold him steady for God's sake – not that way, you fool.' The donkey knew something was up before Mr O'Brien shot him. One moment he was an engaging creature with soulful eyes and twitching ears – the next a lump of meat destined for hounds.

These days it was Fireball who did all the helping with the animals, and he did not have to face anything as appalling as the donkey's death.

Paul got the airgraph off Redmond before Mummy saw it. The words, miniaturised by the camera, were fierce. There were a couple of ink blots like splutters of rage. Nothing for the censor to erase.

'HQ Ghazni . . . My dear Paul . . .', he skimmed through the angry sentences, '. . . betrayal of trust . . . how could you have contemplated . . . far worse than a mere foolhardy prank . . . I need hardly say what a disappointment this has been for your mother and myself. When I return, which I hope will be in the near future since hostilities appear to be drawing to a conclusion, I will consult with Father Hogan about the religious divide which plainly has had a disastrous effect on your morals. I now agree with Father Hogan that the tomfoolery about choosing your faith must cease. I understand your mother has found a qualified tutor on Mr Good's recommendation. Perhaps this man will go some way to rectify the years of idleness you have enjoyed up to now. My hope – albeit a forlorn one – is that with his help you will pass your exams. A good result would go some way in redeeming your disgusting behaviour. I end with feelings of great sadness. Daddy.'

Four hours in the morning, two in the afternoon . . . *indices . . . surds . . . logarithms . . . quadratic functions . . . equations . . . précis . . . comprehension . . . using your own words as far as possible describe the difficulties and unpleasant experiences which John suffered at the railway station . . .*

At dinner Fireball sat in Daddy's place. Agnes stood in the corner, her hands behind her back until called upon.

'Couldn't you get rid of her?' Fireball mouthed amid the clatter of plates being collected.

'Really Julian . . .,' She turned on Paul as a diversion.

'One thing I can't stand is sulking.'

'Paul made a real effort at maths today,' Fireball lied.

At Easter they went to church which was filled with daffodils which his mother had collected and arranged. Another church festival meant that the sparse congregation was swollen with people happy to sing about Our Triumphant Holy Day and pray for the King and the Irishmen risking their lives against Nazi oppression. Mr Hudson pumped away at the organ while the Canon gave a sermon about peace. The plate was passed around, the proceedings going to the Red Cross. Out in the spring sunshine Mummy introduced Fireball to people.

Paul was not to know that apart from the odd funeral that was the last time he attended a Church of Ireland service.

I've got a girl in Kalamazoo.

In the breakfast room Fireball noticed the letters carved deep and wide on the dark mahogany table decorated with garlands and a devil's mask.

'What's that?'

'Oh, Johnny Murphy's initials.'

'Tell me more.'

'He carved them with his penknife one day when he came in to make a telephone call.'

'It looks like the desks at St George's. Is Johnny Murphy still with you?'

'Oh yes, he has been for years. You saw him this morning.'

'The chap who looks like an amiable gorilla?'

Mummy and Fireball played cribbage while Paul read for his exams. *Yon Cassius has a lean and hungry look.* The wireless announced de Valera had gone to visit the German Embassy to offer condolences on the death of Hitler.

'Old toad,' said Fireball.

The swallows arrived and the cherry tree at the edge of the oak wood came into blossom. The wood used to be studded with cherry trees until the Scottish agent who worked here forty years ago deemed them frivolous and had them cut down, except for this one survivor which missed his eagle eye. Mummy and Fireball wandered about the orchard under the apple trees; they, too, were about to burst into flower. Or down the yew walk –'You and yew and me,' said Fireball.

Lady, lady, lady, lady, lady be good to me . . .

After helping to divide the daffodils Fireball groomed Rascal for the summer, cutting off his matted hair so that he looked like a shorn sheep.

'A shaggy dog story.'

In May VE day was declared. Hooray! said Mummy, Fireball and Paul. In the evening they lit a bonfire in the drive and Fireball produced some sparklers and a couple of rockets.

'I saved them for this moment.'

The estate people gathered and watched but only the children showed interest when the rockets surged upwards towards the stars. At St George's there would be loud cheers and a proper bonfire. Mr Good would be putting up a Union Jack and to hell with the gardaí.

'What about Daddy?'

'He'll stay on to help beat the Japs.'

Fireball said, 'He'll be dreaming of a white mistress.'

They decided to celebrate with Jack and Laura.

'Julian's cousins.'

Mummy would attend a meeting to discuss Protestant Magdalens – numbers had tailed off since D-Day. Then they would stay the night in Rathgar after a game of bridge followed by dinner at Jammet's.

'Can't I come?'

'We don't need five for bridge.'

'Please – it's victory.'

'You'd be bored.'

'Jack and Laura haven't room.'

'You've got to work.' So Paul stayed at home with his books.

Interpret the equation of a straight line graph in the form y=mx plus e.

Soon it would be June. He found sleep difficult and his dreams were full of figures and names. He studied feverishly and, to give Fireball his due, the bastard worked with him.

'Thank God I got hold of a Latin dictionary.'

It was stamped *St George's – In Veritate Victoria* and it proved mighty useful.

Fireball helped Mummy rather less and when they went off to plant out annuals he left behind assignments relating to what was forthcoming.

Today thou shalt see me at Phillipi. Discuss.

'Do you think if I pass some things it would satisfy my father?'

'It's not any of my business,' Fireball said. Of course he knew all the details of Paul's expulsion; he knew much more than Mummy did. Mr Good had only written telling her that Paul had bicycled into Dublin by night.

At dinner one evening Fireball passed on the worst part to Mummy *sotto voce*.

'Dolly who?'

More murmuring.

'My God!'

Paul blushed. 'I drank whiskey, that's all.'

'I should damn well hope so. You shouldn't be drinking at your age. Does Daddy know?'

'I got a letter. He's angry.'

'I bet he is. Let me read it.'

'I tore it up,' Paul lied.

'What did he say?'

'I must pass my exams to make up for what I did.' Better not bring religion into it.

'Well go ahead and pass them then.'

There were the practicalities of how Paul was going to take his exams. You had to find a place recognised by the School Certificate people where you would be supervised as you sat and did your stuff. Somewhere like the British Council, but that was in Dublin. Mummy telephoned Mr Good who said that there was no question of such an undesirable influence returning to St George's.

Father Hogan came to the rescue, arranging for him to take exams in the gloomy establishment outside Mountsilver that trained priests. The trainees would be away on holiday during June, but someone would be left behind who was prepared to supervise Paul in return for a substantial donation to the missions. Black babies? Very likely. The School Certificate people approved.

'It's up to you to do your best,' Fireball said at dinner.

'It'll be as much your failure as mine if I don't pass.'

Mummy said, 'Really Paul! Leave the table!'

For ten days he rattled into the village on Bernadette's bike – Mummy gave her ten shillings. In the basket in front he carried ham sandwiches. The place was as big as a prison, bigger if you counted the church in the middle. There seemed to be no priests around, young or old, apart from Father Damien who was there to do the supervision.

Every morning Father Damien and Paul said a prayer – Please God, let me pass something – before the priest took up the big envelope and slit open the day's torture. For two hours they could hear each other breathing and Father Damien gave a regular cough which made echoes in the hall. When the silence and the exam were over and Paul was eating his sandwiches, Father Damien would fetch them both a cup of tea and talk about lions and wildebeest and Lake Tanganyika. Then came the afternoon session, Paul scratching away in front of the tiers of desks used by young student priests learning their stuff. Did they take exams as well? Of course, all the time. About taking mass? Oh, they learnt that as they went along, it was a tenet of faith.

Paul knew that when they said mass it didn't count until they were ordained, lying flat on the ground, watched by their happy relatives. Agnes had seen her brother become a priest in this very place. Whatever happened, Paul would spare himself that.

Father Damien had become a priest a long time ago. He was homesick for Africa where he had spent most of his life.

After two more awful hours had been endured they would say another prayer together.

'Thanks, Father.'

'Poor lad! I still have dreams about not passing exams.'

Paul would ride back to the house over the potholes, the printed exams of the day sitting in the bicycle basket. Fireball would look them over gloomily and question Paul about the answers he had written. He didn't exactly say not a hope in Hell.

CHAPTER ELEVEN

'When's he going?'

Mummy was dabbing on rouge, pale and subtle, not like the ladies in D.F.'s. Six pink cheeks appeared in the triple mirror, passed over with a swansdown powder puff.

'Julian? Not for a week or two.'

'I've finished my exams. I don't need him anymore.'

'He's a help to me.'

Of course he stayed on for far longer than two weeks. Paul took to following the two of them, sneaking behind them, looking for hugs and kisses and worse, or at least a chance of seeing them hand in hand. They wandered round the walled garden picking raspberries and telling Dempsey where to weed. They dead headed roses, Ispahan or Madame Hardy or Rose du Roi à Fleurs Pourpres. Sometimes they sat and smoked on one of the slatted benches and hummed songs.

Falling in love again . . .

Fireball watched when Mummy clipped the grass between the headstones in the dogs' cemetery.

Don't sit under the apple tree with anyone else but me . . .

Sometimes he sat and painted one of his horrible little pictures. He was no Constable.

If it rained they might retire to the conservatory where Mummy fiddled with the plumbago or the vine on which grapes were ripening. Once or twice Paul spied on them in here.

There'll be blue birds over the white cliffs of Dover . . .

'What do Americans know about bluebirds?'

After the rain mushrooms appeared. In past years Paul and his mother had gathered buckets, and for once Mummy did some cooking, producing great fries of mushrooms and bacon. Cook and the maids hated mushrooms. Now the fries were for Fireball, although, Paul had to concede, he, too, was also offered as much as he liked. Fireball and Mummy collected every day. Early one morning Paul went out, walked to the five acre field, and peed on as many mushrooms as he could.

They went hacking on Pav and Parade – did they stop and dismount and do it before they returned? He watched for dishevelled hair or grass stains.

He lay awake at night listening, but the only sounds that awoke him were the hoots of a corncrake. He remembered how an earlier corncrake had infuriated his father to the extent that Daddy brought his gun into the bedroom and shot at it in vain. He got up and crept down corridors.

Boogie woogie bugle boy of Company B . . .

He never caught them at anything.

He couldn't spend every moment of his time day in and day out creeping after his mother. He went fishing. Fireball wasn't a fisherman, and that was good, especially on the day when Paul hooked and landed his first salmon by himself. Years ago Daddy had given him his rod and taught him to cast and stood by when he caught a succession of trout. But never a salmon.

Mummy showed minimum interest. 'Well done, darling!'

There was the usual summer glut when Cook and the maids refused to touch another mouthful of salmon, while Mummy got tired of making mayonnaise, her other culinary achievement. So the cats got most of his fish, not before Paul had taken a series of photographs with his Box Brownie.

He helped with the haymaking. He went up to the high bog and cut turf, which he did not do well, sat with the men, cadged the odd cigarette and talked about the German spy who, so they said, had taken refuge somewhere there. Even if he was a German he felt sorry for him forced to hide away in this desolate spot.

When it rained he talked to the parrot or read. The old *Punch*'s palled. It was a pity there hadn't been an exam on Biggles or Wodehouse or

Agatha Christie. *Certain clues point the reader to the murderer of Roger Ackroyd. Discuss.* For a couple of days, furtively, since he was much too old, he built an elaborate crane with Meccano.

August came and the Japs were swiped with atom bombs. He attended the harvest, taking down sandwiches on the big Sheffield tray to the men working at the reaper and binder.

Still Fireball stayed on and still Paul hadn't caught him and Mummy out.

In the middle of the month Redmond rode up with the post and a telegram. He should have brought the telegram the day before instead of waiting for today's post to come in, lazy devil. Along with the bills was a communication which you could tell at once was exam results. Paul opened it very quickly, feeling sick.

Hello! Not so bad. He had passed four subjects. Four! Four out of eight was halfway.

It had been his own hard work, and perhaps prayer.

'Mummy, I passed . . .'

But Mummy had opened the telegram.

'Oh my God!'

'What's the matter?' Fireball asked.

It was Paul she told. 'Daddy's coming home next week.'

People who have been separated by war can't wait to see each other again.

He peered into Plassey and was delighted to see Fireball packing his bags. Mummy was going to drive him in the governess cart to the station since the Rover was still up on blocks, waiting for Daddy's return. Then she changed her mind. She would go with Julian into Dublin to buy a hat, and it would be Paul who would take them to the station and then return.

The three of them drove in silence to the station. 'Goodbye, Paul – and well done.' This was the moment for thanks but he kept his mouth shut.

On the way back he flicked the whip and made Jessie go at a canter. What would they be doing after buying the hat?

Mummy returned the next day and Paul met her again.

'You will be sweet to Daddy, won't you?'

She put on the new hat and dress she had bought and pirouetted in front of the long mirror.

'How do I look?'

'Nice. How are we going to meet Daddy?'

'What do you mean, how?'

'Governess cart?'

'Oh no. Taxis all the way. Remind me to phone Reilly.'

She took off the dress and slipped a blouse over her bust bodice before putting on slacks.

'We've got to tidy up.'

This was far more than the Christmas cleanup. There was a lot to do, easy things like cleaning out the parrot's cage, harder things like getting in the sweep to clear the jackdaws' nests from various chimneys. All summer long you could hear the voices of the young ones, like rattling tin.

Dempsey climbed up the ladders to remove the strands of ivy and dried pieces of holly left over from Christmas.

'While you're up there you might as well give the horns a dust.' Clouds rose from the Irish elk and the Marco Polo sheep. Frames of family portraits, the Snaffles, King William, King George, Queen Charlotte, the steeplechase prints, and the Lady Butlers were dusted down. Books got a quick wipe.

Agnes was asked to bring in a couple of her sisters to help. She had five. She herself got up on a step ladder to clean the gold eagle on top of the convex mirror before washing down the chimney piece in the drawing room and its frieze of Androcles and the Lion. Then the Kilkenny marble chimney piece in the hall which was flecked with little fossils. Her sisters shook carpets, and swept and polished for a day before tackling the brass and the silver. A silver teapot which had been lost for fifteen years was found in the lift shaft. Spiders were thrown out except for the one in the sitting room which lived up in the corner of the ceiling and which Mummy fed occasionally with milk.

Paul helped clear out Plassey, removing the tray of heaped cigarette butts. He opened the parcel covered with stamps and addressed to his father which had stood on the hall table for three years and found that it contained a box of mouldy chocolates. He groomed Pav and Parade which was a vile job.

Mummy sat in the study looking over bills. She ordered in Jameson, sent the oldest of the *Country Life*'s up to the barrack room and arranged for Dempsey to cut Paul's hair for twenty Woodbines. She called in Mr O'Brien.

Mr Lamb had already gone to the butcher. No one missed him since he had taken to butting people. Borzoi, riddled with rheumatism, shrieking and biting anyone who touched him, was put down.

'He was such a lovely puppy, leaping about like a colt.'

Out on the porch he gave a final shout when Mr O'Brien killed him. At the last moment Rascal, Grasshopper, and the mongrels were added to the death list.

'Big changes, eh, Diana?' Mr O'Brien leered, putting away his poison needle. Dempsey took the corpses in the wheelbarrow to the dogs' cemetery while Mummy washed the surviving dogs in the big copper bath in the west wing and sprinkled flea powder on clean fur.

In the kitchen Paul peered into the big pot where the sheep's head simmered.

'I wonder if that's Mr Lamb?'

The garden was sultry with late roses, chrysanthemums, dahlias, sedums and Michaelmas daisies topped with butterflies. Mummy arranged for Mick to mow the lawns on the day she and Paul would be meeting Daddy.

'And bring in peas and mint and raspberries. Young peas. Not the ones the size of marbles.' Before they left for Dublin she did the flowers. Paul helped her, following her directions, carrying around the ground floor arrangements that echoed the Dutch still life in the drawing room.

The taxi drove out to Dun Laoghaire – Paul refused to call it Kingstown, there were limits – in plenty of time.

'Ah, she's always late,' the taxi man said.

Under the murky sky the sea was empty except for squalling gulls. A fresh wind blew across the bay. Perhaps she had sunk?

They waited nearly an hour before someone shouted 'There she is!' and Paul could make out a thin line of smoke near the Kish. Then the funnel and the hull and gradually the whole silhouette appeared. Within a few minutes, billowing smoke and churning up a frothy wake, the mailboat was rounding the entrance into the harbour. Although the same scene occurred every evening, excitement took over the pushing crowd.

'Get back! Stop yer shoving,' said the man at the barrier.

Not everyone was held at bay. Paul noticed an elderly man being let through. 'Excuse me, excuse me . . .' Mummy went after him, managing to make her way to the front of the crowd and he followed in her wake.

'It's against regulations, Ma'am.'

She was wearing her new dress and hat, tilted to one side, and her fur boa.

'Oh please . . . I haven't seen my husband for three years . . .'

'If y'er quick . . .'

They squeezed through the little gate and walked fast along the empty platform where the boat had docked. Gangways had been lowered. At the stern the first beleaguered returning passengers, poised to make for home, were straining. Suddenly a rope or something was released and they surged down the gangway clutching shabby suitcases towards long tables where customs men waited.

Mummy walked up the other gangway, Paul following, noticing the clip clop of her high heels and the straight line of her stockings. In the first class foyer there was no panic, only stewards in white uniforms, neatly stacked leather luggage, and a smell of cigars.

Two men were standing and talking. They wore striped regimental ties, army coats without badges of rank and bowler hats and had moustaches. Paul could remember Daddy's moustache before he went off to war, but both of these seemed more luxuriant.

'Oh there you are!'

Mummy picked out the right man and kissed him. 'Darling!' The man had taken off his bowler and Paul could see he was fairly bald. There was a little hair left, combed carefully over a bald waste, not doing its job.

'Hello old boy.' Paul had to kiss him as well. 'You've grown.'

In fact Paul was taller than this stranger who must be Daddy, who used to beat him, the writer of letters, who knew he had been in Dolly Fossett's.

'I wouldn't have recognised you.'

Snap! Paul tried to see this paunchy figure as the warrior who had gone off to fight the Hun.

His father turned away and addressed Mummy, 'Remember Tony?'

The other man nodded. 'Nice to see you, Diana.'

'How was the journey?'

'Awful.'

'Rough.'

'Usual delay at Holyhead.'

'The *Princess Maud* is never comfortable.'

'I peered into third class,' the man who was his father said. 'Full of drunks and people being sick.'

'I'd rather be third class on the *Titanic,*' Tony said. 'I'll be off,' he added tactfully. 'See you soon, Gerald, Diana.'

'We'd better get a move on ourselves. Steward! Find a porter, will you?'

They were nodded through customs. Other passengers might have to open their bags, but that didn't apply to his father. They followed the trolley past the Dublin train to the gate outside where a taxi waited.

'Kildare Street Club.'

'Oh no, darling, I've booked us into the Shelbourne.'

'Why, for God's sake?'

'This is a celebration.'

Mummy always disliked the Club, hating the way lady members had to use a separate entrance and were excluded from all the decent rooms. Service you could rely on and a billiard room were of no interest to her. Nor the dining room full of red faces gnawing their way through slices of very brown beef covered in mahogany coloured gravy accompanied by cabbage and little igloos of mashed potato. His father loved the place, having been there back in the week when members protected themselves against IRA bullets by putting fat copies of *Burke's Peerage* behind the front windows overlooking Nassau Street.

In the distant past Paul had to hang around while Daddy talked and laughed with cronies. Catholics were welcomed, provided they were high class, and Daddy always said fun and high jinks were to be had. He told stories of jolly parties ending with hose pipes streaming water down the corridors.

'I don't believe you,' Mummy used to say.

This evening she insisted, 'We'll go somewhere more cheerful.'

'Jammet's?'

'That's for oldies.' Mummy had hated Jammet's since the row over the bloody duck. She had sent it back and then the chef came out of the kitchen and roared at her that she was ignorant of French cooking and it should indeed be bloody.

'The Dolphin would be nicer. Wouldn't you fancy a decent steak after that Egyptian garbage?' Daddy's letters to her, when they weren't complaining about Paul or bills, were filled with descriptions of disgusting milk curd or foul brilliant yellow soup or stringy chicken.

Daddy agreed reluctantly, and soon they arrived at the redbrick dignity of the Dolphin. Paul had never been here before. They side-stepped the red-carpeted staircase – was there really a brothel up there, as some boys in school claimed, a brothel smarter than D.F.'s? How many brothels did Dublin have? They avoided the bar which was men only – what was wrong with women? – and went into the main dining room filled with smells of steak and sounds of loud voices. The frieze around the top of the room extolled the pleasures of tobacco; most people seemed to agree with its sentiments, since the room was foggy with smoke. Along one wall was a fire under a grill where an elderly chef wearing a tall white hat was cooking steaks.

'Can't see anyone I know,' Daddy grumbled.

They sat and unfolded huge white napkins. The head waiter came over to their table. 'Hello Major, back from the wars?'

'Straight off the mailboat, Jack. First evening home in three years.'

The head waiter flicked his finger at a subordinate. 'Have a bottle of champagne, Major, on the house.'

'Very good of you, Jack.' That put Daddy in a better temper.

They consulted their menus. Monkey gland steak sounded odd, even though they were told it was the best that evening. Paul thought it better to be on the safe side and chose rump steak and French fries.

'Oysters, old boy?'

'I've never had them.' He resisted the temptation to say Sir.

'Always a first time. Lucky it's September.'

The oysters tasted like snot, but he managed to gulp them down with the aid of brown bread and lemon juice.

A party of horsy looking men at the next table were enjoying themselves. Someone must have won a lot of money. They kept giving bursts of laughter at off-colour jokes, some of which Paul had heard at school.

The champagne was followed by draught Guinness. Even Mummy had a glass, while Paul pretended he had never drunk it before.

'Only drink that goes with steak.'

Daddy and Mummy tucked into their monkey glands.

'Mustard, please, darling.'

'Waiter! Traffic lights!'

One of the men at the next table had begun to sing loudly.

'*I paid ten cents to see*
The tattooed lady . . .'

The rump steak and fries were delicious.

'*...and around her neck she wore*
The badge of the Anzac corps . . .'

Thank goodness there was too much noise to talk.

'Coffee, darling?'

'Yes, please.'

'Paul?'

'Yes, please.'

'*. . . and on her slender hips*
Was a line of battle ships . . .'

'Waiter, three coffees. And bring me a double brandy.'

Mummy and Daddy lit their cigarettes. Paul longed for one. Daddy used an American Zippo.

'*. . . and round the corner, round the corner,*
Was the whole of Tennessee!'

'Dolphin's gone up in price.'

'Everything's gone up.'

'My steak was overdone. Chef's getting too old for his job. Mixing up orders.'

'You could have complained.'

'Hardly, after the champagne.'

'Darling, it was a lovely gesture.'

'Jack can hardly do that to everyone coming back.'

'Amazing the way he remembered you.'

'Not a soul I recognised. The Club would have been better.'

'It wouldn't have given you champagne.'

'Champagne isn't everything. I hate rowdy drunks.'

Next day Reilly's taxi went through the front gates of Mountsilver.

'What happened to the lion?'

'Lion?'

'On top of the right-hand pier.'

'Oh. Someone knocked its head off the night of VE day.'

'The Roches should have stopped them.'

'They didn't hear anything. And we were having a little celebration, weren't we, Paul? A bonfire. Everyone came.'

'I wouldn't be surprised if the Roches didn't do it themselves.'

Mrs Roche came out of the lodge attended by barefooted children and waved a hand uncertainly. Daddy got out of the taxi and shook it.

'Nice to see you, Mrs Roche. Everything well?'

'Oh yes, Sir.'

'Children grown, I see. How are your eldest boys?' Mummy had prompted him.

'They're well, Sir. They're in South Shields. In the factories.'

'Hardly making munitions now, eh?'

'They'll be coming home, Sir. They don't want to do that National Service.'

Daddy frowned as Reilly continued down the drive. 'You should see to it that she opens the gates to cars coming in. What happened to the big elm?'

'It blew down in a gale last November. It's been keeping us warm ever since.'

'Did those beeches go as well?'

'They did.'

'Nine men on the estate and no one cleared them up?'

'Fitzpatrick has been busy.'

'The drive's in terrible condition.'

'Not from four-wheeled traffic. Bicycles. The most regular is Redmond with the post.'

'Something must be causing all these potholes.'

'Rabbits? Don't be silly, Gerald. They're exactly the same as when you went away.'

They came to the fork, left to the stables, right to the house.

'Laurels need cutting.'

They swept around and there was the house looking grand, the sun shining on the long front where the windows came down to the ground. All the men were there to greet Daddy and so were Cook, Bernadette and Agnes.

'Great to see you, Major. Good day, Major, how are you Major, nice to see you Sir, grand to have you back, Sir.'

The surviving dogs streamed out of the porch barking. Wooster ran up to Daddy, wriggling, flailing his tail and giving a continuous howl.

'Good boy, good boy . . .'

'Like Ulysses and his dog, what's its name.'

'God, let's hope he doesn't drop dead.'

'That was after twenty years.'

'Three years is long enough. Hey boy, good boy, remember the old master? He's got a lot older.'

'Haven't we all?'

'Bring in my suitcases, Dempsey, and take them upstairs. I'll have a look around.'

Mummy's cleaning really paid off as Daddy marched from room to room. Wooster followed whimpering, and behind him, Mummy, Paul and the maids. Daddy didn't bother about the kitchen – he never went down there in the old days. He found nothing wrong.

'Kill Fireball!' cried the parrot.

Mummy and Daddy changed, Paul put on his blazer and they gathered in the study for drinks. Paul and his mother had sherry, his father a couple of glasses of whiskey. A fire shone brightly.

'There's your elm.' There was turf as well.

'Daddy, I went up with the men to cut turf.'

'Did you hear the great Boo? Ha! Ha!'

'No.'

'See any German spies?'

'No,'

'Turf,' Daddy said. 'Nothing like it in England. You could smell it off the mailboat as you came in.'

A fire was lit in the dining room as if it was Christmas Day. Daddy said grace, the first that had been said for three years. The leg of lamb – definitely not Mr Lamb – came up in the lift already carved. Paul met his mother's eye, wondering if the dogs might have got to it. You'd think they would have learned by now down in the kitchen. Daddy suspected nothing and tucked into a huge helping.

Paul introduced pleasant subjects.

'. . . I caught a salmon.'

'Weight?'

'Seven pounds. I hooked and netted it and gaffed it by myself.'

'What fly?'

'Shrimp fly. It took ages to bring in. I took some photos but we haven't had them developed yet.'

'. . . I passed four subjects in School Cert.' Treading on delicate ground.

'Better than nothing, I suppose.'

'Both English papers, history and Latin unseen.'

'No maths?'

'No.'

'Tutor helpful?'

'Oh yes!' said Mummy.

'Raspberries! First I've had for three years.' He took a big helping of cream. 'Pity about the maths, old boy. Everyone needs to know how to add up.' He had a few grapes Mummy had cut from the vine in her conservatory with her special grape scissors. 'And there's more to maths than addition.'

Paul wondered if he would make a huge effort to please Daddy by suggesting he could try again at Christmas. That would mean a tutor. Another tutor? He kept quiet.

Daddy drank a glass of port. So did Mummy and Paul.

'Ah well, we'll talk about things another time.'

They listened to the news, while Daddy lit his pipe and had another tot of whiskey. There was an election taking place in England.

'Churchill should win!'

On the way up where the staircase divided, Mummy and Daddy to the right, Paul to the left, Daddy said: 'It's good to be home!'

He snored. Paul had heard him at the Shelbourne.

CHAPTER TWELVE

Daddy woke with a touch of Irish tummy – too much rich food after the meagre rations they gave you in England.

'Haven't you done anything about the roof?'

He put on a stiff mackintosh and strode outside to inspect the farm with Fitzpatrick. They went everywhere in the rain, first to the yard, where not so long ago the bell had been rung every morning to summon the men to work. Next to the stables to see Parade, Pav, Jessie and the plough horses, to the field where two Friesians grazed, the only cattle left after Sean Lemass insisted on the farm going into tillage, then up to the high fields where ploughing was impossible and a small herd of sheep survived. Men in wet clothes and gumboots saluted him. He went to the orchard and inspected the rows of trees producing far more fruit than the house would ever need.

'Why haven't the apples been picked?' Brown windfalls, half devoured by birds, lay in wet grass all over the place . . .

Wooster followed, wet and shivering, while the other dogs took shelter where they always did, in the tunnel which was used in the old days by servants so they wouldn't be seen from the house.

After lunch Mummy took an umbrella and conducted Daddy around the walled garden, and into the conservatory which smelled of heliotrope.

Daddy looked at the ice blue plumbago. 'You should have dug all this up and planted tomatoes.'

They gave up the outdoor inspection when he said it was too wet to enjoy and came indoors to look at accounts.

Mick killed a chicken for dinner.

'Damn tough. Should have been stewed. Reminds me of Egypt.'

He chewed a leg. '. . . Stupid government insisting on everyone growing wheat . . . we'll get those fields back into pasture right away. Have to be re-sown.'

'. . . We'll have to do something about the Rover. Get it off the blocks. Is Casey still in the village?'

'He closed the garage and went to England. No work for him here.'

'There must be a functioning garage somewhere.'

'There's the one in Wicklow.'

'For God's sake, that's forty miles away!'

'Surely it's just a matter of revving up the battery and putting the tyres back on. Dempsey could do that.'

'A fat lot you know about cars . . .'

Over dessert – more raspberries – he said: 'You seem to have a lot of bills, Diana – Switzers, Brown Thomas – none of them paid for months.'

'I haven't got around to it.'

'Harrods?'

'I haven't bought anything from Harrods since before the war.'

'I can see that. There's a bill dated June, 1939. They seem to have sent it every year. Can't think why they don't close the account.'

'Either they hope to get their money or they are too polite.'

'I'd far rather you'd dealt with one or two of these bills instead of booking us into the Shelbourne.'

'The Shelbourne for one night is a lot less extravagant than keeping up your subscription to the Club all the time you've been away.'

'Parkes must have got in touch with you about the overdraft?'

'I think he wrote once or twice.'

'I suppose you still take the attitude that it is vulgar to discuss money problems.'

'You deal with them, Gerald.'

'Fine mess to come home to.'

Voices had got steadily higher and Paul decided to try and make things better. Besides, he was annoyed with Mummy.

'Daddy.'

'What?'

'I've been thinking.'

'You shouldn't interrupt.'

'I think I've decided to become a Catholic.'

The dining room was silent for a long time. In the corner there was a sound from Agnes – was it a gasp?

Daddy gulped some wine. 'Think! Think! You should bloody well know one way or another by this time!'

Paul picked out a mouldy raspberry and put it at the side of his dish.

'You're sixteen years old and this business had been going on for far too long.'

'Yes, Sir.'

'When did you last see Father Hogan?'

'Uh . . . during Lent . . .'

'Before you were thrown out of school?'

'I suppose so . . .'

'When did you last go to mass?'

'Uh . . . about then . . .'

'Not since February?'

'I've been working at exams.'

'Is this true, Diana?'

Mummy looked blank. 'You were coming back soon . . .'

'What about after exams?'

'I don't have a bicycle to go to mass.'

'What happened to your bicycle? Mummy bought you a new one for Christmas, didn't she?'

'I lost it . . . the time I was expelled.'

'I heard all about that.' Damn Father Hogan. 'You haven't been to confession to deal with your appalling behaviour?'

'No, Sir.' There was another long silence. 'But I do want to become a Catholic.'

'Sure?'

'Yes, Sir.'

'How much time have you spent making up your mind?'

'Lots.'

'When did you decide?'

'Weeks ago.' Another lie.

'You're quite sure?'

A nod and a glance at Mummy.

'We'll that's one damn thing settled. You'll have to do Confirmation. I'll phone Father Hogan first thing tomorrow.'

After dinner Daddy had another glass of whiskey; he had cheered up.

Someone had to lose. No going back now. No great searching of conscience. Trying to make Daddy happy at Mummy's expense. Punishing her. The Rubicon had been crossed. Caesar probably did it quickly. So did Beamish the other way round.

The worst was Mummy. 'If that's the way you want it . . .'

No more dithering. No more bribery.

'The Canon is livid.'

'I spoke to Father Hogan. He told me it was the answer to many hours of prayer.'

'Ass!'

Paul himself had to start saying prayers again. Since taking his exams he had been lax in that department.

'Please God, make it easy.'

Father Hogan arranged things immediately perhaps because he was afraid that if he didn't act quickly Paul would change his mind. He could – sometimes at night, lying awake he considered it. It was awful seeing Mummy so silent. There was no one to argue the Protestant cause now he had made the decision and Mummy had given up. She and Paul avoided being alone together.

Could he have gone on being indecisive indefinitely? But it was too late now. He would take Confirmation with the boys at the school in the town, not the place where the young priests were taught, but the school beyond the huge Catholic church. The Protestant church, nearly as big, tall as a lighthouse, was at the west end. He would have lessons twice a week from

Father McCabe who had never got on with his parents, and for years had been threatening to call in the Archbishop about the state of his soul.

'How will I get there?'

'The boy's got to have a bicycle!'

The new bike, bought second hand, wasn't nearly as good as the one that had been stolen, but a lot better than Bernadette's bone shaker.

The sacrament of Confirmation is a landmark on our spiritual progress.

He was far older than the other boys.

Confirmation is the essential sacramental link between Baptism which marked the beginning of our journey in faith and the Eucharist which we witnessed at our First Communion.

He felt a fool sitting among a crowd young enough to be bijoux.

The Holy Spirit guides us on our journey of fulfillment to our eternal abode with Christ.

Mr Good would hear that Paul was lost to the Protestant faith. *Remember what St Paul described as Fruits of the Spirit which express the character of Christian life – love, joy, peace, kindness, faithfulness, self-control.*

Father Hogan would have written to him. 'We've won!' 'That poor boy,' Mrs Good would say.

Confession, my children, is a necessity of Christian life.

He had to confess to Father McCabe through the grill. 'You told him everything?' his father asked. It was actually none of his business.

He concluded that Father McCabe didn't like him, considering his presence made too much of a disturbance. The other boys found him stuck up. Little brats, four or five years younger than he was.

Ave Maria gratia plena – plenty of those to say.

Prayer, my children, is uniquely necessary for our journey towards salvation.

Please God, make things easy.

My children, we are baptised into the mission of Jesus and called upon to live as His disciples.

He prayed with fervour.

Ave Maria gratia plena . . . Suddenly he was pleased, really pleased he had made up his mind to do the right thing.

He thought of Beamish a few times – Beamish who had made the wrong decision and was now in danger of Hell. Like Mummy. He prayed for her.

Father McCabe asked what confirmation name he would chose.

He remembered the kind priest who was homesick for Africa.

'Damien.'

Daddy had been tolerant about the accumulation of dogs, although he didn't care for them, apart from Wooster whose white jaw proclaimed he wouldn't be around for long. Other things were increasingly annoying. Waste . . . expense . . . unpaid bills . . . too many men on the estate . . . He had a row with Fitzpatrick who wanted to continue sowing winter wheat in the rath field. It nearly came to Fitzpatrick leaving, but they both held back in time.

He went into Dublin to the Club. Old friends had not renewed their subscriptions which had got bloody expensive.

He was furious about the news on the wireless. In England Churchill had lost the general election. 'Ingratitude!'

He thought he'd leave off the news for the time being and play some Beethoven. Paul and his mother never listened to the great composer because they had cloth ears; neither had noticed that the record sides three and four of the Eroica were in two pieces.

Agnes freely admitted breaking the record during an unfortunate dusting.

'I told you, Madam, at the time.'

'Is she getting past it?' Daddy mused, drinking his whiskey.

'It's up to you to sack her if that's what you want.'

'She was here in my mother's time.'

So Agnes, whose presence in 1922 had saved the house, stayed on and continued to stand in the corner of the dining room during increasingly glum meal times.

The Gilbert and Sullivan records were intact, and Daddy spent some evenings listening to those. They did not interfere with the news. The socialists had formed their government in England which was enough for stiff drinks. While fiddling with the knob that made the lugubrious tidings louder Daddy discovered Johnny Murphy's carved initials.

'My God! Do you realise the value of this table?'

'You don't think it gave me any pleasure . . . yes, of course I ticked him off.'

'You should have sacked him. One of these days I'll see he goes.'

'It isn't easy to get good men these days.'

'Good men, I ask you!'

Only one thing made Daddy happy and that was Paul, who was taken into Dublin and measured up for a new suit for Confirmation. Aunt Delia sent down another rosary, which had been properly blessed by the Pope; the war was over and someone she knew had been to Italy and to an audience, dangling a dozen rosaries in front of the Holy Father for people back home.

There were a number of stages in the process of Confirmation including heavy sessions of confession before he got to the wafer and wine part. Daddy and Father Hogan watched while the Archbishop laid hands on him. Afterwards he was introduced, which meant kneeling before the grim inquisitorial figure in lace and billowing skirts and kissing his ring. Everyone smiled.

When they drove back to the house Cook and the maids were at the kitchen window smiling up through the bars. They had been praying for him for years.

Mummy had gone hunting.

He was dazed by his new status. From then on, every Sunday Daddy glowed happily when Paul sat beside him in the Rover on the way to mass, Cook and the maids sitting in the back. In the huge church, which was modelled after Chartres, he sat and picked out details of the sanctuary lamp, the violent-coloured stained glass, and the sad Stations and knelt and said a prayer for his mother. Remembering the drone of Church of Ireland Sundays, once again he admired the slick pace of mass as the priest zoomed through everything in about twenty minutes and all the people including his father, himself, Cook and the maids, the Countess – got their wafer.

Mummy continued to sulk, going hunting by herself, or, defying Daddy, going into Dublin for a shopping spree. She gardened furiously. Her dogs followed her – not Wooster. Whenever Daddy went to Dublin Wooster sat on the front steps waiting for his return. He refused to eat. If Daddy were to die Wooster would lie on his tombstone like Greyfriars Bobby.

At Christmas bent old people came to lunch, the Countess, Sam Seymour, Trigger and Helen, Mary Rooke (Oh Diana, turkey!), Donald and Valerie. In addition to five pounds, Mummy gave Paul a new razor and shaving brush, while Daddy gave him a history of his regiment.

'When I was your age I was preparing for Sandhurst.'

No one wanted to go into the army now.

'My God,' Daddy said after the New Year, 'I'd forgotten how cold the place is.' For a few days the boiler in the basement had been lit and the old radiators gave off heat. That was before he worked out costs.

He began to worry about the maintenance of the house. He broke the dinner silence and the rule about never talking shop at table by mentioning the three dreaded R-words – roof, rain and rates.

Mummy didn't show much interest. 'Why don't you sell up if it's all getting too much?'

'You know perfectly well the house has been in the family for hundreds of years.'

'High time you got rid of it.'

For a brief period Daddy considered the idea seriously. He thought of disposing of the place by letting the Church have it since there was plenty of room in it for a convent. But Ireland had a lot of convents and there was a go slow on acquiring more. He went as far as consulting an estate agent.

Mummy didn't approve his choice. 'Darcy's people all get down on their knees before an auction starts and take out their rosaries.'

Daddy ignored her. 'Darcy says it won't be easy to sell.'

'If I were you I'd give it away with a pound of tea.'

Paul knew he had better take advantage of his father's good nature such as it was while it lasted. Nothing like being called a fool a couple of times to be reminded that Daddy's opinion was precarious. He would never really be forgiven for the business of D.F.'s, however much he had confessed it, however many Hail Marys he had said.

'Daddy . . .'

'What?'

'I'd like to learn to drive.'

'Someone would have to teach you.'

'I thought – Fitzpatrick . . .'

'Fitzpatrick hasn't got a car. And he is not going near the Rover.'

So it was his father who taught him, and for several days Paul bumped and staggered up and down the drive while a lot of Daddy's bonhomie slipped away while the words Bloody Fool resounded in the winter air. But Paul learned the basics and a Sunday came when he drove Daddy and the servants to mass without killing any of the crowd gathered outside. The next day he cycled down to the post office and bought a driving licence with his Christmas money. The good thing about driving licences was that you didn't have to take a test, merely sign a declaration that you weren't a lunatic.

'Typical of this country.'

It meant he could drive for life so long as he didn't have an accident.

Lent was over. Daddy had insisted on a lot of meatless days which made Cook grumble. He caught a couple of salmon on the spring run. Paul had no further luck.

'One salmon does not go far in six weeks,' Mummy said. 'It would be a lot better if you gave up whiskey as a penance.'

Lent or not, it was back to fish on Friday.

Easter came and Mummy had to admit the lamb tasted all the better after fasting. Daffodils were in bloom and so were her tulips, rank upon scarlet rank like a guard's regiment. White bread had appeared for the first time since the Emergency was over, while bananas and oranges were on sale in the shops. The leaks in the roof had been stopped up with tar. Fields were sown with grass seed. The Spring Show would be on soon, time for bowler hats, shooting sticks and prize cattle.

After that, time for a party.

'Celebration of what?'

'War being over.'

'It's been over for some time.'

'Most people are back by now. And all the others, we haven't seen them for years.'

'We've just got over Christmas.'

'The Christmas people will have to be invited.' Daddy endured the Countess because she was Catholic.

'Not that old bag again.'

'You're friend rather than mine,' Daddy lied.

'And her boyfriend?'

'Of course. She won't go anywhere without Sam.'

'Couldn't you put the whole thing off until after the summer?'

'No.'

Daddy ordered copperplate At Home cards from Easons and made lists. Those back from fighting who had returned to their dilapidated houses. So many of his friends were colonel this or major that. Wives and daughters who had served in the WAAF or WRENS. Most had gone into the WRENS because the uniform was so much nicer, particularly the hats. A couple of Queen Alexandra nurses.

Mummy sniffed. 'QA's may be a cut above the others, but they are still nurses.'

Members of the Club. Cousin Lucy over from England.

'Lucy will be doing her imitation of an Irish accent.'

Africa hands. Friends back from India, military men who had stuck pigs, others who had been in the ICS, whose careers were disrupted as Independence loomed.

'The Barnsworths.'

'Those old bores.' Freddy Barnsworth had a shoot in Kerry and Daddy hoped to rejoin him killing birds as he had done before the war.

'Brian White.' Daddy's solicitor.

'Dr Waters and his family.'

'Hardly a hunt ball.'

Mummy had also made a list.

'. . . The Jebbs.' The Jebbs, who also lived in England, continued being rich as Croesus. Mavis Jebb's money came from Wright's Coal Tar Soap or

Debenham and Freebodys or Marmite, no one could remember which. She was rich enough to be forgiven for being in trade.

'Let's hope Mr Attlee will shake some money out of her.'

'They're selling up over there because of the new Labour government and house hunting here.'

'I wonder if they would be interested in Mountsilver?'

'Not if they have any sense.'

'We'll invite them to stay.'

Mummy consulted her list again. 'Harry.' Harry was one of her few relations with whom she kept in touch.

'Of course.' Daddy approved of him because he had a good war, an MC.

'Peter and Charlotte.' They owned a house nearly as dilapidated as Mountsilver. They ate off gold plate which was much easier, since most of their china had been broken.

'Sandy.' Sandy was an Irish lord, one of the few who was entitled to sit in the English parliament after the Treaty. Attending the House of Lords was Sandy's only sort of income; when he was ill he arranged to be carried into the Upper Chamber. He had yet to make his maiden speech.

'The Blackburne-Copes.' The Blackburne-Copes had owned a huge Victorian house which they burned down after a drunken evening because it was so ugly.

'Laura and Jack . . . Julian ffrench.'

'Who?'

'Paul's tutor. He's a cousin of Laura and Jack's.' She smiled in Paul's direction. 'Julian was a wonderful help after you left that awful school, wasn't he, darling?'

Paul was sent off to deliver local invitations on his bicycle in order to save stamps.

'Why can't they be posted along with the others?'

'Don't be so indolent.'

No car. He set off, making his way along avenues as potholed and neglected as the one at Mountsilver. At the Countess's castle, the tall man who came to the door took the envelope. Paul couldn't help asking, 'Are you the footman?'

'I am.' It would be rude to ask when and how often he dressed up and stood behind the Countess's chair. He was a lot more picturesque than Agnes.

'How's the monkey?' Paul remembered its behaviour at Mountsilver with horror.

'Dead. Good riddance.'

'We didn't like it either.'

'Last thing it carried the dog up the tower and threw it down.' Goodbye Pekinese.

The last house he visited was more than twenty miles away; dusk was beginning to gather as he reached it.

'Not Donald and Valerie,' his mother had said.

'Of course,' Daddy had sighed.

'It's more than enough seeing them at Christmas.'

Valerie was Daddy's second cousin married to Donald who was retired from the Palestine Police.

'He was a Black and Tan before that.'

'Jolly them along, Paul. Don't encourage them. With a bit of luck they won't come.'

Their house, down an extra long extra potholed avenue, surrounded by wet rhododendrons, covered with Virginia creeper that grew right across the upstairs windows, shrieked of damp. The doorbell resounded and after some minutes he heard snuffles and coughs, together with slow shuffling footsteps.

'What do you want?'

'I'm Paul.'

'Oh, it's you.'

'Daddy's having a party.'

'What?'

'A PARTY.' Paul followed as he edged his way along on two sticks to the dingy sitting room which was filled with smoke even though the fire was choked with clinkers. The old boy spent five minutes finding his glasses before opening the envelope.

'Oh I don't think so. Valerie isn't well at the moment. Flu. No, no. We can't possibly. Not at all well. Has to keep to her bed. No. Out of the question.'

Paul rode back to Mountsilver delighted to have some good news for his parents.

'Excellent!' Daddy lifted his whiskey glass. 'Cross them off.'

CHAPTER THIRTEEN

The Celtic Swingers were hired from Dublin and crates of drink, including champagne, were ordered from Findlaters. Caterers were called in which made Cook furious; for days she complained how she could have done all the food herself.

Mummy was also furious.

'It's costing a fortune.'

You wouldn't think Daddy had been the one who made all the complaints about extravagance.

'Have you counted how many are coming?' Mummy moaned. 'Do you realise there are over a hundred?'

'I should think many of them won't turn up, like Donald and Valerie. We can only put up a certain amount here and it's difficult for the rest to get down to Mountsilver from Dublin.'

'A lot of them have got their cars on the road again. The others will be here if they have to walk. People will go anywhere for a party.'

'We could ask the Countess to take in a few at the castle. God knows she's been here often enough. It's time she returned the favour.'

'She won't. She might have put up a priest or two, but you haven't invited any.'

'They spoil the fun.'

'The thing is a nightmare.'

He ignored her. 'There's always Macnamara's.' He had written the name of the seedy hotel in Mountsilver at the bottom of the invitations.

'You'll have less friends once they've had to sleep there.'

'Oh shut up, Diana. This is once in a lifetime.'

Again the house was cleaned and once more chandeliers and mirrors sparkled. Agnes called in her sisters again. The floor of the ballroom was polished and sprinkled with French chalk, while Dempsey hammered away at a stand for the Celtic Swingers to play on.

Mummy told Paul: 'The last time the ballroom was used was before you were born.' Paul was born in 1929, the year the Depression began.

Spindly gilt chairs faced each other across the empty ballroom, soon to be filled with dancers eager to foxtrot and waltz – not jitterbug, most of Mummy and Daddy's guests were too old for that.

Dinner plates that hadn't been used for decades were brought out and washed. The parrot was moved down to the dairy. Even though it was May, Daddy decided to have the central heating on; the radiators were dusted again and the groaning machine in the basement had another trial run. Spare bedrooms with their decorations of faded watercolour landscapes by long-dead spinster aunts, were aired and cleared out for people to stay in overnight. Extra blankets had to borrowed from the Countess; if she wouldn't have anyone to stay, she provided those. Very likely not every bedroom would be needed as guests might find the idea of an overnight an ordeal – the obligations of hospitality could hardly disguise a hundred years of decay. Anything for a party . . .

'You'll have to give up your bedroom, Paul.'

'Where'll I sleep, then?'

'In the basement.' In the corridor known as the catacombs in Sheila's old room. That meant an iron bedstead, a pee pot and a couple of coats thrown over him to keep him warm.

'Don't look so miserable, for God's sake. Daddy and I are giving up our room as well.'

The house-hunting Jebbs would sleep in Corunna, the main bedroom, in the sleigh bed in front of the triple mirror across from the bow window with the view towards the river. They would stare at the Flemish tapestry of birds and boats and sea monsters. Giving them the room was providing a kind of bait. Who knew? They might take a fancy to Mountsilver, not that Daddy meant to sell. But it would be nice to have the option.

Daddy and Mummy would move up to Crécy which was on the third floor.

'Only for one night.'

'That's what you think. I bet the Jebbs will make this their headquarters while they are in Ireland. It will save them paying for staying in hotels. The richest people are the meanest.'

Paul wore his father's old dinner jacket, last used before the war. His first duty was to deal with the cars. Fitzpatrick would help, waving the ones belonging to overnight guests into the back yards, while the rest would be directed into the long field where they would line up. Paul prayed there would be no rain and his prayer was answered. The half hour guiding drivers into the field turned out to be the best part of the whole party for him; it was wonderful to be in control of endless purring cars making their way up the drive one by one; for days Mick and Regan had been filling in pot holes.

The drivers deposited passengers at the front door before going to their allotted parking place in the field and then trudging up to the house. After most of the cars had arrived and dusk was gathering, Paul wasted time before returning to the house going around with his torch inspecting them and admiring them. It was amazing seeing this huge cluster of vehicles, after all those years, when just a year ago if you saw one a day it was a miracle. Some had not been improved by being up on blocks throughout the Emergency, but most had come back to life without injury like Snow White or the Sleeping Beauty. The Rolls Royce had been brought over from England by the Jebbs.

Trigger and Helen, together with Mary Rooke, jogged up the drive in the same old Ford V8 that had been run on charcoal. Hurray for petrol.

At the house lights blazed and rooms buzzed with voices of friends greeting one another, many for the first time since 1940. When they weren't discussing the war, they were talking about bankruptcies, abandoned houses, dry rot, the perfidy of servants, friends who had died, the awfulness of de Valera, the coming of Socialists in England, rheumatism, the slump in agricultural prices in voices that sounded cheerful enough.

'Like old times.'

Mummy was wandering around being charming.

'Oh Diana, such a marvellous party!' cried Mary Rooke, her mouth full of smoked salmon.

'How wonderful you look, Diana.' She did, too – a new dress in silver lamé and matching strap shoes bought at Brown Thomas was her price for ceasing to complain.

'Hello Harry darling.' Harry took off his monocle to give her a peck on the cheek. He wore it even when he went swimming.

Julian was there with Laura and Jack,

'Hello Paul. I hear you've been converted.'

Mummy must have told him. Did she write him a letter or did she see him in Dublin?

'Who's this?' growled Daddy.

'Julian, darling, Laura's nephew. Paul's tutor.'

'Pity you couldn't get the boy to pass the maths exam.'

'Not Paul's strongest subject.'

'You tried your best, didn't you, Julian?' Mummy said.

Daddy said, 'I'd have thought a bit of proper coaching might have sorted that out. Paul! See to it the maids and Regan bring in more drinks.'

Paul had been planning to repeat his behaviour of the early summer, keeping an eye on his mother and Fireball. Would they creep away to be alone together? But surveillance was impossible with his father shouting at him all the time to help. Bernadette, Agnes and her sisters, plus Regan, brought inside after the car parking – you couldn't ask Fitzpatrick, he was above that sort of thing – were doing their best running around with trays of champagne. Daddy had given up butlers after Redmond was sacked in 1936; before he departed Redmond tried to burn down the house. Paul had to take over the role which meant that not only could he not keep an eye on Mummy, but he couldn't talk to any of the daughters who had come along with his father's friends.

Mummy didn't seem to be taking notice of Julian, whom Paul saw dancing with a girl whom he himself had an eye on when he peered into the ball room. He could dance better than that – thank you, Miss Watson for all the years of teaching me, I can dance, if I'm no good at Maths. But he never seemed to get the opportunity. *I get a kick out of you . . .* Why was a foxtrot called that?

Mummy was in the drawing room talking to the Countess and Sam Seymour, both of whom were bemoaning the fate of the Pekinese. Paul was offering champagne to comfort them, when his father stormed in waving his whiskey glass.

'Cut your throats, here come Donald Duck and Valerie.'

Paul glanced out of the long window; sure enough you could see by the light in the porch the two old fogeys who had just stepped out of a taxi. By the grim face of the taxi driver he guessed they would have paid their fare in pennies gathered by Valerie in jam jars. She would have another paper bag in her handbag and she would fill it with leftover food; this evening's scavenging would do them for a day or two. They had two sticks each which they were using as if they were skiing across a plain that was deep in snow, and made for the steps very slowly one behind the other, cadaverous Donald leading, fragile Valerie following.

Daddy was furious. 'You told us they weren't coming!'

'I'm sorry Daddy, that's what Donald said.'

'You deal with them.'

So he had to do just that, finding them chairs beside the fire in the hall and a rug for Valerie who still had a temperature which wasn't high enough for her to stay away from the fun. Dr Waters was here and could deal with her if she threatened to die. Paul brought them food, found them a low table to put it on, then more food for Valerie to put away and take home, then champagne for Donald and several glasses of white wine for Valerie, and all the time he had to listen hard as she told him about her weak eyes and chronic indigestion.

'Be a dear and cut up the larger pieces.'

At one time he thought he'd just desert them, leaving them to get along by themselves, but he ran into his father who fixed him with his beady eye.

People were eating steadily from the buffet. He didn't have a chance to get anything himself, only a chicken leg hurriedly snatched from Valerie's plate where he had put two.

'Paul! Paul!' His father was calling again. '. . . get me another glass.' His temper had got a lot worse since Donald and Valerie arrived.

Another plateful for Mary Rooke, who ate as much as Valerie and Donald. Meringues! Early strawberries! Just a spot more cream, if you would, Paul.

When hours had passed and everyone had eaten and Valerie and Donald were dozing, he sneaked off to the ballroom. The Celtic Swingers had smoothed back hair, tight scarlet jackets with gold epaulettes and two of them wore sunglasses. The band leader, whose name was Tom Muldoon, a small dapper fellow with a pencil moustache, was crooning as a saxophone played behind him. Lights were dimmed.

'Come along, young man,' a middle-aged woman grabbed Paul by the arm and led him onto the floor, 'We can't have you shirking.' Mrs Truebody's soft enveloping body pressed against him, he could smell her scent, and surprisingly she moved effortlessly in time to the music.

I've got the sun in the morning and the moon at night.

She also talked loudly about the other dancers, about how the Countess, dancing with Sam Seymour had lost her last husband when he said it was a choice between him and the Pekinese.

'And you know what happened to the Pekinese.'

Mrs Truebody said suddenly, 'What the hell does Diana think she's doing?' He glanced in the direction she indicated and saw that Mummy was dancing cheek to cheek with Julian.

Mrs Truebody let Paul go when the lights went up, a Paul Jones was announced and bad luck gave him Dr Waters' daughter, a plump girl with a face like a boot and nothing to say. No escape. Another foxtrot and he found she didn't know the first thing about dancing. He had to teach her, slow, quick quick slow. After that she clung to him. Oh, hokey cokey! She even had trouble turning round. 'That's what it's all about!'

When he finally got rid of her he looked round. No sign of his mother, but his father was there, demanding the Gay Gordons. No sweat for the Celtic Swingers. 'Keep it quick and cheerful, lads,' Tom Muldoon had told his boys. Traditional foxtrots, waltzes, with the occasional rhumba and the Gay Gordons came naturally. They had specialised in Hunt Balls before the Emergency and it was grand to be playing once again at something of the sort in this barn of a place.

'Everyone join in!' His father's jollity grated on Paul's nerves; he disobeyed and watched from the sidelines as Daddy, red faced and sweating twirled Mrs Fortesque. Twenty or thirty couples one behind the other, women going round and round to cheers. One two, la la, one two, la, whirl, whirl.

'Where's Mummy?' Daddy called out panting as he released Mrs Fortesque.

'Don't know.'

Time for the conga. Paul joined in behind Mrs Truebody, and a lot of people who had got old during the Emergency; the long line stamped round the house which took half an hour by the time it had wound its way through the hall and all the big rooms. One, two three, da! One, two three da! The jaunty music of the Celtic Swingers echoing after them faded as distance increased and then got louder as the line made its way back to the ballroom. How everyone perspired and panted! Dr Waters was at hand if anyone felt really ill. Paul couldn't see Mummy.

The caterers were serving bacon and eggs and more champagne. The sun had come up. Ashtrays were full and people were throwing their butts into Chinese jars or stubbing them out on Famille Rose plates. Paul found a plate for Dr Waters' daughter, about whom he had changed his mind. He learnt her name was Rosemary and she was doing a typing course at a place in Grafton Street. No champagne, no thank you, a cup of tea would be nice. She wasn't all that bad, if dreary. Paul knew she was one of four children and one summer day ten years ago her father, Dr Waters, had put them all in deck chairs on the lawn and taken out their tonsils.

The Celtic Swingers were slowing down.

Going to take a sentimental journey . . .

Time for the windup. Paul pressed Rosemary against his chest, but she pushed back – he should have tried making a pass at her long ago instead of being side-tracked by the fact she was ugly. He had left things too late, although, before she departed he rushed off to the study and found pencil and paper for her to write out her address for him. There was no time for a kiss as she had to go home, her parents were waiting.

When Daddy first talked to Tom Muldoon he had asked if the Celtic

Swingers would end with God Save the King, Tom Muldoon told him he'd rather play *Deutschland über alles*. That was one argument that Daddy lost, and now the flagging dancers under the chandeliers had to stand up for the Soldier's Song. No one in Paul's family had ever before paid attention to the fiery Republican words.

Guests were leaving; some, like the Countess, and Mrs Truebody had already gone. Now Paul had to carry coats. The sun was coming up.

'Goodbye, goodbye!'

'What a lovely party!'

'Such wonderful food!' cried Mary Rooke.

'Welcome back, Gerald!'

'Like old times!'

'Goodbye!'

Daddy waved them all off. Where was Mummy? Paul raced out to the paddock to help the cars on their way. In the low early summer sun they departed one by one. He saw out the caterers who had left a mighty amount of washing up for Agnes and her sisters. The Celtic Swingers were packing their instruments into their van and Tom Muldoon was counting the money Daddy had given him. Then they were away as well.

The line of vehicles made its way slowly down the avenue at about the pace of the conga. Paul waved goodbye to Jack and Laura, noticing that Fireball was not with them. The last car was very full; its occupants included Donald and Valerie holding her bag of chicken legs and meringues, who had left it to the final moments to cadge a lift.

He let out the dogs from the far stable where they had been housed during the party, distant enough for their barks to be almost inaudible. Followed by Wooster, he made his way back to the house, up the steps into the hall. It was very hot; although the fires in the fireplaces had long died down, no one had remembered to turn off the central heating.

The long night had taken its toll. Guests who were staying overnight, had retired to their bedrooms. Cook, Bernadette, Agnes and her sisters were also sleeping, leaving the mess to be cleaned up tomorrow morning. It was morning now. Paul was about to seek out his own room downstairs beside them when his father appeared, his face was blotchy red. He was grasping a cigar in one hand and a champagne bottle in the other – he must have run out of whiskey. Wooster whimpered with delight.

'Seen your mother?'

'No.'

'I've searched everywhere.'

'Uh . . .'

'Have a look round, old fellow, will you?' He sat down heavily on a wooden hall chair and drank straight out of the bottle.

'And look for her bloody friend.'

Paul wandered around vaguely peering into the rooms on the ground floor. The huge spaces were pervaded with cigarette smoke; the big house smelt like an old pub. Empty glasses added to the illusion.

Not a soul in sight. She had probably gone to bed.

Bed . . . Avoiding the hall where his father was sitting, he made his way to the back stairs and climbed up to the third floor to Crécy. He hesitated before trying the door which was locked. He knocked timidly.

'Mummy!'

No answer. He could hear shuffling noises.

'Who is it?'

'It's me, Paul!'

'Go away!'

'I'm sorry – Daddy is looking for you.'

'Oh . . . God – what time is it?'

'Nearly five o'clock . . .'

More shuffling noises.

'What will I say?'

There was a long silence except for squeaks and footsteps.

'I said, what will I say?'

'Oh for God sake! Tell him I've gone out for a walk.'

'A walk?'

'Why not? It's a lovely morning.'

He was about to retreat when the door opened slowly and Fireball emerged buttoning up his starched shirt and carrying his dinner jacket.

Too late. Daddy was there. The notion that something was going on in

Crécy must have occurred to him the same time it occurred to Paul. He must have jumped from the hall chair, and run up the front stairs. Behind him plodded Wooster who was panting hard.

Stupid idiots to have chosen to have their flop in that bedroom. Why hadn't they just gone outside and lain down in the grass? They must have thought they had all the time in the world.

Without pause, without hesitation, without breaking his stride, Daddy dropped the bottle of champagne he was carrying, came forward, pushed Fireball back in the bedroom, seized the key from the inside, slammed the door and locked it.

'Now you and your girl friend can fuck all night long. Night and day!'

He lurched in Paul's direction.

'What the hell are you doing here?'

The locked door rattled.

'Gerald! Gerald! Open the door!'

'Daddy . . .'

'Get out of my way!'

'Gerald . . . please . . .'

'You're a bitch, Diana!'

'Daddy . . .'

Daddy staggered over to the top hall and with great effort lifted up one of the small sash windows which was swollen with damp. Wooster barked as he threw the key out.

He turned and saw his son looking particularly helpless and hopeless. Down the passage the door was still rattling.

'Gerald! GERALD!'

'PAUL! Go to bed!' Which Paul did.

CHAPTER FOURTEEN

He woke in the basement room with a cat lying on his chest.

He looked at the time. One o'clock. His first thought had been how awful the room was where he was sleeping and how could they possibly persuade any maid to stay in it. His second thought was regret that he had not kissed Rosemary. His third thought . . .

He pushed away the cat and dressed hurriedly thanking God he had remembered bringing in some old clothes down here so that he did not have to put on the ghastly dinner jacket again. Upstairs the central heating had been switched off, the sun was shining and already everything had been cleaned up. Bernadette, Agnes and her sisters must have been working since daybreak. Except for the lingering smell of tobacco smoke, you would not have had a clue that anything momentous had taken place yesterday.

In the dining room the fire had been lit once again and the remains of kedgeree and scrambled egg with smoked salmon were left under oval salvers. They were still warm, and he helped himself to a great plateful, together with lukewarm coffee. He sat and ate slowly.

'Where's Daddy?' he asked Agnes.

'He's gone to the races, Master Paul.'

'Where's everyone else?'

'Some are gone with him. The others are after leaving.'

He did not ask about his mother. He wolfed down his breakfast – he was extremely hungry since he had eaten hardly anything during the party – and drank coffee slowly, putting off the evil moment.

Finally with a sigh, he made his way upstairs to Crécy and knocked timidly.

'Who is it?'

'It's me.'

'For God's sake, both of us are tired of this tomfoolery' – that was Fireball's voice. 'Open the door!'

'I can't.'

'Why not?' That was Mummy.

'Daddy threw away the key.'

'How do you know?'

'I saw him. Out of the window.'

'Did you try and find it?'

'I went to bed.'

There was a long silence.

'Where's Daddy?'

'Gone to the races.'

Another silence.

'Look here, Paul. Go and find that key. Or call the fire brigade. Do something.'

He did his best. As he searched under the rosebush far beneath the window out of which the key had fallen, he wondered what his mother and Fireball had been doing for the last six hours. More snogging? Had they shouted? Had anyone heard? Presumably not. The embarrassment of the Jebbs and the servants hearing would have been awful. Old-fashioned country house jinks might be tolerated so long as people weren't found out. He wondered if they could be heard at all, high up as they were.

There would be a chamber pot in Crécy.

He was covered with scratches from thorns by the time he decided there was no point in looking further. Would he ring the fire brigade? The nearest one was thirty miles away and the arrival of a fire engine would be the surest way of letting the whole county know. He found an axe in the wood yard and carried it up three flights where he attacked the door.

'Sorry, I can't make it work!'

'You're useless! Get someone for God's sake!'

So he went off again and found Mick in the yard who followed him up the flights of stairs, took the axe and managed to smash the hinges off.

'Thank you, Mick.' Mummy emerged, dressed in silver lamé. If Fireball had had any style he would have followed much later, instead of stepping out after Mummy in his wrinkled dinner jacket. Mick made no attempt to hide his smirk.

The first thing they demanded was a bath. The water was still hot from the central heating, and Mummy and Fireball retired to the bathroom beside her bedroom with its big copper bath tub. Did they share it? They must have used the new towels provided for the Jebbs. Then Mummy ordered lunch and Cook produced the same breakfast Paul had eaten, heated up remains of the kedgeree and overcooked scrambled egg and salmon, together with coffee which must be bitter by this time.

When she had finished Mummy went back to her bedroom, thrust aside the stuff belonging to the Jebbs and packed a trunk. The first thing that went in was her jewellery case. Clothes and shoes were thrown in with no attempt to fold them.

'Paul! Ring Reilly.' Paul rang for the taxi while Fireball hung about.

'Paul! Julian!'

He and Fireball lugged the trunk downstairs, Mummy following in her highest of heels, wearing her Persian lamb coat, carrying the hatbox she had filled up at the last moment. She went down to the kitchen and said goodbye to Agnes, Bernadette and Cook leaving them torn between disapproval and tears. Fireball scowled when she wrote down the address of his flat in Dublin for Paul.

Reilly took his time and an hour passed before the taxi rumbled up to the porch. No sign of Daddy; Paul didn't know whether to thank God or not. Before they departed, Fireball looking increasingly foolish in his evening clothes, Mummy gave him a peck on the cheek. 'Goodbye, darling.'

'Goodbye.'

'I know your father won't miss me, and I know Julian and I are going to be very happy.'

'What about Bubbles?' Paul asked.

'Oh my God I forgot about Bubbles.'

'Is it wise to take her?' Fireball asked.

Mummy glared at him. Perhaps . . .

Paul went off to find Bubbles who was in the upper yard, where she had been rolling in something filthy.

Reilly helped Fireball lug the trunk into the boot of the taxi – Mummy did not call upon the men to help. But she knew they were watching – everyone was watching, both inside the house and out. She climbed in, clutching the hat box and waved out of the window as if she was going off just for the day. Bubbles leapt in joyfully, her stink overwhelming Je Reviens. She loved cars. Lucky dog.

Daddy returned late in the Rover with the Jebbs. He was wearing his check tweed suit, bowler hat, polished shoes, steward's card pinned over his pocket and his gabardine army raincoat.

He was smiling to himself.

He didn't ask if his wife had gone. He asked no questions and Paul told him nothing. He didn't go up to the top floor to check on the axed door.

At dinner no mention was made of Mummy. Nor did the Jebbs say anything about the mess she had left in the bedroom where they were sleeping. She should have cleared out her drawers and cupboards in the first place before they came to stay. You wouldn't know what lie Daddy told them, but they couldn't be such fools as not to have guessed what was going on. By now everyone on the estate had the story and very soon the whole world, at least all the people who had attended the party would know everything.

Meanwhile the Jebbs talked about how much money they had lost betting.

'Pity you didn't take my advice.' Daddy knew the form and had come away with some winnings. But his wife had gone.

The Jebbs left next day, back to England. They may have lost money at an Irish race meeting, but they managed their finances so Mr Attlee was unable to grab as much as he should have. For years afterwards from their house in the Cotswolds they bored their friends with the story of Diana's love affair, with their imitation of the amusing sayings of the servants at Mountsilver, and their feelings of relief about not going to live in Ireland. They became experts on the island of saints and scholars, a land about which their pals were woefully ignorant. They knew all about the IRA. Tut tut.

Paul was left with his father in a mansion where the smell of cigarette smoke lingered. He could return to his bedroom, which also smelled of cigarettes. He slept on sheets someone had used, he did not know who, and got up to be with Daddy next morning. Over the following days they read thank you letters bristling with insincerity which said how marvellous the party had been. Ill news travels fast.

The routine was much the same, except there was just the two of them. Every morning Daddy woke him if he stayed in bed beyond eight o'clock. He did not come into the bedroom any more, merely stamped up and down outside and if Paul dozed off, the stamping feet would resume ten minutes later. During the day they avoided one another. In the evening they spent solemn silent dinners together.

'Why aren't you wearing a tie?'

'Sorry, Daddy.'

'No excuse for slovenly behaviour.'

Occasionally they discussed Paul's future. 'You should learn something about agriculture so that when the time comes' – code for 'when I die' – 'you'll be able to run this place.' Paul couldn't think of anything else he wanted to do apart from emigrating, and that wasn't on the cards.

Once he broke a silence by asking, 'Are you going to get a divorce?'

'You should know better than that.'

After dinner they would listen to the news, and sipping his whiskey, Daddy would play his classical records or Gilbert and Sullivan or read yesterday's *Irish Times*. He had cancelled the subscription to *Country Life*. Paul read – these days he was tackling Dickens one at a time from the uniform edition on the upper shelf of the study. He spared himself Walter Scott. Or he played patience or tied fishing flies.

Three weeks after Mummy had left Daddy spent a frenetic day getting rid of traces of his wife. In spite of her quick packing the day she left, she had been forced to leave a lot of her things behind, dresses, gloves, shoes, her mackintosh, gumboots, riding habit, jodhpurs, parasol, slacks, face creams, nail files, handkerchiefs, the dress she had worn to Queen Charlotte's Ball, some pieces of Masonic regalia which had belonged to her father and her latest half-finished tapestry, meant for a chair which would retain its leather seat for ever.

Daddy gathered everything that might remind him of her, filled up old suitcases and wooden crates and had Mick take them up to the top floor. They were dumped in the barrack room where two hundred years ago bachelors had been put up for the night. Her books followed – *Rebecca* – Tosh… *The Constant Nymph*… Just what you'd expect… *Elizabeth and her German Garden*… *The Pursuit of Love*… Huh…

'What about the Agatha Christies?' They were spared; Daddy read them too.

There was one evening when he went through Mummy's gramophone records, muttering, taking them out of their jackets and throwing them across the breakfast room. *Boogie woogie bugle boy*…Smash! *Give me a bread and butter woman* . . . Why not? Smash! *It's a hap-hap-happy day!* Like Hell! Smash!

On another day he broke the Rockingham tea service.

He called for Paul to help him lug upstairs the huge portrait of Mummy by Leo Whelan, which showed her in her riding habit, carrying a whip.

He moved out of the breakfast room where Mummy had liked to spend the evenings and went back permanently to the study which Paul associated with lectures on his bad behaviour when he was a small boy. The roll top desk, the rent table, and the *Punch* volumes were there. The wireless had to be lugged in and the chimney swept; sticks and dead jackdaws rained down.

He made no attempt to move back into Corunna which he kept locked after Agnes and Bernadette had given it a clean. He had already taken his belongings into Inkerman and slept there.

He sent Parade off to the horse sales at Ballsbridge. He spared the surviving dogs; they would reduce in numbers by attrition. He killed the spider in the sitting room and had the borders in the walled garden ploughed.

Mick approved. 'What's the good of flowers? You can't eat them.'

Some roses had to be left since they were so prolific they were virtually impossible to uproot. Mummy had grown them from cuttings, Boule de Neige, Souvenir de la Bataille de Marengo. She had loved saying that name to Fireball. The tennis court continued as a hen run.

It was too late in the year to plant potatoes so for this summer Mick concentrated on lettuces; the rabbits couldn't eat enough of them and by the end of the summer Paul and his father could devour forty at a sitting if they wished. Meanwhile Mick had a good time drawing pieces of string tight over the newly manured ground and scattering seedlings, mostly of vegetables that Paul disliked, leeks, carrots and cut and come again spinach.

Mick also planted more raspberries, more than Paul and his father could ever eat. Cook would make jam – more jam than they could ever eat. Daddy told him to forget about watering the plants in the greenhouse – since the walled garden well was threatening to dry up and water was needed for the seedlings. He did not actually ask Mick to go inside to uproot the datura, the heliotrope and the plumbago which Mummy had cared for so much, but condemned them to long painful death from thirst. In the evenings after he had said goodnight to Daddy Paul went out with his torch and watered the greenhouse plants. The scent of heliotrope heated by the sun evoked his mother more than any Je Reviens.

Occasionally Daddy went into Dublin to the Club which had gone to the dogs. Paul yearned for him to go, seizing every opportunity while he was away to cycle into the town to the cinema. Or he would fish, making way down the the river bank, furiously, casting – zing! zing! the Flying Ant Cinnamon leapt across the river and he caught the odd trout which he would fry himself in the kitchen. Before that he would take off his clothes and have a naked swim. It was lonely swimming by himself.

Otherwise the only outside event of the week was Sunday mass.

Father Hogan was invited to stay for a dismal week when he and Daddy spent a huge amount of time wandering around the place, in the rain on long intimate walks as the priest offered spiritual advice, offered to find a convent which would take over the house and estate, and told Daddy to cut down on whiskey. (That was guess work on Paul's part.) All the walking about was too much for Wooster who, following his master every step of the way, stopped beside the stable yard and had a stroke.

Mr O'Brien was summoned and recommended putting him down.

'He's on the way out.'

'I know,' Daddy said. 'But I'm not that ungrateful.'

Some sort of stimulant was injected instead.

'He won't last long.'

'I know.'

'Mrs Blake-Willoughby not here?' Mr O'Brien asked, putting away the needle that was not a killer.

'No.'

For the next two days Daddy nursed the old dog who lay on the big sofa in the drawing room motionless except for the occasional twitch from his tail. He died with his head in Daddy's lap. Daddy was already planning his headstone which would have a poem used for one of the Duke of Ormonde's dogs.

> There are men both good and wise
> Who hold that in a future state
> Dumb creatures we have cherished here below
> Shall give us joyous greetings
> When we pass the golden gate.
> Oh how earnestly I pray it may be so!

Father Hogan disapproved very much of so much attention and emotion being bestowed on a dumb animal, and the sentiment of the planned inscription horrified him. It took him a couple of days to persuade Daddy to record only the basics of the dog's death, WOOSTER 1935 – 1947. Then he had to leave, since clerical duties summoned him. Before he departed he gave Paul an image of Our Lady and the Infant Jesus to be placed in his bedroom, to whom he should direct his prayers.

Paul had an opportunity to take Father Hogan in the Rover, without having Daddy nag and hiss beside him whenever he crashed the gears. But the drive to the station was soured by endless questions about his religious duties. Damn it, he knew very well how Paul prayed, morning and evening, went to mass on Sundays and holy days and in general had plunged into the whole business of conversion and Confirmation with the enthusiasm of belief.

'I know you are praying for your mother.' It was none of his business.

Life must go on, and in a week Daddy had bought a puppy, also a Labrador, also named Wooster.

The second Wooster was another dog for Paul to feed. The daily ritual had evolved on him, and he would feel a surge of depression when he caught sight of Bart from the butcher bicycling up on Fridays with the gigot chops for Irish stew, the Sunday joint, and the sheep's head. The cats got their herring when Clancy from the fishmonger came up with Friday's salmon. Feeding animals was no job for the servants, never had been. Each evening he descended the flight of granite stairs and made his way over the flags to the murky kitchen where daylight came from the barred windows high overhead and every flash of movement might be a mouse. Sometimes the liquid in which the sheep's head stewed was rancid.

He chatted with Cook, Bernadette and Agnes hating the pity in their eyes – poor lonely young man deserted by his mother, bullied by his father. There must have been tensions that he did not observe, since suddenly Cook and Bernadette gave notice. They came into the study on two separate evenings after the news. Daddy put away his glass and heard what they wanted.

'Why?'

Paul had to listen while he interrogated them one at a time like a Nazi officer. Had they other jobs to go to? Were they aware good positions were not easy to come by? Were they dissatisfied with this place? Did they consider they needed a rise in pay? Did they not realise how long they had been here at Mountsilver? Had the work suddenly got too much for them?

'. . . I'm sorry, Sir, my mother's needing me to look after her.'

'. . . please Major, my knee isn't good.'

'You might think that in some way they had been mistreated.'

'I'm wanted at home . . .'

'Of course they were spoiled for years by your mother.'

Everything that went wrong was her fault.

'You might think after her behaviour they would show a modicum of loyalty.'

Only Agnes, pinned by ancient ties, remained steadfast and did not give in her notice. She continued to climb the stairs, breathing heavily, bringing up his father's shaving water, standing as usual in the dining-room corner.

The long drive or Daddy's reputation for being a cuckold may have discouraged the few applicants that he interviewed.

'. . . I suppose they've all gone to England to get jobs there.'

'. . . It's not as if I am looking for a butler.'

Father McCabe suggested another reason. 'I don't mean to intrude, Major, but in today's world girls may be more choosy.'

'Choosy?' That was not a word his father liked to hear from a man who had no idea of how to run a large house. But Daddy knew what he was talking about.

There were ways the kitchen could be spruced up, beginning with a lick of paint. Rat traps, mouse traps. More use of the yard brush. Letting in more light by taking some of the bars off the windows. Replacing some of the blacker saucepans and frying pans. Father McCabe said he would look around for a couple of girls who might suit.

'I need one who can cook.'

Daddy had had enough and needed a holiday, so Freddy Barnsworth's invitation to go down to Mayo for a spot of fishing was welcome.

Paul had not been asked. 'You'll have to stay and mind the place.' Daddy rolled away down the drive in the Rover – at least he took Wooster Two with him. Paul hoped the puppy would be sick.

He decided to go and see his mother. 'I will, indeed, Master Paul,' Agnes said pityingly when he asked her if she would feed the dogs for the evening. He took a train into Dublin, bringing a bottle of champagne left over from the party, a bunch of roses that had survived Daddy's purge wrapped in wet newspaper and the china horse that had stood on the chimney piece in the breakfast room.

Fireball's flat was on top of a house in Fitzwilliam Square. When Paul rang he put his head out of a window and threw down the front door key. Paul made his way up four storeys to what must have been a nursery, small rooms with low ceilings and bars on the windows like the kitchen at home. Too bad if the place went on fire.

'Oh, it's you,' Fireball said.

The student furniture, the photographs of school groups and the reproduction of Van Gogh's almond tree must be his taste. Mummy was lying on a shabby sofa, Bubbles at her feet.

'Darling!'

Paul handed over his gifts. 'Nothing could possibly be nicer. Julian, be an angel, put the horse below Van Gogh, the flowers in water and the champagne in the fridge – we'll have it later. Something to cheer us up after me being sacked. And let's have some tea for the time being.'

By the time the tea came in thick mugs, Mummy had told Paul about losing her job. The decorator's shop – 'I thought Basil such a sweet little man, but he turns out to be a pig.' Trouble arose over wallpaper for Mrs O'Connor's drawing room in Foxrock. 'They ordered white and gold Regency stripe.' Mummy arranged for the room to be papered while Mr and Mrs O'Connor were away in Parknasilla. Unfortunately when they came back and flung open the door of the drawing room, they were greeted with four walls of scarlet poppies. Mummy had got the number of the order wrong.

'Stupid woman – such shrieks. You'd think I did it on purpose.'

'I don't know what you are going to do now,' growled Fireball. 'There aren't that many decorator's shops in Dublin.'

'I'll leave things a couple of days and go back to Basil and butter him up and ask for my job back. He'll give it to me – he's such a snob.' Mummy made the most of her family connections. Whenever her father filled in a form stating his occupation he had put 'Peer of the Realm'.

'I should damn well hope so,' Fireball said. He must also be out of work.

Paul told his news. He left out his father's dealings with Mummy's things and concentrated on Wooster's death.

'Poor old dog.'

He also told her about the staff. '. . . and Agnes is the only one who's staying.'

Mummy looked really pleased. 'Poor old thing.'

Paul went down to walk Bubbles around the square and by the canal while Fireball prepared dinner and Mummy banged at little hard-boiled quails' eggs, taking off their speckled shells with her red painted nails. They ate them together with Parma ham, Stilton from a great drum, caviar, and Carr's biscuits, ending with a jar of crystallised fruit.

'Harrods,' Mummy said.

Daddy would keep getting the bills until he noticed. The champagne went well with the meal.

Afterwards Paul slept on the sofa – pity about them sharing a bed next door, but he had to get used to that sort of thing. He knelt beside the sofa and said his usual prayer for Mummy's soul.

CHAPTER FIFTEEN

'Pity about Cirencester. Too expensive.'

'It's probably a good thing. I'm certain I don't want to do agriculture.'

'Oh, come, Paul, we've talked about this before.' They talked about nothing else. Paul mouthed the next familiar sentence in unison with his father. 'You can't go on hanging around the place doing nothing.'

'No, Daddy.'

'Have you any other ideas?'

Emigration. 'Not really.'

'At your age I was already in the army.' Not again! 'First there was Sandhurst, then your grandfather's regiment.' Daddy repeated himself with a firm decisiveness as if he was making the statement for the first time. 'I can never understand why you don't want to follow the family tradition. It always surprises me.'

'Cirencester would have been OK.'

'Of course Cirencester would have been much better and more appropriate, but we must learn to tighten our belts. However . . .'

Oh God, what now?

'I've been making enquiries about Irish agricultural colleges. Going through prospectuses.' They must have been in the envelopes Paul had seen arriving in the post. 'I've picked out St Fiacre's and have written to the Registrar who says they have a few vacancies.' That was code for the place being half empty. 'Of course I consulted Father Hogan. He says St Fiacre's is excellent and gives an all round knowledge of farming.'

'How does he know?'

'He knows the head brother.'

'Brother?'

'The Franciscans run it.'

'Where is it?'

'Leitrim.'

'Leitrim!'

'What's wrong with Leitrim, may I ask?'

'Rain. Bog.'

He was ignored. 'I have put you down for general farming studies.'

'Can I take up bee keeping?'

'Don't annoy me, Paul.'

In his trunk he had a new pair of gumboots and warm clothing and his bicycle was strapped to the roof rack. He had been given ten pounds. 'For emergencies. I don't think you'll have any opportunity to spend it.'

The Rover reached Leitrim. As it drove through stone pillars and up a long avenue Daddy remembered how he used to come to this place as a boy. The estate had belonged to friends of the family.

'Jolly nice people, but they had to leave. Nineteen twenty-two.'

The avenue, laid with tarmac, was an avenue no longer. There was not a decent tree to be seen. 'I remember a lot of very fine oaks and good specimen trees. It must have taken years for the brothers to cut them down.' They passed a forest of sitka spruce. 'St Fiacre's does a course in forestry management.'

The Rover reached the huge red brick house with turrets and towers to which a concrete block had been added surmounted by a cross. A fat bustling figure dressed in a brown robe and sandals opened the huge mahogany door.

'Major Blake -Willoughby?'

'Brother Ahern.'

'Ah. This must be Paul.' He grasped Paul's hand tightly.

'Uh . . .'

'You'll find out, Paul, how we take in lads from all over the country to learn the rudiments of modern agricultural practice.'

'No girls?'

'Ha ha, very good, Major.' The brother had small dark eyes in a podgy face; laughter launched the rolls of his double chin.

'Do you farm, Major?'

'A little. Five hundred acres.'

'That's a lot more than any of the lads here will ever have charge of. Paul has plenty to learn.' He smiled benevolently.

Damn it, this Brother Ahern must know everything there was to be known – Such a blessing the young man had come into the fold! Mixed marriages are a tragedy! Of course he would be prayed for! We will keep an eye on his spiritual development! An unfaithful mother! All Paul's life's history would have been passed on by Father Hogan.

There was a brief conversation about the relative merits of tillage and pasture before Daddy said, 'Well, I'd better be going.'

'Goodbye.'

'Work hard!'

It was the first time he had been parted from his father since Daddy had returned. The Rover drove off, observed by thirty or forty agricultural students who had finished a day's work.

Inside, the rooms, smelling of Jeyes fluid, had been stripped of all traces of old decency apart from mahogany doors. Another figure in a brown robe appeared to take Paul to his room which was in the new wing. It was small, with enough space for a single bed and cupboard and the crucifix on the wall.

He met a group of students in smelly protective clothing who had come in from the fields, a local farmer's son, a Donegal man he couldn't understand, another with the softer tones of Cork and Kerry.

'What course are you doing?'

'Oh, the basic one – tillage . . . dairy . . . dry stock.'

'Aren't we all?'

A pimply faced youth with broken teeth asked, 'Are ye English?'

'No.'

'My God, ye sound it.'

At supper – the food was almost identical to that of St George's – there was more.

'What part of England are ye from?'

'I'm Irish.'

'If you are Irish, I'm a nigger.'

'Where's he from, then, lads?'

'Hamp-shire. Wilt-shire . . .'

'Oo no . . . How about Ox-ford-shire?'

'Oh no. Oh dear me, no . . .'

'La di dah!'

'Blake-Willoughby . . . Double double!'

It had been a mistake to cling to the double-barrelled name. Blake would have been quite enough. Another mistake was wearing a sports jacket and tie.

Next day he was initiated into farming by mucking out a row of pigsties, work no one else wanted to do. He was given a spade, a fork and a stout brush. After an ineffectual attempt to clean out one corner of a sty occupied by a huge sow and countless piglets, he found the spade snatched from his hand.

'Don't you know anything, Englishman?'

The work wasn't easy, between the lectures – he filled notebooks with statistics and instructions – and the labour and was not helped by having to put up with the continuing chorus of jeers. The boys had gathered he was not exactly English, but something worse.

'Is your father sacking anyone this week?'

He was soon wondering what the hell he was doing in this Godforsaken place sloshing around in gumboots among people who despised him whom he could scarcely understand.

'Ah ye Cromwellian?'

'Oh my goodness, oh no no!'

'Souper!'

'Oh never!'

He did his best with regard to farm management, and maintenance, farm business, cattle, sheep, pig and poultry. Tillage and its mysteries were preferable, but he had no opportunity to drive a tractor which was one of his few skills. Otherwise the simplest job seemed to be beyond his capabilities.

'Straighten your back!'

'He doesn't know how to hold a spade!'

'Why don't you join the Foreign Legion?

He seemed to have to spend a good deal of time with pigs. Or digging – the sort of thing he had watched Mick do most of his life. He spent a rainy week planting wretched little sitkas among the rubble of mature trees that had been felled. He had a difficult time in the chicken run where, to renewed jeers, he learned how to kill. He had spent much time watching Mick chasing fowl with an axe, but this was different, more efficient. Brother Brendan showed him how.

'Hold her by the feet.'

'Not like that! Just below the head . . . pull and twist until you hear her snap!'

'Oh my God! Try again!'

'The bloody thing is still alive!'

'Flapping its wings.'

'That doesn't mean it's alive.'

'It bloody well is!'

'Kill it, Cromwell!'

'You'd have done better in the British army!'

'The Germans would have won with people like you around!'

'If at first you can't succeed, try, try try again!'

A dozen chickens were needed for Sunday lunch. Paul killed one on his fifth try.

Of course he hadn't the faintest knowledge of Gaelic games and tried to evade the hurley afternoons when groups of boys lashed each other with sticks, whacking balls into the air.

'You must know about RUGBY!'

'CRICKET!'

'Garrison games!'

'Oh, my goodness gracious me! CRICKET!'

No point handing this fella a hurley stick and trying to teach him. Could he speak the Irish language? Not a word.

The one thing he had in common with his fellow students was religion.

The drawing room of the house, yet another Siberia, had been turned into a chapel, furnished with a great crucifix, statues of St Joseph, Our Lady and St Fiacre, patron of gardening, and a particularly doleful set of Stations.

He was watched when he pulled out his rosary or went up to take mass.

'Ye're never Catholic?'

He had the sense to say nothing, but continued his devotions without fuss.

The other thing that gained their respect was the fact that Brother Ahern did not like him. Or at the least had problems with him. The little scowl, the Huh!, the fat lips pursed together, signified displeasure.

He was sharply reminded of Mr Good during the regular summons to the Brother Ahern's study. There were differences of course, the religious statuary and the crucifix. Gothic bookcases were similar to those at St George's; they contained files, copies of the *Farmer's Journal* and books on silage, poultry, store cattle, forestry, and veterinary. Paul kept an eye out for *Old Moore's Almanac* which Brother Ahern was rumoured to consult before ploughing or potato planting.

Each time he stood and waited to be scolded, the fat face with the wobbling double chins looked increasingly stern. The vocabulary was similar to that of Mr Good. 'Ah Blake-Willoughby, I've been meaning to have a word with you . . . .I hope you are settling in well enough.'

'Yes, Brother . . .'

The shuffle through papers '. . . The report I have been given on your work isn't entirely satisfactory . . . not paying attention . . . either to your lectures or the work on the farm . . .'

'Sorry Brother . . .'

'Do I make myself clear?'

'Yes, Brother.'

'Perhaps there is something wrong?'

'Oh, no, Brother.'

'I don't pretend that it can be easy for you to adjust to your life here . . . I can only say that your work must show some sign of improvement.'

He must work harder mucking out, digging, milking, dealing with hens, ploughing. And pigs, pigs.

Brother Ahern would continue to keep a close eye on him and pray for him. He would have heard from Father Hogan that the lad's mother had run off with a young man. It occurred to Paul that Father Hogan might well be indulging in a mild retaliation for those sessions in his aunt's convent when he had brought up subjects like the Pope. That had been unwise. Meanwhile he was in everyone's prayers.

He wondered if all the Brothers knew his circumstances – did they sit around and gossip about the boys? He might be paranoid, but it seemed that most of them, tipped off by Brother Ahern, were offhand because his circumstances and his sinful mother made them uneasy.

The other students noticed something and unbelievably they began to be sympathetic.

'Don't worry about those ould fellas.'

While cleaning out sties he even made a friend, John Byrne from outside Mullingar, who wished to specialise in marketing pigs.

'There's fierce money in that, Paul, if you know the system.'

'No thanks.' His new-found knowledge included slurry and its disposal.

'Ah go on, Paul. Bacon, pork, ham – they're always in demand. You could learn from the Danes.'

'If I never saw a pig again it wouldn't be too soon.'

John was amazed at his ignorance. How could anyone who said they lived in a farm know so little about farming? Although the boys had gathered a good deal about Paul's circumstances, they did not know the whole until he rashly confided that his father employed a steward to see other people were kept usefully busy. That he lived on a place as big as St Fiacre's, although with less acreage, which in due course he would be expected to farm.

'Are ye having me on?'

Naturally John passed on to the others the full enormity of Paul's background. Their reaction was unexpected. Perhaps they were amazed by the scale of his home life. Nothing could be stranger. Unbelievable. He was unique. They had never heard the like. They knew by now he wasn't English, he was an ould landlord, one of those who, everyone knew, spent their time evicting and starving tenants. But he was Catholic and Catholics didn't evict and starve tenants. He didn't look the type. He was the last thing they expected to find in the old foe.

They put aside ancient animosities and began to regard him as a bizarre mascot.

He got further into their good books when on their few free Saturdays he accompanied them into the town a bike's ride away where they bought cigarettes and went to the cinema. *Courage of Lassie. Abilene Town.* Afterwards they would sneak into Gallagher's pub, the only pub among many in the town that would accept them without telling the brothers. Gallagher had a running feud with Father Ahern and encouraged the boys into his grimy premises with its bottles and beer casks.

In an atmosphere where it was almost too dark to see Paul stood in sawdust and paid for his round – the tenner his father had given him was put to good use. He passed on a few gamey jokes he had heard at St George's. He taught his new friends some of the songs his mother liked. Keeping an eye open for some sulky brother in brown robe and gumboots, several students found themselves sitting before the cows singing as they milked *Ho di Ho! Hi di Hi!* from Minnie the Moocher or *Was I drunk, was he handsome and did Mama give me hell. Saturday night is the loneliest night of the week.* In return they let him into the lore that passed down from one set of students to the next that St Fiacre was not only the patron saint of gardeners and taxi drivers, but of people with haemorrhoids and venereal disease.

In spite of frowning Franciscans, he had settled in by the time of the Christmas break. He felt something almost like happiness as he packed to leave, his clothes smelling of manure like Crow Foster's used to do at St George's. He got on with people. He liked St Fiacre's better than he had ever liked St George's.

Daddy gave Paul hell when he received a report in which Brother Ahern had been acid. After all the bad reports from St George's over the years you would think Daddy would be accustomed to that sort of thing.

Father McCabe managed to find penitents from the nearest Magdalen home to be maids and cooks at Mountsilver. The first was Sally, who was soon gone.

'A good thing too,' Daddy said. 'She wore lipstick and couldn't be trusted. I'm damned if I am going to put up with any trollop who takes advantage of me.' He had found her with a local boy in her downstairs room.

'Bad enough having an incompetent servant, worse, a woman who plays the game.'

Through Father McCabe's good offices a new girl, Mary was found. How Mary could have fallen at all when she was so plain was a mystery.

'I don't think you will have any trouble with her, Major.'

'Does that mean she won't stray again?'

'Most unlikely Major. She comes from a good farming family and has learned her lesson.'

'Or leave without warning?'

'I think not…'

'Can she cook?'

'Alas, not more than the rudiments.'

You did not like to think of what became of those babies. Mary did the laundry as Bernadette used to. Deidre's cooking was poor, but better than Agnes'.

Paul guessed that the newcomers might last another three months and for the rest of his life Daddy would have to endure servants coming, servants leaving or no servants.

Daddy was spending a day in Dublin.

'Can I come with you?'

'You'd be bored at the Club.'

'I want to do a bit of Christmas shopping.'

After Daddy parked the Rover in Kildare Street Paul raced up to Fitzwilliam Square, carrying in a paper bag a bunch of Christmas roses which had survived the great plough-up in the walled garden. There was no answer when he rang the bell repeatedly until an irritated secretary to the doctor on the ground floor came to the door.

'What do you want?

'Mrs Blake-Willoughby. On the top floor.'

Her mouth stiffened in disapproval. 'They've gone.'

'Where?'

'I wouldn't know.'

He threw the flowers into a bin.

You missed Mummy at Christmas. Daddy made no effort – no decorations, no tree, no gaiety. No drink either – not a sign of even a bottle of sherry. If he was still on the booze, he was doing it in secret. He did not bother to arrange a Christmas dinner. The Countess, Trigger Dobbs, Mary Rooke and the rest had to fend for themselves, while, after mass on Christmas morning, Daddy and Paul drove to Donald and Valerie's house, still suffused in creeper and damp, to share a small chicken. Dinner was made grotesque by Valerie imitating Mummy and producing crackers, paper hats and jokes. *Where do snowmen go dancing. To a snowball.*

The day after Stephen's Day brought post for the first time in a week, since Redmond, who never liked bicycling in the rain, had omitted several deliveries in the days leading up to Christmas.

'I suppose we should be grateful he didn't stick it all into a hedge,' his father said, opening up late Christmas cards. He had not sent any out himself.

He came across a letter for Paul and handed it to him.

'Take it somewhere else to read.' He would have noticed the English stamp.

The English five pound note included in the letter was no consolation for the fact that Mummy and Julian had gone to England where through the good services of Gabbitas and Thring Julian had found a place as a schoolmaster in Somerset.

'Another thing. I'm having a baby in June. xxxMummy.' No euphemisms, no you will be expecting a little brother or sister. She was awfully old to be pregnant, like Elizabeth in the New Testament, thirty-nine. Although Paul didn't know much about these things, he did know of course that it took nine months to have a baby from after the fuck. He worked out that the wretched infant could have been conceived the night he spent in Fitzwilliam Square.

He did not tell his father.

CHAPTER SIXTEEN

Before he departed for St Fiacre's he nicked a packet of twenty Sweet Afton his father had left lying around in the study.

'Goodbye, Daddy.'

'You'll have to do better this term.'

As he bicycled up to St Fiacre's from the station with most of the other boys dusk seemed to have come sooner than expected, helped along by dark grey clouds. By the time they had reached the gates snow had begun to fall, and before they got up to the big building he had to push his bike through a white storm. There was one good thing; Brother Brendan had gone down with tractor and trailer to meet the train and brought up their trunks. The Brother had to do it twice. Just as well; by next morning the snow was eight inches deep.

Jaysus look at the freezing bastard! Did you ever know anything like it! Never enough clothes or blankets – wearing two pullovers was totally inadequate. The brothers shivered in their robes which, at least came down to their sandals. What about underclothes? Vests? Paul had been wearing a woollen vest when he arrived, and he did not take it off. Nor the other one which he added after the first.

He lay in his iron bed, so similar to those he had slept in for seven years at St George's, all his clothes out of his trunk heaped on the two blankets provided, sleepless, thinking of words to describe what he felt – chilly, arctic, glacial, frosty, shivery, icy, bleak, dreary, dreadful, gloomy cold, cold cold. Of course the others felt the same. But if you are about to be hanged it is no consolation if a hundred and thirty others are going to to be hanged as well.

Snowfalls, freezing rain, blizzards by day, frost by night. A world of swollen extremities, and Paul's chilblains were itchy burning radishes. Everyone had them. Brother Donal had a purple nose in addition to his swollen scarlet digits, while Brother Ahern, Paul (and others) were pleased to note, also had a purple nose and in addition purple ear lobes. You wouldn't know about the Brothers' toes since they wore plenty of socks, so that their sandal straps were very tight. Three socks on each foot, Brother Donal, who was good-natured, informed them, knowing well that the boys were having a bet.

The furtive cult of smoking had to be abandoned since soon there was not a cigarette to be had in the whole of St Fiacre's. Apart from Daddy's packet of Sweet Afton. When Paul lay awake shivering he regretted very much that he had not stolen more. Of the twenty he had, he gave half to John Byrne and for ten days they smoked one each in the evening after supper, in the cloakroom by the stairs.

In the morning after porridge the students assembled in the main hall and did exercises before putting on gumboots. There was work to do, and Paul tramped out with the rest, facing into the east wind, picking up his legs to get through the snow. Spades were issued. The school had fifty spades, and they were given out in relays to the boys, half an hour at a time. With so many you could manage quite a clearance, as you dug and dug and swore as to why these fucking big places had such long driveways. Why the hell wasn't the house burnt down in nineteen twenty-two when there was every opportunity for doing it?

Every day, under the dark grey sky they had it cleared by evening and some people were stupid enough to make plans that they would get the afternoon off the next day and make it into the town. But snow would come again in the night and you'd have to start digging again the next morning. It was like that ould legend where the fella had to roll a stone up the hill all the time.

A few spades had to be diverted to clean out the pigsties where the animals moved about unhappily, their trotters packed with snow. Hens huddled together; more shit had to be cleared away to the snow-covered Everest of a midden where it was supposed to rot down. Not in anyone's lifetime. Cows gathered up in the barn mooed sadly and there was no joy in tugging at chill udders with red fingers. With the drive more or less cleared by evening, Brother Brendan would set off in the tractor carrying the milk churns in the trailer behind which one of his favourite boys would be sitting.

A fair amount of sheep had been gathered into one of the barns at the beginning of the major January snowfalls, but many were missing and and for the first fortnight of the term squads of people went looking for them. You did not open gates, you stepped over the top of them. You kept to the hedge line. Now and again someone blundered into a dead animal.

'Another load of stew!' These days they ate nothing but mutton and potatoes.

Working together, Paul and John Byrne found a ewe, which was alive, her black face suddenly appearing out of the snow beside the long wall near the forest. They carried her, struggling like hell, lifting her over three gates, and brought her back into the shed where survivors assembled. 'Good lads' Brother Brendan said, and for a moment Paul felt that this bleak cold day was one of the best of his life. Another good day followed when she lambed. She was one of only eight living sheep to be found, and soon there was no point in going out looking for the rest who were corpses to be found in the spring.

When you were out you could work up a mucky sweat and forgot about the freezing air all around you, but once you shook the snow off your boots and came inside, when your damp dirty coat and mittens and scarf came off, you were facing up to something awful. Every room you were in was chilled, the big dining room where the porridge in the morning and the stew at night tasted grand, the recreation room where the big men fought to get to the fire, and the rest sat and shivered and muttered fuck, fuck the fucking cold, and had no other conversation at all, and the chapel where you knelt on the icy floor and Brother Ahern gave talks about God's will.

They were excused written study, there was no point in it at present, but boys you will have to work harder after the thaw. In the evening there was time for quarrelling and the occasional fist fight. The odd snarling insult came his way, but he was not singled out especially, and in spite of the misery and bad temper he joined in the bonding in the face of difficulty. On the other side of the water the English were still boring everyone by talking of the spirit of the Blitz, but there was a nugget of truth in it – you helped the other fellow if necessary.

The worst was going to bed. No one took off their clothes, only their shoes. No one got a proper night's sleep. No one washed – they were all stinking, but you got used to that. Jugs burst where water froze. After a couple of weeks the one lavatory on the landing froze, so that they had to go to the floor below, and after that froze as well, a hundred and fifty boys had to make their way across the yard to the frozen latrines which would give out a fierce stench in due course. The epidemic of colds affected nearly everyone, and when the electricity went Brother Ahern was snuffling through his red chilblained nose when he announced that everyone should go home for the time being. Train fares would be provided. They could leave their things and their bicycles here, and they would be collected in due course.

They all departed except for the seventeen boys in the infirmary who had flu. In due course five would develop TB. After breakfast the rest tramped down the drive at a solid marching rate, eager to get to the gate before the current snowfall made walking next to impossible. No one bothered about luggage. They made their way through the silent town to the station where the train was two hours late, having broken down twice. For years, through the Emergency, they had all been used to trains being late, but now was a bad time and the oaths they all gave out were disgusting. At last she came, very slowly; the handles of the doors to the carriages were frozen, so it took time to break into the carriages.

'See you,' Paul said to John Byrne when they pulled into Mullingar. But they never met again.

Paul arrived home after a journey that was just a little easier than Scott's trudge to the South Pole. He arrived in darkness. The dogs, who were inside, kept in the inner hall, barked at the sound of the heavy door opening, but recognised him at once, and whimpered in welcome. When he stepped into the hall he found it just as cold as the big hall at St Fiacre's, and also it was dark; the light switch yielded no light. What was new?

He peeled off his coat and scarf and kicked off his boots before crossing in his socks to the study where his father was sitting by a large fire, Wooster Two at his feet, his pipe in his mouth, a glass of whiskey in his hand. On the table was a pile of notebooks and two candelabra with six candles. Gilbert and Sullivan was playing on the gramophone.

'What happened to the electricity?'

'Line blew down.' The electrical link to the town which he had arranged twenty years ago had always been his pride. 'What the hell are you doing here?'

'Same thing happened at St Fiacre's. We were all sent home.'

'They might have let me know.'

'Telephone line was down.'

'Oh.'

'I've had to walk from the station.'

'Sounds as if you have had a long day.'

'Could I have a drink?'

Daddy was silent for a moment. 'Very well. Help yourself.'

The whiskey – without water – was wonderful. Paul sat on the chair opposite and drank slowly, taking in the flames from the fire.

'You'd better get cleaned up. You smell like a badger.'

He ate first, down in the kitchen, attended by Agnes and Deidre the cook; Mary had vanished, but another woman unknown to him called Anne was there; they all watched him, clicking their tongues with sympathy. There was the remains of a big pot of Irish stew – the meat had come from a similar source as the stew at St Fiacre's, frozen sheep stumbled upon by Fitzgerald. It tasted much the same as the mutton he had been eating for the past weeks, but, accompanied by mugs of tea, it was better than ambrosia, or larks' tongues.

A can of water had to do him for washing himself. Agnes piled blankets on his bed and given him several hot bottles. He was warm. He slept. His father did not wake him early in the morning.

Thank god for hot bottles at bedtime, and as many blankets as you needed – that was a great difference between Mountsilver and St Fiacre's. The other difference was the loneliness.

For the time being water was kept from freezing by running the taps a fraction; there was a race between the well drying out and the coming of the thaw. Two rooms only were in use – the kitchen downstairs which the maids kept really warm with the aid of the stove, and the study which Paul and his father shared with Wooster Two and the parrot. For the present they ate their meals there in front of the fire.

Getting up in darkness after Daddy had tramped outside his door to wake him in the morning was unpleasant. The day passed fighting cold. The fire wasn't before six o'clock, and since coal was unobtainable, the fuel used was the turf that had been up on the bog during the summer which had never dried out.

Paul helped his father keep the place going. Similarities with St Fiacre's ceased owing to lack of manpower – nine men and Paul at Mountsilver (and Fitzpatrick too old and dignified to wield a spade), a hundred and fifty at St Fiacre's to dig, dig dig. And at Mountsilver there were only four spades so that clearing the drive was hard going. In any case for much of the time the men had to go and deal with the Friesians, the surviving sheep, the plough horses and Pav restless and sweating in their stables. Paul was one of the four regular shovellers; he had become the world's expert at moving snow. He thought about heat, deserts and barren wastes where snow did not return mockingly each evening.

Sometimes Daddy took a hand at shovelling, since he was determined to keep the drive open for Redmond to bring up the post and to go to church on Sunday. They all managed to clear a way through for the first Sunday mass after Paul had returned. It was a triumph of hard work and prayer, and for once the good Lord who controlled the weather did not send down a snow storm to mock their progress to holiness. For three days no snow fell. Daddy drove the Rover and got them all there, the maids lurching from side to side in the rear seat as they slithered towards their holy appointment and dived through the pillars of the front gate. The church, in semi-darkness, with only two altar candles lit, was full enough, considering the difficulties of transport and in his sermon Father McCabe gave a little talk about God's will.

Paul tried to remember from his Protestant days whether there was any mention at all of snow in prayer book or bible and thought rather not. No snow in Palestine.

After mass all four of them went into Toss Doyle's where he defiantly bought forty Sweet Aftons with what was left of Mummy's Christmas present, and Agnes and Deidre bought their Woodbines. Daddy made no comment to any of them since he was too intent of buying his own cigarettes, together with whiskey, matches and candles. 'Last ones, Major,' Doyle said, but Daddy gave him a pound and got some more. Paul had managed to pocket a couple of votive candles waiting to be bought beside the statue of Our Lady as they came out of church.

That evening the lord of the weather, having received the homage he was looking for sent a snowstorm that holed them up in the house for ten days. They gave up trying to keep the drive open or attending mass. They stayed home and prayed whenever prayer was due. Paul limited his smoking to three fags a day, in his bedroom, away from his father's gaze. His most immediate task was bringing up wood all day long to feed the fire in the sitting room. He helped Agnes clear away plates after they had eaten – more stew. He also resumed the old tried and tested task of feeding the dogs, whose diet had diminished to old bread and gravy. Why weren't they always fed on that?

During these cold days he appreciated the way that snow made him put aside arguments with Daddy. In the face of the coldest winter in living memory they had never got on so well together.

It was typical of Redmond to make his way up on his bicycle between blizzards – you'd think he would take the opportunity of leaving the post for a week or two. The maids revived him with bread and butter and tea. Bills and out of date copies of *The Irish Times* had come over the snow. But one letter was from Father Ahern. With all the boys gone home he had nothing to do all day except write unpleasant communications like this one which suggested that Paul was unsuitable to life as a farmer or at least life at St Fiacre's.

Paul wondered if this had come about after some brother had overheard him teaching his fellow students *Hitler has only got one ball* or telling them about Dolly Fossett's to get through one freezing evening in the assembly hall.

'Ah go on, Paul, say all that again.'

He wouldn't be at all surprised if some Purity Pat among the boys hadn't sneaked his performance to Father Ahern.

'Ah well!' Amazingly Daddy didn't seem to be too upset.

Daddy was not wasting his time while they were confined to staying indoors, but sat in the study inaugurating a three year plan. He wrote and rewrote lists by firelight; these days the candelabra had been put away and they had to restrict themselves to one candle in the evening.

'I have decided to put the place on a new footing. Everything must pay its way.'

Paul was expected to take part.

'Just as well they've thrown you out of St Fiacre's. You'll get more experience here on the place.'

'I am putting you in charge of selling farm produce. The thing is to see everything is in good shape and properly packed. There must be no mistakes. I'm getting rid of a few men. Johnny Murphy for a start.' He glanced at the J.M. carved deeply in the mahogany table beside him.

'Now? In the middle of winter?'

'Don't be a fool. Of course we'll wait until the summer. This is going to take time.'

CHAPTER SEVENTEEN

The thaw did not take place for several weeks, and it came overnight. Pipes burst; the tactic of keeping the taps running ultimately proved ineffective. Getting hold of a plumber was not easy, since the town outside Mountsilver's gates was under water and boats were rowed down the main street to rescue people on roof tops.

It was not until April that the electricity was sorted out and Paul no longer had to creep around in the dark to go to bed. In the study, now bright with light, a series of graphs were prepared which were to show monthly variations in output. The three year plan was about to get under way.

Daddy waited until May before sacking three men, Johnny Murphy as planned, Murtagh, and, surprisingly, Healy, who had been on the place for twenty years.

'He's got beyond it.' Too old, although Paul knew from Agnes that Healy was only a couple of years older than Daddy. So it was off to England for Johnny Murphy and Healy, and the old age pension for Murtagh, while the rest clung to their jobs and Daddy became more and more the landlord.

The quota of milk which families who lived on the estate had taken daily for decades ceased.

'We are not supporting some charity, old boy.'

No more cabbages either for anyone. In the walled garden vegetables were replaced with lazy beds and early potatoes were to be the main summer crop. In the greenhouses, where even the vine had died, tomatoes would replace Mummy's dead plants.

Pressure and sulks from the remaining men on the estate made Daddy relent and introduce what he called a 'tally' system. Good work would be rewarded with sufficient milk and a quota of the potatoes in the walled garden.

'The trouble with most Irishmen is that you have to keep a carrot dangled in front of their noses.'

'What happens if the scheme doesn't work?'

'Of course it will, old boy. Only those who are prepared to do their bit will prosper in life. I want to make certain that there will be no shirkers in Mountsilver.'

Paul would receive a salary. From time to time Daddy grumbled about having to pay him. 'A foetus, Paul, is a parasite on its mother for nine months and on its father for twenty-five years.'

The three pounds a week more than covered Paul's expenses which were confined to cigarettes and the shilling's collection at mass. These days his main duty seemed to be to spy on the men who were left.

'Isn't that Fitzpatrick's job?'

'*Quis custodiet ipsos custodes?*'

So Paul mooched around, watching Mick create the lazy beds in the walled garden and moving tomato seedlings to the greenhouse. Or Roche milking. Now was not the time to demonstrate he could do that just as well, since his father took not the slightest interest in what he had learned at St Fiacre's. He did not sneak on anybody, aware that every day Daddy grew increasingly crotchety and the slightest misinterpretation of orders brought a stream of Damn Fool's.

Daddy was considering the construction of a proper milking parlour, but for the present funds were limited. However, after a long talk with Trigger Dobbs whose barking voice could be heard over the telephone across the study, he half-changed his mind about tillage and decided to plough up some of the lower fields again. Paul went with him to the Spring Show in search of a new tractor. Daddy wore the uniform check suit and bowler hat and carried his shooting stick which made Paul blush in shame. The Mountsilver Friesians weren't up to proper competition yet, but Daddy met a lot of old friends, watched while other animals received rosettes and bought a nice little grey-coloured Ferguson.

The odd hungry fox, the cold, and Mick's axe had done for the last lot of hens and the very last had been boiled during the freeze as a desperate alternative to the mutton stew. A new batch of chicks was raised under a couple of light bulbs in the far study. Agnes cleaned up after them. In only a couple of weeks the pretty things had grown into scrawny adolescents, and soon Paul had new duties, seeing they were fed and watered, and searching for eggs. His time at St Fiacre's never taught him not to be nervous of pecks and he preferred to lift bottoms up with a spade to see if there were eggs underneath. He told nobody about his new skill of neck wringing.

He might protest, but Daddy insisted on pigs as a new venture . A sty was created under Fizpatrick's supervision and the pregnant Berkshire sow arrived which duly gave birth to ten piglets. Paul reneged on the sty duties he had been forced to do at St Fiacre's, and now restricted them to seeing that Mick carried out kitchen garbage and filled up the water trough for snorting mother and children.

He longed to drive the new Ferguson, and do a bit of ploughing – he knew how, in theory, having had a go on the St Fiacre machines. His father was unimpressed when Paul told him, and it was Paddy Smith who was given the job. On the first day out, after been given a few minutes instruction, Paddy drove the machine into the back of a wall.

'I didn't mean any harm, Major.'

There was tension all over the estate while Daddy considered whether or not to sack him. The Ferguson was a write-off, but no one else on the estate could manage the plough horses. So Paddy survived, and so did hairy-footed Kelly and Charlie who had done the ploughing before the tractor arrived.

Redmond rode up with a postcard with an English stamp showing a picture of the interior of Wells cathedral. Although it was addressed to Paul, it seemed Mummy wanted the whole of Mountsilver to learn her news. She must have known that whoever was in the kitchen would turn it over and read it before it came into Paul's hands.

Joe and Philly Roche were back from South Shields at the gate lodge, somehow fitting in the small space once again with their parents and siblings.

Philly soon went off to a job with the ESB fitting electric lines in places all over Ireland. Huh – if the country had started on that a year ago there would have been less candles burnt during the winter.

Joe had a vague idea of going to America if he could get some money out of certain relatives. Daddy gave him the odd day's work harvesting new potatoes, but it didn't amount to much. Paul was glad to spend time with him. When Daddy wasn't around they bathed in the river and did some fishing, Paul borrowing his father's rod. But the weather was too good, after a glorious summer followed the great freeze, and few trout or salmon would rise.

Paul treated Joe to the Astor the odd time. You had to take what came – *The Bachelor and the Bobby Soxer* . . . *The Gay Cavalier* . . . You're wasting your time and your money, Daddy said. He might disapprove, but he could hardly forbid a fellow of nineteen to go off to the cinema. He didn't know about Joe when he saw Paul setting off down the drive on his bike on Saturday evenings.

'You should have better things to do, old boy, than watch Bob Hope.'

Joe claimed he used to have a steady girl friend in South Shields, one of those who tied up her head in a scarf and worked beside him with the munitions.

'So what happened?'

'She married a Yank.'

'What bad luck!'

'I saw her off to Boston with the baby.' Joe licked his lips. 'Whose baby you'd like to know?'

'I don't believe you.'

'Cross my heart and hope to die.'

'Why didn't you marry her?'

'Money.'

Paul was deeply impressed. It was two years since he left St George's where they had been virgins all, and no one at St Fiacre talked like Joe with this personal note in his narrative. Are you sure? Is it true?

Joe was looking for a girl here.

'You'd never get one.'

'How do you think the girls in your kitchen got fucked?'

On Sundays Joe sat in church with his family; butter wouldn't melt in his mouth when he went up to take the wafer. On Saturdays there was the Astor – but Joe kept saying what was the point of *Love Laughs at Andy Hardy* unless you had a girl to squeeze in the seat beside you.

Paul felt restless himself.

Joe asked a number of times, 'Hey Paul, how about the Arcadia?' It was their bad luck that Mountsilver was stifled with religious buildings and there was nothing of the sort within distance. The Arcadia was thirty miles in the opposite direction, a place more sinful than any platform for crossroads dancing.

'We could bike.' But Joe didn't have a bike and Paul was damned if he would offer to take him pillion.

He had a big row with Daddy after forgetting to see the baby chicks were watered so that half a dozen died. Daddy really let fly . . . lazy . . . good for nothing . . . after all that has been done for you . . . what sort of example is it to the men? . . . exactly what I was afraid of . . . Father Ahern was right . . .

'I hate chickens.'

'Get out of my sight!'

He said, 'Mummy had a baby. His name is Nick.'

The silence went on for days. You'd think in a big house they could get away from each other, but routine had to be respected as always, so that in the dining room they ate together without speaking. Agnes was always there as witness. After dinner Paul skipped the evening news bulletins, timing Pav's exercise to take place in the summer twilight – that took him up to bedtime.

He tried 'Sorry Daddy' a few times, and perhaps the words wove a bit of gauze over the gaping wound.

Then Daddy got flu. How you could have flu in the middle of the hottest summer on record?

'Could be a recurrence of malaria.' He didn't call in the doctor but retired to bed. Twice a day Agnes dragged herself up two flights of stairs with a light meal.

Paul looked into Inkerman at nine o'clock where he found Daddy safely in bed, a missal and a bottle of whiskey by his side. His bald head was like a huge egg. He was reading yesterday's *Irish Times*, checking for anyone who had fallen before the grim reaper's scythe.

Paul watched his eye wandering down the obituary columns – peacefully – after a long illness bravely borne – *Ar dheis De go raibh a hanam dilis* . . . Gone Home . . . Rest in Peace . . . No flowers please . . . Suddenly, which was code for heart attack, accident or suicide. Wooster Two sat in his basket, thumping his tail.

'Good night, Daddy.'

'Good night.' After ten days they were on terms of truce. Downstairs in the kitchen Agnes, and the others were listening to the radio.

He waited another hour before making his way to the garage.

The Rover smelt of leather, Wooster and tobacco smoke. In spite of some fear, the excitement of handling a large powerful car on his own pushed away doubts as to his ability. Beside him Joe, dressed in blue suit and garish tie, urged him to put on more speed. He pressed the pedal, feeling as elated as Mr Toad. The empty countryside rushed past, and there were no mishaps apart from an elderly farmer riding his bike whom he narrowly missed. A few miles on he had to swerve to miss a procession of boys his own age, dressed in Homburg hats and black coats marching briskly behind an elderly priest towards a forbidding looking seminary. Speed got them to town quickly. He hooted as he parked awkwardly beneath the statue of the IRA man.

'Jeez, that was great, Paul.'

'Nothing to it.'

He took out the keys with a new confidence, planning future journeys at any available opportunity when Daddy wasn't looking. He had driven so fast that the time was only nine o'clock and the Arcadia wouldn't be properly awake until after the pubs closed. That was the problem.

Outside the cinema a group of youths were studying a poster of Carmen Miranda, her hat topped with bananas. Paul and Joe had the option of spending the next two hours listening to whistle and yells of frustrated boys and men. But Carmen Miranda had already travelled to Mountsilver and they had seen the film.

'We could have another look at her,' Joe suggested. But Paul held the purse strings and they ended up in one of the town's fifteen pubs. Half of it was a shop selling groceries, tea, paint, delph, ling, boots which hung from the ceiling, bike tyres and other things invisible in the tobacco smoke. The rest was space smelling of beer, packed with men, and shaking with the roar of deep voices.

He remembered Gallaghers in the town below St Fiacre's, which was frequented by a lot less people, since grumpy old Gallagher was in charge, and the boys went in the middle of the afternoon. He recalled the pub in Dublin where all his problems had begun. What was its name? He couldn't remember. He wondered if Jeffers Minor had joined up and survived the war.

Perhaps Daddy might wake up and go down looking for the Rover. It was thanks to Daddy and the salary he gave him that he had money in his pocket. Should he keep back something to put petrol in the tank? He thought of the girls assembling in the Arcadia Ballroom in their summer frocks and called for a couple more glasses of stout.

'Jeez . . . thanks, Paul.'

Time passed slowly as people appeared to be getting drunk. Paul talked to a man who said he was a hurler who couldn't understand why he had never been in Croke Park. The place was very hot. He met a man who said he had been in St Fiacre's many years ago.

'Lousy old prick, that Father Ahern.'

Paul agreed, but before he could treat him to a drink, time was called.

'Finish up!' At last! 'Time's up!' Lights were dimmed. A scuffle broke out near the door as a guard forced himself in.

'Time!'

The pub emptied and so did all the other ones. Men, many of them wheeling bikes, made their way up the road towards the Arcadia; the bright lights of the ballroom shone at the end of the road.

'Quiet lads!'

They all approached the door where a burly man dressed in a commissioner's cap and uniform was eyeing the groups of late arrivals. Not many people were actually staggering. Drinking on the premises might be forbidden, but he would have trouble searching them for the half-sized bottles of Paddy the majority carried in their pockets like firearms.

'He won't touch me,' someone said. 'I took out his sister.'

'Was she all right?'

'None better.'

They queued up to buy tickets; from inside they could hear...*when your love wears golden earrings . . .*

'There will be no shortage of girls,' the middle aged farmer behind Paul was saying confidently.

'How do you know?'

'I come here every week. It's easy enough work.'

The young man in front of him paid for his ticket, then rushed off to the men's toilet to be sick. Paul paid for Joe. Inside on the ceiling a revolving crystal globe illuminated the dance floor. Just to look at the dancers made him dizzy. At the end of the room the band played behind the crooner, while down the side a line of women waited for someone to chose them.

...an old love story that's known to very few . . .

'That's not a bad looking one,' said the farmer pointing to a blond smoking a cigarette. . . 'You're a good looking young fella. Why don't you have a go?'

Paul went up and shouted at her: 'Would you like a dance?' She shook her head. He tried another who was also unwilling. Joe got the blond, and the new crowd of men sprinted over to the good lookers and grabbed them.

. . . so be my gypsy
Make love your guiding light . . .

For a time Paul stood and watched the dancers enviously as an elderly guy with slicked black hair showed off expertise with the best looking woman in the place. The music changed to a samba, and he could do that.

'Blast him anyway, the little bugger, for he's taken my girl,' said the youth beside him. 'I'll break his neck.'

'You're a great man for boasting.'

Paul tried again – no luck. The crooner in the band sang another song as the lights dimmed.

If I say I love you
I want you to know

It's not just because there is moonlight
Although moonlight becomes you so . . .

The old fellow could deal with that as well, gliding into an old-fashioned waltz. Near him Joe was swaying about with another reasonable-looking girl, a brunette. What was his secret? Occasionally if a couple were getting too close or intimate one of the hustlers would intervene; a quick tap on the shoulder was enough.

The lights went bright again. Because only soft drinks were sold at the bar, the only place for suitable refreshment was in the safety of the jacks where men were swilling down the stuff they had brought in their pockets as if their lives depended on it.

Joe was there.

'Where's your girl?' Paul asked.

'I let her go. There's more fish in the sea. Any luck?'

'No.'

'The problem with you, Paul, is that you are too stuck up. Anyone would think you were at a funeral.'

He produced a half bottle and invited Paul to take a swig.

'Thank you.' Paul hadn't paid for it.

'Don't put on airs and graces.'

He returned to the dance floor swaying slightly. The opportunity for getting a girl was dwindling as time had moved on. All the good-looking ones had been plucked from their perches and the remaining ones sat in spinsterly disapproval with their legs crossed staring up at the crystal globe. Paul couldn't make out their faces very clearly.

He was surprised when at last one of them agreed to stand up with him. She was thin and wore spectacles. No gypsy. No Carmen Miranda. But her hair was glossy and when she smiled her face lit up.

'I'm not much of a dancer.'

She giggled as they joined the other couples who were making the most of their opportunities before the end. All the girls seemed to have partners now. A group of men who were too late and had missed their chance stood around smoking.

Paul found they had no difficulty negotiating the various steps and they shuffled around the floor competently.Her name was Eileen and she worked in a pharmacy.

'Are you a medical student?'

'No.'

'Are you enjoying your holiday?'

'Holiday?' She must take him for English.

'Whereabouts are you from?'

'Liverpool.' This was an unfortunate choice since she had been to Liverpool where her aunty lived.

'. . . er Mersey . . .'

The lights dimmed before she could ask him more and he could hold her closely for the final dance.

The lights switched on, the revolving globe brighter than ever and the band belted out the national anthem. He was still holding Eileen's hand, only releasing it when they scuttled off to collect their coats before the queues formed. A few patriotic couples remained standing to attention on the floor.

He waited for Eileen to reappear from the ladies. Although nothing had been mentioned, he was hoping for a good end to the evening. It would have caused alarm to suggest anything too soon, but he had put in a bit of bait.

'I have a car.'

Other men were also waiting anxiously, and discussing their chances of success.

'. . . She said her mother is out and the house is empty.'

'. . . I tell you, she's dying for it.'

'I take mine on the back of the bike down the nun's walk. No sweat.'

Eileen reappeared, but she was in company with her friend, Teresa, a large girl whom nobody had wanted.

How the hell to get rid of Teresa?

'I could drive you home.'

'Oh no, no thanks.' With a strange boy you had to be so careful.

It was all up to Eileen.

'It isn't safe to be walking alone at this hour.'

'Don't bother about me, Eileen.'

'Are you sure?' They exchanged sharp looks.

'I'll see you in the morning.'

'Be a good girl.'

Thank God, then, Teresa was walking in the other direction.

What would his father or even his mother think if they knew he was picking up a common girl in a dance hall?

Thank God there was no sign of Joe.

They walked to the IRA statue where the Rover was parked in its glory. Eileen gasped. How could a young Englishman from Liverpool afford anything so expensive?

'I borrowed it from a friend.'

'Oh.' It sounded as if she didn't believe him. She hesitated and for a moment he thought she would go back up the road in search of her friend.

'Like a short drive before going home?'

She hesitated again and then waited for him to unlock the passenger door.

'If it's only for a few miles it won't matter, but Ma will be waiting up for me.'

As he drove out of town they smoked nervously. He switched on the radio and music drowned out any need for conversation. He turned off the road into a rough boreen lined with hedges picked out by the headlights. They went along slowly until the lane widened; probably by daylight there would be a nice view from here.

He switched on the overhead light. 'Another?' He had a packet of twenty.

'Thanks.'

They sat and smoked, listening to the radio. *Chi baba, Chi baba.*

'I like Perry Como.'

She took off her spectacles. She was gazing up at him, her lips partly open, leaning back in the front seat her coat partly open. Her scent overwhelmed the smell of Wooster.

He made to turn off the light. 'No, keep it on.'

She was in his arms.

Some one else sang, he did not know who.

. . . I'd like to get you

On a slow boat to China . . .

. . . all to myself, nobody else . . .

Her warm welcoming mouth and lips, the feel of her body, took away any sense of guilt. The light was on. Music played. *Haunted Heart . . . How are things in Glocca Morra?*

Later, a lot later, he glanced at his watch and realised that nearly two hours had passed since they had left the Arcadia.

I wonder who's kissing her now . . .

'I think we should be going home.'

She sat up, pulled down her dress and reached for her spectacles.

'You're a funny man, Paul.'

For a little longer they sat in silence and smoked. She took a lipstick out of her bag and peered into the mirror.

'Do I look all right?'

He nodded. He was worried about getting back. Suddenly she became nervous too.

'Ma will be waiting.'

He tried to start the car but nothing happened.

'What's wrong?'

'I don't know.' The music was low and the overhead light was dim.

A few palsy kicks from the starter and silence.

He got out, opened the bonnet and peered in.

'You couldn't give a push?'

The headlights weren't working. In the dark, in the mud, in her high heels she got behind and gave a half-hearted shove. Her dress caught in briars.

'Look what you've done! What'll I say to Ma?'

CHAPTER EIGHTEEN

'But Daddy, it was my fault!'

'Joseph Roche has been a bad influence.' Paul should have known better than be dragged into unforgivable behaviour, not quite on the scale of D.F.'s, but thoroughly reprehensible.

'Quite frankly if you don't pull yourself together I can see no future for you in Ireland. You had better go to England for a start, where you would easily encounter the sort of girl you evidently prefer as a suitable companion. I can see that St Fiacre's was a terrible mistake.'

England was too near. Paul daydreamed about going to Australia as a remittance man, or Canada, a country to which Daddy's great uncle Maurice had eloped with a cook. In Australia he could go to some farm in the outback and wield a whip and round up sheep. He didn't know what he could do in Canada. Something with wheat?

He wondered how big a percentage of emigrants left Ireland because they loathed the place.

Meanwhile he had to deal with a crisis, since Daddy was gleeful at the prospect of playing the bad landlord and was determined to use the opportunity to turn all the Roches out of the gate lodge. Getting rid of the Roches would be well worth being dragged from his bed to rescue his son who had taken his car without permission for lustful motives.

'I've had enough with them. I can't have untrustworthy people like that working on the estate.'

'It was nothing to do with Joe. I was the one driving.'

While his father stormed down to the lodge with his ultimatum, Paul got to the phone and Father Hogan came down at once to persuade the Major to reverse his decision. Diplomacy, reverence and respect for the church were brought in to play, and so was another trip down the avenue for magnanimity and cringing thanks from Mrs Roche. Daddy's reputation among the people on the estate was not enhanced but the Roches could stay on, and Mrs Roche continued not to open the gates.

Joe wasn't grateful, but grumbled about how Paul had abandoned him that evening and forced him to do a thirty mile walk. He packed his bags to go and join Phil and work with the ESB. Paul tried to apologise.

'That's all right,' Joe said stiffly. 'You've done me a favour.'

'Are you sure I can't help?'

Joe laughed. 'What good can you do? Hasn't that girl you picked up made a big enough problem?' But he took the couple of pounds that Paul offered.

Paul wondered how many people Joe and Philly would electrocute in the course of bringing light to Ireland.

Father Hogan made some enquiries and learned from Father McCabe that Eileen was a respectable young woman.

'What was she doing in a dance hall?'

'Modern girls are freer than one would like.'

'She should not have been out all night.'

'I wholeheartedly agree.'

Eileen was going to have a little trouble next time she went to confession. So was Paul. But Father Hogan persuaded Daddy and Paul to go with him to confirm Eileen's social status. They all went along, Paul carrying a stupid box of chocolates. The notice on the front gate proclaimed the house's name was SERENE. Eileen's mother, limping with arthritis, came to the front door; she brought them into the parlour where there was an upright piano and a highly polished brass tub containing a scented geranium which grew all over the window and darkened the room. The backs of the chairs and sofas were protected from hair oil by pieces of crocheted white linen; a framed photograph of Eileen's father, now deceased, who had a bushy white moustache like Douglas Hyde, hung over a bookcase filled with a set of the *Encyclopaedia Brittanica*.

'I thought you came from Liverpool,' Eileen said handing around scones and cake. She turned to Father Hogan. 'He said he was over here on a holiday.'

I wonder who's looking into her eyes

Breathing sighs, telling lies . . .

They glared at him. He could not see how association with Liverpool was useful to a smooth tongued seducer. But it was too late and he had sinned, and the untruth, the cock and bull story to explain his so-unIrish voice was seen as a deception, an initiation into debauchery.

There was another silence. At least Eileen had the decency to break it.

'What was wrong with the car?'

'The battery gave out.' He should have remembered to turn off the radio before seeking her embraces.

A stern discussion about the weather followed. He made no attempt to meet her eye.

'Thank you Father, goodbye Father. Goodbye Mr Blake-Willoughby. Goodbye Paul. Goodbye Father.'

Daddy and Paul made up. You could never tell with Daddy. When the Rover came back from the garage he even allowed Paul to drive it. Paul could not make out whether this was merely a surrender, or that his father had simply decided to put him to some use – sending him out shopping, the job that should be done by women. So he had to park the Rover outside MacCarthy the butcher, or Hanafin the grocer before traipsing down the street past the pubs and the cinema into Tracy the ironmonger for a bag of nails or a bucket. He had to order hen food and general groceries and mash for the horses, and soap and three in one oil – the lists his father made grew longer.

On one occasion he had to order coal and drive the long way he went those weeks ago to the town where the Arcadia was located and Eileen worked at the chemist. It was raining and he caught sight of her walking down the main street with her mother, both of them under an umbrella.

He thought about her a lot, her silky skin, her soft breasts, her long hair, the gorgeous kisses and gropings, the fun of it that evening. Forget about her spectacles. Perhaps he would have continued seeing her if the car had started and he had been able to drive home afterwards and give her a final chaste kiss before delivering her to her mother. Perhaps he would have loved her forever if they had not had to stumble about in the dark in the small hours of the morning, herself in her high heels, the dried rutted road beneath them, while he had to listen to the language that came from her lips – nothing foul, she was much too genteel for that – but shrewish stuff, nevertheless, including a stream of ragged insults that continued to sting. But then he would remember the loveliness of her body and the soft words as he clung to her, and damn it, the music playing. Oh, Eileen!

Could they meet again? Sometimes on a lonely Saturday he would think about going back to the Arcadia or even to her house although he wouldn't forget the bitter exchanges in the dark. There were other fish in the sea, the line of girls along the wall.

Daddy sat in his study, sheaves of papers in front of him on the rent table.

'I have been looking at the accounts.' He did that weekly. 'Difficult to make sense of things.'

'I don't understand them.'

'You never did.' Daddy gazed critically at his son. 'Perhaps you think that all our providence comes from the sky and all that you have to do is to sit back and enjoy yourself. At this stage of your life you should show more initiative.'

Paul agreed – the initiative he should be showing was to clear out of this place and go round the world.

He glanced at the letters from the stockbroker, the lists of shares and dividends, all the sort of things his mother used to stuff into drawers. So long as the remittances came in she had never worried. The little man whose job it was to keep them supplied with money never caused trouble, and she had always taken it for granted that, even during the Emergency, the nectar squeezed from 'Trusts' and 'Accounts' was sufficient to keep them in funds. Perhaps you could not talk about luxury.

His father thought differently.

'We will have to sell some Guinness shares.'

'OK.'

'I am not in favour of getting rid of Rio Tinto at present. Its value has gone down.'

'OK.'

Paul sat down to read the pieces of paper his father handed to him, struggling through long lists, Government Securities, Banks, War Loan, Rubber Plantations – 'Thank God the war is over' – Railways, Johnson, Mooney and O'Brien.

'I didn't know we had so much.'

'When you eventually grow to some maturity you will realise that to have a good portfolio needs constant hard work and vigilance.'

Naturally Daddy believed that family shares had gone to pot because of Mummy's neglect. Going away for three years meant that financial ruin had resulted from doing his duty to England. Surely it had been madness to hold on to Irish Hockey Union Shares or Argentine Railway stock? The more he rummaged through the papers the more confused he became. United River Plate Company? Empire Indian Tea? Investing in City of Tokyo and Japanese Government Shares just before the war and then not disposing of them in time had been unwise.

'It can't all be Mummy's fault,' Paul said. 'Fairbrothers has had something to do with it.' But Mummy got the blame, and now was not the time to change stockbrokers.

Daddy put away all the papers into the drawers of the rent table, much as Mummy used to do, and resumed applying his own solution to the family's financial problems. He continued planning his programme of self-sufficiency. For far too long the place had been allowed to amble along on sustained loss, and for the first time he was going to put things on a proper economic basis.

For instance, he did not trust the current rural electrification scheme. He did not trust the government or the ESB to whom he had been beholden for years to light up the chandeliers of Mountsilver. Look how the electricity had failed during the past winter. A considerable amount of money could be saved by damning up the little tributary of the river and acquiring a turbine. Unnecessary bills could be avoided.

He began to think again about cheese. The Friesians – he had bought some more – could be put to proper use.

'Didn't they teach you anything about cheese at St Fiacre's?'

'No.'

'Typical.'

'They were keener on butter.'

'There's no decent cheese produced in Ireland. '

'No one wants to eat it.'

'A good farmhouse cheese is what is needed over here. It would find a market.'

Mushrooms was another idea.

'Did they teach you anything about mushrooms at St Fiacre's?'

'No.'

There were plenty of places at Mountsilver where mushrooms could be grown, including the basement, dark and damp; probably the maid's bedrooms offered ideal humidity. But even Daddy realised that mushrooms were unlikely to find an Irish market and the idea was abandoned so they continued to be confined to the outside, whitening the few fields that had escaped ploughing. The fairy ring beside the tennis court flourished.

The apples were something Paul could do easily enough, manual labour, without specialised knowledge. Six acres of lichen covered trees poured down their fruit yearly more or less unheeded. During the Emergency stewed apple had been as much a part of Paul's diet as rabbit. Daddy now decreed that all this must change, and apples must be sold. Paul must do it.

From early September when Irish Peach ripened, cursing, Paul climbed on a ladder and picked tree after tree, cookers, eaters, Bramleys, the special trees that bore Cox's Pippins and the rest.

The problem was thieves. Apples were a magnet for the children of the village and, together with the dogs, Paul and Dempsey patrolled the orchards, shining a torch in all directions. They had to be careful to avoid trip wires placed between the trees that sounded off an alarm up at the house. On several occasions they caught small boys with their sacks and carted them howling back to the house and the intimidating presence of his father who gave him special praise when several children were arrested on successive evenings and a sack of Golden Delicious was found abandoned in a ditch.

'Not bad work, old boy. In the army the use of intelligence is the best way to forestall attacks.'

The children were threatened with the guard, or worse their parents and let go, blubbing. But trip wires, gun shots, alarms and scoldings gave an edge of danger, and made stealing more fun. Thieves increased in number.

The alarm rang loudly as they were finishing dinner.

'Don't waste a moment.'

There was no time to call Dempsey. In the orchard his torch picked out a sack of apples on the grass. Further on it shone on two men who had discovered the ladder Paul had been climbing for the past weeks. Men, not boys. One ran away, the other tall figure came stiffly down the rungs.

'Good evening, Mr Paul.'

'Oh, good evening.'

'I hope you don't mind. I was having a look around the place.' Paul recognised Sergeant Clarke, who sometimes called on the house for gun and car licences and other matters.

'I heard an alarm go off and I decided to investigate. There's a lot of young lads hanging around.'

He didn't tell his father about that meeting. In fact there was plenty for all, and when he took the endless sorted boxes down to the country market he always found the place choked with rival apples.

Lorries arrived regularly filled with packing cases and machinery. They would be self sufficient in electricity. A second hand turbine came from Belfast with a load of big fat pipes. There were unforeseen delays from the electrification – the fault of the ESB – and the turbine proved faulty.

Paul had many months of being his father's partner, months that were full of incident. There was no time for boredom and when on Saturdays he cycled down to the cinema and sat by himself in the gloomy interior in the stiff seat on the concrete floor sniffing up wafts of Jeyes Fluid and watching – *Johnny Belinda* – *Tarzan and the Mermaids* – he felt the satisfactory exhaustion of a long week's work.

The polished steel vats were for the cheese making; a stable was transformed with newly tiled walls. Recommended by Father Hogan, Miss Collins arrived to make a notable cheese, which would be called Mountsilver.

'I don't want anything with holes.'

'Oh no, Major, we'll work at something much simpler – a type of cream cheese . . .'

After anguished consideration Daddy decided Miss Collins was too superior to sleep in the basement and as a favour gave her Balaclava and allowed her to eat with them in the dining room. She was not to listen to the news afterwards; there were limits, and she was expected to go to her own quarters.

Miss Collins livened up mealtimes with accounts of how she had spent her life; she had been in a convent for some years but had left before the final vows – no vocation. Then a spell in France where she had learned the theory of making cheese. Daddy disapproved of her dark blue slacks; one thing he hated was women in trousers. For cheese making she wore a white coat over the slacks and a shower cap over her hair. First of all she worked out a recipe in a saucepan.

'I've abandoned the idea of a cream cheese in favour of a Brie type. With the addition of some herbs.'

She stood morning and night in the cold new dairy with its cloud of little flies using a knife to the curds or was it whey, stuff poured into a steel vat which in due course would subside into a yellowish blancmange. The dairy got colder as winter set in once more, by which time a certain amount of had been produced and prettily packaged. At dinner, Mountsilver Cheese was served up with Jacob's Cream Crackers and pickled onions.

'There's a slightly sour flavour . . .'

'Perhaps a little too salty?'

'Too many chives? The taste of onion is very distinct.'

'Would you like me to try again?'

'I don't think that will be necessary, Miss Collins. I am sure you know best and it will appeal to many people just as it is. We'll send out some samples and market forces will make the decision.'

Unfortunately market forces did just that.

'Let them choke on their bloody Galtee!' Daddy roared. Galtee, beloved by everyone in Ireland, was the processed cheese ground down and treated with chemicals so that the finished product, cut in triangles, had no rind. As attempts were made to sell Mountsilver to Findlaters and other outlets it became apparent that the country was not ready for anything so sophisticated.

Miss Collins departed, and the cold dairy, with its expensive tiles and steel fittings was deserted. Daddy was still waiting for workmen to come and set up the estate's own electricity, but the fat useless pipes lay beside the useless turbine, and electricity continued to come from the national company.

The milk that Miss Collins had used day after day was taken down to the creamery once again. The pigs might be a failure, the hens got fowl pox, but for successive years the crops of new potatoes made a profit. Vegetables sold off well.

The men on the estate looked on as the Major put on defensive clothes and tackled the beehives. He had bought jacket, veil and gloves, smoker and hive tools from Switzers and Drummonds. In August he had the hives piled in the tractor and, together with Paul and Dempsey, went looking for suitable locations where the bees could get to work making heather honey. He searched the mountains with his binoculars for places where heather spread over the mountains and Paul and Dempsey could lug the spitting hives up hills to where the bees could get to work. He made a map of where they were deposited so that they could be retrieved when the heather faded to brown and the cold discouraged the honey makers. Then it was on the tractor and up the hills again, following the map; however sleepy the bees might be, they buzzed and stung. A few hives were never found. Back at base, carefully stoical about stings, Paul dressed up, and spend days getting the dripping honey into jars, picking up seething blocks of comb, shaking off bees and packaging them for sale.

Honeycomb and sticky jars were a success, but it was obvious that none of the Major's enterprises would make half as much money as a couple of little dividends from Guinness's or Thomas Cook and Son.

CHAPTER NINETEEN

Many things rankled, like being called a fool once a day, and Daddy stamping outside his bedroom door at half past seven every morning to wake him up to a life of muck, bees, apples and hens. Paul was never going to be a willing farmer.

Daddy took up hunting again, buying a new horse, and after it was bought, complaining incessantly how much Bullet cost to maintain. To cut down on expense the plough horses were sold; the tractor did their job. They would end up being eaten in France.

Paul had to hunt in order not to earn his father's scorn, and Pav was still there, waiting to be saddled up on two excruciating days a week. He hated every moment, longing for St Patrick's Day and the end of it for another season. Daddy loved the business and Bullet went well. Father McCabe also hunted, and that was another reason for close ties.

Paul went fishing with his father and they stood by the river in companionable silence; they had just about equal success.

'Good to have a stretch of river to call one's own.'

After the treaty in 1922 the new government had enough to do without taking over the rivers of Ireland which remained in private hands. 'Jolly good thing, too.'

Poachers took their toll – there was Republican justification in going after Mountsilver salmon.

In June they fished on Lough Mask at Trigger's remote and untidy fishing lodge. They fished all day, pounding over the grey water in Trigger's boat, and came back late in the evening for a quick meal and a look into the entrails of various trout to find out what they were eating and consequently choose a suitable fly. Then out again in the long midnight twilight for more. You wanted to watch out for Trigger's casts, since his one eye made them erratic.

That August Daddy and Paul took guns and ammunition and Wooster down to where Freddy Barnsworth had twenty-four thousand acres of shooting, mostly vertical. The group which started off early to climb a lot of mountains included Peter Marsden who was a brilliant shot and took his guns with him wherever he went in case someone would give a day's shooting. Marsden had never been a rich man; when he was young his family in Mayo had been so impoverished it could not afford a proper gun dog and his sister had to put on a bathing suit and plunge into the bog to retrieve dead birds shot by her brothers.

They climbed slowly as the day got hotter and the going more difficult. Freddy's guide led them over a mountain around a valley and back up a higher mountain. Paul did not think that at that latitude anywhere could be so barren of life. They trudged on and on without sight of anything. Paul had ceased to hope when just in front of him several grouse got up. He was not ready.

'Fool!' his father shouted, which was unfair since he had not got a shot in either. Only Peter Marsden got his bird. After they returned exhausted to the car one of Freddy's setters threw a fit. Wooster looked on smugly as Freddy and the guide got the dog going again by rubbing it hard with fresh wet moss, chiefly on its face.

Next winter more hunting. Fun for Daddy and Bullet, agony for Paul and Pav.

At home meals were no longer silent as Paul and his father discussed the latest enterprise and money problems or moaned about the latest financial loss while plans for Paul's future were put on the long finger. Daddy had long forgotten the old rule about never talking shop at mealtimes.

On Saturdays Daddy concurred when Paul biked off to the cinema. *Ma and Pa Kettle. I Shot Jesse James.* Once or twice during the summer, hoping to God Daddy had gone to bed, Paul would go further and bicycle the thirty mile distance to the town where the Arcadia was located. (Never in the Rover.) First thing he would look for Eileen but she was never there.

Then he would spend the evening under the revolving lights and dance with whatever girl would have him. *What part of England are ye from? Are you enjoying your holiday?* Once he cycled with a girl to her home and they stopped and had a snog. But Dolores, who was nice enough, wasn't Eileen.

Daddy went less to the Club – too much effort for too little reward, especially as so many friends had given up their subscriptions and stayed home. His other contact with them was the British Legion. In November Paul was roped in to bicycle round the district seeking out the few people who might buy poppies. Daddy defiantly wore a poppy to mass and Paul had to do the same – from the fuss you'd think those poppies were destined to be converted to heroin.

There was always the drive to Sunday mass, past the lodge, still obstinately full of Roches, past the gate pillars, one with its headless and pawless lion, in that same immortal Rover with whatever female staff was with them at the time; apart from Agnes no one stayed at Mountsilver for more than a few months. Where did they go after they left here, usually without warning? You'd wake one morning and the latest would be gone, and Agnes would be shaking her head.

Nineteen fifty-four blew in with Marian year and a rocky little shrine containing Our Lady and St Bernadette at her feet appeared overnight in the village.

Broken Lance. River of No Return. Casanova's Big Night.

There were times when Paul grew restless, especially after he and Daddy had a shouting match. I can't believe you've been so asinine. Just do what I tell you and shut up.

He saved his money, the salary that Daddy still gave him, allowing himself enough for cigarettes and his few other expenses, and opened an account in the Credit Union. At night he lay awake and planned what to do with it – buy a car? Go to London? Go courting? Dolores, if he couldn't find Eileen? Go and see Mummy? She wrote from time to time; Daddy would see the handwriting on the envelope and pass it over in silence. She would enclose a five pound note as if he was still a school boy and a couple of photographs – herself, looking unchanged and pictures of the little bastard – *Nick's sixth birthday party.*

Cathy was the latest maid who irritated Daddy by a tendency to giggle and the trouble she had with the black uniform and the white cap and apron which looked perpetually creased. She was pretty and cheered Paul up. But Cathy left and Father McCabe sighed and resumed what had become one of his parish duties: finding another servant for Mountsilver.

'You'll have to do something about that kitchen,' he said for the umpteenth time.

'Bring it up!' Trigger Dobbs advised. 'Helen and I have done just that.'

'How could you bring up the Aga?'

'Oh, they can do it. These chaps who fit things are marvellous. Maids love it. Makes all the difference. Life gets easier all the time!'

All over Ireland people were bringing up their kitchens. Daddy came to the idea late.

'How am I going to pay for it?'

There were hours of shuffling through lists of stocks and shares before Daddy concluded, 'Why don't we sell something.' This was the first time that he made up his mind to get rid of something in the house. He had in mind the portrait of King William. Darcy, the valuer, wasn't impressed.

'A hundred at most. King William isn't the height of fashion.'

'What about the other pictures?'

'Hard to tell. They are all in need of a good clean. '

'That's supposed to be a Canaletto.'

'Hm.' Darcy didn't know his arse from his elbow. 'We'd have to call in our experts.' But he admired some of the furniture, including the table with Johnny Murphy's initials. He wandered into the dining room and went into ecstasies over the plate buckets.

'Those things with the gap running down them?' Daddy asked. 'No one's used them for years.'

'They are much in demand. Around 1770 I should say. Good mahogany and brass banding and brass handles.'

'I can't see what possible use they could be to anyone.'

Darcy also got excited about the globes in the drawing room.

Daddy said: 'They're useless. They haven't even got Australia on them.' To his astonishment buckets and globes paid for much of the enterprise.

The new kitchen occupied half the ballroom.

'We won't be having any more dances.'

The contractors came in May and were aided by the men on the estate, which meant that Paul was busier than ever that summer. No time for fishing. The work took until Christmas. Up came the kitchen, up came the Aga, up came the Belfast sink.

Daddy began arguing about expense. A new coolness threatened between him and Father McCabe whose idea the whole thing had been. 'McCabe doesn't know what he is talking about. It's a waste to have two kitchens in one house.'

Another cook was found quite easily, given the enticement of the new premises. Whenever Paul swallowed the food Josie sent across to the dining room, he instantly recalled the meals he had eaten for six years at St George's. Wasn't there a French writer whose memory was triggered every time he ate a little cake?

Father McCabe was invited to lunch to sample Josie's cooking and admire the new kitchen and its shelves and cupboards of Beautyboard. 'Do you like it, girls?' Father McCabe asked jovially.

'Oh yes, Father,' lied Agnes and Josie.

Agnes and Josie hated each other, and if Paul was passing the double doors of the ballroom-kitchen he could usually hear a muted quarrel. In a few weeks the new kitchen took on the aspects of the old, the trail of cabbage stalks and potato peel, the faint rancid smells. Soon the white squares of the linoleum were almost as dark as the black. The cats had found their way up, but the mice were quicker. Paul was amazed by the intelligence of mice. Mouse droppings were one thing, but he wondered how many times a day a mouse urinated. The sink was grubby as it had ever been. The Lord in his mercy be kind to Belfast sinks.

Josie left after Agnes gleefully told her that Daddy had called out, 'What's this muck?' when he was served with her goulash. She was succeeded by Margaret whose cooking was no better.

Another Christmas generated the usual gloom. Donald and Valerie again. Ten pounds from Mummy who was feeling flush, having found another job – you wouldn't think there was scope for interior decoration in Somerset – together with a photo – *Nick winning the egg and spoon race.* Ten pounds from Daddy and a life of St Teresa of Lisieux.

In February, in the cold dining room as they were sitting down to Margaret's Irish stew, Agnes, standing in her corner, collapsed in a faint. Paul and Daddy carried her between them into the drawing room and laid her on the big sofa while Dr Waters was summoned. Alas, Agnes' working days were over. How fortunate she could stay with one of her sisters! How sad after forty years at Mountsilver! She had come as a young girl when Daddy was a boy.

'A pension? It would be a signal for her to live for ever. Always happens when you dole out pensions.'

'Wouldn't a lump sum do?'

'Tricky with all these expenses, old boy. Bloody kitchen. She has the old age pension. And she'll be living scot free with Molly.'

'She'll have to contribute something to Molly towards her keep.'

'I'll see if I can come up with something.'

Paul suspected he did not come up with more than a couple of hundred pounds. He himself raided his Credit Union account and gave Agnes fifty pounds on behalf of his mother. He thought of telling Mummy what he had done when he wrote to tell her of Agnes' illness, but decided that wouldn't be stylish. Mummy wrote back with another fifty pounds. 'Poor old thing – wish her well from me.' But Paul didn't, remembering Agnes' silent fury after she ran off with Fireball. Luckily the cheque had been made out to cash probably because Mummy couldn't remember Agnes' surname. So it appeared that the whole hundred pounds came from Paul.

He told his father.

'Bloody fool.'

Agnes lived with Molly for six months and then died.

At her funeral mass Paul found himself in tears. He had known her all his life and she was as much a fixture as the portraits on the walls or the parrot. In Daddy's opinion she was a representative of the pre-Celtic race. She had been short, strongly built, moon-faced, resolute, grim, faithful and self-sacrificing.

'She left her money to the missions,' Father McCabe said when he came to tea. Daddy had another favour to ask him. Margaret had given notice.

Miss Nolan arrived at the same time as the machine for washing clothes that Father McCabe insisted upon.

'She did duties for a priest in Castlebellingham.'

Miss Nolan was awarded a room on the third floor. She did not stand in the corner of the dining room at mealtimes, but stayed in the new kitchen, because she was always busy cooking. Daddy summoned her between courses with a silver bell.

She planned the cleaning of the house day by day, Monday drawing room, Tuesday dining room . . . She found time to polish the brass and the silver gleamed. Her cooking was acceptable. She cleaned the bottom of the parrot's cage. Daddy might criticise – he did that constantly, it was a habit like stammering – but he was able to report to Father McCabe that there was much that was acceptable about the new domestic help.

'Pity about her clothes.'

'For heaven's sake, Major!' Father McCabe had come over for his reward, another substantial contribution to the parish funds. But he may have felt some sympathy when Miss Nolan brought in the tea – home-made scones and cake – and he could inspect her thick stockings, the puce sweater several sizes too big, the stained skirt and the gym shoes.

Daddy dabbed at his pipe. 'Pity she can't wear a maid's uniform.' But Miss Nolan was no skiv. She called Paul by his Christian name, no Master or Mister Paul.

Father Hogan invited himself to stay. He did this occasionally for the usual reasons – to check on how well Paul had adhered to his faith, and to see whether or not Daddy was drinking.

Daddy planned a luncheon party in his honour.

'Important to keep up with friends.'

'Not the usual suspects?' asked Paul.

'We haven't had them here for years.' They were silent. Not since before Mummy left.

'If you don't like my friends, invite your own.' Fat chance.

'Trigger and Helen and Mary Rooke are Protestant.'

'So?'

'Father Hogan hates Protestants.'

'Don't be a fool, Paul.'

'So are Donald and Valerie. Protestant.'

'Father McCabe is also coming. Bringing a friend, some sort of cleric. Even things out.'

'Why don't you invite Dr Schmidt?' Dr Schmidt was the German who had bought the neighbouring estate.

'Don't be a fool.'

The day before the party Daddy tackled Miss Nolan about her appearance. Paul read her thoughts which were to do with the difficulties of cleaning a huge house and hearing constant criticisms. When you considered how many women had passed through the battered caravanserai since Mummy's departure, you'd think Daddy would have learned by now.

'I don't mean to be impertinent but do you think you could wear something a little more appropriate tomorrow?'

Windows sparkled and the main rooms smelt of polish. The dogs had been shampooed. The weather cleared and the grey house in its circle of trees showed much of its ancient dignity.

The first to arrive was Trigger guiding his new Austin past the potholes.

'Next time I'll sue you for damages.' Helen and Mary Rooke climbed out, easing their arthritis with the aid of sticks. Ritual Anglo-Saxon kisses were exchanged. The Countess drove up with her latest companion – 'my cousin, Michael' – followed by Donald and Valerie. Father McCabe came with an American friend, Father McCarthy.

In the drawing room the fire blazed, even though it was late in May. Sherry and gin and tonic together with a saucer of lemon slices waited with a saucer of peanuts.

'Oh Gerald, how well the place looks!' cried Mary Rooke, her mouth full of nuts, and everyone agreed. Light streamed through the windows and Miss Nolan had wiped the crystals of the chandelier. There were bowls of flowers. Daddy was never able to get rid of all Mummy's flowers;

the wall flowers whose seeds she had stuck in the walls bloomed in spring and so did the daffodils, including those that were planted nearly thirty years ago and spelt out *Gerald and Diana 1928*.

In the dining room Father Hogan said grace. They sat and Daddy rang his silver bell.

This was the moment when Miss Nolan should have brought in the soup. Father Hogan was praising Marian year. Trigger talked about his gardener.

'Paddy has a car! Turned up for work driving it. Can you imagine-whatever next! A car!'

Daddy rang again. Surely this time Miss Nolan must have heard the demanding tinkle? Around the table conversation lapsed as he glowered at the door to the kitchen. At last the soup came in, two plates at a time, so it took several minutes before everyone was served. Parsnip soup, nice, but lukewarm. Paul noticed Miss Nolan had on her puce jumper and her gym shoes.

After that unfortunate first course Miss Nolan got into her stride, serving up roast lamb and new potatoes. She brought in strawberries accompanied by crisp meringues she had whipped up. Everyone felt cheerful. Father Hogan always enjoyed a good tuck in, while as usual Mary Dobbs and Donald ate as if they hadn't touched food for a week.

Trigger boasted how some bovine he owned had won a prize at the RDS. They discussed capital punishment which they all believed in. For a while Father McCarthy held the floor. The Protestants listened politely as he described how he had had a wonderful time touring Ireland; he had been to Knock and said a mass and climbed Croagh Patrick. Next week he was going to climb Skellig Michael and say a mass for the hermits who lived at the top a thousand years ago.

Daddy watched as Miss Nolan cleared the cheese plates. 'That will be all.' He caught the Countess's eye; she rose majestically from her chair and the other women followed her out of the room. They would take the opportunity of visiting the lavatories and then settling down to the coffee which should be waiting for them.

Daddy passed the port, adjusted his hearing aid and described the landing at Anzio.

'Bloody Americans.'

Father McCabe, who knew a horse when he saw one, turned the conversation to the Derby and speculated on the winner. Trigger agreed with his choice. Father Hogan was steering the conversation back to ecclesiastical matters when he was interrupted by a knocking on the door to the kitchen. Behind they could hear Miss Nolan's voice.

'May I come in, Gerald?'

The men looked up in surprise since there was no further need for Miss Nolan's services. If there was one thing Daddy really hated it was a member of the lower classes calling him by his Christian name.

The door opened and they saw that she had removed her clothes, except for the stockings attached to her suspender belt and her gym shoes. Flesh bulged in unexpected places.

'Oh Gerald, you didn't like me dressed!' she giggled.

'GET OUT!'

Miss Nolan was smiling as she slammed the door shut.

They all got up hastily leaving their glasses half filled. Paul could not help grinning, and his father noticed. The priests were blushing.

'Hard to get good servants these days,' Trigger said.

CHAPTER TWENTY

Rain drumming on the bedroom window. As usual Daddy had marched past his door stamping his feet, clearing his throat.

'I've a bit of a cold,' he lied, shouting through the closed door.

'What?'

'I've got a COLD. Could be FLU.'

That kept his father outside.

'I'm off to Arklow for the spare part. Back for lunch.'

Paul would lie in some more, snuggling under the bedclothes before getting up and getting his own breakfast. Bernadette was not back yet after the Christmas holidays. Was she the third Bernadette? She wore shoes with pointed toes and stiletto heels and took no notice when Daddy ticked her off. She probably wouldn't come back at all.

Max curled up beside him. For the first time Paul found it good to have a dog to call one's own. He would have to get up soon and let Max out for a pee. He lay and lit a cigarette and tried once again to remember the things that had happened during the past year.

The Pope died. De Valera was elected President. Trigger also died. Father McCabe was annoyed that Paul and his father were going to a Protestant funeral; the Archbishop and his cohorts, forbade such practices in case good Catholics picked up something in the damp interiors of Protestant churches that would send them to hell. Trigger's gardener, Paddy, together with his maids, waited outside cravenly in Paddy's car, but Daddy and Paul defied Father McCabe and the whole lot of them. Later Daddy, who may have been drunk, told Paul how Trigger had to leave the army because he had rogered a guardsman.

Pav had also died (twisted gut), which was a relief. Daddy went hunting on his own or rather with Father McCabe.

Only Dempsey and Mick were left among the men. Daddy had seen to it that they left one by one, although some had gone on their own. Dan Roche and his family finally abandoned the gate lodge after they were given a council house in the village, departing overnight without a word. Weeds soon surrounded the empty lodge; letting in the jungle. Joe and Philly went to America.

Last summer Paul bought a car, an Austin several years old, and drove to England to see his mother. Daddy didn't try and stop him. Nearly ten years had gone by since Mummy had run off. Paul crossed in the mailboat and drove shakily across Anglesey. It was the first time he had been out of Ireland and the feeling was exhilarating.

Mummy and Fireball lived in a small Georgian house they had rented in a pretty village.

'You don't get houses like this in Ireland. Or villages either.'

They had been offered a cottage to rent, which Mummy had declined, believing thatched houses vulgar. She still worked for an interior decorator in the nearby town, and had raided it for the chintz curtains in her drawing room. The flowers in the little garden bloomed in profusion; Paul recognised the same things she had grown at Mountsilver.

'In spite of moles. That's one good thing about Ireland, maybe the only one – no ghastly moles.'

'What abut snakes?'

'I prefer snakes to moles.'

Nick, who was attending the village school – 'you couldn't do that in Ireland' – was a brat.

Mummy dressed as well as ever, had very few wrinkles and her hair was still fair.

'I have it dyed regularly.'

'You've changed your scent.'

'Je Reviens belonged to another time. And the name is a bit unfortunate under the circumstances.'

'What are you wearing now?'

'Mitsouko. It means mystery in Japanese. It's hideously expensive.'

Fireball who must be at least thirty-five by now, wearing his old school tie – Haileybury? – and highly polished shoes, had grown fat. He managed to hold down a job in the local prep school; the day before Paul left he showed Paul around and pointed out the similarities to St George's.

Paul stayed a week and everything went swimmingly. He even began to tolerate Fireball. Pity Nick was spoiled. No talk of anything contentious like religion or money or Daddy's feelings or what was Paul going to do for the rest of his life? Mummy didn't care.

'Give my love to Daddy.' Her fingers may have been crossed.

Paul finished his cigarette and stubbed it out in a bowl piled with butts as Max moved restlessly, telling him it was time to get up. Too late; he had wandered over to the corner and peed. Paul took the mop he had standing behind the door and mopped up.

In the kitchen he made himself a huge fry. After breakfast he fed the dogs; tins of dog food were the greatest invention since the wheel. The cats were fed, so was the parrot. He put on his mackintosh, stiff as a board and went outside to feed the hens. Dempsey would deal with the pigs and milk the cows. The rain dripped down the back of his neck and he took the servant's tunnel as a short cut back to the house. He carried in turf and wood and made himself a huge fire in the sitting room.

He settled down to read, Max in front of him, muzzle to the fireguard. Not *Térèse Desqueyroux*, which his father had given him for Christmas to add to *The Desert of Love* – Daddy continued to pelt him with Catholic writers. He picked up the *Old St Georgian* to which he had recently subscribed. He wondered why he suddenly felt an interest in the bloody place; perhaps it was meeting Fireball again. The odd time he went into Dublin he usually ran into one or two boys from school. Dublin was so small, the odds were every time you walked down Grafton Street you would encounter someone, even if you didn't know more than twenty people in a lifetime. Hello Sheridan. Good to see you, Mercer. How are you doing?

But most of the people from school could have gone up in smoke, and the *Old St Georgian* offered reassurance and satisfied curiosity. Old boys got married, and the *OSG* carried the details, and then again announced children being born. He felt twinges of envy. He went through the section with details of what people were doing – Beamish running his father's haberdashery, Mulligan in the Hong Kong police, Sheridan a doctor in Derby.

Mr Good had died and in this issue of the *OSG* there was an account of the memorial erected in the chapel to the school's wonderful headmaster at a ceremony attended by Mrs Good who would probably live for ever. The current headmaster called Simpson, was probably English like the Goods, since the school never encouraged Irish headmasters.

The school was building a new science block. He recalled the old lab where he was supposed to have been taught chemistry at the time when Mr Good had been desperate enough to allow Mr Hartley a spell as science master. The informal atmosphere of the lab had totally undermined his indulgent regime. 'What is that pandemonium?' listening visitors asked. 'Oh, that's just Mr Hartley's class.' The governors had not liked it when on a surprise visit they found Mr Hartley's boys grilling sausages over their Bunsen burners. Science became duller when Bunsen burners could no longer be used because of the gas shortage.

Mr Hartley must surely be Obit by now. Paul was startled to find Cusack had also snuffed it. How? It didn't say. He had never spoken again to Cusack after the fiasco of Dolly Fossett's and he tried to suppress a feeling of satisfaction. Plenty of people died in their thirties.

His eyes were dropping through other names and careers when the doorbell rang and Max barked. He peered out of the window.

No one likes seeing a police car outside their door.

Hat in hand, Sergeant Clarke was polite. What a job! 'I am sorry Sir, there has been an accident involving Major Blake-Willoughby.'

'Oh God. Where is he?'

'I am sorry, Sir, he is deceased.'

Suddenly.

There was so much to do that he didn't have time for grieving. He had to identify Daddy. Apart from the blow to his temple that had killed him, he looked fine, lying straight as an effigy.

Father McCabe helped with arranging the funeral mass and burial. Paul suddenly found himself an instant authority on removals, and funeral masses, the two bites of the cherry that the Catholics have for their corpses. He put his foot down when there were suggestions of exposing Daddy in Keane's funeral home for people to file past.

Someone had said an Act of Contrition when they found him lying by the crashed car, so that was all right. Who? A fellow from Carnew, Paul could thank him at the inquest.

He felt guilty about being annoyed with Daddy for waking him this morning.

He phoned his mother. 'Oh,' she said and there was a long pause. 'Thank-you, darling, for telling me.' She posted over a shoe box full of bunches of snowdrops.

There was the matter of Wooster who had been killed as well. Paul had him brought up to the house and buried him himself in the dog's graveyard next to his namesakes.

Bernadette returned the same afternoon Daddy died, full of coy sympathy. He put her to work at once, cleaning out the drawing room and removing the parrot before he went in and sat receiving visitors. Although a big fire was lit, the room was cold and people did not stay long. Most of the men who had left the place, all the Roche family and many people from the town turned up; so did two of Agnes' remaining sisters whom Paul hired on the spot to help after the funeral. Whiskey had to be ordered, a ham, and plenty of white bread and butter.

Father Hogan came down to offer comfort, although Paul felt he was grieving more than he was. Aunt Delia came, tearful for her brother and his soul. Paul spread his mother's flowers on the coffin on top of Daddy; everyone knew who they came from.

The church was packed. Before the mass began Father McCabe announced: 'The toilet is situated behind the church.'

There was an abundance of wreaths and Protestant flowers, winter flowers because it was January. Carrying their wilted offerings, mostly tied with embroidery wool, the Protestants walked up the nave with as much enthusiasm as horses entering a burning stable. They sat firmly in their pews or stood stoically while the rest of the congregation bobbed up and down and crossed itself.

Father Hogan gave the oration, singing Daddy's praises and you would never think he and the Major had ever had any disagreement. Father McCabe also told everyone what an amazing person Daddy had been, before splashing the sides of the coffin with holy water and spreading the incense, something else which made the Protestants wince.

With the aid of workers on the estate, past and present, Paul held on to a corner of the coffin and lugged it out into the hearse – no squeaking trolley for Major Blake-Willoughby as there had been for poor old Trigger. His right hand ached after shaking several hundred hands. The undertaker manoeuvred the hearse through the broken down gates of the family graveyard where the coffin had to be carried yet again, this time to the freshly dug grave beside Grandad. Granny was nearby, she who had made the family Catholic.

Father McCabe did the final business, Paul threw clay into the gaping hole, and Johnny Murphy, who had chosen to forget that Daddy had sacked him, brought out his fiddle and played Danny Boy. A lot better than the 'Dead March' in *Saul*.

At Mountsilver the lower classes gathered in the part of the ballroom that hadn't been turned into the kitchen and drank whiskey. The upper classes, like the Countess, Aunt Delia, Father Hogan and Daddy's pals from the Club, assembled in the drawing room, and got tea and ham sandwiches. Father Hogan and the Canon talked nervously to each other as if they were cold war antagonists.

The inquest had to be endured. A verdict of accidental death, although everyone (except Paul) knew there was more to it than that. Months afterwards, when Paul was helping Mick with the milking, Mick told him what the whole of Mountsilver knew. The Rover, lurching from right to left across the Dublin road, Daddy's voice booming *she could very well pass for forty-three in the dusk with the light behind her*. The St Christopher medal on the dashboard that did no good. The young guard who should have known better, and who had since been transferred to west Kerry, calling the car to a halt, leaning in the car window and catching Daddy's breath. You didn't arrest the gentry or even caution them unless they had committed bloody murder. Here was gentry with tweed jacket, tie and white moustache.

'Drive home carefully, Major.'

Paul was by himself with nothing more to arrange. Father McCabe persuaded Mary, Agnes' younger sister to stay on for the time being while he looked for another domestic; it would hardly do for Bernadette to be left alone with him.

The letters and mass cards Redmond carried up every day had to be answered. Thank you for your kind thoughts. I appreciate your condolences. And then after Daddy had been dead for a month more letters including those from soldiers of his old regiment. Paul made a trip up to the convent to take part in one of the masses Aunt Delia was arranging to knock off Daddy's time in purgatory.

Bills in plenty, some going back for years. We would be grateful if you would settle this account . . . prompt payment . . . legal action. He remembered what Mummy used to say: 'Don't pay until you see the whites of their eyes. They can always hang on, and remember, that for them, having a Mountsilver account is a privilege.'

Tax to deal with. Paul would be a lot poorer off after death duties. He discovered a bulk of correspondence from his mother and her solicitors about separation and a possible divorce. Letters from Father Hogan agreeing that there was no way that could come about. Never. Mummy could sing for her divorce and little Nick could continue to be a bastard.

All now utterly changed since Mummy was now a merry widow. Was she going to marry Fireball? Had she done so already?

He found the metal tag he had given his father all those years ago on Mountsilver station just before he left for the war. *Major G.L. Blake-Willoughby.*

In Daddy's bedroom he opened the left-hand cupboard door and discovered the pile of empty whiskey bottles. On a moonlit night he used the wheelbarrow which usually held pigs' swill to take them down to the river where he threw them in.

He remembered that when Daddy came back after the war he had quite seriously considered getting rid of the place, so he needn't feel guilty if he decided to do the same. He could sell up and go round the world, singing a vagabond song. Buy himself a Harley Davidson. Build a bungalow with proper heating.

He was old before his time. He could hardly go down to a dance hall or even go to the cinema locally.

Did he love the place? Willoughbys had been here for nearly three hundred years – Cromwellians, the boys at St Fiacre's had been right.

Max wagged his tail.

He thought of the times he had planned to turn the place into tillage – barley would do, as the wheat yield was always unsatisfactory. Dig up a lot of hedges and widen the fields. Buy a new tractor and do much of the ploughing and sowing himself. He could retire Mick and just continue with Dempsey. He might keep the Friesians for the time being. He would stop growing vegetables, they never paid for all the work they involved. He was not a bloody Dutchman.

He was very sorry about Daddy but he found it difficult to suppress a feeling that he was ashamed to identify as satisfaction.

He might continue things the way they were for the time being.

Bullet would have to go.

He would buy a television set.

CHAPTER TWENTY-ONE

After Daddy died Mummy visited Mountsilver twice, bringing Nick with her each time. Fireball never bothered to accompany her. When she came, a year after the funeral, Paul took her to see his grave. He was proud of the stone he had provided, which had good clear lettering listing Daddy's ancestors and achievements.

'You've everything there except his dental records.'

She went round the house and estate trying to find traces of her old life. No garden. None of her gramophone records, none of her books, none of the clothes she had left behind. The tapestries on the chairs had faded.

In the evening he lit the fire in the breakfast room and gave her a gin and tonic. Nick had disappeared; she didn't trouble to go looking for him.

'Daddy did a good job getting rid of reminders of me.'

'He was angry.'

'He might have left a bit of the garden.'

'The potatoes do well there instead.'

'Even the mimosa has gone.'

'That wasn't Daddy. It froze in the bad winter.'

'Time you got rid of the place.'

Most days he thought about that very thing.

'It's a shambles.'

'It wouldn't be easy to sell.'

'You could find a Kraut.'

For a start, Dr Schmidt owned the neighbouring property and he would have plenty of friends from the Fatherland looking for estates in Ireland.

When he came back from mass on Sunday Mummy said, 'You can give up that nonsense.'

'I can't.'

'You only became a Catholic to please Daddy.'

And to annoy you. Simple idiotic reasons for the biggest decision of his life.

'You don't understand. It's my faith now. I believe it. Like Daddy did.'

'What about me?'

'What do you mean?'

'What do you believe will happen to me when I die?'

'I suppose a spell in purgatory.' Let's not start talking about Hell.

'I'll stick to the C of I – C of E in England. We have such a beautiful little Norman church in the village.'

'Most churches like that in Ireland were destroyed.'

The day before she and Nick were scheduled to leave Nick disappeared and they feared he had fallen into the river. He had hidden in one of the attic rooms and appeared gleefully after the guards were called.

'He needs a good hiding.'

'Mind your own business,' Mummy said and Paul learned that you do not criticise children to their parents.

Three years later she came back with Nick who was twelve by this time.

'Nothing changed?'

'Nothing much. Max died. I've got a new Labrador.'

'I suppose it's called Wooster.'

He kept a cupboard full of tins of dog food. In case of Armageddon Wooster would be fed.

'You'd do better to get a wife.'

'One of these days.'

'You don't know where to start. No girl in her right mind would dream of coming to live here.'

He knew that. Even Rosemary, Dr Waters' daughter turned him down when she called in for tea one day and he proposed to her.

'You should get rid of the place,' Mummy urged again.

'One of these days.'

That time Nick did fall into the river, but managed to swim ashore.

When Nick was seventeen Mummy sent him over to Mountsilver to stay. He brought a friend named Ben with him. The visit was a disaster and Paul felt Mummy was to blame. Maybe the weather. Rattling windows, creaking doors and overflowing gutters were not his fault. The boys had to stay indoors and play billiards.

'Pity about the tear in the baize.'

'You did it.'

They never stopped complaining.

'Boring.'

'Stately home of Ireland, huh!'

There was a nagging strain in Nick's voice that reminded Paul of Mummy.

'Talk about damp.'

'God, what a kip!'

He knew more or less what they were saying without overhearing. But most of the time they said things to his face.

'Paul, haven't you heard of people called plumbers?'

'Roof menders? How many slates have you lost this week?'

'Why don't you have colour television?'

'If you had a proper aerial you might get BBC.'

'The bath water was cold again.'

'You've never heard of the Rolling Stones?'

'Paul, there's a black spot in this potato.'

'Not corned beef again!'

'Cabbage, yuk!'

'Why don't you have cream instead of custard?'

Paul drummed his fingers on the table and grimaced. 'If you don't shut up I'll tell Marie to cook a rabbit pie.' That kept them quiet for a few minutes. They had seen corpses of animals with myxomatosis all over the place.

'Can we go shooting again, please, Paul?' They were sick of bashing croquet balls and shooting was one thing that appealed to them. When they arrived they had a couple of days with the shotgun.

Paul himself shot regularly. He still went down to Freddy Barnsworth's mountains behind Dingle, tramped over expanses of bog, and went after grouse or snipe which rose suddenly and zigzagged in front of him. He aimed his gun low, left and right, following the bird into the distance. Crack! Afterwards Guinness and steak at the Butler Arms.

Woodcock were another challenge; remembering his father, Dan Parsons invited him regularly to his estate at the foot of the mountains behind Portumna where the woodcock flew into the woods at the October full moon. And Averil, Dan's wife, would have the day's limp corpses cooked. They would appear on toast, black feet curled, before her guests, who picked at little brains and crunched marble-sized skulls. Jolly good.

Quite often when he was back home and went outside the house he carried the shotgun with him. You never knew about intruders these days.

The other bout of killing he enjoyed was fishing for salmon in the river. Nick and Ben were not interested in fishing. In the first week they were here Paul had tried to teach them to cast but they had neither enthusiasm or skill.

'Why don't you use a net, Paul?'

'Oh Christ, rain again.'

'Can't even go shooting.'

'Nothing to shoot but dying rabbits.'

The last thing he wanted was to continue entertaining these two young monsters. Nick and Ben loathed being in this house as much as he loathed having them. They hated him for wearing a bulky tweed jacket patched with leather and for the tufts of cotton wool on his lugubrious face where his razor had nipped his skin.

Why had Ben been included on this visit? Ben was Nick's friend, that's why. Why had Mummy phoned and asked if they could stay at Mountsilver for a couple of weeks. By themselves, not with her?

It was only after the boys had been at Mountsilver for ten days that he got around to asking Nick, 'Why did Diana send you over here?'

'She wanted to get rid of me.'

'Oh?'

'She wanted to be alone with Dad. She's trying to shore up her marriage.'

'Oh?' Nice to have a bit of good news.

'Dad's found another bit of skirt.'

'Skirt?'

'Emma's younger than he is. A lot younger.'

'Sad for you,' Paul said with satisfaction.

'Emma isn't a bad sort. Poor old Mum's past her prime. Do you know she's ten years older than Dad is?'

'Nine,' Paul corrected. 'And Ben, why did you want to come over here?'

'Keep Nick company.'

Nick said, 'He saw a picture of Mountsilver. Mummy has this big photo in our drawing room to impress people with all those pillars and windows.'

'I've never been to Ireland before,' Ben said. 'And never again if I can help it.'

'You thought it would be shamrocks and leprechauns. You're like all English people, don't know a thing about Ireland.'

'You don't know anything about it either.'

'At least I have Irish parents. You were taken in by looking at pictures of the bloody portico.'

'I thought it might be interesting.'

'You're a snob. Just as much of a snob as Mum.'

No doubt Nick had told him he would inherit the place when Paul died. No doubt he was now saying, 'Who would want a house like this?'

Ben grumbled more than Nick about uncomfortable beds, lumpy custard and the lack of hot water. Bowls and buckets on the stairs and in the corridors catching rain water had ceased to be a joke.

'Big house cliché.'

'It's all cliché. Anglo-Irish squalor. Dogs mess and draughts.'

'The lavatory makes you fear the worst.'

You'd think with all that rain there would be more water in the tanks, but when either of them drew a bath he was lucky to get a rusty brown trickle.

Both Ben and Nick's voices were public school Cockney – they attended one of the very best public schools. How had Mummy and Fireball paid for Nick?

'Dad isn't short. Good old inheritance for Julian. His great aunt.'

'The boys are glad to leave,' Mummy told him over the phone.

'I'm sure.'

'Why did you send them over?' He wanted her version.

'I needed a little time alone with Julian.'

'Nick told me.'

'It's no good. He's going off with a little tart.'

'That's terrible,' Paul said gleefully.

'We've gone our separate ways as the newspapers say.'

'I'm sorry.'

'There's no such thing as an amiable divorce. That's an oxymoron.'

'I'm sorry.'

'In some ways it is a relief. It gets harder the older you are to keep up with someone who is a bit younger.'

'I'm sorry.'

'Stop saying that for God's sake. One had to keep trying so hard. Face cream, lashings of it, the sort that promises eternal youth. But you can't stop the face getting leathery. The wrinkles begin to show.'

'Won't he have to give up his job?'

'He's always hated teaching.'

There was another pause which must have cost a shilling. Paul said 'You know, you can always come back here.'

'I'm used to England.'

'I would even put up with Nick.'

'I don't think so, darling.'

When that rates bill arrived at the same time as the yearly demand for insurance Paul panicked. Who to consult? Naturally he had visited the family solicitor, genial Brian White in his dingy office in Leeson Street. For thirty years Brian had dealt with Daddy's affairs; he was a family friend. Never have a solicitor as a family friend – or as a friend at all.

Mummy's Uncle Charles had gone further with a clause in his will that disinherited any of his daughters who married a solicitor (or a Catholic).

'Nice to see you Paul. How's the little residence?' All pleasant chat and jokes; Brian had joked the last time Paul saw him when he was sorting out his father's will and together they had pondered the considerable amount of money Daddy bequeathed to Mummy.

The huge black box marked BLAKE-WILLOUGHBY in white letters was opened up and Brian shuffled through a pile of documents before writing down ideas on a half piece of white paper with a scratchy biro.

There was no need to sell anything at all. Paul could get rid of the twenty acre river field that abutted Dr Schmidt's estate – Dr Schmidt was sure to snap it up, and the asking price would not only cover bills and debts, but leave money over. Paul could still fish on the west side of the river since fishing rights would be shared between himself and the Hun.

Thanks Brian, I leave everything in your hands.

They did not even have to approach an estate agent as Dr Schmidt was delighted to make a generous offer. Things moved slowly. Signatures were exchanged, a deposit was put down, time passed and Dr Schmidt paid up, letting Paul know immediately that the river field was his under a caretaker's agreement. In a week Paul could see how the good doctor was fencing it off, even along the banks on his side; an army of men hammered in barbed wire between high concrete posts in the shape of hockey sticks. Then Dr Schmidt filled the field with deer, being determined to introduce the Irish to venison.

Paul went down and inspected the deer regularly from his side of the river. The does herded in the field took against the weakest of their number and bullied her, biting her, lashing at her. Her fur was staring and soon she had one eye. Worse than hen pecking.

The does gave birth, and still Brian had not sent Paul Dr Schmidt's money. Paul rang his office timidly from time to time, knowing that each call would cost him thirty pounds on the final legal bill. A question about rights of way, the fishing rights had to be sorted out, a little problem with the deeds, nothing to be concerned about . . .

'But the sale has gone through. He's got his deer in the field.'

'Don't worry Paul, all will be sorted out in a week or two.'

Two months later Paul sold off some Guinness shares to pay the rates and waited. He made another call. Mr White is not here at present. He will phone you back. Another call. At the fourth call the secretary put him through at last and he heard the cheery voice. Hello Paul, how's things? What's happening Brian? A slight hitch in the registration process but the cheque will be with you in a week.

When he went into Dublin again, back to the frowsy office in Leeson Street, Brian was not there, only his secretary who glared at him through her thick glasses and advised patience.

'Mr White is not the sort of gentleman to let down his clients.'

Widows and orphans wept during radio interviews as details of Brian White's dishonesty and the depths of his embezzlement emerged. At least he had the decency to shoot himself, but that was no real consolation.

Mummy had been unsympathetic when Paul rang and told her. 'I could have told you he was crooked. Daddy always insisted he was a good friend. But if he swallowed a nail he would shit a corkscrew.'

Dr Schmidt legally owned the river field since Brian had seen the purchase was completed so that he could add Paul's thousands to the millions he had squandered. The good doctor put a stag called Heinrich in among his does who stank and oozed sex. Smelling him across the river, Paul envied him. Dr Schmidt used pieces of antler for buttons he wore with his lederhosen.

What to do about the next rates bill?

The problem was solved when a man in a Volvo estate car trundled up the drive. He wore a bright yellow check jacket. He took a card out of his pocket on which was printed 'Brendan O'Byrne. Fine art consultant.'

'As I happened to be in the neighbourhood, I thought I might give you a call.'

In the hall Mr O'Byrne said, 'What a wonderful collection you have here, Sir.' He peered at a red-faced judge in wig and gown. 'A pity that isn't a woman.'

In the library he was attracted to the tiger skin on the floor, the head of which had lost a glass eye.

'You don't often seem them in such good condition,' Mr O'Byrne lied, and seemed impressed when Paul told him it was a man eater. From his inner pocket he took out a roll of money and peeled off two fifties. 'I will throw in another tenner for luck.'

He looked around the breakfast room and caught sight of the table with Johnny Murphy's initials.

'Ah, what a pity.' He picked it up and turned it over. He examined the dark mahogany, the bow legs, and the grotesque mask. 'Not bad quality and you have to admire the workmanship. Nineteenth century copy. But because I like it I'll give you two hundred quid.' Between that and the price Mr O'Byrne offered for the judge the rates were paid for another year. Paul was not to know that the old judge had been painted by Joshua Reynolds.

CHAPTER TWENTY-TWO

Paul lived alone, cooking for himself, managing quite well considering, disliking visitors. Perhaps he carried his shotgun too casually when he went outside and he learned from Dempsey that he had a reputation for aiming it at intruders.

'They'll call the guards in, Mr Paul.'

Dempsey was the only man left on the estate and he and Paul did not get on.

'Who does the gobshite think he is, giving me orders?' he would ask rhetorically at Toss Doyle's, just as he used to when the Major was alive. Because he lived in the upper yard house free of rent did not mean that he was paid enough. When Paul made suggestions – 'Oh Dempsey would you mind . . .' – he would tell him, 'That's not a good idea.' Dempsey's favourite task was cleaning up rubbish which he put into hedges – all the way around the estate tins and empty bottles gleamed.

It wasn't as if Paul really intended to shoot anyone. When Joe Roche's son, visiting from America, drove up asking to see the gate lodge where his father had grown up, he put away the shotgun immediately and went down the avenue with him to inspect the little ruin.

'Gee. You mean to tell me seven people lived in that?'

He waved the gun at Miss Collins when she drove up one spring afternoon to give him advice about his hen enterprise which he had kept all these years since Daddy died.

She was unafraid. 'It's only me.'

It took time to recognise her. Cheese. Mountsilver cheese. 'Come in, Miss Collins.'

'Call me Moira.'

He gave her a mug of tea in the study where he had been wrestling with demands and ultimatums where they reminisced about his father and Mountsilver cheese. She had given up cheese making for chicken sexing.

'You have to look very closely.'

He remembered that she had once wanted to be a nun.

He took her around the grounds. All his ideas of tillage farming had never come to fruition. He showed her the pigs with mud up to their bellies, the broken panes of the greenhouses, the unhappy hens still pecking on the old tennis court, the addled eggs . . .

'Things can be sorted out,' she told him. She drove away in her Morris Minor which had a thin stiletto image of Our Lady on the dashboard. The next day she returned.

They dealt with the poultry first. When she had done the job on Paul's latest batch of chicks she suggested hanging dead rats on wires over the hen run so that within three weeks in summer healthy protein-filled maggots would fall down on the hens. Paul spent damp summer evenings shooting rodents.

She helped him empty some of the buckets catching drips from the roof. 'It's all a bit run down,' he told her.

'I'm sure it can all be dealt with,' Moira said. He began to court her.

'One way of solving your household problems,' was Mummy's comment when he rang and told her he was engaged. 'I'm pleased. I've worried in case you were a pansy.'

Mummy was still in Somerset where she ran her interior decorating business. Wasn't it vulgar to call it Lady Diana? Oh, no, darling, it's the sort of thing the English love. She had not been in Ireland for years, and although he missed her, he was thankful. Every few months they exchanged news – Julian living with his ghastly Emma in Maida Vale, Nick running his own firm.

Paul and Moira were married by Father McCabe in Mountsilver

church. He dutifully invited his mother.

'No thanks, darling. I hate weddings. I prefer funerals.'

They had a reception and meal of cold chicken and ham in the Macnamara's Hotel, since Moira quite rightly did not consider the house to be in the best state for a celebration. For a quiet wedding there seemed to be a good many members of her family. Father Hogan was present, so was Aunt Delia, both very old.

The house was taken care of and the animals fed by Dempsey while they went to England. They stayed for a night in Somerset so that Moira could meet Mummy and be shown her garden which contained a white garden, a nuttery and a lot of box hedging.

'How delightful your mother is!'

Paul did not tell her how Mummy had winked at him when Moira was not looking. But she gave them five hundred pounds.

Back at Mountsilver he had thought hard about the big bedroom which his mother had used, but in the end decided against it. Instead, he and Moira slept in Waterloo and with Dempsey's help they dragged the four poster down the passage and across the hall to its new position. Dempsey told everyone at Toss Doyle's about the new arrangements.

All winter Paul and Moira snuggled close together under an electric blanket which only covered the middle of the bed. They lay on the Odearest mattress Maura had bought, the name giving them opportunities for gentle love banter. Their love life was restrained and they never wandered off the missionary position.

'I never slept better.'

'Another cup of tea, dearest?' Moira asked.

He yawned, although the time was well after nine. In the kitchen, warmed by the Aga, everything was neat and clean. The black and white linoleum and the formica table which his father had installed all those years ago shone. The disinfectant that had been wiped over most things smelt of roses, but combined with the pleasant odour of beef stew. He knew there was freshly made sponge cake in the large tin covered with pictures of wild flowers. An image of Our Lady stood on the window sill between two pots of scarlet geraniums. Outside Moira had set up a table in the shape of a little house to which flocked a good many small birds for the crumbs she laid out.

Wooster lay at his feet.

'When Wooster passes away, dearest, we won't replace him.' She was allergic to dogs.

Prickles, eighteen years old and blind in one eye, was the only cat. Although Moira had reduced the feline population by drowning kittens, no mouse dared show its ugly face.

'Here you are, dearest.' She served up eggs and bacon on mats which were decorated with pictures of vintage cars and ladies in Edwardian clothes. Paper napkins lay beside them. The Ironstone plates and dishes had been put away, since the patterns on them tended to fade in the new washing up machine, and now they used a set she had bought with the aid of green stamps.

There were a few drawbacks to his happiness like the fact that she wouldn't let him drink whiskey.

'Dear heart, you don't want to go the way of your father.'

This morning she had on her pink dressing gown and her hair was in curlers. She would put on her slacks in due course and then go and deal with the hens, whose eggs were bringing in a profit at last. Cheeping fluffy chicks had reappeared in Paul's life; they grew into contented hens running around the tennis court and laying again properly. She would give Dempsey orders about the pigs and the vegetables in the walled garden, which were also selling well. Happy pigs bounded their way joyfully to the slaughterhouse; she arranged for their meat to go to good restaurants. She would also contact the butcher about the lambs. She would see the milk from the Friesians was taken down to the co-op and do the paperwork on the quota. Under her direction apple trees were pruned, sprayed and cropped in a brisk sequence that Daddy would have envied. A new lad called Jim was hired to help with the potatoes and vegetables in the walled garden. Most of the land was set. Others did the ploughing, the sowing and the harvesting and Paul got the money.

He didn't have much to do. He might take the gun and go after rabbits which had recovered from the first terrible plague and were making their way back. He might go fishing.

He had an idea of recreating the garden that was here once before his ancestor got taken in by some follower of Capability Brown. There were old plans in the library.

He did not mind looking at bills, which seemed more manageable these days since Moira helped to sort them out. She had changed the study's appearance quite a bit. The furniture there was more modern than in the past after she had banished a lot of the old pieces to the barrack room and the attics where there was plenty of room for storage.

What estate and family papers remained took up little space. Paul's great grandfather had destroyed a good many, telling his family they needed no recollections of the past so long as they knew they were descended from honest men.

The new sofa, covered with a pattern of zebra stripes, and the easy chairs were all a lot more comfortable than the armchairs the family had used in the past. On the chimney piece were two sets of Lladró figures in pale blue and grey and a small bronze bust of John F. Kennedy. In here Moira dispensed with pictures altogether apart from a print of an oriental lady with a blue face. On the bookcase was a vase of lifelike artificial flowers. The television was very large and the aerial that made its way out of the window up to a chimney high above the diocletian window brought them English programmes in vivid colour. In the evenings they sat drinking cocoa and following the doings on *Coronation Street*.

'You're like Oblomov.' his mother said when he next phoned her and talked of how good life was.

'Who?'

'Russian. In a novel. Lounges about doing nothing. Spoilt by his housekeeper.'

'I don't lounge about. She's no housekeeper, she's my wife.'

'The phone bill is terrible,' Moira complained. 'Perhaps, dearest, in future you should let your mother do the ringing from her end.' But he knew that if he tried that he would never hear from Mummy at all.

Never mind Mummy when things were going well for him. Happiness had been a long time coming.

He ate well these days, especially the sweet things that Moira excelled in preparing, favourites he had liked when he was a boy. The rolling pin and the electric whisk were her slaves. The flour and the butter were humbled by the muscles in her arms, the egg whites and whipped cream were like a winter's day. Her pastry crisp and perfect, her apple pie to die for. Add jam, her home-made raspberry, strawberry, plum. Queen of puddings. Sponge. shortbread. One cake after another.

The rest of the food was good as well. Today the odour of boeuf bourguignon drifted out of the kitchen many yards across the main hall to where he was sitting.

He had stopped biting his nails.

Life is just a bowl of cherries . . .

He had never been so happy in his life.

His cup had run over after residential domestic property rates were abolished.

On Sundays they drove to mass together and sat up near the front of the church as Daddy had always done, the big people from Mountsilver being superior to the rest of the congregation. Paul grumbled about Vatican Two and murmured about going to a Tridentine mass, but Moira made him keep quiet. In February she took him to Galway for the Redemptorist novena. They climbed Croagh Patrick on Garland Sunday and spent a weekend on Lough Derg in their bare feet. While Moira dutifully fasted, Paul cheated by eating a bar of chocolate in the lavatory. When the new Polish Pope came to Ireland Paul and Moira were in Phoenix Park with a million others to greet him.

Moira soon had the measure of Dempsey, giving him a good shouting if need be. It took Dempsey a month to pull the bottles and tins out of the hedges and he did more muttering at Toss Doyle's. You don't want to take notice of that ould one, the wrong side of fifty. The Major had the halo, the son was useless, the place was going to the dogs, he'd leave and work for the ould Hun next door.

Paul produced the card that Mr O'Byrne had left. Fine art consultant.

'What about selling some more of the old stuff?' He told her about the tiger skin and the old judge.

'Oh, no dearest, you must not sell things that belong to the family.'

'What do you suggest?'

'We could try the Georgian Association.'

'What good would they do?'

'We might get a grant.'

He knew all about the Georgian Association, a group dedicated to the survival and restoration of mouldering old houses in a country where people who liked ramshackle eighteenth century architecture were in a minority. Few wanted the survival of gaunt discomfort, welcoming the coming of the bungalow. At heart Paul felt the same.

The Association had an uphill struggle persuading the indifferent that there was merit in trying to preserve houses like Mountsilver. Its nosy people wrote to him regularly checking to see the glorious old place was intact.

Its president drove up one day and asked if he could have a look round. Paul recognised the curly hair at once. 'Hello Poodle.' Poodle had been at St George's for a very short time. He hadn't stayed longer than a term before his parents realised the deficiencies of Mr Good's establishment and packed him off to Eton. In due course Poodle had returned to the family home in Ireland, which was definitely not tumbling into ruin. Paul got regular news of him from the *Old St Georgian* and *The Irish Times* – the lavish hospitality, the film star friends, the rock star friends, the sumptuous furnishings of his beautiful house, the Impressionist pictures.

More importantly *The Irish Times* reported on the activities of the Association, with accounts of the houses that had been saved from the jaws of bulldozers. You had to take your hat off to Poodle. After his mournful letters appeared in *The Irish Times* stating that somewhere or other some gorgeous place was falling down, there was a better than even chance that it would be saved.

Paul had let him look around the house, although the place was not looking its best. He followed him half listening . . . splendid fanlight, rusticated columns – Italian Baroque of course – something wrong with that roof, ooh – wonderful stucco-work, possibly Franchini, not on the scale of the work at Kilshannig, the putti are similar – damp – the balance of those pillars should be adjusted – marvellous detail – magnificent saloon, pity you had to ruin the ballroom – my goodness, Ducart at his best – Neo-Palladian influences – blocked gutter – pity the pavilion wings were knocked down, dry rot up there, Paul, you should have that dealt with, there's a chimney piece very like that in Florence Court, fine flying staircase, more dry rot . . .

After the tour Paul entertained him with a mug of Nescafé and they talked about St George's. One term had left Poodle with a range of memories; he remembered very clearly the conflict of faith shared by Paul and Beamish. When he departed, leaving the feeling that a thing of beauty was not a joy forever, Paul heard no more.

Moira and Paul listened to leaks falling into buckets, as regular in his life as the ticking of clocks.

'The Association might give us a grant.'

He did not know how to proceed and she took the matter in hand, dictating the letter he wrote to Poodle whose reply showed some interest. There was a hint that they could arrange some sort of grant from the government, if the house merited repair or restoration. The letter also contained a request – could a small group of members of the Georgian Association come and visit Mountsilver?

He clutched his head in despair.

'I'll deal with it,' Moira said.

Forty people, no more, and only for tea.

She dug out the tea cups that were thrust into the cupboards in the back pantry among the empty Gentlemen's Relish pots which Daddy had collected over the years, and crystallised jam, labelled with dates that went back to the nineteen thirties. Several cups had been broken and stuck together with Seccotine, but more than enough remained – tennis parties at Mountsilver used to consist of very many people.

He left everything to her, cleaning up, arranging, producing cake and sandwiches and tea with a touch of Earl Grey made in large aluminium teapots. Together with Poodle, the members of the Association arrived in a bus and Wooster barked his heart out. They were nearly all Protestants – he could tell a Protestant a mile off. Some Paul recognised as old friends of his father. Some English people. Many old Americans, much more colourful, with their cameras, the men in their white peaked hats and pastel tweed jackets, the white haired women with their sleek coiffures, couturier clothes and handmade shoes. They were very rich; Paul knew that the Association milked Americans for funds.

'Do you keep sheep?' asked an old lady craning her neck upwards and aiming her camera at a nice piece of plaster work. Musical instruments; two hundred years ago members of his family had not been tone deaf. Gods, goddesses, cherubs.

'Some.'

'I have a small herd of Cheviots grazing in my front garden. I have them laundered every day.'

Click, click went the cameras. 'Davis Ducart . . .' The Americans had a detailed knowledge of the house and its architect which Paul lacked. Their enthusiasm for eighteenth century Irish architecture had led them to be invited to join the Georgian Association and gave them the privilege of donating large sums of money towards shoring up houses like this. Davis Ducart – the sound of his name was like a whisper. He wished the damn fellow had stayed in Sardinia instead of covering Ireland with unmanageable buildings.

They drank their tea, ate Moira's delicious sandwiches and little cakes and debated among themselves whether the portrait over the fireplace and eighteenth century could be by Gilbert Stuart, who was considered an honourable American. They admired the parrot.

'Isn't that just darling?' Pity the bird shouted fuck.

Poodle said, 'Pity you had to get rid of so much of the furniture.'

'It hasn't been got rid of. It's up in the attic. We've found the modern stuff is more comfortable.'

Poodle must have noticed the religious statues that Moira had scattered around liberally. He was too polite to comment, but Paul read his thoughts. 'I see the nuns got you in the end.'

But on the whole the day was successful and in due course the Association arranged for a grant for the roof. A small grant. A very small grant.

'No need to put away the buckets.'

'It's a beginning.'

'Poodle is filthy rich. His wife flies to Paris regularly to get her hair done.'

'Of course he doesn't pay for repairs to houses himself. That's what the Americans are for.' Moira's voice was brisk and full of enterprise. 'We'll arrange more visits like that in exchange for more grants. We'll make them regular.'

But Poodle told them, frankly, Mountsilver was not smart enough. He called in from time to time with a photographer to take pictures of the plaster work which illustrated the book he was writing about superb Irish houses.

CHAPTER TWENTY-THREE

On each anniversary of their marriage they celebrated. This sort of thing was new to Paul; because their wedding had been so unpopular his parents had never indulged in anniversaries. Every year Paul and Moira exchanged gifts and went into Dublin for dinner in a restaurant – not the Dolphin – that had gone – and a visit to the cinema. He was reminded of the evenings with Mummy before the start of school term.

Evenings were spent watching television while Moira knitted patchwork blankets in aid of St Vincent de Paul. She persuaded him to give up smoking. No rowdy parties, just Christmas lunch cooked by Moira and served out to some of her Collins relations and old Father McCabe. No crackers or paper hats, and only a small artificial Christmas tree put up in a corner of the sitting room.

The farm made a small profit and what dividends remained helped to keep the wolf from the door. Thank God he had never been tempted to become a member of Lloyds like several of his father's old friends who had suffered and had to sell up. As Moira said, 'You don't get something for nothing.'

One proposal for making money that they considered and discarded was to hire the house out for weddings. Another was to link Mountsilver to a group of big houses joined to promote high-class bed and breakfasts. Americans again. Attracting rich Americans, bless them, with romantic dispositions offered lucrative possibilities. The idea was to recall and imitate the past, provide old-fashioned sleeping accommodation combined with breakfasts in the fire-lit dining room offering kippers and kedgeree and other Edwardian delights under domed silver plate platters. In the evening there would be formal dinners, with Paul dressed in a velvet dinner jacket moving among the guests, romantic rich Americans, bless them again, while Moira served up a four course meal with good wine and brandy afterwards. They abandoned the scheme after they had done their sums. The drive would have to be tarmacked, new beds would have to be bought and Moira would have to do an expensive cooking course at Ballymaloe. The old furniture would have to be brought down from the attic and people would have to be hired to help with the serving.

Although Paul mourned Father Hogan's death as someone he had known all his life, he felt guilty relief that his shortcomings were no longer under regular scrutiny. They had masses said for him and also for Aunt Delia. Her convent was finding it increasingly difficult to recruit new nuns; Paul thought it was because these days they were forced to wear civilian clothes. He saw Aunt Delia shortly before she died, diminished in her grey dress and cardigan, like a swan plucked of feathers.

The Countess died. 'She'll have quite a spell in purgatory,' Moira considered.

Mountsilver had its first burglary last year, lads from the village, everyone thought. Nothing much had been taken, since Moira heard them from the bedroom and came running down the stairs after them. He would have run as well, only he tripped on his dressing gown cord. The thieves left a mess as they opened drawers and scattered papers and one of his guns was stolen. You should keep a dog, the gardaí said. Nothing like a couple of dogs to put off intruders. But Wooster had died and had not been replaced.

They decided not to increase insurance premiums on the house since Moira considered health insurance to be a better idea.

'Why? I'm fit as a fiddle. So are you.'

'Sweetheart, one or other of us is bound to be ill one of these days. Something is waiting round the corner.'

'Cheer me up.'

'Look how that heart attack caused poor Father Hogan to pass away.

There's stroke, dementia, and the problem that old gentlemen are prone to. And of course, dearest, one must face up to the danger of worse things happening . . .'

He knew she meant cancer, but that was a word to be avoided like actors not talking about Macbeth. Even pronouncing the word was to encourage it. When she heard that someone had cancer, she gave great groans, insisting the victim was doomed. No point in telling her about advances in treatment.

'If you don't join fairly soon, dearest, you'll be too old. Sixty-five is the age limit.'

He took out health insurance for both of them. The cost was terrible, and the company refused to pay anything arising from Moira's asthma, but he knew she was right. Every morning, he was reminded of coming problems after she had gone to make breakfast, and he pulled back the bedclothes, put on his frayed dressing-gown, and went to the window to see if it was raining. He would stand for a few minutes looking out and flexing his muscles to alleviate twinges in his arms and legs. Arthritis and dry rot were the big house inheritance. Bending down to put on his socks took patience and stoicism.

He would put on a freshly ironed shirt. Moira loved ironing; she ironed the dish towels. By the time he had dressed, done up the laces of his well polished shoes, washed and shaved – an electric kettle provided hot water for early morning tea and shaving – he was stiff as a board. Downstairs he could expect porridge with cream from the Friesians and a boiled egg. Getting there was the problem. It didn't seem long since he was able to run up and down without loss of breath.

This Sunday morning they drove off to mass where Paul sat back and listened to the drone of Father Dunne, the priest who had succeeded Father McCabe. The first careless rapture of his entrance into the Church, had subsided, and his faith had dwindled during the years he had lived by himself; now it was now a matter of routine more or less based on his alliance with Moira.

He sat gazing at the sanctuary lamp and mused as to whether he could be considered a cradle Catholic like Moira, who used the term proudly.

Something half way. They stood up and shook hands with people to the right and left of them. When did that custom come in? It seemed very early Christian.

Lunch would be late, chicken, already prepared to go straight into the oven. Cabbage, which they ate regularly, came from the walled garden. Moira had been told that Poles, Russians and Chinese were less prone to get that disease whose name must not be mentioned because of their cabbage diet. Apple pie would follow, another demonstration of her wonderful light hand with pastry.

They were sitting in the kitchen, drinking their weekly glass of sherry, waiting for the chicken to cook, when they heard the throb of the doorbell. In the old days the sound of barking dogs would have alerted him, but after Wooster died there was a great silence. Paul peered through the window and there was Reilly's taxi and an old lady in a mink coat was climbing out followed by a small dog on a lead.

'Goodness, it's Mummy.'

Reilly ran through the rain piling luggage against the pillars beside the front door. When Mummy paid him he scowled at her tip. Some habits die hard.

'Why didn't you let us know you were coming?'

She was sipping sherry, making a face. 'Mouthwash.' They only kept Cyprus sherry.

'No time. I've sprung myself.'

'Sprung?'

'I couldn't stand that ghastly place a day longer.'

He remembered her complaints over the telephone, the long telephone calls which went down on his bill.

'It was a bit like running away from my finishing school.'

Mummy had been sent to a Swiss finishing school at the age of sixteen to learn poise, good manners and how to get a husband. She had run away in the first week and managed to rejoin her mother who was holidaying in Rome. She had not been able to remember the name of her hotel, only that it began with the letter D; it took the taxi four attempts before the

Hotel Doria was discovered.

'I didn't have to go back then, any more than I'm going back now to that horrible granny farm. '

'What's wrong with it?'

'I'm not going to go on living among dim whiskered old women without a word between them. Being given Marietta biscuits with their afternoon tea. Who is Marietta?'

'It's a town in Georgia where the biscuits were first made.' Moira said.

'Give me another glass' . . . 'All gaga in that place, every single one.'

'Surely not' said Moira.

'Loonies . . .'

Paul knew that it was too late to teach her to say things like physically challenged, intellectually disabled, psychologically impaired, visually impaired instead of cripple, idiot, mad, blind.

'. . . There's Anne making out lists and doing accounts for the shop she ran thirty years ago. And Elizabeth clutching her empty bag and sitting in the hall glowering at everyone going by. Anne and Elizabeth are the sanest. Were in Elizabeth's case; she was by far the nicest. And I suppose Joan is just about *compos mentis*, horrible woman. None of the rest are the full shilling and most can't talk at all. You say good morning and the response is a ghastly grin.'

'I thought you liked the thought of moving into an old people's home.'

'I changed my mind.'

He recalled how the idea had come up six months ago after the conversations about the pains in her arms and legs, her occasional black outs, and poor eyesight. And her birthday.

'I'm eighty-five. You'd be surprised how many people sent me birthday cards with EIGHTY-FIVE written on them in huge letters. You might as well have cards saying SHINGLES or HALITOSIS or BUBONIC PLAGUE. Or showing a man in a hood carrying a scythe.'

Little by little he had learned her plans . . . 'It's lonely since I have had to give up bridge.' 'I'm stone blind of course.' 'Sooner rather than later.' 'Nick thinks it's a good idea.'

Now he asked her 'Couldn't you go back to your own house?'

'It's been sold to pay for my stay in that hell hole. I could live in the Ritz for the price.'

'I suppose after a spell here we'll have to make arrangements for you to get a little flat somewhere – in Somerset, perhaps . . .'

'I can't live on my own. I can't see a thing.'

Moira said, 'I'll lay an extra serving.'

Mummy peered at the mat with the Edwardian lady sitting in a car before eating heartily. 'Best meal I've had in six months. They gave you garbage.' 'Apple pie – nice.' She dabbed her lips with the paper napkin and lit a cigarette while Moira served Nescafé. 'You couldn't smoke in that place, you had to go outside. I nearly died of pneumonia.'

The dog made a puddle. 'Could Diamond have some chicken as well? And a bowl of water?'

'Diamond! What a pretty name!'

'He was named after Isaac Newton's dog, the one which chewed up his *Principia*, after he ate Nick's passport. Of course I don't have a passport now; I'll never go abroad again.'

'Where was he when you were in the home?'

'Boarding with Mrs B.'

'Mrs B?'

'My char. I paid her a fortune and I'm sure she was beastly to him. He had to escape as well.'

Paul said, 'We'll get dog food tomorrow.'

'Don't you have a dog? How can you not have a dog? What happened to Wooster?'

'He died.'

'Wooster the third?'

'Fourth.'

'Why didn't you get a fifth?'

Moira said. 'Unfortunately I am allergic to dog's hair.'

Mummy grunted. 'I have measured out my life in small dogs.'

'. . . I left partly because of the row over my teeth. Bloody nurse wanted me to go to the dentist. I knew he'd yank everything out, they're loose.'

'You soon get accustomed to dentures,' Moira said.

'Too late to start.'

'Was that why . . . ?'

'Oh no, lots of other reasons. The old women are always dying and I hate that. The nurses and carers – carers, what a word! – they bring out the black clothes which they keep in their cupboards. They have special outfits for funerals and of course they get to wear them regularly.'

'. . . Just before I left Elizabeth died. Cancer.' Moira took an intake of breath. 'They whisked her off to hospital and that was the last one heard of her. Her last words were "I don't want to die on such a lovely day."'

'Oh, how sad!'

'There was this other woman, Joan Simpson, in the bed beside her. Tough as old boots. Joan was the one who came back.'

'At least that must have been nice.'

'No it wasn't. Joan's a pot of poison. When her daughter told me about Elizabeth dying I said to her "I wish it was your mother."'

After lunch Mummy toured the house, leaning on her ivory handled stick. 'Not ready for a zimmer frame yet. In that Chinese death house the loonies have them piled up by the front door.'

It was a long walk, going in an out of each big room, noting the changes.

'Of course I can't see . . .'

'We don't use these rooms too often.'

'It's not a good idea to keep them completely shuttered. Black as pitch. You ought to let the light in. Hello darling.' She greeted the parrot who said fuck.

Paul told her 'Nick taught it that – all those years ago.'

'It'll probably need another ten years to forget. If ever. It used to say nothing but Polly wants a biscuit.'

'It never says that now.'

'Myself I try not to say fuck or bugger except on the telephone.' She went up and down the house, '. . . You seem to have a good cleaning woman' . . . 'I can't see much. Lead me across the hall to the breakfast room, will you Paul? And will you put Diamond out or he'll do another pee?'

In the breakfast room Mummy asked, 'Where are all the things that were in here? '

'We moved it upstairs to the attics. Don't you think Moira's made things a lot more comfortable.'

'I'll sit down for a bit.' She consulted her talking watch which said in an American accent THE TIME IS FIFTEEN MINUTES PAST THREE.

Paul lit the fire. 'We'll make up a bed for you while you rest. Would you like the television on?'

'No good – I can't see a thing.'

'Where would you like to sleep?'

'In my room.'

Paul and Moira had to lift her up the stairs between them.

Diamond made the biggest immediate change. Paul hadn't realised how much he had missed having a dog in the house. He followed behind him, mopping up puddles before Moira caught sight of them.

Nick came to see his mother and stayed for a week.

'You should do something about that mouldy lion on the gatepost. No head, no paw. And nothing on the other side.'

Paul hadn't clapped eyes on his half brother for more than twenty years. He was middle aged now.

'Nick's made pots of money, haven't you darling?'

He was put into Inkerman. 'Same old raindrops keep falling on my head.'

'How is Fireball?' Paul asked.

'Who?'

'Your father.'

Nick and Mummy both laughed. Paul didn't confess that he had not thought up the name himself.

'Julian's fine after his bypass.'

Mummy said, 'I hope it keeps on hurting him.'

'He and Emma live in a flat in an Elizabethan manor house. They have nurses there to keep an eye on them. And a live-in doctor.'

Paul caught Moira's eye.

Nick treated them all to a lunch at The Courtyard which had opened up in the village and had an Egon Ronay recommendation. Paul ate mussels which were lukewarm and beef which was brown even though he had asked for underdone. Profiteroles, also lukewarm.

Mummy said 'Ghastly!'

Nick didn't hear, he was too busy telling Paul and Moira about the people he knew . . . the Dalai Lama has a good sense of humour, I sat beside Denis Thatcher last week, my good friend, the crown prince of Bhutan . . . Mother Teresa, wonderful old lady – Moira gave a gasp.

Mummy ordered a brandy.

'No ice.'

The waiter misunderstood her and brought along a glass with a couple of ice cubes which she sent back.

'I bet they'll just fish them out with their fingers.'

She went to sleep.

Nick was still talking – the Arab sheikhs all hate Britain which is on its last legs . . . no one in England writes good books now – only the Irish and Americans . . .

The waiter came and he pulled out his magic card to pay. 'Wake up Mum, we've got to get going.'

She couldn't be woken.

'Wake up!' he shook her, but she didn't stir.

Everyone in the restaurant turned around and looked and there was much calling for doctors and an ambulance. Moira felt her pulse and a nurse from one of the far tables came over and did the same. Mummy sat with her mouth open looking absolutely dead and stayed that way for ten minutes, while mobile phones rang and people's meals went cold.

Nick gave her a final desperate prod, and she woke up, and consulted her watch. THE TIME IS TWENTY MINUTES PAST THREE.

'I'm all right. This awful place is stuffy.'

'An ambulance is coming.'

'I don't need an ambulance. No, I don't need to go to hospital.'

The restaurant owner was mighty relieved when the party shuffled out; nothing puts guests off their dinner more than a fellow dead guest.

Back at Mountsilver Dr Hartigan was summoned.

'Where's Dr Waters?' asked Mummy.

'He died years ago.'

Dr Hartigan said, 'A pacemaker will put you to rights.'

Nick left without any suggestion that he might take Mummy with him back to England. She stayed on. Paul was ordered to bring down the old furniture that used to be in the breakfast room and Moira acquiesced.

'Where's the table with Johnny Murphy's initials?'

'I sold it.'

'How much did you get?'

'Two hundred pounds.'

'My God!'

'Better than being burgled.'

'Burglaries only happen when you don't have dogs.'

She ordered Paul and Dempsey to rearrange the breakfast room. Moira removed the Lladró figures from the chimney piece and the print of the blue-faced lady.

Mummy said, 'People would rather admit to being rapists than lacking taste or a sense of humour.'

At Christmas she gave Paul a Labrador puppy. She arranged her gift through the vet, not Mr O'Brien, he was long dead, but a woman vet called Jacqueline. The puppy sat in a basket under the Christmas tree with a red ribbon round its neck and a label saying WOOSTER.

'I chose a Labrador because I know you like them the way Daddy did.'

'I do.'

'I don't. Labradors are fine, gentle and strong and all that, but there's something smug about them – they are the Swiss of the canine world. But there's always been one here.'

They knew Mummy would be with them for some time to come when she ordered a stair lift.

'Nick will pay, he thinks it's a good idea. It will only cost a few weeks stay at that ghastly granny farm.'

A lorry arrived and two men took two days for the installation. The stair lift with its padded arm rests, did not look very suitable in its surroundings. Every evening, after they had watched television and her watch announced THE TIME IS A FIFTEEN MINUTES PAST TEN or TWENTY MINUTES TO ELEVEN as the case might be, Mummy made her way slowly across the hall to the foot of the bannisters. She climbed into the contour seat that swivelled and locked her in before she touched a button on the remote control. Shaking, rattling and rolling, directed by Mummy wagging the joy stick, the chair ascended the staircase like something in the Swiss Alps before wiggling around at the divide and making its way up the left fork. Diamond would be running upstairs along with it, barking every step of the way. Paul could never bear to look, even though the swivel invariably opened just when it should and deposited Mummy gently outside her bedroom.

CHAPTER TWENTY-FOUR

Every time Paul read an issue of the *Old St Georgian* he braced himself to read the Obit column. He was reminded of the engraving in the inner hall, *The Roll Call after Balaclava*. Old age, someone said, is the time when you are punished for things that are not your fault. Someone else said ask not for whom the bell tolls.

Notice of the reunion arranged by Squinty Stan, tempted him. Squinty Stan must be in his eighties.

'You should go, dearest,' Moira said. 'You've never kept up with your old school friends.'

'I keep in touch with Poodle.'

'Don't call him that.'

'A reunion? Fifty years on?' Mummy said. 'Grotesque.'

The foyer was crowded with old men in Old St George's ties, gathered around a table waiting to collect identification tags to pin to their jackets. Although he didn't think he knew a soul, he knew that couldn't be the case. For a start, he immediately recognised Stan who sat greeting each newcomer and giving him a tag.

'Glad you made it.' Yes, there was the squint, and the thin hungry face with remnants of wild hair falling over his ears. The face that had sneered at Paul's incapacity for understanding the simplest question had crumpled into deep wrinkles.

Stand up, Blake-Willoughby and explain how two trains coming from the same place and at different speeds reach point x at the same time.

In those days Stan's yellow teeth had been fanged like a wolf's. The teeth were straight now, and very white; like Paul, he must use Fixodent. Today there was nothing antagonising in the expression that looked up. He even smiled.

'How are you?' He must be saying that to every walking wounded here this evening.

'Wonderful to see so many old familiar faces,' Paul lied.

He pinned on the tag with PAUL BLAKE-WILLOUGHBY 1942 written in capital letters – Stan must have spent days doing them all – and then wandered off, looking for anyone else he knew, joining others at the bar which was crowded with old boys trying to renew ancient friendships. The idea was to partake in a get-together before the meal. Those who had kept in touch with one another over the decades huddled in groups talking loudly. The rest were furtively peering through bifocals at names on the tags.

'Ah Vaughan!' What a relief to find someone he knew. The red hair was grey, the freckles were still there. They chatted and a couple of minutes informed him that Vaughan had gone into accountancy, married a girl from Waterford and had two boys, now in their forties.

'They are both doing extraordinarily well.'

Paul gave a censored version of his own circumstances and they fell silent. No need to bring up Jeffers, chapel, Mr Good, religious problems, Mr Rowse. Vaughan had been a prefect under Sheridan. '*. . . betrayal of trust . . . sullied his role as prefect . . .*' No need to bring that up either.

'Is Sheridan still in Watford?'

'He's dead.'

Someone tapped him on the shoulder, and he turned, glancing hastily at the tag.

'It's BW, isn't it?'

'Darby!'

Good God! Darby had been his best friend for almost a year. During breaks they would steal off to smoke in the High Wood.

It's been a long time. All around them people were saying, or rather, wailing, the phrase.

'What have you been doing these days?' Paul had a moment of cognitive whatever and couldn't remember Darby's Christian name.

'I was in Fairbrothers. Stockbroker. Retired, now, of course.' The word retired echoed across the bar like a bell. 'And you? Still in that old house?'

'Yes. Doing a spot of farming.'

Time for a drink. He fumbled with his twenty pound note.

'Anything smaller, Sir?'

'Sorry.'

Typical of Darby not to take over and pay. He had always been a mean bastard. Paul remembered him stuffing himself with cake from his tuck box.

The barman suffered the note and handed over much needed whiskeys. In the crowd Paul recognised someone else, Dixon, from the north of Ireland, still tall and angular, with the mistaken appearance of a loveable old rogue. Dixon hadn't shaved well; pale rank hairs were stuck to his cheek and a couple of nicks on the chin didn't improve his looks. Paul wondered if he still jeered at Catholics. Would he know that Paul had become one? Please God he wouldn't start talking about the Troubles.

Yes he did, but from an original point of view, describing how he was making a fortune buying up property in Belfast which no one wanted at present because of the bombing.

'But our time will come as the shinners might say.' He still had that awful voice. Needless to say he supported Ian Paisley. He told Paul about his vintage cars worth a hundred thousand which he took out on vintage car parades. There must be almost as many of those in the north as there are Orange parades.

A puffy red face loomed on Paul's left who needed a bit of time to work out the features. 'Hello, Cunningham.' Cunningham was the junior who had inherited Paul's nanny, and Paul had always wanted to know if he had been beaten with the hair brush the way he had. Somehow now did not seem to be the time to find out.

He was getting into the swing of things, and by the time he had downed his whiskey, had identified and spoken to several people. Metcalf the Wog, whose black curls had become white like a sheep – hello Neil. Lestrange was in line for a hip operation, nice to see you Ian. Beamish

– Gosh, it's a long time. Beamish, the Protestant by choice, would have a better bush telegraph than Dixon, and was bound to know about Paul and his choice. But we don't have to talk about that. You retired? Still living in Cork? Paul wondered what had become of his sisters.

Moore gave an account of his triple bypass. You're looking well, Tim, Paul lied. After all these years they were on Christian name terms at last. Moore told him Crow Foster had died, poor old Crow who smelt of manure. And Thorne – he had been a junior.

You didn't want to talk about health if you could help it. Forget erectile problems or incontinence. If possible make no mention of prostate or strokes or cancer. Death's fetid breath was at all their backs, but worse than death was the hovering spirit of Dr Alois Alzheimer. Moore's hesitations reminded Paul of the doctor who had given his name to progressive oblivion. Everyone in the room must dread that possibility. A forgotten name, an appointment not kept, or any small episode of forgetfulness draws people towards the sort of terror they try and reproduce in horror films. The word you can't think of, and the longer time it takes to slip back into the memory.

Mild cognitive impairment happened to Bertie Wooster who must have been a hell of a lot younger than anyone here. '*One moment the mind a blank, the next the fount of memory spouting like nobody's business.*' Bertie forgot, and then had an episode of recall when he remembered the name of the fascist Roderick Spode's underwear firm. Eulalie. Did Wodehouse have any direct experience of the Eulalie Syndrome or did he just use Bertie's memory loss to forward the plot of *The Code of the Woosters*?

This was not the place or the time to be brooding. Paul had a word with Hamilton, shouting at him because Hamilton had become very deaf. Thank God for the name tags or he would never had recognised Brown who was wearing a black patch over his right eye. Doctor, solicitor, soldier, rich man, poor man.

No sign of Poodle who was far too grand to attend a function like this one – you could be sure there were no Georgian enthusiasts here. Poodle was probably sitting in his mansion entertaining a film star or a member of the royal family.

In the dining room the current headmaster stood up at the end of the long table that accommodated them all. Thirty-two people were present.

'I want to welcome you . . .'

He looked positively boyish, and if you thought about it, he was far the youngest of anyone here.

Stan stood up and they all stood up together while he muttered the long Latin grace. It made Paul, for one, shudder.

After they were seated and white napkins had been spread across laps the man with the luxuriant moustache who sat beside him on his left bellowed in his ear. He had difficulty in placing him until he said his name was Joly. Of course! Vamp Joly! Paul remembered very clearly the charming youngster with the sparkling blue eyes, a bit clouded now. Almost everyone in the school had been in love with this particular bijou. Mercer Mi, the previous beauty, had grown tall and spotty by the time Vamp Joly entered Junior House. Paul, himself, had felt a frisson. From the moment he arrived messages would be passed from the senior boys and even from the prefects down to the junior table. A flirtatious smile and a secret glance would confirm that a note had safely arrived and many boys' hearts were broken. Poor Sheridan had been an admirer.

'Pretty good turnout considering,' Joly said over the soup. Considering how many were dead. It took time for Paul to find out what had happened to the little bijou after he departed from St George's leaving a trail of broken hearts. He had gone to Sandhurst. A good regiment. Korea, promotion. Suez, promotion. North of Ireland, promotion. Desk job, promotion, retirement. Final rank brigadier. Same wife all along, the Colonel's lady, Ha! A son who had gone into his regiment. Voluntary work for the Legion.

'And you?' Joly asked, wiping soup off his moustache.

'I do a spot of farming.'

'Are yes, you've got that big old place.'

The brigadier showed no further interest and turned to his left to talk to Hamilton, one of those who had been most assiduous in courting Vamp when he was a little junior.

Paul talked to the very old man on his right who introduced himself as Jack Turner. That rang no bells. Another who was deaf as a post and Paul let him do the talking. Apparently Turner had been at St George's in the late 1930s before his own time there. Interesting chap – turned out he had been in the RAF during the war, Lancasters, and afterwards worked as a pilot with BOAC – had actually flown Comets before they packed up – bad business.

He tried to work out the old pilot's age, reflecting on the great divide the war made; most of the people here, however old they might be, had been too young to fight. You had only to do your sums. This old boy must be pushing ninety and chances were he wouldn't attend another of these bizarre reunions, that is, if Stan was going to organise any more. Turner confirmed the thought by muttering 'Health not too good' and calling the waiter to bring him a glass of water to get down a couple of pills. If he failed to do so would he fall dead?

Opposite, across the table Paul met eyes set in heavily jowled features. Henderson. My God, who would have thought it? But yes, he could see, looking at that fat face, that inside was a thin school boy trying to get out. Henderson seemed to be the only one present who had dyed his hair, which was a dull marmalade. Paul remembered the endless beatings he had endured from Mr Good; he would surely have been expelled if his father had not been a governor of the Provincial Bank of Ireland.

He had never liked Henderson and a lot of others hadn't liked him either. Of course that did not stop him from doing well in life. He had become a surgeon; the *Old St Georgian* gave periodic fulsome descriptions of his success. One of those penis-enhancing professions like conducting orchestras, directing films or being a high priest. Aztec priests combined both occupations, stretching their sacrificial victims over a narrow stone and carve out their beating hearts before butchering the bodies so they could be eaten ritually. Twenty thousand on a good day.

Perhaps becoming a surgeon followed the first step on the road to achievement when Henderson had stripped down Drip Fitzgibbon's trousers and lit his farts.

'Look at the blue flame,' he had called out to the circle of boys who surrounded the unfortunate victim. Another match struck, another fart lit. No one tried to put a stop to the torture, they all just giggled nervously,

Paul among them. Amazing those farts. What was also amazing now was that Drip was sitting beside Henderson laughing. They seemed the best of friends.

Soup was followed by what was billed as wild salmon.

'Bloody cheek, that's not wild,' complained Joly. 'I've fished enough rivers to know the real thing.'

Paul had as well, but he couldn't tell any difference in the taste. 'Better than lumpy porridge and horse meat,' he ventured. The brigadier barked a laugh and fell silent. Why was it the most vivid memories of school involved the dining room? – the squeak of chairs and shuffling of feet, the smell of burnt cabbage and the radiators behind which they threw rotten potatoes. Paul felt faint at the recollection. He remembered the smear of butter, intended to last a week. Rose hip jelly. Liver.

Now he was served with duck, which wasn't bad, although a challenge to his teeth. He finished his ration of wine and called for another half-bottle – must have something for the toasts that were bound to follow. The dessert was vanilla panna cotta, better than Murphy in the bath. Joly laughed, again.

Paul had another word with old Turner who assured him that the food served up before the war had been just as vile.

Time for speeches. Who's that fatso at the end of the table who was getting up and beginning to read from his notes? Pages of them. Drummond, Joly told him in a hoarse whisper and Paul could hardly believe it. Drummond had been another darling, always outrageous, fluttering his eyes like any young girl. Now his face was as lined as a drought-dried river bed. Another who went into law, and Paul knew, from reading the *Old St Georgian* and *The Irish Times*, had ended up as a judge. High court. From time to time the Irish government appointed the odd Protestant judge to show how liberal it was. You could imagine the sheepskin wig covering what was once fair hair.

Pompous jokes were intoned.

'I never could stand the brute,' Joly whispered surprisingly, his voice drowned by general laughter at one of Drummond's efforts which would not have made it into a Christmas cracker. Rivalry, of course – the flirts had always competed furiously. But time had passed, and Joly, having said his piece, was willing to give the devil his due, clapping with such enthusiasm that he spilt his wine.

Why can't the ass shut up? There was another round of clapping as Drummond recalled the occasion when St George's had beaten Holy Name. That had certainly not happened during Paul's time. Drummond dwelt on the exploits of Blennerhasset, now sadly no longer with us, and his wonderful try. His memories were sweet. St George's appeared to have been wonderful to him. Never trust anyone who liked their school. But Paul clapped with the rest.

'BW!' someone called out from three places to his left. Paul knew him at once, Arsehole Butler, the bullying prefect, several years older than he was; Arsehole had gone off to fight a couple of years before the war ended. Before that he had control over Paul's miserable junior existence. Clean these plates, make tea, make toast, clean my shoes, bend over. Junior boys were invariably given a vicious kick at the end of their labours. Feeling the old surge of loathing, Paul wished him a bad back, the remainder of his hair to fall off, lice in his beard and the compulsion to get up four times in the night to pee. But he returned the smile. Hello Butler! How are you keeping? Not too bad! Good to see you!

The current headmaster got up again and began a serious speech. He said nice things about the school in the past under the inspired headmastership of Samuel Good, about whom he knew nothing, of course, and hoped that this evening would bring back many pleasant memories. What a memorable occasion this is – thanks to Stanley Parsons so long associated with the school – applause – for organising this reunion. Perhaps he would organise another?

Laughter. Clapping. A few hoarse cheers. That's a grisly idea.

He dealt with the things that were happening under his aegis – the new computer room, the generosity of old boys like you who give so much back to the school (count me out, Paul thought) the number of entrants to university, the first girl to be prefect – how proud we must all be of St George's and its continued fine reputation. You will know the attributes that a St George's boy or girl carries through life – decency, self-respect, respect for others.

'We have the honour of the presence of one of our most distinguished old boys. I want you first of all to give a round of applause to Sir Wilfrid Jeffers, who has done so much for British industry, and who is now a senior advisor to the Conservative government.'

Remembering the last time he had seen Jeffers Minor racing off on his bicycle from Dolly Fossett's, Paul could not bring himself to clap.

The headmaster turned and indicated the old fellow to his right, another whom Paul had not noticed throughout the evening. 'How pleasant and remarkable it is to have two masters who taught many of you present this evening. You have already paid tribute to Stanley Parsons. Now I would like you to raise you glasses to Neil Erskine who happens to be in Ireland at this moment to receive an honorary degree from Trinity College.'

'What's he done to deserve that?' Paul asked Joly, who seemed to know everything.

'Fingers? He's pretty famous. Taught at Harrow or was it Charterhouse for some years, then started writing historical novels about Roman emperors, didn't you see any of the ones they made into films? Best thing on telly for a long time.'

Now Ireland was honouring her own, although Fingers was about as much Irish as Jeffers Minor. Or Francis Bacon, another honorary Irishman.

Paul stared at the skull-like head, marble maybe, yes, just like an ancient Roman. Unmistakable. Fingers must be at least ninety. The cottage in the mountains. The tea parties. The boy scouts. Fumbling. The great survivor. The wicked flourishing like the bay tree.

It was amazing how Paul was still prone to a surge of raw emotion at the sight of Fingers in the same way as he felt hatred for Arsehole.

Outside the club it was raining. In the foyer they were saying their goodbyes.

Stan said, 'Paul would you do us a great favour? See Mr Erskine into a taxi? Share it with him?'

Why Paul more than another? It occurred to him that people were avoiding Fingers.

He overcame his reluctance, since courtesy was another attribute of an old St Georgian. He made his way out beyond the the porch into the rain giving Fingers his arm as the bent figure went down the steps very deliberately, one at a time. Groups of Old Boys clutching umbrellas were slowly filtering into the street. A car splashed past and a few lights gleamed. It would be a wet night.

CHAPTER TWENTY-FIVE

Mummy could hear well enough with her aid stuck in her ear, pink, fleshy and shining with wax. In the evening after supper, they turned on the television.

'I can just see a few things. Dimly. Hardly anything.'

'...*Coronation Street*? All the loonies used to watch it.'

'...*Glenroe*? I can't see anything of course, but it sounds pretty dire.'

'. . . I quite like programmes about Hitler.'

'. . . That man's wearing a wig.'

'. . . Not another programme about wildebeest? . . . Now they're crossing the river. Come on crocodiles! Gnus! Lunch!'

They sat through repeats of episodes of *Brideshead Revisited.*

'Castle Howard? I stayed there the year I came out. Later on they had an awful fire, burnt a lot of the place down. Plenty of insurance. A fire like that is exactly what we need here.'

At the final episode, when Laurence Olivier crossed himself she gave a shudder. Definite proof that she could see some things.

After the television was switched off she tottered to the bottom of the stairs and settled herself in the chair lift.

'. . . I won't be with you for long. I am old and blind. I'll be dead very soon like Laurence Olivier.'

'Moira, would you mind sewing these onto my blouse. I can't see, of course.'

'Would you be a pet and have a go at washing my cashmere cardigan? Not in the washing machine.'

'I've a spot of ironing . . .' But Moira loved ironing and piles of neat warm clothes were assembled several times a week.

Paul and Moira could hardly remember the time when they had been on their own.

New dogs appeared. The fault lay with Jacqueline the vet, who conspired with Mummy and brought up one puppy at a time. Jacqueline was expensive. In the old days when Mummy used to summon Mr O'Brien to deal with sick animals there had been far less of all this injecting, dosing and inspection. If a dog got distemper or fleas or a rash of ticks it was sad, but too bad.

To be fair Mummy did pay many of Jacqueline's bills.

Paul was in a dilemma since he found he was ridiculously pleased to have dogs in the house again.

'. . . Dearest, you realise those dogs cost more in vet's fees than the pigs?'

'. . . Sweetheart, your mother does not seem to realise that I am allergic to animal fur.'

Mummy was gardening again. She took back a swathe of the walled garden and had Manzie and Paul replant it in much the same way she once had it. She didn't do any digging personally, but sat on a shooting stick directing Paul and Manzie as they fought with bishop's weed and nettles, and planted out viburnums, daphnes, lilac choisia, lemon verbena, swathes of wall flowers and roses.

'Things that smell nice . . . I can't see anything.'

'. . . Over there. A deeper hole. Put more muck into it.'

'. . . Careful, Manzie. You trample plants the way a goose tramples her goslings.'

Manzie was the old boy she hired to come up twice a week and help her, and, to give her her due, she paid him. Elsewhere in the walled garden Moira and Dempsey struggled with the vegetables.

'. . . Fragrant Cloud . . . Didn't Edward Heath have a yacht that name? I can just see, it's a vulgar sort of colour, but what a marvellous smell!'

The rambler Daddy had spared had spread all along the south wall of the walled garden.

'It has flourished because Blossom is buried beneath it.'

Along the avenue new daffodil and narcissus bulbs were planted. There were plenty of old ones, and the patch beside the lawn still spelled out *Gerald and Diana 1928*. Those daffodils that had gone blind – 'Hah!' said Mummy, 'like me!' – were dug up and divided by Manzie. She insisted on more tulips.

'Did you know tulips are examples of beauty without utility? They never had any medicinal role, and for some reason that's why they excited the Dutch.'

Bulbs were also grown indoors, in spite of Moira's protests, since she was allergic to the scents of most sweet smelling flowers. as well as dog's fur. Every evening throughout the winter Paul carried bowls of newly flowering hyacinths or narcissus out of the breakfast room into the hall before the three of them settled down to watch the evening's television. Other plants could stay. As spring approached the window sills became crowded with pelargoniums, cuttings and seedlings, sweet pea and tobacco plants. A hop was being trained to circulate. Mummy – or rather Paul at her instruction – fed the plants with liquid fertiliser like foie gras geese. Moira coughed and wheezed.

Moira, you are so good to me, never losing your temper.'

'Oh, I wouldn't say that, Diana.' It had taken two years for her to bring herself to call Mummy by her first name.

'Full of conscience, caring for others. Giving buckets of money to St Vincent de Paul.'

'We should all donate to charity.'

Mummy never donated a brass farthing to anything apart from buying the smallest sized poppy on Remembrance Sunday.

'You're not only good but you're nice, which is unusual since you are also a Catholic.'

'Diana, I will not have a word said against my religion.'

'I was only teasing.'

'You know I would die for my religion, Diana.'

'You terrify people because you make us realise how horrible the rest of us are.'

'Speak for yourself, Mummy.'

'Horrible or not, I won't be around for long. It's no fun being old.' Paul waited for what was coming next. 'I suppose there are a few advantages – no more curse, hot flushes over, the hairs on one's legs growing less thick. But one is so shaky.'

'. . . Remind me to ask Nick to get one of those things to wear round your neck which you press when you need help.'

She seemed to get most things she needed from Nick. Apart from paying Manzie and Jacqueline, she contributed nothing towards household expenses, except to make some dramatic gesture, like that installation of the stair lift. Occasionally Paul sneaked a ride on it; Moira never. Mummy also contributed an even bigger television set, a dishwasher, a new clothes washing machine and had a bidet installed in the bathroom beside her room. Nick paid.

Moira offered up her thoughts at confession after she and Paul had a couple of little quarrels *sotto voce.*

'Dearest, do you think it's possible Diana broke that statue of Our Lady on purpose?'

'Oh, no, darling, it's just that she's old and clumsy.'

'She shouldn't call the image of Our Lord on the Cross the grisly hallmark of Christianity.'

On Sundays when Paul and Moira drove off to mass Mummy stayed in bed. She got up when they returned, and dressed herself very slowly, sometimes shouting for Moira to come and assist. Then she came down when Moira had cooked, and the scent of the roast permeated up the great staircase. Time for gin and tonic. You'd think she might have descended beforehand to peel the potatoes.

'I can't see to peel. I'd cut my fingers.'

She never went to church herself, because the Protestant church in Mountsilver was in the hands of a woman.

She and Moira agreed about a few things. They disapproved of AIDS. They never sorted out AIDS, believing people caught it like flu.

Neither of them liked the idea of women priests.

'I can't stand clergy persons. They're all over England now. Ghastly woman used to come and see me regularly when I was in the home. Almost made me want to become a Catholic.'

They also disliked Quakers and Methodists for different reasons, although Moira was too good a person to voice her opinion which was something she took to confession.

Mummy said, 'Quakers are smug, so pleased with themselves about all their good works. Feeding people during the Famine was their high water mark. Poor old Methodists never had anything like the glamour of Quakers – you can hardly get excited about a religion whose best known member after John Wesley is J. Arthur Rank. Let's not talk about those scruffy Presbyterians.'

Moira said, 'You know, Diana, you would live longer if you went to church. I read that people who go to church at least once a week have a twenty-five per cent lower mortality rate than those who don't.'

'I don't want to live longer. I'm waiting on tip toe this side of the River Jordan. Any moment. Ah . . .'

'Are you in pain, Diana?'

'Not really. A little ache. You know yourself rheumatics are an automatic part of old age. On the Beaufort Scale of torture slight discomfort is number one.'

Every meal time she spread around a dozen pills on the table.

'The pebbled shore.'

They were not only for whatever was wrong with her, but different coloured pills full of antioxidants, vitamins and minerals, and shining ovals the colour of amber that contained beneficial oils and essential fatty acids. 'They might help in keeping me going a month or two longer.'

'You'll see us out,' Paul said grimly. His hair was white – at least he hadn't gone bald like Daddy – his teeth were gone, and he walked as if he had been wound up. His back went for weeks after obeying Mummy's directive as to the planting of an azalea.

Whenever a priest appeared on television in handcuffs because of the awful things he had done to small boys Mummy tried to hide her satisfaction as Moira grew sorrowful. Having suffered at the hands of

Fingers, Paul could never understand what the fuss was about. Sometimes he wondered whether it would be too late to reveal all and bring Fingers to court. But the wicked old rogue died full of years and honours, earning a long obituary in *The Irish Times* and the *Old St Georgian*.

The difficulty was that Paul liked having his mother in the house. She made him laugh. She might be tottering here and there, helped along by her ivory handled stick, but there was an energy about her presence which had not been there when darling Moira had sole responsibility for everything. Things were not dull any more. He liked listening to her humming the old songs. *He left me for a damsel dark, damsel dark . . .* even when the hum was followed by a moan – I'm a very old woman, and won't be with you much longer. He liked the dogs, he liked all the flowers and plants, he liked the gin and tonics she had reintroduced.

Dempsey also liked having Mummy back, and at Toss Doyle's had good things to say about the ould hoor.

Moira was the one who ran the farm, boiling potatoes for the chickens, finding tasks for Dempsey to do, seeing the cows were milked. She tried her hand at making cheese again.

'Uneatable,' was Mummy's verdict.

Paul thought back to the calm old days with Moira before his mother had arrived and tried to decide fairly which he preferred, then or now.

He never dared ask Moira her opinion in case he got the answer, either she goes or I go. Instead, Moira took Mummy's orders or criticisms or jeers calmly, never making a complaint. She took to going to mass more often – several times a week.

'I put in a little prayer for her soul.'

On two occasions a year apart, Mummy tried a spot of entertaining the way she used to long ago. Not a Christmas party, that would be too hard to arrange, but a lunch in midsummer when the house would not have to be heated.

Moira cooked fish pie, carefully removing any bones she could find, and laid the big table in the dining room – the mats with the vintage cars were forbidden. Half a dozen very old people turned up for lunch – no dinner parties, nothing in the evening, they lived thirty, forty miles away and none of them could see to drive in the dark. They were frail, and one of them was knocked down by Wooster.

'No harm done.'

Paul did not recognise them since the old friends who used to come to Mountsilver like the Countess, Trigger, Donald and Valerie were long dead. Where had Mummy found this lot? They were strangers except for Mary Rooke, who looked exactly the same so many years on.

'Oh Diana, marvellous fish!'

'Moira cooked it.'

Three out of the six present were deaf, and one was vague. They ate in silence, and Mummy said, to nervous laughter, 'I might as well be back at that bloody old people's hell hole.'

Paul and Moira sincerely hoped that was the end to lunch parties, but a year later Mummy insisted on another.

'This time you'll have to lock the dogs away.'

The same old folk minus the two who had died during the year were summoned; lunch was stewed chicken garnished with a mild curry sauce. After the meal the old folk were ushered into the drawing room for coffee. While they sat sipping, next door thieves broke in to the dining room and stole the table.

Burglary was nothing new at Mountsilver; thieves were taking things fairly regularly . . .

'Dearest, the dogs are useless. You'd think they would bark.'

The grandfather clock which spent the week slowly revealing a caricature of the moon had gone. The lady with the moustache in the drawing room wasn't much of a loss. The silver candlesticks, and the silver fox that stood on the dining room table at Christmas had gone and so had the tapestry of the Judgement of Paris in which the woven naked goddesses were a soft faded pink.

'Dearest, I do believe that is a good riddance.'

A shabby little chair with bandy legs in the drawing room went at the same time as the tapestry. Paul seemed to remember that Mr O'Byrne the fine art dealer who had bought Johnny Murphy's table had shown interest in that chair. He wondered if Mr O'Byrne had anything to do with the burglaries which had begun after his visit.

'Nonsense,' Mummy said. 'It's tinkers.'

'Travellers,' Moira corrected. She was always correcting Mummy about that. Mummy never cared for the travelling people since one of the Connors tried to sell her a horse with mange.

'They covered the mangy bits with boot polish. I happened to stroke the bloody creature . . .'

Now Moira said, 'I may say, Diana, there is absolutely no proof that travellers were responsible.'

'Of course it was tinkers. They've been to almost every big house in Ireland. They've made burglary into a cottage industry.'

'How do you know?'

'Philip told me.'

Philip, whoever he might be – where had Mummy met him? – was a tall thin old man wearing an old Etonian tie whose eyes had lower lids drawn right down showing tinges of red like a bloodhound. Throughout lunch he had been totally silent and Mummy, who was sitting beside him, had said: 'Pull yourself together.'

That was until the table disappeared. The excitement, ringing for the guard, letting the shrieking dogs out, and Paul and Moira running in vain down the avenue, had been extremely good for the company, and two of them quite lost their symptoms of dementia.

'Philip says the tinkers take all the stuff they steal down to their headquarters in the country. There are some antique dealers in Dublin who race down in their cars every weekend to look at what's new and take their pick. After that anything the dealers don't want is shipped to England. Goodbye, dining table.'

Once again a couple of plain clothes detectives drove up to look for fingerprints, dusting a few doors and windows. They were lost in admiration, marvelling at the brass neck of the thieves in lugging out the table, putting it into the van parked beneath the French windows and driving away when the house was full of people. It was a tale to add to their criminal exploits. All over Ireland thieves were robbing rich people or people like Paul and Moira who might give the impression of wealth; their doings made them comparable to Robin Hood and his merry men.

'Everyone knows who they are, don't they?' Mummy asked the guards.

'We may have our suspicions.'

'They are tinkers, aren't they?'

The detectives looked bland. No proof. No proof whatsoever.

Six months later they returned to Mountsilver; this time some pictures were stolen, including the huge Ramsay copies of King George and Queen Charlotte in the drawing room and King William at the Boyne. One of the detectives, a bull-like man with a Republican background obviously felt that anyone who kept pictures like that had no right to sympathy and deserved to lose them.

'King William?'

Although he had been familiar with the triumphant king all his life, Paul could not recall details of the painting.

'Can you remember, Sir, if the king was wearing armour?'

'Armour? I don't think so.'

'What about the horse?'

This he was sure about. 'It was rearing up. The battlefield was behind it. It was brown.'

'Brown?'

'Yes.'

'I thought King Billy rode a white horse.'

'Not at the Battle of the Boyne. The white horse came later.'

'Get alarms, get new locks on all the doors, keep the dogs barking outside,' they said before they departed. They weren't interested. They had too few resources and there was a drug problem in the village, and no one minded if people in big houses lost their possessions.

'Dearest, we must think about more insurance.'

Their premiums had increased remorselessly, and even so, the insurance company was getting restless. But although it grumbled, it did pay up, and King Billy covered the stupendous cost of the plumber's latest visit.

Three months later, when Paul was on a walk with the dogs down towards the bog field he discovered King William's picture hidden under a bush.

Whoever had thrust it in there had tried to cover it up but some of the branches had blown away. A part of the elaborate gilt frame shone in the sun, the king's face had been slashed and the eye of the rearing horse gouged out.

He didn't tell anyone about his discovery, least of all Moira. She was too honest and would have insisted on informing the insurance company and repaying it.

Why not burn it?

He did so the next morning, first filling the wheelbarrow with sticks. Mummy had not got up, while Moira had gone to mass and Dempsey was planting out young leeks.

He placed the equestrian portrait on the pile he made. 'God save the King,' he thought, splashing paraffin over the royal figure. Without the Battle of the Boyne the course of Irish history would have been different. He lit a match but the wind blew it out. He tried again and at first nothing happened. A small flickering light ebbed and wavered and then the sticks caught; he could feel the warm glow of the flames as he stepped back from the bier. How many other paintings of the victor of the Boyne had perished?

He watched the small blisters that broke out on the brown rump of the royal charger and dimpled its well-shaped leg. The crackle of sticks increased and soon the bier was covered in a pall of smoke.

He returned to the house and gave himself a gin and tonic even though it was before midday. Next morning he returned to clean up. The prancing horse was incinerated and most of the king, all but his head that lay in the still smouldering ashes, gazing up, looking solemn and forlorn with its singed black wig and protruding fleshy lips.

Paul couldn't bring himself to start the fire up again. He went back and searched for a receptacle. Moira was at mass, Mummy in bed. He had plenty of choice in a house so full of clutter, and chose a large biscuit tin which was the perfect size to contain the surviving piece of canvas. He buried King William's head in the dog's cemetery.

He never told Moira. A year later, with Mummy still comfortably installed in the house, he thought he might bring himself to inform her. He never considered bringing up his action at confession to Father Dunne, since in recent years his faith had slid away, and his appearances at mass were more to please Moira than to keep his soul safe.

But before he could bring himself to confess to her, Moira died. Suddenly.

No one was there in the breakfast room when she collapsed with an asthma attack before the sweet smelling hyacinths and narcissi that covered the window sills.

In his misery there was one thing that comforted him, that she did not die of cancer. She would have hated that, as she would have endured it patiently.

'Moira was that formidable creature, a good woman,' Mummy said. The flowers she brought to the funeral were very beautiful. The church was packed.

'Heaven awaits her,' Father Dunne said.

With Sympathy and *We Are Here For You* said the mass cards.

Mummy didn't stay long in the house afterwards, but, leaving him with Diamond, went off to live in the most expensive old people's home in Ireland. Nick paid.

CHAPTER TWENTY-SIX

Thieves continued to sweep through regularly and the house was largely stripped of furniture. They never took books; the old *Punch*'s, the P.G. Wodehouses, the Agatha Christies, the Dickens and Scotts, the books by Francois Mauriac, G.K. Chesterton and Hilaire Belloc, the Little Flower's autobiography were safe. Nor did thieves trouble with alarm clocks and Paul kept half a dozen on top of the bookshelf in his bedroom replacing them one by one when they ceased to tell the time. The latest, which he had bought a month ago, told him when to get up.

Hot water bottles accumulated under his bed since it was easier to buy another than bend down groaning and peer under the mattress to retrieve any that had fallen out of reach. He had not used an electric blanket since Moira died.

He was in his old bedroom, Minden, the one he had slept in from the time he was a schoolboy. Among the garments in his clothes cupboard were suits he had worn at St George's. Thieves never stole clothes cupboards or their contents. In the bathroom down the passage he seldom used the bath with the heavy taps except occasionally for washing bed linen. Mummy's bidet worked splendidly.

People did not have to live like he did in the twenty-first century in the era of the Celtic Tiger. He was constantly being nagged by those who intimated they had his well-being at heart. The idea of soldiering on in a crumbling Georgian mansion was an old old story, long out of date. Poodle had written saying he knew of someone eager to buy Mountsilver and restore it. Mary Lou, the wretched woman who was supposed to be keeping an eye on him, suggested if that did not appeal, he could sell off a few acres to install creature comforts. But he wouldn't go that way again, repeat the huge mistake. After Dr Schmidt gave up deer farming he turned the river field into a caravan park and Paul could see the tops of the caravans from his bedroom window.

Father Dunne, another who constantly recommended him to sell up, wanted Paul to go into a home where he could maintain his independence. He was constantly reminded how his mother had made the right decision years ago and was now as happy as Larry.

'Give me patience!'

He managed perfectly well on his own. Once a week he took the car, an old Toyota, to Tesco or Aldi and stocked up on his few wants, baked beans, tins of stew, dog food, tea and whiskey. Soap. Etc. Food for the parrot.

Before he went out he would fill his wheelbarrow with the few things left in the house that he valued – the silver gilt candlesticks, his wallet containing his driving licence, travel card, Visa card and health card, Mummy's pieces of Meissen wrapped in newspaper and the Dutch still life which was one of the few pictures left. And his gun wrapped in a sack. Thus far thieves had never found it. He would transfer everything from the wheelbarrow into the car boot which he locked before climbing gingerly into the front seat.

The interior of the car was filled with newspapers, old envelopes, and papers in which sweets and chocolates had been wrapped. There also had to be a couple of cheques from O'Connor, since he couldn't find them elsewhere. Sometimes as he drove along he would hear a rustle behind him which might be a rat. He drove very slowly. Never at night. Kindly Dr Hartigan would probably allow him to continue driving unless he became stone blind, or had an accident which would mean he would have to hang up his keys. Careful!

He had given up farming, apart from keeping a few chickens in Moira's memory, and let most of the land to O'Connor. 'My dear fellow,' he would drawl at O'Connor who considered him a soft touch. When he came to call, Paul would lead the way to the kitchen and watch him bracing himself for stale biscuits, weak tea and the filth. The man knew it was worth it for taking advantage.

At present there were puppies in a stained cardboard box beside the cooker; their mother, a mongrel, had walked up the drive a year ago.

On Sundays Mary Lou drove him to mass. Again the wheelbarrow was used and she allowed him to bring out his possessions and put them in her car boot. Otherwise, as he had made it plain to her and to Father Dunne, he would have stayed home. But he quite liked the Sunday routine. Putting in his false teeth and attending mass broke up the week. Quite recently he realised that all the effort made by Daddy and Father Hogan and Father McCabe, all the prayers of Aunt Delia, all Moira's very special prayers to get him to accept the claptrap that had plagued his life, had been wasted. He went to mass because Moira would have wished him to, and got down awkwardly on his knees and got up and sat and watched Father Dunne in his regalia and people crossing themselves and mumbled a little prayer for Moira and another for Daddy and gazed at the Stations and the sanctuary lamp as he had done when he was a boy. At the right moment when the bell quivered and tinkled he turned around and shook hands with fools beside him and behind him. A good way to spread flu germs. He queued up and took Holy Communion to keep Father Dunne happy before Mary Lou returned him and his things to the house.

In the breakfast room he sat in a deck chair checking *The Irish Times* with the aid of a magnifying glass. The copy he was reading was six months old, since these days he took his time. The letters page – Dear Madam . . . *The Irish Times* had a woman editor. A jam jar full of unopened daffodils was on the chimney piece. Thieves had not taken the print of the woman with a blue face that Moira had liked. There was no other furniture in the room apart from a box containing croquet mallets and balls, a hedge trimmer and his gun.

Wooster lay beside him, twitching, his nose almost touching the electric fire. He was old and as stiff as Paul, something he demonstrated when he got up and began barking at the sound of a vehicle crunching on the gravel. This was not the right time of day for the post. The post office van, was driven by another woman whose name Paul didn't know. She brought bills.

Not the post woman. It could only be Mary Lou come up to keep an eye on him, hammering repeatedly on the knocker, sounding the shrill bell shouting, Oh Mr Blake-Willoughby, I know you are there!

There was no time to hide. He had made the usual mistake of parking the Toyota outside the front door instead of taking the trouble of driving it into the stable yard. He looked out of the curtainless window – no, it was not Mary Lou's car, but a bright red sports car. A fat man wearing dark glasses was running through the rain. Courtesy, tinged with curiosity led Paul into the hall where he opened the front door in a gesture of surrender.

'Terrible day!' The man puffed and panted.

He recognised his half brother; behind him was an expensive red sports car of the sort only rich old men could afford. He could make out the number plate: NIC 1.

There was eighteen years between them in age which meant that Nick was over sixty, but Paul thought he looked older.

'Been over to see Mum. Sorry to come crashing in like this. I tried phoning.'

Paul made it a rule never to answer the telephone after ten o'clock in the morning.

'Come in, my dear fellow.' Well mannered as ever, preceded by Wooster he led him across the hall where the giant elk horns towered. Thieves had not been able to reach them.

'Careful. Don't step there. Loose board.'

In the breakfast room he watched for the look of dismay he regularly observed on the faces of Father Dunne, Mary Lou, O'Connor and Dr Hartigan.

'Whiskey?'

It was always good to have an excuse to share a drink. He poured out two measures of Jameson in clouded tumblers, taking for himself the one with the chip. The water in the jug had been there for a few days, but he was not going to make the effort of travelling to the kitchen to fill it just for the sake of a casual caller.

Nick asked: 'What are those things you have hanging from trees all along the drive?'

'Do you mean the foxes?'

'I suppose that's what they are.'

'I shoot them.'

'I shouldn't think the local hunt would approve.'

'There's no need for the hunt to know.'

Some had been dangling for a long time. The most recently dead, still fat with winter fur, were on their way to carrion. The melting carcasses of those shot last year slipped from suspended bones. The reek of decay replaced the vulpine musk of those which had perished before them.

'You have no idea what damage foxes can do.'

What did Nick want?

'How is Mummy?'

Nick said, 'She's determined to make me bankrupt and live for ever.'

'I saw her on her birthday.' Paul had taken her a bottle of Mitsouko.

For years the nursing home had disliked her imperious ways and high anglified voice but now it was proud of her. She was a trophy; she had her picture in the local paper surrounded by grinning nurses blowing out a candle.

'The place is too mean to provide a hundred. They only stuck in one. And the cake was horrid. Bought in Tesco's.'

She told Paul: 'I saw to it that ghastly Reverend Susan didn't know the date. She insists on coming to see me every week. Can I say a little prayer? I tell her, certainly not. I far prefer the nuns.'

A couple of nuns had been dumped in the home after their convent had been sold for building land. 'They are skinny and healthy. Why don't nuns make money by publishing the Nun's Diet?'

In Mummy's room, hot as a sauna, she sat in her chair with headphones in her ears listening to a talking book. *Last night I dreamt I went to Manderley again.* When she wasn't reading, she listened to the news on the little portable radio Nick had provided her with, about calamities in the Middle East, items on tropical forests being cut down, whales being slaughtered, and polar bears staggering from ice flow to ice flow.

'. . . I'll be dead long before the polar ice cap has melted.'

She wore a silk dress, a long gold chain, a big ring on a gnarled finger and polished high heeled shoes.

'The loonies keep on their furry bedroom slippers. I won't wear bedroom slippers as long as I live. Not very long.'

She showed Paul two cards which she had received. One was of the President of Ireland who had sent a pleasant letter of congratulations that Mummy was a hundred years old and over two thousand euros.

'How are you going to spend it?'

'I'm getting in lashings of Bombay Gin. And Teresa needs some money to bribe someone back in the ghastly Philippines to get her family over here.'

It puzzled Paul that she accepted her life in this place, so similar to the old people's home she had rejected in England all those years ago. She had stopped hating nurses and didn't even mind them calling her Diana.

'Teresa's a chum, she dresses me, cuts my toe nails and helps me to write cheques. She realises I'm as blind as a bat. I suppose I'll give something to charity . . . lifeboats . . . injured jockeys . . . saving orang-utans . . .'

The other card showed Queen Elizabeth in a yellow dress and a diamond brooch and a message wishing Mummy well.

'No money from her, mean cow. One thing, I'm determined to do and that is to live at least another year which will mean living longer than her awful old mother.'

'How did you qualify for the Queen's card? You're Irish.'

'I lived long enough in bloody England. When I was a debutante some woman, can't remember her name, I must be going ga ga, had to teach me to curtsey to her ghastly grandparents. Took a week. Step and bend to King George, step aside and bend to Queen Mary.'

Nick accepted a second glass of whiskey. He told Paul about the places he had been to lately . . . Ladakh, I was there for the moon festival, Uruguay, covered with summer flowers and long rivers down which it took me days to paddle with friends to go fishing. Huge fish – he made the conventional sign for a big catch. Plenty of condors. Kodiak, those bears are astounding . . . Galapagos – not the usual island tourists are taken to, but a little one where someone I know is counting tortoises . . .

What did he want?

'The house is looking great,' Nick lied. 'Do you have any plans for its future?'

'You mean when I die?'

'Oh, come now, of course not,' Nick lied again.

He was his nearest relation. Did he know Paul hadn't yet made a will?

Why should he leave his property to this fat fussy little old man and then to his children who must be verging on middle age? Of course he had thought long and hard about what to do with the place. Day after day Paul made plans and changed his mind, there was no hurry and sometime he would bring himself to decide on Mountsilver's future. He could give it all away to a charity that appealed. No money to Africa. They made a mess of things in Africa. Nothing to St George's. At least once a month he received messages from the old school pleading for money for a new science laboratory. A gymnasium. An extension to the library. Nothing to the Church, that was for certain.

He had not made a will yet. He wrote out his ideas every day on scraps of paper and stapled them into a notebook. Meanwhile he was alive and well, and his finances were sufficient, although the roof was a lost cause.

'The old place must be getting a bit hard to keep up. Especially for one person.'

Damn cheek. What did he want?

'Would you like some lunch?'

He could offer eggs with baked beans, the eggs fried in vegetable oil bought cheaply.

'No thanks.'

He sighed. 'Would you like to see around?'

Nick put down the whiskey glass and followed Paul and Wooster across the expanse of the hall.

'What happened to the furniture?'

'Thieves.'

In the drawing room the parrot cage sat on the floor. Nick laughed self-consciously. 'I remember teaching it a bad word.'

'It doesn't say anything these days.' Thieves never took it, although Paul had a hopeful daydream that one day they might remove it like Shergar. He should make provision for the wretched creature; he would contact Dublin Zoo. It would probably need an endowment.

'Careful where you tread. Safer to come this way, around the edge. There's a plank there that isn't safe.'

Nick said, 'Beautiful detail . . . .wonderful ceiling.' A lot he knew.

'I'm afraid things are a bit run down.'

'Is that dry rot?'

There were light bulbs that did not work, mildewed wallpaper and dark places.

'Mind that board!'

He took Nick upstairs. 'The stair lift still works. I use it the odd time.'

Then they went downstairs to the basement; Nick peered into little rooms with flaking plaster floors and followed Paul, trotting down flagged stone passages and the line of maid's bedrooms, the room with the piles of potatoes and coal, and the room into which Paul threw tins and eggshells; through the open door they could hear a rustle.

'Amazing old kitchen.'

'Needs a bit done to it.' Paul pointed out the balcony near the ceiling from where his grandmother used to throw down the day's menu to the cook.

Wooster barked with joy when they went outside and climbed up the basement stairs. The rain had ceased. Nick showed interest in the laundry house, the steward's house, where Fitzpatrick had lived and the line of stables which were altogether in better shape than the house. The granite walls had lasted well since the stables had been solidly rebuilt when the heiress married into the family a hundred and fifty years ago. First things first.

Paul made no attempt to open the half doors; no need for Nick to inspect the debris that had accumulated, the turnip grinder, the old Ferguson tractor, broken furniture.

Nick said, 'You'd be surprised how old buildings like this can be restored to different uses.' He mentioned a stable block in England which had been successfully converted into houses for retired couples.

'I hope I'm not putting you to any trouble,' he said. It was the sort of remark that did not merit a reply.

In the walled garden they waded through weeds past the skeletons of greenhouses.

'That rambler was planted by Mummy.'

They went out into the open fields.

'How many acres?'

The impertinence. But Paul told him, 'Four hundred and sixty.' Forty acres sold to that damn German.

Suddenly he guessed. Perhaps it was a gesture on Nick's part or just following his glance past the cattle grazing on the rented land among the park trees. The place might be a little neglected but the oak wood and the fat lime trees in a line were magnificent.

Greens.

He had seen what had become of Freddy Barnsworth's place after he attended Freddy's funeral. He had seen for himself the transformation, the Jack Nicklaus design, the artificial lake, the club house, the putting greens, the shop that sold golf clubs and the sites for houses to be bought by well-endowed clients.

'Golf.'

After Paul mentioned the four letter word and cleared the air Nick became articulate. Only in outline so far. Only with your co-operation. Of course you would be a partner in the venture which would attract major funding from all over Ireland and elsewhere. You would have a choice of one of the new houses to be bought by well-endowed clients or you might prefer a bungalow in the grounds of Mum's nursing home. You would have complete independence, but on the other hand, there would be some sort of help immediately available if by chance you were to need it.

Paul listened.

This is a superb location not too far from Dublin. The house would lend itself to a spectacular development, although naturally its original features would be maintained. A carefully planned addition at the rear would provide suitable bedroom accommodation for the four star hotel.

'What about the trees?'

'There would have to be some casualties. But screens of conifers would be planted as part of the layout.'

They returned slowly towards the house. Paul was humming to himself at the thought of a cup of tea. Such mood swings are common in the elderly. Rooks were settling on the trees and the lines of windows reflected the dying sun.

'I never showed you the old servant's entrance.'

It was over sixty years, before the war in fact, since the last unsightly maid, invisible from the main rooms of the house had bicycled down the tunnel towards the kitchen.

'This way.' Down more steps. 'Have a look.'

Nick continued to humour the old boy. Paul slammed the door on him and shot the bolt across. For quite some time he listened to banging and shouting.

The kitchen was warm. The floor was covered with empty tins and a good many pieces of newsprint sprinkled with rodent droppings, articles he had torn out of the paper because they interested him. After he read them he usually dropped them. A chicken he had killed some days ago lay on the table waiting to be plucked. What an adventurous day. He liked nothing better than the prospect of relaxing with a mug of Earl Grey – not the wretched tea that came in bulk from Aldi. The delicatessen in the street behind also supplied Gentleman's Relish which he might have on a slice of toast.

He would have to do something about that car. He would have to start up the tractor.

The puppies whimpered in their cardboard box. He could pay for Jacqueline to dispose of them humanely or dump them into a bucket himself. Tomorrow, perhaps. He turned on the radio.

Damn. Mobile phones.

One of the articles lying on the floor which he had read a week or two ago had been about Vodafone. Mary Lou had tried to persuade him to get one of these things in case of emergency. Nick was bound to have one.

Ten years ago no one had mobile phones.

The kettle was boiling and the dented teapot with the black wooden handle and silver pineapple on the lid was waiting. If nowadays there was no servant to give it a polish, tarnish did not spoil its graceful lines.

He thought about his gun. First things first. He would have the mug of tea afterwards, together with the Gentleman's Relish.